"That will do. Now you can start on my chest." He leaned back against the rim of the tub and folded his hands behind his neck, looking utterly relaxed.

Beast! Satan's spawn, she cursed silently, holding on to her anger and nurturing it as she ran the cloth across his chest. The dark hair glistened in the suds and her fingers tingled as if they had fallen asleep and suddenly awakened. A current shot through her veins as she realized this invader stirred something in her. She chanced a glimpse into his dark, blue eyes and noticed the gleam in their depths. Quickly she looked away. She could not bear for him to know her thoughts.

"Do not forget to wash all of me, slave," he said, laughter sounding in each word.

Damn him! Bethany closed her eyes. Pretend he is dead or so ancient that he cannot lift his decrepit body without help. Good, if she thought of him as a helpless old man, it would make the task bearable. But when she washed down his chest and followed the thin line of hair down his belly . . . Her face flamed and she jumped back from the tub. There was no way she could pretend he was old!

* * *

"Outstanding . . . a winner."
—*Rendezvous* on A YEAR AND A DAY

FROM AWARD-WINNING AUTHOR
JO BEVERLEY

Hearts Victorious

MARIAN EDWARDS

ZEBRA BOOKS
KENSINGTON PUBLISHING CORP.

ZEBRA BOOKS are published by

Kensington Publishing Corp.
850 Third Avenue
New York, NY 10022

First Printing: June, 1996
10 9 8 7 6 5 4 3 2 1

Printed in the United States of America

Dedication

To a woman of remarkable courage and a man of great compassion: Lillian and Edward Jastrzembski. Your children and grandchildren are grateful for your wisdom and love.

To my son Pete, who had the wisdom and great good sense to set the date, and to Denice who was wise enough to wait. May the years ahead be blessed with happiness and love.

To all my soul sisters—Maggie, Joan, Suzie, Kathy, and Laura, the red-ink ladies. What a team you are!

Prologue

Normandy, 1044

The metallic taste of blood filled William's mouth. One eye was nearly swollen shut and several teeth were loose from the blows received.

"Etienne, leave the little bastard alone until the baron arrives," said the man building the camp fire.

William prayed the advice would be heeded as he hung like a limp shirt in Etienne's fists.

"We should kill him now and have done," Etienne said as he shook William like a dog would a bone.

"Non, Veryl will do it. It is his plan."

Though he was nearly unconscious, the information burned into William's mind. His abduction and assassination had been planned by his own baron.

Cuffed like a cur, William fell to the ground and welcomed the hard earth as a soft cushion. With his hands bound behind him, unable to defend himself William offered no resistance. As he drew a deep breath, a haze of pain enveloped him. The assailant's boot had not bruised his ribs, but had broken them. Though his body was bludgeoned and beaten, his spirit was not. He drew short, even breaths to stem the wave of nausea and fight the unconsciousness. When his assailants made a mistake, he would be awake and seize his chance for escape.

With his ear pressed to the ground, the dew-soaked grass soothing his sore face, he felt the gentle vibrations that announced an approaching rider. The partial vision left in his right eye slanted to the two assailants huddled before the camp fire. Deep in dinner and drink, they were unaware of the rider. William smiled. From the men's lax behavior, he inferred that the baron was not expected until later.

In the dead of night, Gowain Mactavish galloped through Normandy. As he bent forward in his saddle and urged the animal on, clumps of wet earth and crumbled leaves churned up behind the racing steed. Suddenly, the animal's gait changed and Gowain pulled back on the reins. Finished with the mercenary's life, he wanted to be out of this cursed land and home in Scotland, but he would not lame a horse to do so. The animal had strained a muscle, and he was still hours from Calais and his departing ship. Through the dense trees, Gowain noticed a flickering light in the distance. A campfire so close to where he must make camp could not be ignored.

The trees gave way to a clearing where an armed party of two gathered around a meager fire. As Gowain rode into the site, his sharp eyes caught the shape of a tied and struggling youth. Without showing a flicker of interest, he focused his gaze on the men at the fire.

"Do not be alarmed," Gowain said, noticing both men had covered the hilt of their swords at his sudden appearance. "I am Laird Gowain Mactavish and my horse has thrown a shoe."

The firelight shone on the angular features of these two men as they faced the Scotsman, but only one advanced. "I am

Soren, and this—" He swung his hand toward his friend. "—is Etienne. We are on our baron's business."

The condescension in the Norman's voice drew a thin smile from Gowain. "What business sees a boy bound and gagged?"

The Norman held his ground. "This bastard is a threat to Normandy." Soren moved forward, a sneer on his lips. "What say you now, Scot?"

Gowain returned the contempt, his gaze hard and sharp. "I have little interest in Norman politics." Then, still watching the man, he slipped from the Norman language into the heavy burr of his homeland. "And even less interest in cowards and traitors. God smite these Normans!"

Gowain turned his horse as if to leave, but it was merely a ploy to unsheathe his sword undetected. Before Soren could offer a defense, the Scot's weapon pierced flesh and sank deep into the soldier's chest. Etienne ran forward with sword drawn, but he was little match for Gowain, who easily dispatched the Norman to hell.

Gowain quickly dismounted and untied the bruised and bloody boy. He had been sorely used by those who meant him harm. "So, lad. You are considered a threat to the Norman throne?" Gowain could not hold back his laughter.

Though the boy was outmatched and weak, he rose to face his rescuer proudly.

"Mactavish, if you hate the Normans so, why then did you spare my life?"

Gowain was shocked that the boy understood his language. He studied him. Though his face was misshapen with one eye swollen shut, the remaining eye was clear and held his gaze. "I dinna like the odds. Besides, I dinna hate all Normans." He gave the lad time to absorb his words before adding, "But make no mistake, lad, when you are full grown and wish to meet me on the field of battle, I will honor that fight. Scots make war on men, not children."

"Gowain Mactavish, I am in your debt. I will remember your

honor. If there ever comes a time when you need my assistance, you have only to ask."

"You are a bold lad." But even as he said the words, Gowain knew the lad's promise was no idle boast. "What is your name, boy?"

"William, Duke of Normandy. Remember it. You will hear it again." The words were spoken as calmly as the others, but this time there was a passion and conviction that even the laird who had scoffed understood.

Though it obviously caused the lad great pain to bend over, young William searched the dead men's bodies. "They carry a king's ransom. Mine."

Gowain let the exaggeration pass; he thought the boy a high-born aristocrat who, in the heat of excitement, colored his importance. The pouches of gold lay at Gowain's feet. "Where will you go, William?"

"Back to my stronghold, from whence I was abducted."

The boy asked for no help and, it appeared to Gowain, needed none. Extraordinary, in light of the circumstances and the danger. There were still powerful men who would shed fortunes to have a bairn murdered. Gowain stared at the pouches of gold.

"Ride with me, lad," Gowain offered.

Young William nodded his head in agreement, then removed a ring and handed it to Gowain. "Remember this night. For your kindness you have earned a place in my affection. And I am true to those I trust."

Mactavish smiled indulgently at the boy. There was something exceptional about this lad, but surely he was not the Duke of Normandy and monarch of this land. Yet, he could almost picture young William on the throne. Unbidden, the image formed in his mind of William as the *conqueror of England.* It was an uncanny and unsettling vision. Though he tried to shake off the thought, it persisted. His gaze was drawn to the gold. A king's ransom, he thought, then pondered—could it be?

"Bring the gold, Gowain. Our destiny awaits," said young William.

And without question at the tone, or the command, Laird Mactavish followed.

Chapter One

The smell of stale ale and warm bodies assailed Royce de Bellemare as he entered the crowded inn. With the necessary papers tucked safely against his chest and the disappointment buried deep in his soul, Royce surveyed the dingy surroundings until he spotted his brother seated at a far table.

"William has ceded the castle and estates of a Saxon in North Umberland."

"I am sorry, Royce. I know it is not what you wanted." Guy accepted the pouch of papers from his brother, then hailed the innkeeper for another ale. "Perhaps your betrothed will find life in England exciting," Guy said with a knowing smile as he looked over the land titles.

"*Non,* she will hate it," Royce said, thinking of his lovely Damiana, a Norman lady of exceptional poise and grace. "By God I will have this union. Lady Damiana's standing would mean my acceptance at Court. I cannot abide being referred to as a base-born knight, nor do I want to pass that legacy to my heirs." Royce took a long draught of ale. "But this piece of

English dirt—" He grabbed the land title and accompanying papers from his brother and held them up. "—tis all I have to offer her."

"If she loved you, brother, it would not matter where you lived." The harsh contempt was not hidden from Guy's words or his look as he met his brother's stare.

"If?" Royce slammed his tankard down and glared at his brother. "Damiana has waited for me to make my fortune."

Guy shook his head and leaned forward as if to share a confidence. "Damiana sent you off to war in hopes that you would die and release her from the marriage contract, or win such glory that William would reward you with an estate in Normandy."

"Guy, this animosity you harbor for the lady colors your judgment. You are greatly mistaken about her character, *mon frère.*"

"Am I?" Guy drew his sleeve across his mouth and leaned back in his chair. "Then send for Damiana and watch her reaction to the fruits of your labors."

"That I will, after you and I have taken possession of the castle."

Northern England, 1066

Murder and mayhem. Screams of terror. Shouting reigned as men ran through the castle slashing and hacking anyone who stood in their way. Blood flowed from sliced bodies. Children whimpered, cowering in corners, staring at the carnage.

Bethany awoke bathed in sweat. The nightmare seemed so real. No doubt the horrible images were prompted by the harsh news that filtered to them from the fleeing, war-weary, wanderers. William of Normandy had defeated Harold's army at Hastings; and with the king's death, England's spirit had folded. Rumor held that William would be crowned king on Christmas Day.

A terrible shiver engulfed her. If William became King of

England, even this far-northern outpost could not escape the Norman heel.

Throwing a coverlet around her shoulders, Bethany left her bedchamber. The castle was quiet—too quiet. The absence of familiar sounds was unnerving. She walked out to the unmanned battlements and stared toward the southern horizon. In the distance, like a burning patch in the night-dark sky, the crimson-colored clouds reflected the red glow of a raging forest fire. The wind rose, whipping the blanket about her in the October night. A bitter chill with a hint of moisture permeated her nightclothes and she welcomed it.

"Please, let it rain," she whispered. As if in answer to her prayer, thick dollops fell. Smiling as the rain sluiced her face, she stared at the empty battlements. Now, maybe the men could extinguish the fire and return to their posts. Meanwhile, the deserted walkways filled her with dread. They were at war; and without the castle guard, they were defenseless.

She closed her eyes to blot out the vulnerable scene; and in the darkness, the image of her mother's face appeared. Though five years had passed since her mother had left this world, her voice sounded in Bethany's mind as clear and familiar as if spoken yestereve. "Bethany, 'tis time for you to take my place."

With tears in her eyes, Bethany had knelt at her mother's deathbed, ready to receive the two precious heirlooms that had been handed down from mother to daughter for untold generations over a period of nine hundred years. "Protect our family and take care of our people," her mother had said, placing in her daughter's hand the jeweled dagger with the Roman coin embedded in the hilt, along with its own special woven tapestry sheath. " 'Tis your only duty. Fulfill your birthright. Do not fail those who have gone before."

While her mother watched, Bethany had solemnly placed around her hips a rich girdle embroidered with their rare history. In fine detail, the pictorial vignettes told the simple story of their ancestor—a Northumbrian bride vanquished by a Roman conqueror only to become the victor. Love had conquered lust, and the Roman soldier had decreed that for all time the oldest daughter of that house would inherit the land and castle. Bethany unsheathed the ancient dagger that held the Roman soldier's coin. Both the dagger and the girdle were a symbol of her legacy—an inheritance through the matriarchal line.

"Aye, mother. I will take care of them." Bethany had said as her fingers instinctively traced the ancient coin. "I vow it."

The image faded and Bethany sighed at the last memory of her beloved mother. She was dead. The responsibility of their people now rested solely on Bethany's shoulders. Even if she took a mate, he could never own the castle or the land. He could merely act as a guardian.

Her eyes opened and the deserted rain-slashed walkways met her gaze, the emptiness mocking her for her decision. She had ordered the old captain of the guard, Cedric, to take his men and fight the fire. The people, property, and livestock threatened by the approaching fire had prompted her decision, but now she questioned the wisdom of fighting the immediate fury of nature while ignoring the imminent force of man.

She missed her father's counsel and sent a silent prayer heavenward for his safe return. Brave warrior that he was, he could not have foreseen two invasions. He had taken all of the village men and most of the castle's soldiers to Stamford Bridge, joining forces with King Harold to thwart the King of Norway's attack. As a precaution, her father had left behind the most experienced twenty men to defend the castle. Would he have done as she had? Her shoulders slumped as an inner voice whispered, *probably not.*

The rain pelted her clothing and drenched her, but she did not feel the cold. Like a lone sentinel, she paced the storm-slick walkways.

At the back wall, she halted and stared off into the black sheet of rain. Her father's clan, the Mactavishes, lived only several leagues to the north. She had sent a missive to her uncle, apprising him of their need and requesting men.

The Scots were fierce warriors, but she could not be sure

her uncle would involve his clan. She had hinted at the wealth this demesne possessed and made it known that her gratitude would be generous. If that could not sway her uncle, nothing would.

Bethany took a deep breath and sighed. The alternative was not pleasant. She would be forced then to make a marriage match. If her uncle could not supply warriors, he should be pleased to arrange an alliance. There were many clansmen who would willingly give up their name and assume hers for the land she controlled. All she wanted in a husband was the protection and strength he could bring her demesne, yet she could not afford the months the negotiations would take!

She turned away from the north and headed toward her rooms. All she could do was wait. Her frustration made her feel as helpless as a leaf twisting in the wind. Her vow to her mother weighed heavily on her shoulders. She must find a way to keep her family and her people safe.

Goose bumps covered her flesh by the time Bethany reached her room. The draft seemed worse than before. She added another log to the fire and peeled away her clinging nightdress. The sodden material fell to the stone floor in a dark puddle. Briskly rubbing her chilled skin, she grasped a clean dry nightgown from the chest. The hem barely had time to touch her ankles before she leapt into bed.

The heavy bed robes had just covered her when lightning filled the room with a ghostly light, followed by a thunderous boom that shook the very roof. The door flew open and her little brother, Bret, careened through the room and straight into her arms.

"I'm scared." His muffled voice sounded against her chest.

Fear also dwelled in her heart, but not fear of the storm. "Don't worry, Bret. You are safe with me." In mocking answer, lightning and thunder occurred instantaneously. Wrapping her arms around his small frame, she slipped down beneath the covers. Crooning the same lullaby that had comforted and reassured him since their mother's death, she felt his tense muscles relax. Bret snuggled into her embrace and was soon asleep. A lump formed in her throat as she felt his hand slip into hers. Softly smoothing the flaxen hair from his brow, she tenderly kissed the child who was more son than brother and whispered, "I will protect you. I vow it."

"Bethany, are you coming to the chapel with me?" Mary asked, standing in the kitchen with her Bible in her hand, seemingly unaware of the commotion around her.

Bethany dried her hands on the linen sheet wrapped around her waist and sidestepped the young children playing on the floor to join her sister. "Not today, Mary."

"But the holy friar will be distressed," Mary insisted.

"If the good friar will come and do my work, I will gladly spend an hour in chapel," Bethany said heatedly. "Today, we are preparing the cabbage in brine; tonight, the beets. Tomorrow, the potatoes, carrots, and rutabagas have to be sorted and stored in the cellar." Bethany wiped her perspiring brow and wondered how her sister could not see the village women hard at work to preserve the fruits of the field for the long winter.

At her sister's hurt expression, Bethany felt a twinge of regret and softened her refusal. "Tell Friar John that I will say my prayers tonight when I walk."

Mary nodded, mollified, and turned to go to chapel. Bethany shook her head. Mary was so pious and good, it was hard to reproach her. After her hours in prayer, she would come to the kitchen to help. God first, life second.

Bethany did not share the same priorities. She believed God helped those who helped themselves. Intent on resuming her work, she turned and noticed Bret playing with children from the village. Their childish laughter echoed around the room. Hearing the innocent joy in their voices, she could almost believe everything was all right.

But it wasn't.

Three days had passed since the rainstorm, and the men had

not returned from the fire. Nor had her uncle sent a reply. Though she went about the business of running the castle, she feared she was losing a battle with time. The Normans would come; and when they did, life would change for every Saxon.

"Your sister is a good Christian," Maida, the cook, said with a knowing grin as she handed Bethany another head of cabbage to shred.

"Aye." But Bethany believed Mary could pray just as well in the kitchen while she worked as in the chapel. The sinful thought was typical of her and confirmed what she already knew. She was not cut from the same cloth as her sister or the Church.

Indeed, she was as opposite to her sister in temperament and looks as night was to day. Mary was the essence of an angel; with flawlessly smooth skin and pale, silver hair, she lacked only a halo to complete the picture, while Bethany could have been an imp come to life, sporting a unruly mane of red-gold tresses and a full dusting of freckles across each cheek. A wry smile curved her lips as she attacked the cabbage and met Maida's merry gaze. "No doubt our endeavors will be blessed by my sister's diligence."

Maida returned the smile, not deceived by Bethany's words. "Aye, prayers will nourish the soul, but not the body."

"Maida," Bethany gasped in feigned shock. " 'Tis blasphemy. Perhaps my sister is right, and I should spend more time in the chapel. It could not hurt."

Cook laughed out loud. "But would it help, my lady?"

Bethany's smile grew. Cook had known her too long. "Probably not," she conceded and accepted another head of cabbage.

The day proceeded as the others, her time spent helping in the kitchen and handling disputes. When she put Bret to bed, she felt exhausted and worried. With a shawl around her shoulders, she stepped out into the night. As she walked softly across the battlements, her attention centered on the woman standing guard, a troublemaker who stood the four-hour duty as a reminder that quarrelsome bickering would not be tolerated beneath the castle roof. Bethany ignored the villager and continued across the walkway.

The bright moon lent an eerie light across the landscape. She had always felt safe behind these walls. Tonight, she did not.

"Lady Bethany."

The deep male voice startled her, and she whirled around. "Friar John."

"I am sorry, child. I did not mean to frighten you."

" 'Tis nothing, Friar. I was lost in thought."

"Praying?"

Bethany could easily lie, but Friar John was a man she respected. "Nay, I was thinking."

"About the overdue men."

"Aye. I fear . . ." She hesitated.

"Go ahead, child. You do not have to pose a brave front for my benefit."

"I have missed our talks, Friar," Bethany said, trying to avoid the compassionate eyes of the cleric.

"So have I. Perhaps if I came to the kitchen tomorrow, we could spend some time together. I think Mary should join us with the chores. She spends too much time in the chapel. Hiding."

His suggestion so closely mimicked her own thoughts that Bethany burst out laughing. At his puzzled expression, she said, "Thank you, Friar John. I feared I would be damned in hell for the very same thought."

He chuckled, "Then we shall be in good company. See to your sister; she will listen to you."

"I will, Friar."

"Now, let us talk about you. Dark circles shadow your eyes, and I have noticed that you spend your days and nights laboring like a servant rather than supervising the cooking and cleaning as befits the mistress of the castle."

"Idle hands are the devil's playthings," she quipped to lighten the mood.

Without warning, the friar clasped her hands between his. His gentle inspection exposed the rough skin and callused fingers. He raised an eyebrow in her direction. "These are not the hands of a devil's plaything."

Bethany did not want to comment on the obvious, nor did she feel like discussing her fears. As if understanding her reluctance, the friar gave her a blessing and admonished her to seek her bed.

It seemed as if Bethany had just fallen asleep when Maida awakened her with a shake. "My lady, come quickly."

The urgency of her voice reached Bethany's exhausted mind. Throwing on her clothing, she followed the cook to the walkway.

"There, my lady. Do you see?" Maida pointed to the field directly before the gate.

A shadowy figure moved slowly forward. Painstakingly slow. The form approached, and Bethany strained to make out the shape.

" 'Tis a horse with something strapped to its back," Maida said.

The hairs on the back of Bethany's neck rose. It was a man.

"Open the gates." Bethany ran down the battlement and into the courtyard as the horse plodded in. Dear God in heaven.

A lump of bloody flesh lay over the saddle. The torch in Maida's hand moved closer, and Bethany recognized the face of the captain of the castle guard. "Cedric." She reached out and touched the matted hair on his cheek.

He moved slightly, the effort causing him pain as he groaned.

"Help me!" Bethany commanded Maida.

With her customary efficiency, Maida bellowed, and several villagers came running. The women assisted Bethany in lowering Cedric from the horse and carrying him into the castle. Worried faces and whispered fears abounded as the awakened women stared at the injured soldier. Immediately, a place was cleared in the crowded great hall for the wounded man, and Bethany knelt beside him. "Cedric, can you hear me?"

His voice was weak as he tried to grasp her hand. "Forgive me, my lady. I have failed you."

"Shh," Madia said, kneeling by the wounded soldier. "Let us care for your wounds first."

"Nay." He gripped Bethany's hand tighter. "They are all dead."

Mary knelt by her sister's side with a bowl of warm water and cloth. "Who is dead?"

At the sound of her voice, Cedric turned toward Mary. His eyes held hers. "The castle guard."

Maida caught the bowl of water that fell from Mary's hand.

The reaction did not escape Bethany. Reality had finally intruded into her sister's world.

"Mary," Bethany said, grasping her sister's hand. "Go sit down. We will take care of Cedric."

Mary stumbled away, and Bethany briefly rued her inability to comfort her sibling before returning her attention to the wounded soldier. "Rest, Cedric."

"Forgive me." He drew a ragged breath. " 'Twas the Normans, who ambushed us. They are coming, my lady." His voice faded away as he slipped into unconsciousness.

Bethany's insides roiled with the news. "Dear St. Bede," she whispered, invoking the North Umberland patron saint. The Normans were near the village. Tales of the horror of war and her own nightmare returned to haunt her.

Immediately, women crowded around, their faces pinched at the revelation.

"Tayte, I will need my healing tray," Maida instructed the nursemaid without looking up as she assessed Cedric's wounds. Tayte started at the cook's voice, then turned to retrieve the needed supplies.

" 'Tis bad," Maida said to Bethany, peeling back the blood-encrusted coverings.

Thankfully, Cedric remained oblivious during the removal

of his clothing. The soiled garments lay in a pile on the floor, and Bethany marvelled that he had made it back. Hardly an inch of skin showed, for the wounds covered his body.

Tayte handed the cook the required aids as Bethany cleaned the oozing wounds of dirt and dried blood.

"Some will need sewing, some searing," Maida said as she handed a knife to Tayte to place in the fire.

Bethany felt the perspiration break out on her forehead. She had tended many wounded men and knew the danger of searing. Her eyes met Maida's over Cedric's still form and held the older woman's gaze.

As if understanding Bethany's fears, Maida said. "I have no choice; he will bleed to death without the searing."

With a nod, Bethany acknowledged the cook's assessment.

"You and Tayte must hold him still." Maida held the red-hot knife above the first wound. Bethany threw her weight against Cedric's chest as Tayte held his arms. Cedric convulsed when the searing started but thankfully remained unconscious. Maida worked quickly and efficiently, laying the knife upon the wound and quickly drawing it down the length of the gash, moving on to the larger wounds. Bethany's admiration for the woman grew, for even she had to struggle to keep the bile from rising at the acrid smell of burning flesh.

With the serious wounds seared, the three woman sewed the others and packed each with poultices.

Dawn was breaking when the trio finished dressing Cedric's injuries.

"His fate is in God's hands now, as is ours," Maida said, washing the blood from her hands.

"Amen," Mary chanted from her seat across the hall. Sitting alone like a lost soul, her eyes wide and her face pale, she turned to face her sister, clearly seeking answers to this madness.

Unable to offer comfort and at a loss as how to reach her, Bethany said, "Hurry, Mary, or you will be late for chapel." She sighed, feeling horribly inadequate and overwhelmed by her responsibilities.

"Nay, sister. I am needed here in the castle."

The adult voice and sure conviction startled Bethany.

"Yes, Mary, you are." Bethany gave silent thanks for her sister's uncharacteristic gesture.

Bethany moved to cover the wounded Cedric. There was nothing more she could do for him. The village women started the day's tasks, and Bethany moved to the courtyard. The weak morning sun did not warm her. She did not mind the cold. She was numb with worry. What in God's name was she to do?

Midday brought an answer from her uncle. The missive hung in her hand like a death sentence. He could not send men. If she wished asylum, he would be glad to offer her and her people a home—but for a price.

Bethany shook her head. There was naught to do but comply. She could not defend the castle without men, and she would not surrender her people to Norman slavery.

Bethany moved quickly. She ordered carts filled with the castle's valuables. Women and children ran through the castle, their arms laden with heirlooms. Urgency permeated the air and spurred the villagers on. Fear shone in their faces, and the quiet panic that resided in their hearts showed in the frenzied movement of their work.

Tears misted in Bethany's eyes as the treasures of many generations, for the first time, left their honored place.

She bundled the wall tapestry that chronicled the amazing story of her matriarchal ancestry with great care. This was her heritage and it must not go unattended.

The silver, gold, and everything else of value was stripped from the rooms and loaded onto the carts. At sunset, when they had finished, seven carts of wealth and one of food stood ready to leave.

Though the women were anxious, every face that met hers was filled with trust. It humbled her that women twice her age looked to her for guidance. The responsibility weighed heavily, and she prayed she would not fail them.

Tonight, the carts would leave under the cover of darkness.

Carrying the castle's wealth and the wounded soldier, they would be in Scotland by morning. Tomorrow, the women and children would depart. After their work today, the children would need rest to endure the long march.

Now, she would name the six women who could drive the carts. Friar John would handle the food wagon. He had the most experience; and though they would need money to buy their way in Scotland and perhaps purchase mercenaries, they needed the food more.

After all, armies, even those made up of women, moved on their stomachs.

Chapter Two

"Dear God," Bethany whispered as she stared down at the Norman army before the castle gates. They had run out of time.

"Put your weapons down and open the gates. Surrender and all those within will be treated with clemency. Resist and no mercy will be shown."

At the sound of the Norman's voice, everyone in the castle turned and looked at Bethany for answers. Only Mary seemed capable of movement, and that reaction was obviously fueled by panic. She ran heedlessly from the courtyard, tripping on the stairs as she climbed up toward the empty battlements and her sister.

Bethany knew that the Norman words—harsh, curt, and foreign—fell on the Anglo-Saxon ears like unintelligible noise, sounds without meaning. Only she understood the foreign tongue and wished she did not.

"What do they want?" Mary asked as she joined her sister at the wall.

"They say if we surrender, they will be kind masters," Bethany said, staring at the Norman army from the safety of the walkway.

"What will you do, sister?" Mary's face grew pale. She looked around, as if suddenly a miracle would materialize.

Lady Bethany took in the frightened faces of the women as they clutched their children to their sides before turning back to answer Mary.

"You must lead our people through the tunnel. Go to our uncle in Scotland. He will shelter you."

Mary blanched. "But the journey is long."

"The border is only ten miles from the tunnel exit," Bethany said, giving thanks that the loaded carts had left last night. "You must do it. Follow the cart's wheel-ruts."

Mary began to wring her hands. "I am frightened. Bethany, you must do this."

"Would you rather stay here and face the Normans?"

The little color left in Mary's face drained away. "Nay. I will lead them," she said and bowed her blond head. "What of you?"

Bethany smiled wanly. "I will stay behind and create a diversion to give you time to be away."

The pain in her sister's eyes was hard to bear. They embraced, and Bethany walked to the wall. Leaning over the edge, she stared out at the vast army of Normans. She had learned the Norman tongue from her father when she was but a child. Speaking the language through the years had been a game, shared between her sire and her, to exclude others from the conversation. She prayed her memory would not fail her. But a woman's voice would not be questioned if she were the interpreter.

Bethany took a deep breath and shouted from the high walkway. "Norman, the lord of this castle bade me speak his words. He says there is no need for senseless bloodshed. He will send out his best warrior to face yours. The winner will determine the fate of the conquest."

One rider, a huge warrior, advanced. "What trick is this, Saxon?"

"Nay, 'tis no trick. One of our soldiers will face one of yours at midday, when the sun is directly overhead, on yon field."

She pointed across the landscape. " 'Tis said the Normans fear nothing. Mayhap we were misinformed."

"I accept your lord's challenge, my lady. But be warned, this is resistance."

"Aye, Norman. But if your man fails, *you* will surrender."

The warrior laughed and led his horse back to the column of men.

Bethany nearly sagged with relief. She had feared the Norman would not accept her challenge.

Now that he had, she would not allow herself to think of the outcome. It would be far better to die than meet the fate the Normans had for Saxon women.

In the courtyard, Mary stood surrounded by the growing crowd. No one listened to her. Bethany shook her head. Mary was such a timid creature.

Shouldering her way through the milling villagers, Bethany raised her hands. "You will leave with Mary. If you wish to live, you will keep your children quiet and make haste for the border." Bethany faced her sister and handed her their father's ring. When she started to remove the girdle and dagger worn only by the eldest daughter, Mary took a step back.

"I could not, Bethany. Do not ask this of me. By our custom 'tis yours to pass to your daughter. I can only receive it," she paused, her voice catching, "if you die without an heir." Mary pushed the girdle and dagger back into her sibling's hands, refusing the honor of the possessions and the accompanying responsibility.

Bethany understood her sister's hesitation and did not press the point. Soon enough the matter would be taken from both their hands. She turned to the village women. "Go now and Godspeed."

"God's teeth, Royce. Why did you agree to those terms? Legally, the castle belongs to you."

With his attention on the castle, Royce answered, "Simply

put, brother, it will expedite the matter. After the outcome of this contest, the Saxons will be unable to question my right of ownership." Royce noted that the stone blocks did not need to be remortared. The castle had been well maintained.

"I should have known you were not reacting to the Saxon's taunt. Logic, not emotion, rules you." Guy slapped his brother on the back and noticed Royce's serious expression.

Royce continued to stare at the castle. "Do you not think it is strange that no one is on the battlements?"

His younger brother, Guy, gazed up and studied the walls. "What do you make of it?"

"Take a complement of men. Look for a tunnel or cave. I suspect there is a plot afoot, and I will not be out flanked by Saxons."

Guy nodded his head and turned his horse to do his brother's bidding.

Royce faced the castle. It would be his final conquest. He needed the respite from war. God, he was tired. Death and destruction drained a man's soul. He longed for the life of a quiet country lord for which he had worked and fought. Now, all that stood in the way was one soldier. He would meet the man himself. Too much was at stake to send another.

As midday approached, Bethany searched through the squire's clothing. "This one, I think," she said holding up the tunic and tights of a young page.

Her old nursemaid, Tayte, and the cook, Maida, remained behind to help her dress and mount her steed.

Maida placed woolen batting on her shoulders and across her chest.

"What are you doing?" Bethany asked.

" 'Twill ease the chafing of the armor," Maida explained as she wrapped the heavy batting around Bethany.

"Nay. Take it off."

Maida hesitated, then said. "The wool padding will make you appear larger."

"Very well, Maida. Let it stay."

Bethany was unaccustomed to the chain mail and felt her shoulders sag from its heavy weight. "How do they carry all this metal?"

"They have considerably more size than you, Lady Bethany. You do not even look like a boy in this suit."

"Never mind. It will not matter. Let them laugh at the soldier sent out. The more time wasted, the more time our people have. Once I am through the gates, board them, then make your escape. Pray God you reach safety."

Tayte had tears in her eyes. "My lady, we owe our lives to you. I wish there were another way."

"So do I, but there is not."

Maida was not as sentimental. "There is always hope you will carry the day."

Bethany smiled at that quip. "Aye, Maida, as much chance as sprouting wings and flying." She did not add that she did not expect to live past the hour. Reverently, she picked the girdle and dagger from the pile of clothes and handed them to Maida. "Make sure my sister has the symbols of the legend." When her eyes finally met Maida's, it was clear they both knew her situation was hopeless.

The appointed time came, and Bethany spared one prayer. She asked God to see her people to the northern climes and safety. Beyond that, she had no other request of her maker, not even for herself.

Weathered trees, stripped and dark, stood ready for winter's onslaught; and damp, decaying leaves littered the ground as she rode out of the castle toward the designated area. The autumn wind nipped at her skin, and she welcomed the numbing chill. The crisp, clean air filled her lungs with the pungent smell of wet soil and long-past harvested fields. Danger heightened her awareness, and she breathed deeply, inhaling and savoring the unmistakable tangy musk of the season.

Norman soldiers lined a ridge overlooking the field. In the clear light, their numbers looked less. But their strength was unimportant. A hundred men could storm the castle, but all that mattered was the contest.

She blocked out the insults and slurs, the laughter at her size. Her horse stopped at the end of the field, and she waited as one rider approached. He was massive, his chest wide, his arms as large as tree limbs. This soldier needed no padding to fill his tunic. She knew she would not last the first contact.

"Be you ready?" a deep voice behind the helm asked in the hated Norman tongue.

Her back remained straight as she refused to give any indication she understood the Norman language.

His hand covered the hilt of his sword as he inclined his head in her direction.

Afraid to trust her voice, she nodded.

He drew his sword and waited for her to do the same.

The broad sword was difficult to unsheathe, and she struggled with it before finally managing to pull it free. The weight of the sword pulled her arm down, and she needed both hands to hold it upright.

The champion laughed at her struggles. "Do they send a boy to battle for a castle? Hold the sword steady, boy. The wavering makes me dizzy."

Swinging his sword, he advanced, and Bethany knew the sudden taste of fear. She raised her weapon in a valiant effort to repel the force of his strike and felt his blow clear to her shoulders. Perspiration dotted her upper lip as she struggled to bring her skittish horse under control.

Fear lent strength to her limbs as she pulled back hard on the reins while raising her sword for another attack. Steel met steel with a loud clash, and the teeth-jarring contact dazed her. Her arms were numb, and through a dizzy haze she saw the sword swing towards her again but could not block it in time. The flat of the blade bruised her ribs, the force knocking her from the horse. She tried to rise, but the weight of the armor held her pinned to the ground.

The warrior dismounted and stood over her, his sword pressed against her throat. "Do you yield?"

"Nay," she whispered, forgetting to disguise her voice.

The sword tip withdrew, and he knocked the helm from her head, spilling her hair out across the ground.

"God's teeth! What is this?" His voice sounded like thunder in a quiet room.

"Have done, Norman," she spat, panting to catch her breath.

He reached down and grabbed her chain mail, lifting her clear off the ground with one hand. Suspended in midair, she found herself face to face with him and glimpsed the dark eyes behind the helm. A shiver went through her at the coldness that stared back. She prayed it was a trick of light that made this man's eyes seem so merciless.

"A woman! They dare send a woman to do battle?" He shook her, expressing his disbelief.

Her teeth rattling and her heart pounding, Bethany struggled in his grasp as his men advanced, bringing his mount.

He threw her over his horse and rode toward the castle with his men in tow. Slung over the saddle like a sack of grain she bore the jolt of each stride in her ribs. Though the ride back to Renwyg was short, by the time they reached the castle, her lungs felt beaten and she had to fight for each breath.

On their arrival, the Normans found the doors barred. The mighty warlord barked an order, but no one answered from within the castle.

"Lying Saxons," he snarled, then turned to the soldier beside him. "Vachel, climb the wall and open the gates. Show no mercy to those inside."

A stout Norman soldier dismounted, yelling orders to the others to throw ropes with hooks to the upper battlements. Several soldiers scaled the wall after Vachel and disappeared behind the stone edifice. In a matter of moments, the doors opened and her captor was informed that the castle was deserted.

With a growl, he rode inside the empty courtyard and dragged her from the horse. Walking into the main room, he threw her to the floor. "Where are they?" he demanded.

Bethany remained silent. Brushing the rushes from her hands, she looked around the room. Through her terror she felt a small measure of satisfaction, and a wan smile touched her mouth. She had saved her people.

He advanced on her, overshadowing her with a sheer physical presence that was both menacing and overwhelming. Though she felt substantially cowed, to her credit, she did not cringe.

"This is your last chance to answer me. Where are the serfs?"

"Far from here," she gasped, finally catching her breath. She had beaten this mighty warlord. Inhaling deep, long draws of air, she added in defiance. "Enjoy your spoils. Without the villeins, your castle is worthless."

The warlord towered over her like an ancient pagan deity, vengeful and displeased with his worshipper. Casually, he removed his helm. The absence of the face guard should have softened his appearance, but it did not. His features were as uncompromising as the face mask. The angles and lines of his face were strong and so boldly defined that his expression could have been hammered out of bronze.

Bethany should have been afraid, but her own safety had ceased to matter. If fate decreed that she die at the whim of this Norman, then she would do so bravely. Never would she disgrace those proud and noble ancestors who had gone before her.

His hands rested on his hips. "We will see, mademoiselle."

Men crashed through her home, throwing open doors and running though hallways. But Bethany rejoiced that these thieves from Normandy would not line their pockets with looted treasure from her demesne.

"My lord." Vachel stood before his leader. "The castle is stripped of all worth. There is nothing left."

The black-eyed gaze of the warlord rested on her as he spoke to his man. "Find the tunnel."

Bethany looked away, afraid he would see the truth in her eyes.

"It exists." He hauled her to her feet. "Where is the escape route?"

Though the Norman words were strange to her, she spat them out. "I am Saxon. I will not betray my people."

"You have already betrayed your people by challenging a Norman soldier."

He pulled her along after him as he walked from room to room. In the doorway of the barracks, she spied her clothing on a pallet. The rich fabric and jeweled neckline lay where the nursemaid had left them. He walked over to the garments and picked them up. After a moment's examination, he turned to her.

"Your clothing, my lady?"

"They belong to the mistress of this house."

"*Non*, they *belonged* to the mistress. Now they belong to me."

Bethany lifted her chin and stared into his face. "It is merely fabric, warlord. Nothing more."

"It would cover your meager frame." His gaze slowly ran the full length of her. Then he smiled. "Your present garb leaves little to a man's imagination."

Her face flamed from his words. Still she tried to brazen out his stare. 'Twas a war of wills and one she intended to win. But when his smile slid to a full-blown grin and his eyes sparkled with a knowing light, her gaze fell beneath his smug, masculine expression.

"*Oui*, my men will appreciate the spectacle."

Swine, she thought. He was trying to goad her temper—and succeeding. With effort she raised her eyes. "You and your men are not my concern."

"You think not? We are very much your concern."

"On the morrow you will be pillaging another Saxon village to take the treasures to the bastard William," Bethany said, nearly trembling with the effort to contain her outrage.

The warlord pulled her close. "My days of sacking are over. This is now my demesne and you, poor substitute that you are, are my only serf."

Her face paled. She had not considered the possibility of his staying! As though he read her mind, he called Vachel forward. "Place our only serf in the tower so she does not decide to join her people and leave us totally without servants."

Exiled from the familiar and imprisoned in darkness, Bethany sat in the cold cell, terrified. The ululant wind swirled around the tower like the cry of ancestral spirits wailing in shame. Tears of misery slipped unheeded down her cheeks. She was utterly alone.

Though she had put up a brave front today, inside, her heart was breaking. Wrapping her arms around herself for warmth, she felt the rough clothes of the squire. Skimming over the short tunic and tights, unconsciously her fingers slipped to her hips, missing the girdle, the symbol of her status. The thought of the legacy gave her a measure of comfort and wiping away the tears, she took a deep breath. A North Umberland woman did not bend nor break. She had nine hundred years of pride to uphold. With her family and people safe, she would resist the invaders and, if possible, escape. Her mind raced with sudden ideas. Though the Normans were unaware of it, Renwyg Castle had not one but two escape routes. They would find the northern tunnel, because that's what they were searching for, believing southern escape route to be useless to the Saxons and easily discovered by the advancing army, marching from London. She silently blessed her ancestors for their forethought; if an enemy approached from either direction, an escape path existed for retreat. If only she could flee the tower and make her way to the unused passageway, she could join her family in Scotland.

* * *

The following evening, Bethany was led by Vachel from the tower into the great room and pushed into a chair. The Normans had neither molested nor mistreated her. Now, she wondered if that would change.

Across the room, the warlord stood listening to a report from a soldier. It was obvious they were related; their builds and features were too similar. Both men were a striking sight, with raven-black hair and eyes so dark that on first glance they appeared black, but were in truth a midnight blue. Bethany thought the warlord's features were the more arresting. He was not as handsome as the younger man, yet his rough-hewn face possessed character and seemed more commanding and interesting than the other's near-perfection.

The Norman leader listened intently to the soldier, then a slow smile crossed his lips. She was struck by the difference the expression made in his appearance and frightened by what had given him such pleasure.

"Come here, mademoiselle."

Bethany remained where she was. She would not answer the man's summons.

The soldier standing beside the warlord shook his head at such insolence and started toward her. He pulled her from the seat by the scruff of her tunic and dragged her back to the warlord.

"Brother, why not just beat her?" the younger man asked.

"I have already beaten her in combat, Guy," he said, then turned toward the soldier standing by the portal. "Vachel, bring them in."

Bethany glanced past the burly guard opening the door, then gasped as Mary entered, followed by the women and children of the castle.

A counterpoint of sounds echoed off the walls. Whimpers, wails, and hiccupping sobs of frightened children joined their mothers' comforting voices, blending together in a composition of fear.

"We tried, Bethany. Truly we did," Mary said.

Bethany nodded her head and blinked her tears away; in that span of a heartbeat she suffered all the impotent anger, and devastating frustration that travels in the wake of conquest.

They were truly beaten.

"You will translate my words to them," the warlord ordered.

Bethany stared at the villagers who were herded like sheep into the great room. Their frightened gazes locked with hers, seeking assurance, and pain stabbed her heart.

"I will not translate." She croaked the Norman words out, trying hard to swallow her tears at such a humbling display.

The tall Norman raised an eyebrow at her refusal. "You will not?"

He pulled his sword free of its sheath. Bethany drew a deep breath, steeling herself for the blow.

At the gesture, a smile of pure contempt crossed his features, then he pointed the weapon straight at her sister. "Bring her." Two soldiers grabbed Mary and hauled her kicking and screaming over to the warlord.

Bret chose that moment to run from Maida to Bethany. Clinging to her legs, he stared in terror at the Norman holding a blade to Mary's throat.

"Nay, do not harm her," Bethany shrieked as her gaze pleaded with the warlord for clemency. Searching for and finding no mercy in his dark eyes, she held his gaze and nodded slightly. "I will speak that which you wish translated." Bethany waited until the warlord replaced his sword, then disentangled her brother's tight grasp and picked him up. He wrapped his arms around her neck and hid his face in her tunic.

"The prisoners will kneel and swear fealty to the new lord of the manor, Royce de Bellemare."

The words clogged in her throat, and Bethany closed her eyes, unwilling to watch her people give their allegiance to this Norman. She despaired that her plan had failed them so completely.

Still whimpering, Mary knelt before the warlord and said her vow, then whispered to Bethany. "Pray forgive me."

Bethany struggled to smile encouragingly. "It is all right, Mary. You did your best."

Shamed at seeing her sister on her knees, Bethany turned and faced the warlord. "I will not swear allegiance to you."

"It is not necessary. They are serfs, owing me only partial service, but . . . you you are a slave."

"I am no slave, least of all to a Norman master."

"You challenged a Norman in combat. You lost." His tone was matter-of-fact.

She almost hated him more for his lack of gloating. Though several of her father's favorite curses came to mind, she kept them to herself. Silently praying for guidance, she placed a kiss on her brother's forehead, then tried to hand him over to her sister, but he immediately began to fuss. Bethany refused to give in to Bret's beseeching gaze and tearful pleas. He would be safer with Mary.

"Tell the women to prepare a meal for my men," the Norman warlord commanded.

Her eyes, smarted from tears and she choked out the order.

The women dispersed immediately, though their furtive glances strayed to their young mistress. Mary also stared at Bethany; but unlike the serfs, she remained in the middle of the hall, holding Bret and looking helpless and terrified.

" 'Tis your sister?" Bellemare asked Bethany as he eyed Mary speculatively.

"Aye, Mary is my younger sister," Bethany replied, worried that the warlord's contemplation boded ill for her beautiful sister. "You will not harm her," Bethany insisted.

"She is a daughter of this house and as such will be treated with respect."

Bethany almost sagged in relief.

She translated the words to Mary and saw the fear lessen in her eyes.

"Guy, take the Lady Mary upstairs," Royce commanded. When Mary cringed at the soldier's advance, Royce added, "Tell her 'tis my brother, Guy. She need not fear any harm from him."

The handsome soldier came forward and bowed with courtly grace before Mary, while Royce restrained Bethany from going to her sister's aid.

"Who is the child in your sister's arms?"

"Our brother," Bethany said defiantly, knowing he believed Bret to be her son and, therefore, deserving of sharing her fate.

" 'Tis a shame you did not surrender, then you would share your brother and sister's status. Since you dared to challenge me, you will remain dressed in the squire's clothes so all may see your disgrace."

Bethany raised her chin. "My only regret is that you did not perish by my sword."

"You will have much time to ponder your foolishness. You will attend to my needs. See to a bath so I may wash this filth away. And, slave, make sure the water is hot; I cannot abide a cold bath. After that, have my belongings placed and stored in the master chamber."

Bethany whirled about and left the main room. *Attend my needs.* Oh, she would indeed see to his needs, but he might wish she had not. *A bath.* Fine. She had a few surprises for her Norman warlord.

Bethany hauled the water to the master chamber and heated it in the large kettle over the fire. She looked sadly around the room. It was her sire's, and she could not bear the thought of the invader making free with his home. This room above any other was special. Her parents had enjoyed their private moments here. Often Mary and Bethany had spent the day sewing with their mother by this very hearth. She closed her eyes to the memories. That life was over, gone with the advent of this new lord. She hated him.

"Is the bath ready?"

His voice startled her and she nearly dropped the pot of boiling water she carried. Without a word she poured the last container in the tub and watched with pleasure as the steam rose to the ceiling. *Boil, you son of Satan.*

"Aye, 'tis ready."

"Is it hot?"

She had to suppress the smile that threatened her lips. "Aye 'tis hot."

She started for the door, but he called her back.

"Hold. You are not dismissed."

She turned around, hating the superior tone of his voice.

"Since my squire is busy, I will need assistance."

Bethany gritted her teeth and approached him, then waited for him to speak.

"Do you not know what to do?"

She knew, and damned him to hell for his baiting. Her father had not allowed his daughters to attend a guest's bath. He did not hold with the custom and now she knew why. It was humiliating.

"This chore is usually reserved for the lady of the house. Do you wish me to call upon your sister?" he asked, one eyebrow raised as he awaited her answer.

Bethany felt the blood drain from her face. "Nay. She would find it as distasteful as I."

His deep rich laughter filled the air. "Then hurry before the water grows cold."

That remark gave her pleasure. Cold? It would take half the night for the water to cool. She reached up his chest, feeling the cold chain links beneath her hands, but the tips of her fingers barely brushed the fastening on his shoulder. Although the closure proved just out of her grasp, he did not sit to make the job easier, and she would be damned before she asked his assistance. Standing on her tiptoes, she stretched to undo the armor, her arms and back feeling the strain as each strap slipped through her fingers. She nearly dropped the heavy woven metal rings, and when the covering was free, the weight dragged her arms down.

He smiled at her predicament and stepped out of the heavy garment at his feet. She glared at his arresting features. The sum total bespoke harshness, but taken slowly, each individual trait became, if not truly handsome, then somehow . . . pleasing. Angrily dismissing the thought, she turned and pulled the chain mail across the floor.

"Have a care, slave. The less you abuse my armor, the less work you will make for yourself when you clean it."

Bethany let the heavy links slip through her fingers. Damn him. The chain mail hit the floor with a heavy thud. She turned and walked back to the warlord. He waited with insufferable patience for her to continue.

Her hands shook as she loosened and unlaced the ties down the front of his tunic, revealing a thick mat of dark curly hair. The ropey muscles beneath his skin rippled and quivered under her fingertips as she slipped the material off his broad shoulders and down his powerful arms.

Bethany blushed from the tip of her toes to the top of her head and she tried to finish removing the tunic without looking at or touching the man. Her hands fairly tingled from the brief contact.

"It would seem you have never done this before."

Bethany turned and stared at him. The laughter in his eyes raised her ire. "Stripping an invader holds little interest for me."

"Someday you may find the experience rewarding. But I will take pity on you. See to my clothes while I finish removing my braies." His hands moved to the belt at his waist.

Relieved that she did not have to strip him naked, Bethany whirled around. This one tiny kindness humbled and humiliated her more than being beaten in battle. Bethany had never been, nor would she ever be, an object of charity.

She moved to the clothes chest his men had deposited in the room and opened the lid. Behind her she could hear him moving around and the sounds of clothing being dropped. She could not wait for him to get into the tub.

Covertly, she removed his tunic from the floor and waited for the yell of pain. She heard water splashing, but no pain-filled cry.

"Ah, the water is comfortable. Remember, slave, this is how I prefer my bath water."

Lord, he truly was the son of Satan. She kept her back to him as she folded his clothes, trying to block out the splashing sounds. The water had been poured straight from the kettle to the tub and would be scalding hot.

"Hand me the soap, Saxon."

Unable to look at him, she picked up the chunk of soap from the tray and took a cautious step backwards. Careful to keep her eyes averted, groping for the rim of the tub, she thrust the soap behind her.

Hot water splashed her hand and she cringed from the heat. He was a devil.

"Closer, mademoiselle; I cannot reach it." She moved a foot back and thrust her hand farther behind her, fearing she might accidentally brush his warm skin, which on a normal man would be boiled and blistered by now.

Another spray of water hit her back and she gasped, jumping away from the tub.

Laughter filled the air and, forgetting herself, she spun around.

He stood half dressed on the other side of the tub. "The water is just a touch too hot. You will have to fetch two buckets of cold water."

Bethany seethed. It was not being the brunt of a jest that bothered her, but the frustration of not being able to best him.

She snatched up the buckets and stormed from the room, his mocking laughter following her all the way down the stairs.

"Lady Bethany pardon me," the nursemaid said as Bethany filled the buckets.

"What is it, Tayte?" Bethany asked, noticing the strain and hesitation on her old friend's face.

"We would have made good our escape if not for the noise that led the Normans to us."

The children, Bethany thought sadly. "Children cannot be expected to understand the gravity of the situation."

"Nay, the children, they were as good as angels. It was your sister who betrayed our hiding place."

"Mary?" Bethany gasped.

"She heard the soldiers searching for us and became frantic. I wanted to box her ears after the sacrifice you had made."

"Mary," Bethany repeated in bewilderment, then remembered the nursemaid. "I am so sorry, Tayte." Knowing that her own sister had ruined the plan hurt more than she could say. "I will try not to fail you again."

"No one blames you, my lady. We all know the length you went to assure our safety. It breaks my heart to see you as a slave while your sister is treated like a lady."

" 'Tis done."

"Take care you do not rile the Norman," Tayte said, a fearful expression clouding her aged features as she met her mistress's gaze.

" 'Tis too late. I think I was put on this earth to do just that."

She bid Tayte farewell and climbed the stone steps with the buckets.

The bath was tempered by the cool water, and she immediately went to finish the chore of unpacking the invader's belongings.

"What are you called?" he asked from the tub.

"I am Bethany of North Umberland." She said her full name, unable to keep the ring of pride from sounding in her voice.

" 'Tis a weighty title and much too formal an address for one such as you. Never mind, slave; I shall think on it."

There was silence for a moment, then his voice rang out.

"Annie, fetch my clean clothes."

"My name is Bethany," she said through clenched teeth.

"Annie, fetch my clean clothes."

This time, Bethany did not argue. Snatching his clothes up, she stomped over to the bath and laid his clean apparel by the tub.

"I am called Royce de Bellemare. But you may call me *my lord*," he said with droll amusement in his voice.

Bethany swore neither name would pass her lips. "Is there anything else, warlord?"

"*Oui,* slave." He extended his hand with the chunk of soap resting in it. "Scrub my back."

Bethany swallowed hard as the soap dropped into her palm. She moved around him and held the rough soap by her fingertips. The stretch of skin across his back was wide and bronzed by the sun; the muscles beneath his flesh rippled when she drew the soap lightly down his back and across his shoulders. Her face burned at the intimacy and yet, she could not look away. She was fascinated by the difference between them.

"Slave, you may not be familiar with bathing, but you need to scrub to get the dirt off." He held a cloth over his shoulder.

Bethany gritted her teeth at the insult. She had never been as filthy as she was now, covered in mud and ground-debris from her fight with him yesterday.

She took hold of the cloth and dug the rough material into his shoulders. The flesh was red from her harsh treatment, but he did not complain. However, she noticed that his muscles tensed every time she started another stroke. A smile spread across her lips. By the time she was through, he would not have an inch of skin left that was not red and sore.

"Slave, that feels wonderful, but you have yet to scrub the skin below the water."

The smile on her face vanished. Below the water. She closed her eyes and lowered the cloth down beneath the waterline. So intent was she in finishing her task that her arm swung madly across his buttocks and sloshed water over the rim.

"That will do; now you can start on my chest." He leaned

back against the rim and folded his hands behind his neck, looking utterly relaxed.

Bethany did not know if she could. She moved to the front of the tub and stared at the floor. This was beyond any humiliation she had ever suffered.

"What delays you, slave?" he asked, his tone serious.

She lifted her gaze to his and saw the amusement in his eyes. Damn the man. He was laughing at her! Her chin rose a notch and she lathered the cloth with angry strokes.

Beast! Satan's spawn, she cursed silently, holding on to her anger and nurturing it as she ran the cloth across his chest. His dark chest hairs glistened in the suds and her fingers tingled as if they had fallen asleep and suddenly awakened. A fine current shot through her veins as she realized this invader stirred something in her. She chanced a glimpse into his dark, blue eyes and noticed the gleam in their depths. Quickly she looked away. She could not bear for him to know her thoughts.

"Do not forget to wash all of me, slave," he said, laughter sounding in each word.

Bethany closed her eyes. He knew what he did to her and was making her endure more. Damn him.

Pretend he is dead or so ancient that he cannot lift his decrepit body without help. Good, if she thought of him as a helpless old man, it would make the task bearable. But when she washed down his chest and followed the thin line of hair down his belly, it was not a limp rod she felt but a firm shaft. Her face flamed and she jumped back from the tub. There was no way she could pretend he was old.

"I have finished. Will there be anything else, warlord?"

"Oui. From this night forward, you sleep there." He pointed at the bed. "With me."

"Never!" she exclaimed.

"Never, mademoiselle?" An eyebrow arched in disbelief as he held her gaze. "Have you not yet learned that opposing me is futile?" He pointed again to the bed. "Upon yon pallet, you *will* rest your head next to mine."

Frustration and fury burned within her. "Why?" she demanded, unable to believe his command.

"Because you are my slave," he replied in a quiet, patient voice clearly reserved for the weak of mind.

Bethany squared her shoulders. "As your slave I will do any menial task you assign, but I will not play the whore."

His eyes narrowed slightly. "You will do what I say. This is not a request, Annie. It is an order. You will sleep in my arms."

"I will not!" She flung the cloth into the tub, splashing soap and water into his face.

He wiped his face and stared at her. "Do I have to get out of this tub to prove my point?"

Terror surged through Bethany, and she took a step backwards before standing her ground. "Nay, I will fetch my clothes," she lied, bartering her integrity for ingenuity. She needed time to outwit him.

"Slave," he said, halting her rush to the door, "do not put me to the trouble of looking for you."

Chapter Three

Royce watched the Saxon girl depart. She was a fetching sight. When the door closed he let his smile show. Now that the villagers had returned, he found his mood improved and his disposition towards the maiden changed. God's teeth, when he had found the castle deserted and realized it was her fault, he'd wanted to throttle her.

Serfs were the key to success and, by all he held dear, he would make this land prosper. Once he set his mind on a goal, he never wavered. He planned to be a wealthy landowner and a powerful lord.

He rose from the tub and towel-dried his skin. The memory of that comely Saxon wench turned his thoughts from the future, a rare feat. But his goals were nearly attained; and after seven long years, he was reaping the rewards. It was time for him to celebrate.

He poured himself a chalice of wine and raised the rim to his lips. As the bitter-tasting brew slid down his throat, he wondered what was keeping the maiden.

* * *

Bethany wondered how long it would take before the Norman warlord came looking for her. Strange, the perceptions of youth. This secret place had always seemed so cozy and secure. With the passage of time, it was still snug—rather too much so— but the serenity and security had vanished with her childhood.

The other children had never found her hiding place—a narrow space between a low pallet and a window alcove in the tower. Now the chill from the wall and floors reminded her that this was not a game and she was no longer a child.

Adults, she had learned, also played games, but the stakes were higher and the forfeits costlier.

Bethany took a deep breath and rested her head in the cradle of her arms. Her home was now a prison. She could not move about with any freedom to seek another resting place, nor could she return to the Norman's room.

A shiver went through her as she remembered his muscular body and the feel of his skin. He would find her. She was only putting off the inevitable. Still, it was all she could do. She thought longingly of flight to Scotland. But she could never leave without her sister and brother. And even if they managed to escape, how could they enjoy their freedom, knowing that their people still lived in bondage?

Bethany heard someone bellow and huddled deeper into her hiding place, making herself as small as possible. The musty odor of mold that clung to the damp corners wafted through the air. The disturbing smell had not been present when she was a child, but then, neither had the invaders.

"God's teeth, Vachel, find the wench!"

"My Lord Royce, the maiden is not to be found," Vachel said as his steps echoed in the great room. "The castle guard swears she has not left by the gates, and the barricade to the secret passage has not been moved. She is here, my lord, hiding."

"Very well, Vachel, I will deal with her on the morn."

Bethany heard the soldiers' footsteps retreat. She settled down again until Royce's voice penetrated her hiding place.

"I know you are within the sound of my voice, Annie. You are playing a very foolish game. Show yourself now, and all will be forgiven and forgotten."

Did he think her so lack-witted as to believe his promise? She would face him in the morning when his desire had waned and there was little chance of being ravished at the hands of this Norman. Whatever the punishment, it could hardly match the fate that awaited her now.

She would get through each day in the same way, doing her chores obediently, then disappearing when dusk brought on the warlord's lust. Settling down to exhausted sleep, Bethany congratulated herself on her cleverness.

Taking a deep breath, Damiana leaned forward and tried to concentrate, a frown settling across her brow as she struggled with the words on the paper. Reading was such a chore. Like ciphering and scribing, reading was generally too tiresome a pursuit. After all, one could hire someone trained in such menial tasks. Unfortunately, if one wished to keep one's business private, then sacrifices must be made.

Why did Royce use such long words? Slowly, painstakingly, she sounded out each syllable. After several attempts, she understood the message.

England! That godforsaken isle? He expected her to live there? Why had Royce survived? If only he had died, she would never have to leave her beloved Normandy.

She paced the room, formulating her reply. Then, thoughtfully, she reformed her acceptance into four small words she could spell. *I wil come soon.* She blew on the ink to hasten the drying then smiled at her handiwork. She would not cross the channel until the last possible moment. With the curt missive written, she placed it aside and thought of the fun she would have visiting her friends before her exile.

"Morgana!" Damiana bellowed for her maid.

The young girl rushed into the room, looking like a scared rabbit.

"Pack my belongings. And mind that you do a good job or I will have you whipped." There were so many important families to bid farewell to. It might take months.

The serving girl moved in a frenzy. Her obvious fear brought a smile to Damiana's face. She enjoyed her station and the power it held.

England. No doubt the serfs there would be worse than here. The thought was appalling. She was going to live among the savages.

Damiana boxed Morgana's ears. "How many times must I tell you to fold the tunic in thirds, not halves?"

Tears glistened in the young maid's eyes.

"Do not rouse my ire again," Damiana said, indifferent to the servant's weeping, but vowing that if one teardrop stained her clothes that girl would rue the day she was born.

Bethany rubbed the sleep from her eyes and listened to the early-morning sounds. For an instant she was back in her warm bed, then reality intruded and she remembered how she came to be in her hiding place.

If only she could lie here and pretend all was as it should be. Even as the thought formed, she stretched, knowing she must rise and face the day, no matter how unpleasant it would be. The image of the warlord materialized in her mind. He would be angry after her escape last night. It was time to face her folly.

Bethany rose and began her long climb down from the tower, almost amused that no one had thought to check the very room she had been held in just two nights before. Swiftly she moved to the kitchen and started the fire for heating her water. She would not face that man another day looking like a filthy urchin.

The water was heavenly and she reveled in it, washing away the layers of dirt that coated her skin.

"My lady . . ." a shocked voice gasped from behind her.

"Maida, you gave me a scare." Bethany said as she took a deep breath to still her racing heart. "I did not expect anyone."

Maida rolled up her sleeves to begin the daily preparation for breaking the fast. "People who bathe in public should not be surprised at being discovered."

"There was nowhere else to bathe."

Maida eyed her strangely, then abruptly turned away and went about her chores.

Bethany shrugged at Maida's strange behavior. "Can you help me rinse my hair?"

Maida answered the summons silently and seemed unable to meet her mistress's eyes.

After Bethany stepped from the tub and towel-dried, the silence continued, creating an awkward tension she could not tolerate. "What is bothering you, Maida?"

"I feared you were . . . injured last night." Maida said, twisting her linen waist-covering into a tight rope.

"Heavens no! I outsmarted that dim-witted Norman."

"Then it was not your screams I heard in the middle of the night." Maida said with relief and released her wrinkled apron.

"Screams? What screams?" Bethany asked with growing panic as she clasped Maida's hands.

"The pleas for help. Where were you that you did not hear them?"

"In the tower, but . . ." Bethany raised her hands and let them drop, conveying her helplessness. "I must have been more tired than I thought." Bethany dressed quickly in the squire's clothes. "Who could it have been?"

Maida made the sign of the cross. "Whoever it was, my lady, she needed help."

"Maida, you must find out for me."

"What good will it do to know who suffered last night?"

"Mayhap there is something we can do to help ease the pain. I will not let this go unanswered."

"My lady, take care. The warlord had all his men searching

for you last night. I thought for sure when I heard the cries much later that they were yours."

"I will heed your warning," Bethany said, filling a bucket with hot water. The Norman would probably want to wash before breaking the fast.

"This should improve his mood." She grabbed a flagon of ale and, at Maida's look of alarm, kissed the cook's cheek before leaving the kitchen.

At least she would be safe today. The warlord's lust would have waned with the night's sleep, and she would only have to worry about his baser instinct at eventide.

Her arms felt as if they had been pulled out of their sockets by the time she climbed the stairs and reached the bedchamber. Timorously, she tried the handle. The door had not been barred and opened under her slight pressure.

She peered in and noticed with relief that the warlord lay beneath the bed robes still asleep, his heavy snores testament to his sound slumber.

Thank you. She directed the silent message heavenward as she entered the room. Tiptoeing across the floor to the table at the window, she crept past the bed.

Bethany kept her eyes averted from the sleeping pallet. Curiosity ate at her restraint, but she would not tempt fate and look at the Norman, afraid that gazing at him would bring him awake. His snores continued to fill the air, and Bethany poured water into a bowl without alarm at the noise she made. Then she placed the flagon of ale next to it and looked around her for the goblets.

"Are you looking for these?"

The goblets were shoved before her eyes, and her gaze skittered from the hand that held them up an arm to a shoulder and finally a face. He was awake and fully dressed, and she had not heard a sound! She glanced to the bed. The mound remained unchanged, but now the snoring noise came from the figure before her.

"You were awake the whole time?"

"*Oui.* A warrior does not sleep so soundly that an enemy can approach and place a sword in his gullet."

She inhaled slowly to calm her apprehension. "I have brought you warm water to wash and ale to ease your thirst."

"Such a thoughtful slave. Where were you last night? I had a need that was not met."

Her face burned from the question and she tried to turn away and slip to the door. His massive hand seized her shoulder.

"You will never make it."

Frustration and anger filled her. "I am not afraid of you."

A smile actually creased his lips. "I have noticed that. But, from now on, you had better fear me. I want your clothing brought in here. This is where you will reside. Do I make myself clear?"

Bethany nodded. "I will bring my clothes."

"Annie, I seem to remember warning you that if I were put to the trouble of looking for you, there would be consequences."

Bethany stared at him. Hostility and loathing filled her gaze and she did not bother to conceal her hatred. "If it pleases you to beat me over this, then I will speak my mind and tell you I would rather take a beating than share your weight in bed."

"It is fortunate for you that I do not take you at your word. I tell you true, maiden, you try my patience to the limit."

Bethany looked at him curiously. Although women had ruled this demesne, she was well aware that elsewhere things were difficult. And she was mindful of the beatings and punishments women frequently incurred at the hands of their husbands, let alone masters and lords. She was surprised he had not already retaliated.

"What will you do when you lose your patience?"

"You question me? Do you have no instinct for self-preservation?"

"I must know what manner of man rules my land and people."

"*Your* land and people?"

"Aye, they look to me and I am responsible for them."

"Not anymore," he said with finality.

"I am responsible for them. If I were not, I would have left last night, not hidden."

"That brings us around to the topic. Where were you last night?"

Bethany swallowed the lump of fear. "It does not matter."

"You asked what I would do when you pushed me beyond my limits." His gaze narrowed and seemed to bore into her. "If my question remains unanswered, you will know."

Bethany took a step backwards. She felt trapped. An inner voice warned—*tell him, you can find another hiding place tonight.*

"The tower. I spent the night in the tower until your lust waned and it was safe to return."

His eyebrow raised and he stared at her as if she had uttered gibberish. "Safe to return?"

"Aye, safe. The sun has risen," she said and, at his puzzled expression, expanded, "You will not be abed when there is work to do. Besides, 'tis daylight. Surely you do not want— *that,* in the daytime."

The Norman stared at her, blinked, then stared again as though he did not believe the sight before him. Laugh lines crinkled from his eyes, and he covered his mouth trying to clear his throat.

She hastened to pour him a goblet of ale. "Here, drink this," Bethany instructed.

Though he complied, she noticed an expression of humor in his gaze, but she did not comment on it. She was at enough of a disadvantage without showing her ignorance.

"You are right about one thing, *cherie,*" he said finally, handing her the goblet. "I have a very busy day ahead of me." He smiled, showing bright white teeth, and the expression lit up his eyes. Leaning forward, he brushed his knuckles across her cheek. She felt a rush of heat clear to her toes.

A deep sigh passed his lips as he pulled away. "Work must be seen to first." With obvious regret, he withdrew his hand, turned, and left.

Bethany felt warm all over. The man was truly handsome. For a Norman.

Rolling hills of gray and brown, and drab forests of tall trees and dark vegetation were all that could be seen as the Norman warriors galloped out of the castle toward the north.

"Royce, what brings a smile to your lips?" Guy asked as they rode to check the one perimeter of the estate that presented concern. Their demesne bordered Scotland.

"The Saxon slave."

"After last night I did not think anything to do with that woman would ever bring a smile to your face."

"She returned shortly after sunrise." A chuckle escaped his lips. "Did you know that she believes a man's passion is ruled by the time of day? Apparently, a man's lust is uncontrollable between sunset and sunrise, but during the day his baser instincts are displaced with the business of the day."

Guy chuckled. "I hope you set her straight."

"I did not have time. But, never fear, brother, I will correct the girl's misunderstanding and take great joy in doing so." He chuckled again, enjoying his good fortune and imagining the pure delight he would have at her expense.

"I have not seen you this happy in a long time."

Royce thought about that. It was true he had never allowed himself to enjoy life. He was always pushing harder, reaching further.

"Soon, I will have what I want," Royce said.

"I hope, brother, obtaining what you have dreamed of is as fulfilling as desiring it."

"What the devil do you mean by that?" Royce snapped, annoyed.

"Often, I have learned, the reward is not as sweet as the victory."

"You make no sense," Royce scoffed.

"Or perhaps I make too much sense," Guy replied with quiet assurance.

"Enough. Damiana is the *lady* I have chosen; and for family peace, you had best accept my decision."

"As you say, enough."

That piece of irreverence warranted a cuff, but Royce put no force into the blow. "I should have sent you back to the monastery as Mother wished."

"It is too late to bemoan your decision. As I am your brother, you now have a loyal sword to protect your back and gentle advice whispered in your ear to safeguard your soul."

"Gentle advice?" Royce roared. "Your time, and that of the good friar's, was wasted thinking you would ever make a good cleric."

"I agree. I do not have the temperament to turn the other cheek. But just because I did not choose the church does not mean my time was wasted there. You are making a mistake with Damiana."

"It is my mistake to make. Have done. I grow old and weary of your chatter."

"Shame on you, Royce," Guy mocked, but could not contain his smile. "Would you have me ignore the Bible? Am I not my brother's keeper?"

Royce roared with laughter. "*YOU* were never that pious. Look to your own love interest or else I will find more pressing matters to occupy your time."

"As you wish, Royce. I have no desire to stand night guard nor train raw recruits."

Royce nodded his head, accepting his brother's acquiescence, although he knew it was only temporary.

"I want watch sentries posted here," he said, pointing to the far ridge. "See to it, Guy."

"Do you expect trouble?" he asked, his manner instantly alert.

"*Non,* but I would be a fool to be unprepared. The Scots are unpredictable and I have no desire to find myself at their mercy."

" 'Tis said they are heathens."

"Heathens be damned. They can paint their bodies and set their hair afire, I do not care about their beliefs. It is their military strength that interests me. William's reports call them the fiercest warriors and strongest strategists."

"Do you think we will encounter them?" Guy asked as either apprehension or anticipation sharpened his features.

"If we do, brother, stay close. I do not wish to write our mother that her youngest son foolishly underestimated the enemy."

"Verily, that would be a terrible duty. Mother does dote on her favorite."

Royce quickly responded to the lifelong jest. "*Oui*, she felt sorry for her youngest son, being weak of limb and wit."

Guy grinned at the remark, his eyes sparkling with amusement.

Royce thanked God his brother was with him. His loyalty was unquestionable even if his manners left much to be desired. But Royce would not change Guy, nor his blunt honesty. The truth, though difficult to hear, was oftentimes harder to speak.

"Mother called me aside before we left Normandy and beseeched me to look after you, Royce. She has always feared that blow to your head injured what little brains you possessed."

Royce laughed, then said casually, "We have been under surveillance. To the north and west, small bands of men have followed our moves."

Guy continued to smile as he furtively gazed about, then looked directly at his brother. "How long have you known?"

"Since you asked if we would meet the Scotsmen."

"What do you think they are doing?"

"Deciding."

"On what?"

"If we are worth the trouble to fight."

Guy stared at the trees just beyond the rise. "It does not anger you to be spied upon?"

"Non! In a match of wills I shall not be found wanting," Royce said.

Guy shook his head. "If ever you lose your iron resolve, the church bells shall sound the funeral dirge and I, myself, shall conduct the ceremony."

Royce smiled. "A leader must be in control. I will never willingly bow my head to another."

"What about William?"

"William has my loyalty. He has earned it as I have earned my position. In this respect we are equals. Outside of you and William, there is not another for whom I would lay down my life."

"I have similar loyalties," Guy said. Then he turned and scanned their surroundings again, as if enjoying the view. "They are still there?"

"Oui, they watch for now," Royce replied. "Later, perhaps, they will strike. When they do, we will be ready."

Royce turned his horse and the men followed his lead. They were headed back toward the castle.

"Leave Vachel behind," Royce ordered his brother in an undertone. "He is the best. If they are following us, we will be well advised."

Vachel received his orders and nodded curtly to Royce.

As always, Royce settled back to ponder his situation. Something was afoot here, and he needed to know what it was.

Chapter Four

"My lady, the Normans are returning," Maida said breathlessly as she rushed into the room.

Bethany folded the letter into thirds and returned it to the warlord's trunk. Discreetly, she brushed away the moisture gathering in her eyes.

"Thank you, Maida." Bethany dragged the trunk containing his personal papers back to its original place next to the clothes chest. She stepped back to study its position. Satisfied, she turned to Maida. "He will never know."

"Did you find a weakness, my lady?"

"Aye, he has a fondness for his family." Bethany shook away the thought. She did not want to see this man in any light other than ruthless conqueror. "I must find a way to defeat him," she said aloud.

Maida dabbed at the perspiration on her brow and upper lip. "If he finds you sneaking through his belongings,—"

"Do not worry, Maida," Bethany said. "I know what I am about."

"That is why I worry, my lady."

Bethany did not reprimand Maida. Her words were honest, and spoken from the heart.

Maida left the room, and Bethany quickly restored order to the chamber. There were only a few articles out of place; and while she was busily setting them to rights, she heard a strange scraping sound. She stopped to listen carefully, but she did not hear it again and could not be sure she had not imagined it in her nervousness.

Suddenly Mary's voice startled her, distant yet urgent. "Come quickly, Bethany," she called.

Bethany threw open the door and immediately stumbled, falling straight toward the balcony rail. Her face cracked into the top of the balustrade and slipped passed the rail. She hung over the great hall, catching her forward momentum with a death grip on the rail.

The room below swam before her eyes as dizziness engulfed her. She had nearly careened over the rail to the floor below. Taking deep calming breaths to still her racing heart, Bethany sank slowly to the floor, cradling her sore cheek with her palm. Her gaze travelled to the doorway and lighted on the object she had tripped over.

God's teeth, she could have sworn she had placed that bucket safely out of harm's way. If not for her luck at grabbing the rail, she would have been seriously injured, if not killed. A shiver went up her spine as she contemplated her close call.

Bethany closed her eyes and gingerly felt her aching cheek. Sharp pain sliced from under her eye to her temple as large tears trailed down her face. From now on, she would have to be more prudent. Her eyelids opened slowly, revealing the bucket rolling back and forth in an arc on the hall floor. Despite the evidence before her, it was still hard to believe she had been so careless.

But she had had much on her mind, and in truth, had been sneaking around trying to find out information about the warlord. St. Bede, she had no one to blame but herself. Quickly, she wiped the moisture from her face, causing another wave of pain. Willow's bark would help alleviate the ache, if only Maida had some on hand.

"Bethany! Are you all right?"

She looked up to find Mary hovering above her. "Aye, sister." Bethany accepted the hand offered and pulled herself up. "Why did you call me?" Bethany asked.

"To tell you the Normans are returning," Mary replied, releasing her sister's arm.

I knew that, she felt like yelling; but of course Mary could not have realized that. Bethany frowned to keep the anger within, and the grimace caused her to moan.

"Oh my, your face," Mary gasped, staring at Bethany's injured cheek.

Bethany shook the cobwebs from her brain. She cared little for the appearance she presented. "I will survive. What matter if my face is misshapen?"

Mary shook her head. "Your cheek is swollen and bright red. It must hurt dreadfully."

Bethany took a deep breath. Her little sister had a talent for understatement! She wondered, not for the first time, if the eight years Mary had spent in the convent had slightly stifled her wits.

"It will heal," Bethany said, trying but failing to keep her frustration out of her voice.

"What will you say when asked how it came about?" Mary asked. The innocent concern and beseeching expression on Mary's lovely features made Bethany feel guilty for her uncharitable thoughts.

"Do not look so worried, sister. This is one time when the truth will see us out. It was an accident."

"Bethany, do be careful," she cautioned as her frail arms wrapped around Bethany in an embrace. Mary clung like a vine, as she had when they had been small and frightened. Then, as now, Mary offered the only comfort she could—her warmth. The gesture touched Bethany's heart.

"Mary, you worry too much." Bethany leaned back from the

embrace and brushed aside the pale hair from her sister's delicate cheek. "I was appalled to hear that the screams heard late last night came from your room. Mary, love, what terrified you?"

Mary lowered her heard as if ashamed. " 'Twas a nightmare, no more."

"I want Tayte to sleep in your room. She can awaken you if you should start to dream again."

"Before the Normans came, I never suffered ill dreams. They have changed our world. I want them gone."

"We all want them gone." Bethany tried to see her sister's downcast face. With a finger placed gently beneath Mary's chin, Bethany raised her sister's gaze to meet hers. "And we all must do our part."

Amazement flashed in Bethany's mind. Mary's tear-filled eyes burned with passion! "If the holy saints died unafraid as martyrs in a righteous cause, then I can do no less. What would you have me do?"

Bethany had never suspected this core of determination. But what she must ask of Mary would take courage and she hesitated to place her sister in danger.

"Do not treat me like a delicate child," Mary said, apparently guessing her sister's thoughts.

The words decided Bethany. "Court the Normans' favor. You can move within their circle. Gain their trust. Be my eyes and ears." Bethany held up her hand to forestall her sister's objection. "I know you do not speak their language; but when we were children, I taught you their dialect. I believe if you are surrounded by their speech, your memory will return and you may understand their conversations, or a part of them."

"Ask me anything but that. Our people will think I betray them."

"Nay, I will see to it that they know you do this for our good."

Her momentary bravado seemed to waver as Mary wrung

her hands. "I will do it, although I am afraid," she admitted, backing up to leave.

"You will do fine."

Bethany watched her timid sister walk away and wished her safely in Scotland.

Somehow Uncle Mactavish *must* be notified. Though an arrogant Scotsman, he would not turn his back on her plea to save his kin. At least she hoped he would not.

She would send him a message. As their only male relative, he might be able to rescue at least Mary and Bret. That would be one worry from her mind.

The tinker travelling north could carry her missive.

By now the caravan should have arrived safely in Scotland. She knew Bram Mactavish to be an honorable man. He would not spend the money, but he would arrange to control it if the opportunity arose. Laird Mactavish had never understood the Umberland legacy or his brother's willingness to give his name and power to protect and defend the land belonging to his wife. But she was sure that, despite their differences, he was a man who would not turn his back on kin.

Hearing the sound of horses clamoring over the stone courtyard, Bethany pulled herself together for the coming ordeal. Through the chamber door, she noticed steam rising from the bathing tub and grimaced.

The Norman's bath awaited the master of the house. That thought soured her mood even more.

This was her home, not his. With frustration and anger, she rose and grabbed the offending bucket. She would store it safely away this time.

Well after sunset, the candles and torches were lit and the fires burned in the hearths. The aroma of baked bread and roasted meat filled the air with a mouth-watering scent. Renwyg Castle exuded its warmth and hospitality, unaware of the difference between family and foe.

All was ready when the warlord, followed by his men, entered the great hall, filling it with the boisterous noise of hungry soldiers. Bethany lowered her eyes, the sight of the returning conqueror a painful reminder of her loss.

She hated the foreign conversation that floated to her ears. She kept her eyes on the rushes and prayed to St. Bede for patience when the warlord's brother made some particularly unpleasant comments about the flavor and fare in Saxony.

"No worse than the homely women who live on this isle," said Royce.

Her head snapped up and she found herself staring into the laughing eyes of the warlord. He knew she could understand their conversation; and by the pleased look on his face, she could tell he had purposely baited her.

Suddenly, his humor vanished and his face grew solemn as his gaze flicked over her cheek. "Who struck you?" he demanded.

When she remained silent, unable to understand his interest, he grabbed her chin and tilted it upward for closer inspection. "I know the mark of a heavy hand when I see it. Who did this to you, *cherie?*"

She did not want his concern; and, what was worse, she did not want to explain. "Leave me be."

She tried to pull away, but he held her within his grip. "Do not refuse to answer me, Annie."

Bethany struggled for a moment, but her effort was wasted against this giant of a man. She drew a deep breath to show her frustration and release the building tension. " 'Twas no one's fault. I had an accident."

At her explanation, the tense lines about his mouth and eyes disappeared. Softly, he touched her cheek. "Take care, *cherie.* A face so lovely should not be marred."

Beneath his gentle caress, she felt a warmth surge straight to her heart. His tenderness and flattery unnerved her. She did not want to let her guard down. To feel anything besides hatred for this man would be traitorous. She steeled herself to retreat behind a barrier of anger and mistrust.

A slow smile teased his lips when she squared her shoulders and jutted her chin up in order to look down her nose at the invader. When he winked at her, she whirled around and picked up a flagon of ale.

"Ale? After today's ride I favor wine," he said.

"Are you lack-witted, brother? This country's wine is a far cry from Normandy's. Sour is the taste of Saxon grapes," Guy said.

"I agree, but I prefer wine to ale," Royce said to his brother, then turned to Bethany. "Remember that, slave."

She slammed down the flagon of ale and went in search of the wine. She hoped it was the sourest vintage they had ever made.

Storming past Maida, she ran down the steps to the cellar and inspected the wines. Rows of oak barrels, stacked from ceiling to floor, lined one wall. In the flickering torchlight she read the charred letters burned into the wooden covers conveying the date and name of each wine. She moved down the aisle past elderberry and dandelion to the last stack and filled the flagon with their worst wine.

When she entered the kitchen, she noticed Maida pouring cider vinegar into milk to curdle it for bread. She should not even contemplate the wicked thought! Then, as if all the good intentions dissolved with her common sense, she placed the flagon of wine on the table and reached for an empty pitcher.

"Maida, pour some of the cider vinegar into this vessel. How dare he say our wines are sour!"

Maida's face paled. "Please, my lady, this is not wise."

"Nay, I will not allow that man to insult my home."

"My lady, he can do anything he wants. Our lives are held in the good offices of his whim. Would you anger him needlessly?" Maida asked, shaking a flour-covered finger at Bethany.

" 'Tis I who will bear the brunt of his anger. Please understand, Maida. I must do this."

Maida shook her head, but partially filled the empty container with vinegar and then eyed her mistress carefully. "What will you do tonight, my lady?"

The concern in Maida's voice relieved the tension between them. Bethany added the wine to the pitcher containing the vinegar, then smiled at Maida. "I have that all worked out. Do not worry," Bethany said.

"I cannot help but worry," Maida said.

Bethany gave in to Maida's curiosity. "The Norman is smart, but I am smarter."

"Forsooth?" Maida intoned in disbelief.

Bethany ignored the sarcasm. "I have set a little intrigue in motion, and by bedtime the Norman will have more important matters on his hands than bedding a Saxon."

Maida once again shook her head and turned away, a subtle rebuke that was not lost on Bethany. "Do not worry, Maida. All will be right."

"Aye, as you say, my lady, all will be right. But for whom?"

Ignoring the warning in the cook's words, Bethany transferred the wine and vinegar mixture into a flagon and carried it out to the table where the warlord sat with his brother and her sister. As she poured a generous cup of the liquid into his chalice, the pungent smell filled the air.

When he raised the cup to his lips, his nostrils flared. Quickly, she turned, hiding her satisfaction from his sharp-eyed gaze. She hoped he choked on the bitter brew.

"Ah, this wine is very distinctive. I insist that Lady Mary try it."

Bethany whirled around, knowing that he had discovered her ploy. "Nay, my sister does not like wine."

Ignoring her, he turned to Lady Mary. "Would you like a cup of wine, Lady Mary?" He thrust an empty chalice into her hand, then raised his goblet to signify his intention. "You will join me in a toast."

Mary looked helplessly at her sister. The Norman had cleverly left her no way of refusing.

"She will not drink with you. If you must have a toast, propose it and I will lift the cup." Bethany shook her head to mock him. "You must think it poisoned the way you go on so."

He smiled at her, but the look held not humor, but retribution.

"Here." He handed her Mary's chalice. "Fill it and join me in the toast."

Bethany was aware he watched her as she filled her vessel from the flagon containing the wine-flavored vinegar. Though she would have liked to pour only a small quantity in her cup, to do so would give her away. To allay suspicion, she filled the brass goblet to the brim.

"To the people and land of North Umberland." He raised his chalice to her.

She swallowed the lump in her throat and raised the cup high in the air. The strong fumes stung her eyes and she blinked several times to relieve any tearing. "To the people and land of North Umberland, may they be free of the invader's heel." The added toast gave her a small measure of satisfaction.

The Norman slowly drew the chalice to his lips, waiting for her to do the same. His midnight-blue eyes were visible above the rim, that steely dark gaze fastened on her every move.

To hesitate now would admit guilt, which she would never do.

Taking a deep breath of courage, she gulped the tainted wine. It burned her throat and erupted like a lightning bolt in her stomach. Tears streamed down her face and she gasped for air.

Through a watery blur she saw the warlord shake his head. "Verily, you are the most stubborn woman I have ever met." Soft laughter filled the air. "Next time, Annie, choose something that does not alert the senses. The smell of vinegar is unmistakable."

He was absolutely right. The next time she would choose some odorless poison. She looked at the half-filled cup of vinegar, then to the warlord, then back to her cup. Flinging it in his face would not be lethal; but oh! would it be satisfying.

"Annie,—" His deep voice carried an edge of warning. "—do not even think it."

She stared up at his face and wondered how he knew her thoughts.

Still, it would be worth the punishment. Just as her heart won over her common sense, she noticed Mary's pale features. This whole episode was obviously terrifying her timid sister. She would not have her revenge at the price of Mary's peace of mind.

With frustration, she slammed down the tankard. Damn. Being meek did not have its rewards, no matter what the good book said.

Several deep breaths brought her emotions under control, and slowly she raised her gaze to meet the insufferable Norman's.

The expression of humor that clung to his eyes and lips bespoke the sport she was to him. The very idea that Bethany of North Umberland was the jester to this barbarian humiliated her.

Though it was difficult, she squared her shoulders beneath his scrutiny and held his gaze.

"Slave, see to my bath."

With those few words he reminded her of the hopelessness of the situation. Bath. Ah yes, his bath. Though she would not acknowledge the vivid images of his body, the memories of the rippling muscles and hard, firm flesh that had made her fingers tingle refused to be buried. Like a specter they haunted her.

This was harder than she could ever have imagined. She nodded, unable to trust her voice. The deep huskiness would betray her thoughts and that was the last thing she wanted.

She had made a fool of herself with the vinegar; that would not happen again. Consoling her bruised and battered pride, she reminded herself of the coming night. She had it all planned.

Tonight, he would play the fool.

The image of the mighty warlord calling out for his slave and searching hither and yon without success tickled her.

She could almost hear the townspeople snickering under their breath at the foolish conqueror. Their voices floated to her in a delicious fantasy of revenge. "A North Umberland woman commands, being born and bred to lead, not follow," they would whisper among themselves, shaking their heads at the folly of the outsider.

With renewed energy, she headed up the long stairway. Tonight, she would be the victor. Outsmarting this Norman would restore her pride.

Chapter Five

Fires burned in all the hearths and ale flowed freely in the dark, brown stronghold by the loch. Shadows shimmered along the walls as the invited clan lairds left their kinsmen in the great hall and assembled in the lesser hall. Colorful plaids brightened the dour room as men who had met in battle now shared a mug in honor of Mactavish's call. Several chieftains removed their smocks and sat only in their plaids as the warmth in the room rose. A few who were further into their cups removed their plaids and sat as bare and bold as the day they'd entered the world.

"How powerful are you?" Laird Mactavish asked the clansman from the west who stood before him, while covertly checking Friar John's sign. As agreed upon beforehand, the cleric circled the filled chamber, gleaning either favorable or unfavorable information about the prospective candidates to help aid in the selection process.

"You need not worry. I, Killian Macleod, dinna have to watch my back," the young Scotsman said with a touch of arrogance.

"The man is dangerous," Mactavish warned, testing the metal of the man before him as others looked on with avid interest.

"For the Lady Bethany's dowry, a third of the wealth in yon room," Macleod said, pointing to the room that housed the North Umberland treasures, "I would march into hell." His emphatic response brought nods of agreement from the crowd.

Mactavish ignored the cleric's frown at the remark and responded, "I knew you were the man for the job."

"The lass, she dinna know of your plans?" Killian Macleod grabbed a chalice of ale from a passing servant.

"Nay, but she will agree," Mactavish said.

Cedric, the wounded soldier from North Umberland, leaned forward on his crutch to address the clansman. "You need not worry, lad. She is a comely lady."

"I dinna care if she resembles my horse." The man paused to down his whole cup, then dragged his sleeve across his lips. With a sardonic smile, he returned the laird's stare. "I care for the wealth she brings."

The man only spoke the truth, yet his callous words pricked Mactavish's conscience. And Lord knew, the burden he carried in his soul had festered too long. Yet he managed to reply with practiced ease, "There is only one problem, but it is a minor obstacle for a Scotsman. A Norman solider stands between you and the money."

This chieftain, like all the others in the room, stared at Mactavish as though he had gone mad. "Not for all the wealth in England would I cross the Normans. You will have to find someone else who is hungry for money at the expense of his life." Macleod lowered his tankard and turned to leave, several men falling in behind him.

"Is there not one man among us that would brave the Normans for the wealth of a laird and the sweet gratitude of a comely lass?" Mactavish's insult hung in the air.

At the shuffling of feet in the silence, Mactavish drove his point home, ridding himself of his anger and frustration. " 'Tis a poor day when no stouthearted man canna be found."

"I, Fenrir Gunn, will wed the wee lass," one voice boomed from the background. "Though I have no bloodline, I wouldna leave a lass in such distress. And unlike those who eat your food and enjoy your hospitality, I fear the Normans not."

Grumbles of dissent arose at the comment, and several men left the room. Those who remained raised their chalices in a toast to the young man.

Mactavish felt a measure of relief, but he did not show it as he looked at the man. The colors he wore denoted he was a clansman from the north. Strange men they were. But no one could dispute their bravery.

"I will need to know, lad, if you plan to share any of this wealth or if ye have any objections to my guardianship." Even as he posed the question, he knew there were more important things than money or clan. A lesson he had learned too late.

"Nay, I dinna risk my life for you. The money and lass are mine, Mactavish. If your kilt is threadbare, look to another clan for wool."

"Aye, you are a smart lad. So be it," Mactavish said, relieved to have a man who would rescue his kin. They were Mactavish's responsibility, but as laird he could not involve his clan in a war. This way, the north clansman would bear the burden and weight of the invader's wrath.

Bram made his way to Fenrir's side. "She is a bonnie lass, make no mistake, lad. But you will be obliged to bring her family also."

"I dinna have a problem with that." Fenrir raised his chalice and drained his cup.

"Then we are agreed. You will rescue the North Umberland lady and her family."

"North Umberland." The man paused, rubbing his chin. "Aye, the name rings a bell. They must possess great wealth for me to recall the name."

"Aye, lad, but 'twill not be easy. The Norman has claimed your bride as his slave."

"Ah." The north clansman shook his head in a gesture of understanding. "Her family opposed the Norman."

"Nay, lad. She did."

"A woman?"

"Aye. Much like her mother, she possesses the strength and courage of a warrior, but without the brash and bluster." Mactavish caught the cleric's warning expression and cleared his throat to cover his lapse into the past. "Bethany is a woman of strength and fortitude. She gave the people of her demesne time to escape. 'Tis a brave lassie you will be getting."

Friar John slapped the lad on the back. " 'Tis a lucky lad you are, Fenrir Gunn, getting a bride as bonnie and brave as Scotland with a heart of gold and a spirit of iron. What more can a man ask for? Not to mention the reward in heaven for the good and right deed of saving an innocent angel from the devil's own clutches."

The young Scotsman covered the hilt of his sword. "Let us be away."

"Nay, we leave in the morning," Mactavish said, a smile touching his lips for the first time that night.

"If the Norman will not give her up, will you stand with me?" Fenrir asked.

"Only if you share the dowry, lad. Otherwise I will not risk my life, or the clan's safety." If there were regret in his tone, no one heard it except that damned cleric. Men who listened to confessions could hear remorse in any response.

"Nay, the dowry is mine," said the north clansman.

"Then the fight is yours," Mactavish responded.

"Aye, 'tis fair."

Mactavish watched the man walk with the others into the great room for the dinner feast. The room emptied except for the friar. When they were alone, Friar John joined him by the fire.

"For your part in this intrigue, friar, I expect you will fry in hell."

Instead of being insulted, the religious threw back his head and roared. "Bethany assures me that I will be in good company." The cleric turned to him. "What about you, Bram Mactavish?"

"My hell began nineteen years ago, the day I watched my brother, Gowain, take as his bride, Hayley of North Umberland. Damn that legacy."

"You have been given a second chance, Bram Mactavish. You can rescue the children of that union."

"Aye, and by all that's holy, I swear I willna fail them as I did their mother."

Bethany waited for the warlord in the master chamber. The steam curled toward the ceiling as she sat by the bath tub, remembering the smile on his face as he'd proposed that damn toast. She hated him and hated herself for being so stupid.

What in the world would her people do without a strong protector? She had to be cleverer. She could not just make up plans as the day began. No, she needed a strategy or a powerful ally. Since there were no powerful Saxons left in England, only Scotland could provide safety and protection. But she had no way of getting her family and friends there. *Think, by all that's holy, think. And be resourceful. People are depending on you.* She sighed. Being responsible for others left a terrible burden on the soul. She would gladly align herself with the devil himself if he could help her people. She was fresh out of ideas and needed to find some quickly.

Royce de Bellemare strode into the room with a smile hovering on his lips. Oh, how she hated that smirk. He looked as if he possessed a secret to which she would never be privy. Some men asked for animosity just by being alive. This man was one of them.

The way he studied her irritated Bethany. She could feel his gaze upon her; he watched her every move like a cat about to pounce. Did he not have any diversions? Suddenly, it occurred to her that she would have to create less of an appeal or she would not escape tonight.

"Is the bath ready?" he queried.

"Aye."

"Then, if you will help me . . ."

She remained quiet as she undid his fastenings and tried not to think of what she was touching. Still, though she would have it otherwise, his body held a fascination for her. For a brief second she closed her eyes, marshalling her defenses against him.

It was a near-futile task for he insisted on talking to her, making it impossible to block him out.

"You are making this much harder than it needs be," he said. "If you will but allow yourself to relax, then the night should pass agreeably."

The arrogance! Bethany raked her nails down his back as she peeled his shirt away.

"Sorry, did I hurt you?" she asked solicitously.

"*Non,* Annie. It would take more than those little scrapes to wound me."

"Pity," she muttered, wishing she had injured him more so that he would think twice before pursuing her.

"What?"

Startled that he had overheard her remark, she responded quickly. "Nothing, I was clearing my throat."

That damn smile was in place and instinctively she knew it did not bode well for her.

"You look unusually pensive tonight, Annie. Is there something churning within that Saxon mind that causes you unrest?"

Bethany ignored his comment and reached for his sword. She tried to hold it steady when he placed it in her hands, but the damn blade wavered like a reed in the wind.

"I forgot, you have trouble with these." He took the sword from her.

If only he would trip and fall on his weapon . . . what a pity to be skewered! She would spare him one prayer out of Christian charity.

But he made it to the table without harm, and Bethany felt disappointed and a little miffed that her wish had gone unheard by the Almighty. But not the warlord. As if he read her thoughts, he chuckled at her expression. "If I were a suspicious man, I would think you wished me harm."

"Me?" Bethany feigned innocence, laying her hand over her heart. "Why would a slave wish a master ill-will? I cannot picture the image in my mind." Though her expression remained benign, her voice took on an edge. "Verily, the slave sees how much better off she is to lose her home, land, and freedom."

" 'Tis the lot of the vanquished. If you had had men to protect this demesne, the outcome could have been different," he said as he came toward her and held her shoulders in a gentle grip. "Annie, in every confrontation since the dawn of time, there has been a winner and a loser. That is the way of conflict and contests."

Though true, his words cut to her soul. "I see. Then my life is merely a game."

"A game you should not have played if you were unwilling to pay the price. Do not cry foul now."

"I never cry," she said, refusing to be pitied. Determined, she untied his braiel and moved to place the breech-girdle in the chest.

"You are so shy, Annie. Whenever you almost uncover the interesting parts, you run and hide."

"I am putting away your clothes—or would you prefer I fling them about the room?"

"I would prefer you over here. Not scurrying and skittering about the chamber beyond my reach. Come here, Annie."

Bethany rose as if she were going to her execution. "I do not fear you," she said with false bravado, trying desperately to present a courageous mein.

"Good. I would not like to see fear in your eyes. Especially when I hold you in my arms."

Unconsciously, Bethany took a step backwards. "No matter, Norman. You will never see fear in my eyes, only hate and loathing."

"I care nothing for the other emotions as long as you do not fear me. I find it extremely hard to bed a frightened woman."

"Bed!", she gasped. Where in God's name was her sister's diversion?

"Yes, bed. What did you think, Annie? That I would not lie with you?"

A loud crash followed by a bloodcurdling scream made Bethany start.

"God's teeth," Royce swore and strode from the room half naked.

The moment the door closed, she picked up a wolf pelt, wrapped it around herself, and scurried from the room. Bless you, Mary, she whispered as she tiptoed up the steps to the battlements.

With the fur covering, she felt warm and cozy as she settled into her new hiding place, and a smile of pure joy crossed her lips as several moments later she heard the warlord bellow for her return.

This time when she crept back to Royce's room, Bethany was wary. The sunrise lit the way as she hauled the water and carried the wine. Last night she had been victorious, but today could see her defeated. Her stomach roiled with every step taken toward her adversary. Matching wits and wills with Royce de Bellemare was dangerous. Though she hated to admit it 'twas not his strength but her weakness that placed her at a disadvantage. For the first time in her life, she was aware of the opposite sex—and not just any man, but the one who had conquered her land. She took a deep breath and reached for the door handle. Thank goodness it was daylight.

The door swung open and she peeked inside. The mound of bed covers was piled high, and she kept her gaze on the robes as she entered the room. Suspiciously, her gaze travelled full circle, but the Norman had to be abed. There was nowhere else in the room he could hide from her sight.

Satisfied, she placed the wine on the table and poured the water into a basin.

"Where did you go last night?"

The gasp caught in her throat as she whirled around. "Where did you come from?"

He stood with his arms crossed over his bare chest and looked down at her imperiously. "Annie, I am not the mystery. You are."

He was too close for her to think. She tried to step back, but the table was behind her. Carefully, she tried to ease to one side, but the warlord leaned closer and grabbed the table on either side of her, stopping her escape.

"I am back now," she said with a false brightness. When an answering smile was not forthcoming, she tried to ease her weight from one foot to the other to wedge a little space between them.

He moved closer, a handsbreadth from her face, effectively ending her bid for breathing room.

"*Oui*, Annie, you are here now."

She was becoming confused by his nearness. "Is that not what you want? A slave to serve your needs?"

A smile spread across his lips and the sight of it warned her before his hands closed around her arms. "That is exactly what I want."

"Nay, 'tis daylight!"

"That, my dear, would serve you well if I had any duties that needed my attention."

"But you have duties every day. Everyone does," she said, feeling a rush of panic. Could it be she was mistaken that men's lust rose in the night and diminished in the day?

"Today I entrusted my brother with more responsibilities."

"Why?" she asked, wary of his answer.

"Because you seem to keep disappearing at night."

Her heart plummeted. Oh Lord! She had made a grave error. Bethany stared into his eyes. She knew the time for outwitting him had past. Her knees began to tremble but she fought the panic. Fear would impede her escape.

"Would you force a maiden?"

" 'Twill not be force, my dear."

Bethany relaxed. If he would not force her, then there was nothing to worry about.

"I am relieved to find you are a man of honor."

"Honor?"

"Aye, you will not force me; therefore, I need not fear you any longer."

"Have you never lain with a man before?"

"Nay, I have not yet chosen my mate."

"You would do the choosing?" His question mirrored his disbelief.

"Aye."

"You have strange customs here."

"Our customs are different. I am sure you would not like being at someone's mercy, yet you expect me to be overjoyed."

"Enough. I realize it is better to be among the victors than the vanquished. But you cannot expect me to feel sorry for you."

"I did not ask for your pity."

"Oui, that is so. You ask for nothing. I actually admire you." His hands had started to travel up her arms, and a delicious warmth spread across her flesh not only from his touch, but from his words.

"Why would you admire me?" Bethany asked, baffled by his response.

"You were the only one who resisted. You are very brave."

She lowered her head. This was such a complicated matter. She did not understand her ambivalent feelings. "Please, I do not wish to hear kind words from you."

He lifted her chin so he could look into her eyes. There was a gleam of amusement in his eyes. "Would you rather hear curses?"

Her throat constricted. Why did he have to look at her with such warmth in his gaze? Why did this man have to produce such a disturbing reaction in her?

"I would rather you moved away and let me think."

But his hands slipped softly to cradle her face. "Why do you make it so hard, Annie? Is compliance to a Norman betrayal? . . . Is that why you fight me? There is nothing you can do. Nothing. I have won the right to you, and I mean to enjoy it." Softly, he released her face, then his fingers danced quickly down her back, causing tingles where they travelled.

Her thoughts flew apart. She shivered, unable to hold onto any of the important ones.

"Why?" she managed.

The question hung between them for several seconds before he answered her.

"Because you are a beautiful woman."

She stared at him as if he jested.

"Me? I am afraid you have me confused with my sister."

"Non, cherie. Others may be fooled by your sister's pale image of perfection, but I am not. I know whom I hold in my arms. A warm vibrant woman."

The words were powerful magic to a girl who had been raised in the shadow of a beauty such as Mary.

"Do you play me false? Surely, my lord, there is livelier sport to be had than to cruelly tease a plain woman."

He stared at her for a moment before pulling her over to the polished metal in the corner of the room.

"Look at yourself. Can you not see your image in this looking glass?"

She stared at her reflection and saw nothing that would inspire great fits of passion. Instead, her attention centered on the image next to hers. Royce's strong profile and virile body captured her sight and imagination. The lines in his face had been etched by hardship and . . .

"Well?" he inquired.

"Well what?" she asked. "It is my face, the same one I have owned for eighteen summers."

"Can you not see what I see?"

She stared again, this time concentrating on her image.

"Red hair, too many freckles, and eyes the color of fields

newly churned for planting." She recited her faults and flaws as if he were blind.

Royce looked at her strangely, then a grin split his features. "What's this, Annie? Fishing for compliments?"

"Nay. I know my looks are passable. They would not cause a mother-to-be to lose her child or turn a man's face away, but then they have never earned a second look or wishful comments that the next generation possess even one attribute. Nay, warlord, I hold no illusions. I am Bethany of North Umberland, plain and simple."

Royce's features seemed to soften as he gazed at her; and when he spoke, his voice held a huskiness she did not remember. "I see hair, a rare color that I have never seen before." He lifted her tresses and let them drift through his fingers. "The shade of your mane has all the warmth and fire of a flame, yet each lovely strand is as cool and soft as a rose petal. The delicate angel kisses on your cheeks beckon a man to kiss each one. The proud chin, the bright eyes, the lovely mouth that has driven me wild each night with images of its touch and taste. No, my dear. You need to see yourself through my eyes."

" 'Twould no doubt be grand, but I must live with the face God gave me, not the one you wish me to see. You are an overlord, not the Almighty."

He roared at her serious comment. "Verily, I will see you as I wish and you can believe what you will. Although, may I remind you, I am the master of this demesne and my word is law."

She shuddered as his hands continued to work their magic, stroking and massaging her skin with feather-light touches that left her both chilled and on fire.

"Please. I cannot think when you distract me so."

"Passion is not a matter of the mind, Annie. I am a man and I cannot resist your creamy skin or the feel of your silky hair. It's as if, plain though you say you are, you call to me with a secret song that only my ears can hear."

His soft lips grazed her cheek. "Are you a witch?"

"If I were, I would not be a slave. Please . . ."

"Please what, Annie?" His warm lips moved over each feature of her face, touching and tantalizing. A shiver of pure delight rippled over her nerves, and she could not seem to hold onto the meaning of his words. Then a strange weightlessness came over her, as if her bones had dissolved and her support came from him.

"Just trust yourself." His breath caressed her ear, then his lips did the most incredible foray over her chin and down her throat.

Grasping for air, she held his head. "Please, you do not know what you are doing to me."

A smile, soft and sensual, crossed his lips. "Annie, it is what we do to each other."

"Then you must stop."

"Why, Annie? Does this not feel right?" His lips descended, covering hers.

Right and wrong no longer mattered. Bethany was lost to the sensual assault. To a maiden never kissed, the sensations he created overwhelmed her. His lips felt warm and firm as he drew the kiss out. Suddenly, his tongue touched her mouth and a shower of sparks burst in her senses. She had dreamed of being kissed many times, but the glorious reality far exceeded any of her fantasies.

His skin felt warm beneath her fingertips as her hands moved over his bare shoulders. The muscles beneath his sun-bronzed skin rippled at her touch and it amazed her that he reacted so strongly to her. It was as telling to her mind as her sigh must have been to him.

His lips nuzzled her neck, then her shoulder. His arms slipped behind her and suddenly she was lifted and held against his broad muscular chest. She could hear his heart pounding, the fast cadence matching her own as he crossed to the bed.

Just as she was about to protest, his lips covered hers again and she felt the bed beneath her.

He joined her there, his hands straying over every inch of

her body. The tunic she wore lay suddenly untied and around her waist. Her gasp echoed with the sound of pleasure as his lips grazed her breast. Her resistance crumbled; Bethany was lost. She could no more stop him than she could stop the rain from falling.

His hands roamed over her with sensual skill, exploring every curve and plane to discover the places that caused a shiver. He whispered words she had never dreamed existed, his voice vibrating through her, striking her senses with a chord of desire.

She felt him tug on his braiel and in a daze suffered the brief separation as he rid himself of his waist belt and tights. Before her senses could clear, he returned to her with a kiss that made her weak.

She wound her arms about his neck, drawing him closer in a silent acceptance.

He gathered her in his arms, embracing her within a caress that promised much more. His mouth descended, and his tongue slid across her parting lips, teasing, stroking, and tasting, before consummating the kiss.

Suddenly, a loud pounding sounded at the door. "Royce, are you in there?"

She felt him tense as he raised his head and glared at the door. "God's teeth! What is it, Guy?" he called out, his voice husky.

As the door opened, Royce cursed, hitching up the cover to shield her naked body from his brother's sight.

"Royce, we have been watching the advance of a Scottish entourage. They have sent an envoy ahead to ask for an audience."

"What is it they want?"

"Within the hour they will be at our gates with a man who swears he is your slave's betrothed. He sends word that he will challenge you to fight for the maiden."

"What?" Royce turned his dark gaze on her. The warmth that had singed Bethany moments before vanished, leaving her chilled and shivering under his cold regard.

"Who is he, Annie?" he demanded.

When she remained silent, he said, "You told me you had not yet chosen a mate."

"My uncle must have taken matters into his own hands."

"When the Scotsmen arrive, send the intended up here," Royce said to his brother.

"Nay," Bethany said, grabbing Royce's arm. "Would you shame me thus?"

"I wish to see how much the man desires you."

She looked at him perplexedly.

"It is very simple, Annie," he explained, taking her face between his hands. "If your intended walks into this room to find you thusly and still wishes to fight, then greed, not lust, drives him."

Apparently, he saw the confusion still on her features, for he smoothed the lines from her brow and smiled. "There is still the matter of your missing fortune. Did you think I had forgotten it?"

Chapter Six

By the time Guy shut the door, leaving Royce and Bethany alone, her faced burned as though scorched by the sun. She tried to refasten her tunic top, but her task remained impossible for the covers were trapped beneath Royce and he refused to move.

Her whispered prayer, begging the Almighty to open the earth and swallow her to avoid this indignity, went unanswered. In the hallway, several pairs of forceful-sounding footsteps approached and she drew a deep breath to steel her courage, but she could not help letting out a little cry when the door opened. Apparently, her distress touched a chord within Royce. He relented and shifted his weight slightly, allowing the covers to slide beneath him so she could pull the animal skin up to her chin.

"Bethany," her uncle said. He took a step forward and reached out to her before he censured himself. Stopping just inside the door, he stood ramrod straight and faced Royce.

"Uncle Bram, what are you doing here?" she responded, and tears misted her eyes before she lowered her gaze.

"Translate," Royce warned her as he turned to his brother and ordered him to bring the other Scotsman up.

Bethany's head snapped up in defiance of his command, but she did as he asked. "This is my uncle, Laird Bram Mactavish," she said to Royce with a proud tilt to her chin. Then she turned from him to address her uncle in Saxon.

"This arrogant son of Satan is the Norman warlord who stole my lands when you, loving uncle, refused to send clansmen to help me protect my holdings." When she noticed her uncle tensing, she donned a sweet smile and rushed on. "Do not give me away, uncle. As you can see, this lout does not understand our language."

Though her expression never changed, her uncle's did. He seemed to take a great pleasure in her words.

"What did you say?" Royce demanded, studying her suspiciously.

With a demure look she turned to him. "I merely introduced you to my uncle."

"I would not wish my worst enemy to suffer as you would if I found you are not translating accurately." Royce grasped the animal skin and smiled as he gave a light tug.

Bethany gripped the fur covering as though her life depended on it.

Guy appeared in the doorway with another Scotsman. "Verily, the blushing bridegroom."

Royce's brother leaned against the door frame as the man he escorted gaped at the couple in bed. Then, nonchalantly, Guy covered the hilt of his sword in subtle warning.

Royce nodded his head, obviously pleased by his brother's diligence while noting the telling reaction of his guest. The warlord rose from the bed and picked up his clothes. With his departure, Bethany pulled the covers more firmly around her. She was amazed that Royce seemed unaffected by his own nudity in the presence of others.

He dressed slowly, assessing each man carefully. "You will sit at my table today and share our bounty." As Royce strapped on his sword, he turned to his brother. "We will take our guests downstairs. Bethany will join us in a moment."

Guy and Royce ushered the Scotsmen out of the chamber and closed the door.

The moment the latch sounded, Bethany drew a deep breath. Serenity would be impossible, but she forced herself to lie in the bed for a moment and gather her composure. The coming ordeal must find her at her best.

Suddenly, the door opened and her heart skipped a beat at the sound. Royce stood in the doorway, his profile to her as he closed the door. When he turned around to face her, she felt the impact of his full attention. Under his intense regard, she began to feel uncomfortable but would be damned before she let him know he affected her.

"I thought you would still be abed and might need a gentle urging to hurry." With a soft chuckle, he moved toward her.

He was too pleased with himself, and that worried her.

"Annie, your bridegroom was once a catamite."

"Catamite?" she asked haughtily, not knowing the meaning, nor caring. "What matter of importance is it to you where yon Scotsman hails from? You are from Normandy. Verily, your place of birth is not a crime, nor is his." She looked away, and under her breath swore. "Only a lack-witted Norman would judge a man by the color of his cloth and the richness of his pockets."

Royce rubbed his beard, failing to hide his smile. "Oh, Annie, to teach you a lesson, I should let you wed him."

Holding the covers to her breast, she rose up to a kneeling position as he advanced. "Would you?" she asked. The plea in her words was reflected in her eyes. Warmed by his unwavering gaze, her lips parted softly.

"Never," he whispered. He leaned forward and covered her mouth with his. The softness of his lips surprised her once again. Since his body was so hard and unyielding, she had not suspected his kiss could be so warm and sensual. His lips moved over hers, like velvet drawn against the naked flesh, his touch soft, soothing and terribly decadent. Her lips responded to the lush and yielding mouth as the warmth of his kiss consumed her.

A fire of passion burned within her, scorching her very being, and the depths of desire this man uncovered both excited and alarmed her. His hands moved over her shoulders and down her back, fanning the heat already out of control, but she dared not give in to the flame. To forget her responsibilities and position would be unforgivable.

Though it took a great deal of will, she slanted her face sideways and ended the kiss. His lips trailed across her cheek to her ear, nuzzling the skin with a gentle caress that sent more shivers down her spine.

Her lips, still warm and moist from his kiss, moved against his cheek. "Will you permit me to marry?"

Gently, his hands stroked her back, "With a face and form such as yours, it is hard to believe you are such an innocent." He rested his head against hers. "You would not wish me to gift you in marriage to a man such as your betrothed."

"Why?" she asked, leaning slightly back from his chest so she could study his face.

He took a deep sigh and with a resigned expression looked into her eyes. "Annie, trust me. Verily, you would not like being married to such a man."

"Why?" Bethany asked again, her eyes narrowing at his silence. "Do not treat me like a half-wit."

"As you wish, Annie." He massaged the muscles in his neck, as if forming the words in his mind, then looked at her. "But remember, it is you who insisted upon the truth. A catamite is a boy who sexually serves a man . . . someone who prefers the same sex."

"What!" Bethany screeched and pushed him away. Appalled by such blasphemy, she shuddered.

"You did not notice that the man's gaze feasted more on my naked body than yours, Annie?"

"You are beyond all wit. He probably found himself too stunned at your lack of modesty."

"Lie to yourself if it saves your pride."

"I do not lie," she spat, her vehement denial sounding false even to her own ears.

Royce laughed, but the sound lacked amusement and held skepticism. "Oh, my little Saxon, you bend the truth better than a trader hawking his wares on market day."

At his thinly veiled insult, she threw back the covers and leapt from the bed. Forgetting her state of undress in her anger, she fumbled, then tied her fastenings as she muttered under her breath.

"What did you say?" Royce inquired, obviously unable to refrain from baiting her.

"I said I would be better off with a catamite than you. At least he would not look at me as you are wont to do."

"How do I look at you?" Royce asked.

"Like you were starving for food and you could eat me alive," she shot back.

" 'Tis true. I admit I have a hunger for you. Annie, you are not aware of it, but in time you would find your intended's disinterest in you as loathsome as you now find my interest."

"I doubt that very much."

"We shall see. Someday you will make a meal of those words while you beg for my attention."

Her eyes widened in disbelief, then narrowed as she stared at him with open antagonism.

"Are you ready?" he inquired, moving forward and clasping her arm before she could utter her objection. "Your uncle and intended await my pleasure."

Bethany marched by his side. Her betrothed preferred men. Could her uncle be of his right mind? Then she accepted the painful truth—no one else had wanted her. Not even her dowry was incentive enough to rescue a plain bride.

Uncle Bram, her intended, and Guy de Bellemare sat at the great table with Mary and Bret. Scots and Norman guards filled every empty space. Bethany noticed that her sister and brother seemed apprehensive and confused. She could see them quite clearly, for the warlord had led her to the middle of the room and left her there to be the center of attention. Then Lord de Bellemare walked to the fireplace and leaned against the stone wall.

She raised her gaze and stared into her uncle's eyes. Could it be pity she glimpsed or a trick of light that had showed compassion before he turned toward the warlord.

"I am Bram Mactavish. Bethany, Mary, and Bret of North Umberland were sired by a Mactavish, and I have come to offer them sanctuary," he said, watching the warlord's reaction while Bethany translated.

Instead of responding, Royce merely crossed his arms in front of his chest.

Her uncle's face turned a bright red, but to his credit his voice remained calm when he spoke. "I have arranged a match between my niece, Bethany, and this young north clansman, Fenrir Gunn."

As Royce listened to the translation, Bethany held her breath, daring to hope her release was at hand.

"Bethany can no longer fulfill your obligation. She is answerable only to me, as my slave."

Royce's edict echoed in her mind, and her throat constricted as she repeated the Saxon words for all in the hall. She would never be free. Until her death, she would remain a Norman's slave. Humiliation covered her shoulders like an ill-fitting mantle. She refused to meet her uncle's eyes. Earlier his gaze had held compassion for his brother's child, but her uncle had never approved of the legacy. Now she feared her new status would garner his gloating. Finally a North Umberland woman had received her comeuppance.

Royce moved toward the table and poured a chalice of wine. "You may take your other niece and nephew, but Bethany remains here."

Bethany repeated the words and noticed her uncle's dark

expression as he watched the warlord drink his wine with an easy, relaxed air.

Bram Mactavish turned and whispered something to the intended bridegroom. The young man stood and faced the warlord.

"I will fight you for the maiden," Fenrir said.

Bethany was stunned as she relayed the message.

"Why would you bother?" Royce asked. "It is obvious you have no interest in her, or any other woman."

Bethany's face flushed bright red. She lowered her eyes as she translated the Norman's words.

Her uncle blustered in a heavy brogue about the insult to her and to her champion. Apparently, Mactavish missed the Norman's true meaning.

The young man did not appear afraid or ashamed. "I will fight for the maiden," Fenrir repeated, bowing his head to Bethany as a sign of respect while she spoke his words.

"Do not raise your hopes, Bethany. Remember your champion, is practically a woman. He will hardly be any competition for me," Royce said in French. Bethany bristled at the snickering and guffaws she heard throughout the room. The Saxons did not understand Royce's words, but every one of his soldiers did. Oblivious to her anger, Royce told her to repeat his terms.

"If I fight you, will you accept defeat and never return or seek revenge?" Bethany asked in Royce's name, curious of the champion's reply.

"Aye," the Scotsman replied, dispelling her hope of a future rescue.

"What about you, Mactavish? Will you accept the outcome?" Bethany translated and watched her uncle smile.

"When you best me in battle, Norman, you will have my promise and nay before." Her uncle stood tall and straight as he faced his adversary, and in that moment Bethany felt prouder than ever before.

"Then, Mactavish, we will meet someday." Royce waited until she had translated his words, then turned to the young

Scotsman. "I will honor your request. Satisfaction will be given on yon field."

After translating, Bethany turned to follow the men. She was not going to be fought over as if she had no more voice than a piece of grain.

"I have not agreed to this contest." Her French halted the Normans in their stride. All male conversation subsided as every pair of eyes focused on her. Half of the crowd's gazes reflected admiration—the rest, shock—at her brass.

Royce turned around slowly and pinned her with that damn stare she had come to know and hate. "Slave, you have no more voice in this than you had when I defeated you on the field of honor."

"What if you lose, warlord?" She raised her chin a notch to shoulder her pride. "Do I not have a say then?"

He thought about it for less than a second as he approached her. "You need not fret, Annie. I shall not lose." With a smug smile he leaned forward and, before all present, took her in his arms and kissed her soundly.

Within his embrace she noticed a subtle difference. There was passion, but there was always passion when he was near. No, this kiss held something more. Inexperienced, she could not name it, but she felt it all the same. It was . . . a mark of possession. He was branding her as his in front of everyone! She tried to fight, but just then his lips softened and moved over hers with a sensual giving—not taking—which she found impossible to withstand. To offer any comfort to the enemy meant treason to the Saxon cause. She did not understand how she could respond to this Norman . . . a man who had made her a slave. . . . Yet, in his arms she forgot her country, her people, and her pride, knowing only the mastery and magic of his touch.

He pulled away and touched her cheek. "Do not worry about the contest. I would never let a passionate woman waste away with a man who did not appreciate her charms."

Royce's men voiced their approval with cheers and whistles,

while the Scotsmen grumbled loud enough to be heard in the next borough.

Dazed, Bethany watched Royce leave, unable to remove her gaze from the strength and surety of his gait.

Clicking her tongue in disapproval, Mary joined her side. "What, pray tell, will happen now?"

"Now we will bear witness to a fight that will be little enough contest for our warlord—but may very well be the death of a gentle man who thought only to save us from disgrace." Bethany sighed as a whimpering Bret broke free of Maida's hold and charged toward them. She nearly lost her balance when he threw his weight against her, wrapping his arms around her legs and hanging on for dear life.

Unable to soothe his crying, Bethany picked up her brother and hushed his fears. "Do not worry, Bret, I will always take care of you."

Bethany carried Bret out of the castle and past the courtyard to the very field where she had met Royce in battle. Soldiers rimmed the area. Anxious faces, both Norman and Scottish, looked to the battleground with eager anticipation. The men would fight afoot after selecting their weapons.

As she gazed at the two combatants in the center of the field, a painful image of her defeat flashed through her mind's eye. The Norman had beaten her soundly, and yet she knew he had not fought in earnest, thinking her a boy.

The Scotsman would not stand a chance.

Her uncle made his way through the throng of men and joined his family, standing between Mary and her. "The wagons made it safely to our clan."

"I prayed they would. How is Cedric? We had no word," Bethany asked, wondering about her valiant soldier.

"He will live, lass. Though he wished to return home, his wounds needed to mend."

"Lady Bethany," Friar John touched her arm.

"Friar, I am pleased to see you." Her eyes filled with tears and she quickly blinked them away. "I have missed your counsel."

"All went well with the caravan. With God's blessing, we made the journey to Scotland without a mishap. I wish our villagers could say the same."

"Aye, as do I," Bethany said, lifting Bret to a more comfortable position. "At least this thief does not possess our wealth. With our fortune safe in Scotland, an army can be raised to free our people."

"Nay, lass," Mactavish said as he took hold of her shoulder as if to brace her. "I could not find a bridegroom for you except this one. He is the only man who did not fear the Normans."

"No one is willing to fight even for our wealth?" Bethany asked.

" 'Tis not simply this warlord's army, lass, 'Tis all of William's forces. If any Scot invades, he knows William will consider it an act of war. Other than a little raiding of crops and cattle, our hands are tied."

"Lord have mercy, sister. What is to become of us when the day has dawned that a Scotsman fears a Norman?" Mary cried.

"Watch your tongue, child. Kin or no, I will take a broom to your backside," her uncle threatened, and Mary looked instantly on the verge of tears.

"Uncle Bram, Mary only jests."

"Still protecting all Saxons, Bethany?" Friar John asked.

"They are about to start," Bethany said to change the subject. She shifted Bret in her arms so he could not see the soldiers fight, but he twisted and turned until he had gained a full vantage for the combat.

Everyone was on the ridge, watching. Norman and Saxon stood side by side, while the Scotsmen were off to the left in their own gathering. Royce de Bellemare stood with his legs braced and his sword held ready.

The clansman was no less impressive a sight. But from the sound of the crowd, the Norman was easily favored to win.

The signal sounded and the men began to fight. From the moment steel crashed against steel, it was apparent to all that this was going to be more than a simple match. Despite the difference in size, these two men were more evenly suited than expected. The clash of swords rang out time after time until the sounds merged together as one.

Bethany could not believe Fenrir's skill. Royce had made her think of him as less than a man. She had been wrong. And so, it seemed, had everyone else. There was a real possibility that her intended could win.

The Normans grew quiet as they watched the fight. Some of the soldiers even moved their bodies with each blow, as if their movements would help their leader.

Bram Mactavish wore a cocky smile and the friar a benign expression as the Scots cheered for the first time.

The combatants looked exhausted. Both had drawn blood. The warlord's left arm was sliced open and hung like a useless appendage while the Scotsman's chest bled from a gash that stretched diagonally from his shoulder to his hip.

Royce swung his broadsword with such force the Scotsman staggered under the blow, yet he held his ground. The Norman seemed possessed and wielded his sword as though he would drive his enemy into the ground. Time after time he hit his mark with deadly precision and force.

Suddenly, Royce stumbled and the clansman charged forth. Bethany held her breath. Fenrir Gunn had the advantage, but just as he raised his sword, the Norman shoved his foot deep into the man's gut. As the Scotsman doubled over, Royce knocked the fallen soldier's weapon clear. With a quick movement he was on his feet, holding his sword to the clansman's throat. "Do you yield?"

"Aye," her intended panted heavily.

With a curt nod, Royce lowered his sword. " 'Tis done."

Bethany watched as Royce and the beaten Scotsman approached. Covered in blood, dirt clinging to their clothes and hair, their garments torn and ripped, they were a far cry from the men who had entered this field. Though one was Norman and the other Scot, they both resembled wild heathens.

Her uncle took a step forward to meet them. "You have won, Norman, and I dinna dispute it."

Bethany translated.

"Know you this, Scotsman, I have beaten your intended bridegroom for Bethany and allowed him to live. The next man will not be as fortunate. Tell any prospective bridegroom that, henceforth, the fight will be to the death."

"Aye. That I will do, Norman," Mactavish said, then pointed to his family members. "About my relatives."

"You know that I will not release the slave," Royce said and watched Bethany as she spoke the words.

"Aye. You have made that clear. But my niece, Mary, and nephew, Bret?" he asked as Bethany hopefully restated his request.

"They may go—when you return the wealth of this demesne," Royce replied.

Numbly, Bethany repeated his words.

The silence that swept over the group was as deafening for its lack of sound as the loud cheers had been earlier. Royce had merely been toying with them! Bethany looked to her uncle and saw his anger.

"Do you go back on your word, Norman?" Bram Mactavish challenged.

Glaring at Royce, Bethany spat out her uncle's accusation.

"*Non*, they will be released when the riches that were sent to you are returned to their rightful owner—me."

Chapter Seven

Royce turned to Bethany, waiting for her to relay his demands.

She simply stared. He knew about the caravan. Slowly she recovered her wits and translated the words, knowing the others were in as much shock as she.

"Until we meet again," Uncle Bram said and nodded his head in salute. "With your permission, might I take my leave of my brother's children?"

"Oui. You may bid them *adieu,* with hope to see them soon. When you decide that family is more important than gold and silver, on that day your reunion will occur and not before."

When Royce stepped away, Bethany laid her hand on her uncle's arm. "What can be done, uncle?"

"I do not trust him to release Mary and Bret when I return the goods." Bram stared over her shoulder at the man in question, his eyes narrowing, then his gaze returned to her and the anger that had been present was replaced by sadness. "I can not barter for you, in any case. He willna let you go."

"That does not matter. I want Mary and Bret safe."

"I will do what I can." He kissed her cheek and whispered,

"Courage, lass, there is always a way." Then he picked up Bret and, holding him aloft, said, "Take care of your sisters, lad, and dinna be afraid."

At the boy's sharp nod of agreement, Bram returned him to the ground and mussed his hair. "I know you will honor your father's memory and name."

Mary stepped forward, looking as serene and demure as an angel. "Uncle Bram, I will keep you in my prayers."

"Mary, lass, your mother and father would be proud of you." He hugged her in his arms.

The gold chain around Mary's neck caught the light and through Bethany's watery gaze seemed to shine like a rainbow. "Father's ring," she whispered to herself and brushed the moisture from her eyes.

"Mary, give Father's ring to Uncle Bram. He should have it to remember his brother by as we may not see him again."

"But, Bethany—" Tears spilled over and slid down Mary's cheeks. "—Uncle Bram has all our wealth. This is all I have of Father's."

"I know, Mary," Bethany soothed, glancing over her shoulder to be sure that those Normans who had not yet returned to the castle were not watching them. "But Uncle Bram has nothing personal to remind him of his family, while we have each other." Mary slipped the chain off her neck and, with a pout, placed the ring in her sister's hand. Bethany wanted her uncle to have the memento. Should he fail them again, his conscience would prick him every time he laid eyes on Gowain Mactavish's ring.

"Remember Father." Bethany ceremoniously handed the ring to her uncle and watched him smile as he placed it on his finger.

"For a North Umberland woman, Bethany, you are not a disappointment. Keep the way you are. Do you ken?"

Bethany shook her head at his words. "Uncle Bram, see you remember us."

"Dinna act witless, lass. With this ring, how can I forget you?"

Bethany chuckled. She did like the man.

Her uncle returned her smile. "Be of good heart, lass. All is not lost."

Uncle Bram threw his arm over her shoulder and turned her toward the castle. Hugging her to his side, he escorted her through the gate to the courtyard.

The warlord approached them and stood by her side, sipping wine and looking around with the nonchalant gaze of a man in charge of all he surveyed.

His intrusion irritated Bethany and with a mock smile on her lips, she said, "How I despise this black-hearted knave. God's teeth, I will die before I let a usurper take the North Umberland fortune." She took a deep breath to calm her racing heart and fortify her courage. She knew what she had to do. "I will send Mary and Bret to you tonight. Keep a man posted at the tunnel entrance. When the castle guards are drugged from Maida's sleeping powder, I will keep the Norman busy. Then, God willing, Mary and Bret can join your man and escape. I vow it on my mother and father's souls. I will see that they are at the crossroads. Wait for them."

Bram glanced nervously at Royce. "I fear you play a dangerous game, lass. Take care you dinna outwit yourself."

"Do not worry, Uncle Bram. He is as lack-witted as he is mighty and tall. What the Maker gave him in physical abundance, He obviously denied in mental prowess. The poor man is strong of body and dim of mind."

"Hush, lass. Dinna underestimate your enemy."

"I do not. But he is strangely infatuated with me. All that will be needed to take his mind off his duties are a few coy smiles."

"If you are wrong, the price will be paid by morning and you will have no one to blame but yourself and that abundant North Umberland pride."

* * *

The moment the Scotsmen had cleared the gates, Guy de Bellemare approached his brother. "Royce, you need to attend your wound. The duties can wait or I will see to them."

Royce grasped Bethany's arm. "I have need of your services, slave."

She did not argue. The blood from his wound soaked his tunic and tights. 'Twas a miracle he still stood after the loss of so much blood.

Bret wrapped his arms tight around her legs, and Bethany bent down to whisper in his ear. "Mary needs you, Bret. Remember your promise to Uncle Bram. You two will leave for Scotland, and I will join you later," she lied to soothe her brother's fear.

With a sniff and a nod, he released his tight hold and went to Mary. When she picked him up, he gently wiped away her tears. "Do not cry, Mary. I will take care of you."

Friar John stepped forward. "I will take Mary and Bret to the chapel." He wrapped his arm around Mary's shoulders, then offered a parting smile. "Bethany, come and see us when you can."

"Thank you, friar. I will."

With the departure of the friar and her family, Royce tugged on her arm and she accompanied him through the castle to the master chamber with apprehension. When she entered the room, he shut the door and barked, "Attend to my bath. I cannot be about my duties looking like this." She whirled about to do his bidding.

"And, Annie," his voice, low and strained, stopped her in mid-stride, "find a healer who can attend these wounds."

When she turned to face him, Bethany drew a sharp breath at the raw pain etched in his features. Not until they entered this room had he allowed the true extent of his injuries to show. She refused to admire his stoic behavior. Royce de Bellemare, a Norman soldier, was her enemy. All she would acknowledge was relief that he had his health on his mind instead of pleasure. With the practiced eye of one who has attended many injuries, she stepped forward to examine the wounds and knew only one was serious.

"What are you about?" he snapped.

"If it needed searing, I would send for Maida; but I am skilled in the art of healing. This," she said, pointing to his arm, "requires stitching." Bethany turned away and pushed the kettle of water over the fire to boil, mentally listing the herbs needed from the pantry to treat his wounds.

When she caught his skeptical expression, she almost laughed aloud. "You will not be maimed by my hand, warlord."

"What makes you think I will trust you?"

"You already have my obedience. If you are afraid, all you have to do is hold a sword to my throat."

"Non, Annie, 'tis not your own survival you hold dear, but your brother's and sister's. That is why you are a slave. How foolish to place another's well-being before your own."

Bethany did not answer but merely turned on her heel to leave.

"Annie, I take no joy in threatening your family, but you bring it upon yourself. If you were not so willful but accepted your lot, the need for threats would not exist."

Her voice was soft and sure, but she knew it carried to him. "Like an animal, I am to submit meekly? Know you well, Norman, every fiber of my being rebels at the sound of the whip and the voice of the master."

"Meekly or no, you can do naught but submit," he said, running a hand down her back.

She shivered and pulled away. "I can do much else," she replied fervently, and rushed from the room.

"If that is how a catamite fights, I shudder to think if they send their warriors against us," said Guy.

"See that the men are drilled three times a day. If we are to meet them, we should be ready," replied Royce.

Bethany heard the tail end of their conversation as she entered the room and feigned disinterest. With her brother and sister's escape set into motion, she felt much better.

At the scowl on Guy's face, she turned to the warlord and said calmly, "If you wish, I can come back later."

"*Non,* now will do." Royce waved her in.

But his brother stopped her. Removing the tray from her hand, he inspected the herb pouches one by one. She glared at him as he spoke to Royce.

"There are no fairy wings or bat's eyes in the lot. Still I would not trust her." Guy chuckled at his own jest, then grinned at her.

Bethany did not return the smile. Norman humor, she thought was singularly without mirth.

"She knows the punishment should she fail," Royce said.

"Remember the vinegar," Guy said pointedly.

A smile actually crossed Royce's face. "She suffered the consequences of that folly."

"Still, if she had the nerve to try it once, I am of the mind she would try something similar again," Guy said, watching her with mock horror, as though she might sprout horns and stick him with a pitchfork.

"I am sure she will. It seems Annie does not like being a slave. But slave she is, and will obey if she wishes to see her family live."

Like salt poured into a fresh wound, his words were a painful reminder of the hold he had over her. Tonight, if all went well, his threat would be for naught. "If you would prefer to treat your own injuries, you have only to say so and I will be gone." She put down the bucket she was carrying and held her shaking hands together, unwilling to show her pain.

"*Non.* You will stay and attend my needs," Royce said.

Guy shook his head in disagreement as she picked up the bucket and went to the tub.

Royce slapped his brother on the back. "I am safe enough. Go and see you that my wishes are carried out. I shall need no assistance but that of Annie's gentle touch."

As Guy handed her the tray, he said, "Know you well, Saxon, if my brother suffers at your hands, I will avenge it."

She watched him leave, then spoke to the warlord. "Your brother takes much pleasure in trying to cower me."

"*Non,* Guy is not mean spirited. He only does for me what you do for your siblings. In this, you two are more alike than not."

Bethany ignored his remark and shifted her tray to her hip. She pointed to the stool. "Sit, and I will stitch your arm before the bath." She brought a basin of fresh water and a container of potato whiskey. After pouring the spirits into the water and over her needle and thread, she held it poised above his arm. "Are you ready?"

"I need no false courage. Proceed."

As Bethany poured the strong alcohol over the wound, she heard his swift intake of breath, but he said not a word; and when his glance met hers, his eyes were lit with resolve. Taking up the needle, she threaded it and began the tedious process of closing his flesh. Each entry of the needle made him stiffen, but still he did not cry out. Though he seemed unaffected, she felt the sharp puncture of the needle as if it pierced her own flesh.

"I know it is painful. If you wish to yell out, or even cry, I would not take it amiss."

"Cry!" he bellowed, clearly offended.

"There is no one present but you and me. You do not have to be brave in front of me."

"Saxon men may bleat like sheep in front of their women, but Normans do not."

"Pigheaded swine reasoning," she muttered in Saxon, allowing his arrogance to help raise her anger and get her through the gruesome task. Her fingers were bloody and shook so badly she needed a calming, medicinal sip of wine, but dared not drink for fear of losing her stomach. Though it was a mercy that the wound was clean cut and not jagged, it took all her concentration to close the gaping flesh. Still, when the last stitch had been tied, she felt weak in the knees and needed all her willpower to stand, while he sat looking as fit as a man just risen from a long night's sleep.

A pox on him, she thought as she deposited her tray by the hearth and picked up the bucket for his bath. Taking several deep breaths, she tried to calm her unsettled stomach. The task of stitching his arm had strangely unnerved her.

Steam curled up from the bath as she added the cooler water. Trailing her fingers across the top, she knew the temperature was right, but delayed telling him. She dreaded this intimate chore.

"Lend a hand, Annie. I have enough trouble getting out of this when I am not injured."

His words brought her head up. Bethany met his gaze and tilted her chin in agreement, though she did not want to see his other wounds. She was not usually squeamish, but the thought of them disturbed her.

"It was stupid and senseless to fight. Only a man would settle his dispute by force," she spat in Saxon, knowing he could not understand her. She carefully peeled his tunic back. None of the other wounds needed any more than a salve. Strangely, this brought her anger to the fore. "God's teeth, you are a reckless fool. Did it not occur to you that you might have been planted in yon field?" she muttered, then added every Saxon curse she could remember.

He raised an eyebrow at her tirade, but mercifully did not ask for a translation.

Quickly, she bent to undo his braiel and peel off his dirt-stained tights, throwing them onto the pile of his blood-soaked tunic and waist girdle. She averted her eyes when he braced his hand on her shoulder to carefully step over the tub's rim. With slow movements, he eased his body down into the warm water.

Ironically, her tirade seemed to expel her anger, for the minute she took the cloth in her hands to scrub his skin, her touch turned gentle, almost feather-like. Though her lips could decry the man, her touch could not.

"You are sure none of the slashes need searing or stitching?"

"Nay, only your arm needed stitching. The other wounds are not as deep."

"Then do you think you could scrub the dirt from them?" he mocked.

Immediately, she dragged the cloth across the open cuts and watched him flinch.

"Why did you goad me into hurting you?" The moment the words were out, she covered her mouth. She had not meant to ask the question aloud and in Norman.

There was a long silence before he spoke. "I will gladly weather your hate, but I do not want your pity."

"You mistake compassion for pity. Do not the mighty Normans feel compassion for the wounded in battle?"

"*Non*, an enemy is an enemy. I do not think of them as men. If I did so, it would bode ill for me on the battlefield."

He was absolutely right. Royce de Bellemare was a Norman and her enemy; under no circumstances should she begin thinking of him as a man. A very attractive, virile man.

Absently, her cloth-covered hand stroked his back in long soft sweeps. She could feel his muscles ripple beneath her palm and traced the ridged outline of his spine, straying, now and again, across a rib or raised scar. Only a thin piece of linen separated her fingers from his flesh. How she ached to touch him and feel his response. She shook her head to clear her mind of the wayward thoughts. But though she wished it otherwise, the image and feel of the soldier remained. When the time came, could she possibly injure someone she had come to know? Even murder him?

God's teeth, she was the leader of her people. She held the hopes and dreams of others in her hands. *Remember the legacy.*

Remember it and let it guide you, a silent voice in her head intoned.

Bethany stopped washing his chest. "I think I will fetch your meal from the kitchen."

"*Non,* I will dress and eat downstairs with my men and your sister."

Bethany panicked. Her sister and brother were preparing to meet their uncle later tonight.

"My lord, you must not move about so after the stitching. My handiwork would be for naught." Bethany bowed her head. It nearly killed her to act so subservient. "Pray, let me fetch your food and wine."

"*Non,* there is no need." He grasped her hand. "I do not hunger for food. Besides, Annie, you cannot run off when you have yet to treat the rest of my wounds."

Suddenly, she felt trapped in a prison of her own foolish making. "Very well," she acceded, trying wildly to think of a way out. "But I cannot treat your wounds when you are in the bath."

A smile creased his lips and the expression of amusement reached his eyes. She did not like the look or his smugness. "Reach the linen and hand it to me, Annie."

She unfolded the white cloth and held it out to him as he rose from the bath. There was literally nowhere to look. She avoided his body by holding his gaze and staring into his eyes. Damn the man, he found her dilemma amusing.

He took his damn sweet time drying off. Bethany wished she could throw him outside to dry, like clothes left draped over a bush. Frustrated, she turned and retrieved her healing pouch. With her back to him, she began mixing the herbs and grease to make the ointment.

She heard him sit and turned around cautiously to find he had the linen wrapped around his hips. With relief she smoothed the soothing salve into his cuts. The plantain would stop the bleeding and the garlic would keep the wound free of fever.

She saw his nose twitch at the smell. " 'Tis a healing balm," she said, taking pleasure in his discomfort.

"But it reeks."

His disgruntled remark actually brought a smile to her lips. "If you would prefer to treat your own wounds, I will remove the potion. But I do not think the smell so bad."

"From a Saxon who rarely bathes, that is not reassuring."

"Aye, we know little of good manners. Perhaps the kindly Norman masters can teach their ignorant slaves to wash!"

She turned away from him, too angry to say any more and too upset to control her temper.

"Perhaps you are right."

She screamed as he lifted her into the air. Resting against his chest, she stared at the mock determination on his face and the amusement in his eyes.

"You would not dare!" she gasped indignantly, guessing his intent as he headed for the tub of water.

He did not respond, but a wide smile split his lips.

Chapter Eight

"Warlord, you must not get these wounds wet now," Bethany said.

Royce smiled, enjoying her protests. She did not think he would really do it. She did not know him.

"I do not intend to ruin your hard work."

She relaxed visibly in his arms. What a trusting innocent she was. He almost felt a twinge of regret. Almost, but not quite.

It was incredible. She was so light in his arms, weighing much less than his mail. Even dressed in the drab soldier's garments he commanded her to wear as punishment for challenging him, she did not look like a boy. He silently admitted liking the tunic and tights. They offered an alluring outline of her shape, and the view of her legs was scandalously enticing.

He approached the tub. There was such a soft sweetness in her gaze that he paused for a moment. "Annie, I only wish to return the favor. You are so used to my body, I would know the same of yours. Tonight, even though you do not need a bath, I will play your serf and bathe you."

She stared at him with incredulous disbelief. "Nay, you will not treat me thusly."

He started to lower her into the tub. The moment her soft leather boots touched the water, her arms tightened around his neck. "Nay," she shrieked. "My clothes will be ruined."

" 'Tis only water, Bethany."

"I beg of you, do not do this. I do not wish to bathe now."

"Annie, when will you learn? You have no choice in the matter. You are not a servant, but a slave to your sovereign lord."

Her eyes flashed like fire coals as he lowered her into the tub. As the water sloshed against her neck and chin, leaving only her head above the bathwater, she folded her arms across her chest.

" 'Twill make the job easier if you divest yourself of your clothes."

"Will it? In that case, I will remained dressed."

"Pity," he taunted, pulling out his knife. Instantly, she shied away. "If you will not remove your clothes, I will do it for you."

With a huff, she grabbed hold of the hem of her tunic and tried to peel her top off. It was no easy task, for the material was sodden and heavy and she had to literally wrestle the tunic and tights from her body. He wanted so badly to help but restrained the urge.

Never had he seen her more beguiling. The wet material molded to her feminine curves like a second skin that craved a man's touch. Though petite, her delicately shaped form tantalized his senses. When the garment clinging to her flesh like a lover's embrace was slowly slipped back, it revealed silken skin now slick and shiny with rivulets of water streaming downward. He felt his need grow painfully evident as water washed against her breasts, while below the undulating waves, her flesh shimmered white and beckoning. He could not stand much more.

She covered her breasts with her hands in a futile attempt to shield herself, but although she was embarrassed, her pride remained. She would lift her chin and brazen out his looks. She did not cower and he admired her for that.

She extended her hand for the wash-linen. "I can do this myself."

"*Non*, Annie." He held the cloth out of her reach. "I will do it."

Sparks fairly glowed in her brown eyes and it was evident once again that she was unaccustomed to being told what to do. For a brief moment he wondered about the stories he had heard and the strange pictures on her elaborate girdle. Then he dismissed the thoughts. No matter what her status had been before, she would have to accept her lot now.

She turned away from him, but not before he saw the quiet rage seething within her gaze.

As he started scrubbing her back, her shoulders shook with a silent sob and he paused. He could not credence her reaction, but neither did he want to deal with her tears.

"Here." He let the cloth slide over her shoulders. "That is how it is done. You can finish up."

She did not look at him, but merely accepted the cloth. Sensing her need for privacy, he moved away from the tub. He would never understand women, nor did he intend to try. But there were certain rules of conduct he adhered to.

Though it would have been easy to force her, and there would have been none to stop him, he had never used his size or strength against a woman. God had made women different for a reason, and he would not take advantage of the fact.

No, there was a simpler and a much more enjoyable way. She could be seduced. No maiden had resisted his charms yet; and though this one professed to hate him, he knew that would change with a little gentle persuasion.

Every woman had her price. He thought about it for a second. *Non*, he would not leave her demesne, nor would he release her or set her people free. It seemed this maiden's price was far higher than any he had ever encountered or, for that matter, was willing to pay.

The thought disturbed him. Was she really so selfless? Oh, he might believe it of her pious sister, but Bethany possessed a passion that simmered just below the surface. She did not fit the mold of a holy woman on bended knees. An erotic picture of Bethany lying naked in his bed with her hair spilled out across his pillow and her arms beckoning to him filled his mind. That thought fired his brain and tortured his loins. He swore he would see her like that soon.

He could hear soft splashes as she went about her bath. The noise of the water sluicing across her skin teased his senses. God, there had never been a maiden that had so lingered in his mind. In his vivid imagination he could see her lovely skin with the water drops glistening in the firelight.

Needing a diversion, he moved to the table and poured two goblets of wine. He savored the taste on his tongue before he turned and held the goblet up to Bethany. "Do you wish any?"

She lowered her gaze and did not respond.

He carried the goblet to the tub and placed it in her hand, then moved to the fire to sip from his own cup.

She was a strange puzzle that presented a challenge he could not resist. Yet he sensed that when he placed all the intricate pieces together and completed the picture, he would be no closer to solving the mystery than he was now.

A pounding at the door interrupted his unsettling thoughts.

He walked to the tub and strategically stood between Bethany and the portal. "Come."

The door opened and Maida, the friar, and Guy de Bellemare filled the doorway.

"I do not know what they want, but it is evident they wish to see your slave," Guy explained to his brother.

Royce studied the two for a moment, then moved aside.

"What is it?" Bethany asked, her face full of concern.

"My lady, you must come." Maida's voice dropped a notch. "Some of our men have returned."

"Be careful, Maida. They may not speak our language, but you are acting suspiciously," Bethany said as she looked speculatively at each Norman. At their blank expressions relief swept across her face and she turned to Maida. "How many returned?"

"I do not know, my lady."

Royce walked back to the tub and handed Bethany the white linen. "What do they want?"

"There is an injured villager who needs my help. Please, I must go."

Royce turned to his brother. "Take them downstairs." When the door closed, he turned back to her.

"Will you let me treat the Saxon? I did no less for you." Standing, she wrapped the white linen around herself, then looked at her sodden clothes on the floor.

"You may treat the injured villager. But," he said as he helped her step from the tub, "if I find you have deceived me, the penalty will not be pleasant."

A thank-you was on the tip of her tongue, but she could not bring herself to say it. She knelt down and with her finger and thumb picked up the soaked tunic and tights. The sodden material created pools of water as she held them up and away from her body. There was no help for it, she would have to wear them.

He took the clothes away from her and let them drop in a soggy mound. "You may wear your own clothes from now on."

She looked up, stunned. Had he read her mind? She noticed, then, the half smile playing about his mouth. Amazing how that one expression could transform him from the fierce Norman warlord to Royce de Bellemare.

"Although I must confess I will miss the tunic and tights," he said, his eyes reflecting his smile.

After a moment, lost in his soft expression, she remembered his words. Her own clothes. The thought filled her with joy. She had not realized how much her pride had suffered from having to dress as a man. And to wear her girdle and dagger would give her the extra confidence she needed to forebear.

"If you will pardon me, I must dress and leave."

"Your manners leave a lot to be desired, Saxon. No expression of gratitude for the boon I have granted you?"

"Thank you," she gritted.

"Thank me with a kiss, Annie, and I will count the matter done."

Warning bells sounded in her head. Her instinct screamed refusal. She did not want him to kiss her, but it was small payment for his boon and it would expedite her departure.

As she approached him, the linen wrap clung to her damp skin. His gaze made her all-too-aware of what was revealed by the flimsy cloth, and she wished for more adequate covering. Stealing herself, she stood before him, but he made no move to initiate the kiss.

"You will have to kiss me, Annie."

Kiss him? She did not know how to go about it. But with a determined air, she placed her arms on his shoulders and stretched up on tiptoes. Her lips touched his and she pressed them lightly against his mouth. When she pulled away, he was shaking his head. "That weak offering will not gain my favor. You will have to put some passion into your kiss."

"I am afraid that is impossible."

"Then, you will miss treating your Saxon because, unless I receive a kiss of a generosity that matches mine, you will remain here."

"Blackmail suits you," she snapped and stepped closer to him. With anger in her heart, Bethany grabbed his shoulders and fairly pulled herself up and against him, then slanted her lips across his. She wanted to get this matter over with as quickly as possible.

When she started to pull away, his arms went around her and his mouth responded to hers. His fingers tunneled beneath the edge of her wrapper, tugging the linen sheet free so it sagged in the back. He slipped his hands up and down her back and she felt a cool breeze caress her skin, yet her flesh felt on fire wherever he touched her.

For a moment, just a moment, she turned herself over to the

new feelings of passion coiling within her, then reality intruded and she pulled away gasping. God's teeth! How could she allow herself to respond to him?

She quickly strove to soothe her pride. It had only been an act, one necessary to gain her freedom. Then she met his smoldering gaze and admitted the truth. 'Twas no act. And what was worse, he knew it as well. The only defense was to brazen it out.

"I have paid your price, Norman," she said with as much distaste as she could convincingly inject into her words. Then she added, "Am I free by your leave?"

" 'Twas a beggar's payment." His finger traced a soft path down her cheek and she felt the tingle of his touch travel clear through to her center. "A poor reward for a service granted," he replied.

His devilish smile took the sting out of his words. He merely baited her with a jest.

She took his teasing like a godsend, relieved that she could reply in kind. "Someday, Norman, you will ransom a kingdom for my favors."

"With you, my little Saxon slave, I might be tempted for the first time." The way he looked at her belied the jesting.

Her throat tightened, and her heart raced at the intensity in his eyes. "Would you?" she whispered before she could stop herself.

He stared at her for a long time, then pulled away. "Verily, no woman is worth my kingdom."

Bethany turned around and recovered her over and under tunics from the chest. She dressed quickly. Not for all the world would she admit that his words wounded her.

With determination and pure strength of will, she banished Royce from her thoughts. She had her people to think about. The men had returned. Perhaps her father had survived and they would be reunited. For so long she had thought him dead that the possibility that he lived was breathtaking.

Deep in thought, she did not hear Royce approach. "Take

my mantle," he said, wrapping his warm cloak around her. "The air has a chill and I would not see you catch a cold for lack of proper clothes."

Why was he being kind to her? Bethany did not want to accept the wrap.

"If it sets your mind at ease, I have no desire to have a sick slave," he said, correctly interpreting her hesitation. "There is nothing else to consider about the gift, and you will wear it because I order you to do so."

"In that case, I have no choice." She would gag before she thanked this man again. Still, it was a warm mantle and, without it, she would have suffered the bite of autumn's breath.

"Take care to return early."

She nodded her head in agreement, a bit stunned by his kindness and understanding.

When she opened the door, a scream froze in her throat. Mary stood in the opening.

"You must be careful, Bethany, lest the Normans discover our men."

Bethany raised her finger to her lips and silently but firmly pulled the door closed behind her. With Royce safely in the bedroom and the hall clear of eavesdroppers, Bethany turned to face Mary.

"Why have you left the safety of the chapel?" she asked, wondering why Mary had not followed the plan.

"My movements are not watched or questioned. Besides, sister, it will raise suspicion if Bret and I go into seclusion. Do not worry. Friar John will take us when the castle retires and fewer men are on duty. Maida has prepared the brew that will make the Norman guards sleep."

Relieved, Bethany touched her sister's arm. "Where are our men?" she asked, knowing her sister brought information.

"At the crofter's stable."

"Aye, that makes sense. How many have made it back?"

"I do not know. Here, take these." Mary thrust something into Bethany's hands.

Bethany's mouth dropped open when she recognized two of Royce's daggers. "How did you come by these?"

"Were you not paying attention? I come and go at will."

"Why are you giving me these?" Bethany juggled the weapons in an attempt to grasp them.

"The men will need weapons. All of the village women are taking turns carrying food and clothing to the returning men. I think it fitting that they have the warlord's own weapons."

" 'Tis a good plan," Bethany said hesitantly, appreciating the irony of stealing Royce's weapons, yet knowing who would bear the consequences. She dismissed the disturbing thought while looking for a place to put the daggers. Finding a concealed pocket within the folds of Royce's mantle, she dropped them inside.

"I am not as helpless as you think I am, Bethany."

"Forgive me, Mary. 'Tis sometimes difficult to see my little sister as an adult." Bethany prayed she would see her sister one last time before Mary left for Scotland. But if not, this would be their goodbye. Bethany struggled to keep her emotions at bay. She did not want to break down before Mary.

"I love you. Be careful." Bethany hugged Mary, then hurried from the castle. She brushed away the tears that gathered in her eyes. Her sister and brother would be safe; that was all that mattered. The sorrow and pain of their separation must be borne, and never shown to the Normans.

The crofter's stable was a goodly distance, and she took pains to make sure no one followed her. Several times she looked over her shoulder until she was convinced her departure had gone unnoticed.

At the stable, Bethany rested her hand on the door while she turned around once more to make sure no one was watching before she entered the barn.

The interior was dark and smelled of this season's hay and oats. Cautiously, she called out. "Is anyone in here?" When no one responded, she walked further into the barn. " 'Tis Lady Bethany. Come out from where you are hiding."

"My lady," a tentative, tearful voice responded as one soldier emerged from his hiding place followed by four others.

Their gaunt faces told her they had suffered more than she could imagine. It would take more than a few good meals to replace the flesh that had melted away. There was more than loss of food; there was loss of spirit. She saw the look on their faces and felt like weeping.

" 'Tis over, my lady."

"What happened?" she asked Hadden, a soldier who was in truth her age, but now looked more like her father's counterpart than hers.

" 'Twas a bloody battle that we lost. Your father, brave man that he was, fell in the first hour. Soon after, the tide turned against us and we were all left for dead. Only the five of us survived, my lady, and only because our enemy was in too much of a hurry to check the fallen for survivors."

She shuddered at the thought and laid to rest her secret hope that her father lived. "You are home now."

"But, my lady, defeated soldiers and those who hide them are not safe."

"Nay, I will see you safely into Scotland," she said with determination, unwilling to desert these loyal men in their time of need.

"My lady, we wish to remain," he said and, though drawn, his face mirrored his resolve. "This is our home."

"But your home is occupied," she protested.

"As is all of England. Where would we go? Our families are here," Hadden replied, and the other four nodded their heads in agreement.

They were right, of course. But she could not get their families out, too. She had tried once and failed. If only she could think of a way for the men and their wives to travel from this demesne . . . a means that would not be questioned by the Normans. Ten leagues to the Scottish border might well have been ten thousand.

"We will swear fealty to the new lord," Hadden said as he

put his hand on her shoulder. "We are farmers, my lady, not soldiers."

She knew Hadden was right. These men were not her castle guard or the trainees that fostered at her demesne; they were, indeed, tillers of the soil.

They would be sorely needed to keep starvation from the door. A lump formed in her throat at the enormity of her failure.

"You are right," she said, swallowing the bitterness and defeat. Though her voice did not waver, the pain sliced deep. The measure of a good ruler was the well-being of the humblest peasant. Her farmers and their families needed protection, and she had failed them.

Suddenly, the door to the barn opened and Bethany gasped.

Royce de Bellemare entered with a complement of his men. " 'Twould seem I am not as surprised to see you as you are to see me," he said in the emotionless tone of authority that she hated.

The five men and Bethany were easily surrounded.

She stared at the Norman soldiers, so large and well-fed, with thick muscles that had been honed in battle, making them look like giants instead of men. Then she looked to her little half-starved band, their eyes sunken, their bodies emaciated with the aftermath of war. Next to the Norman force, they were a pathetic match. With each sunrise, the responsibilities on her shoulders increased and weighed her down.

"Warlord, these men have returned home, wishing asylum. They are willing to swear their loyalty to you." The words were difficult, but she managed to say them.

"Where is the wounded villager you were suppose to tend?" he responded.

Her chin went up and she glared into his dark eyes. "The villagers came to me for help."

"Then you lied to me."

"Aye."

"I will deal with you later," he said, raising his gaze to the men behind her.

"Please, do what you will to me, but show mercy to these brave men. They have been through so much," Bethany said, grabbing his arm.

He covered her hand. "Would you come willingly to my bed to save these men?"

Her face flamed, but she met his gaze. "Would you want a woman who had to be bribed?"

"Non," he said tersely, then directed his attention to the Saxons as he spoke to her. "Tell these men that they will be welcomed back after their oath. But once sworn, they will give their allegiance, and their life if need be, to protect their lord."

The men listened to her words and easily bent their knees. They had seen too much of war.

"Take the men back to the castle and see that they are fed and given decent clothes," Royce said to his man-at-arms, Vachel.

Bethany started to follow them until she felt Royce's detaining hand on her arm. He remained silent until the last man left the barn and the door closed.

"I understand why the villagers approached you; but from now on, you will not involve yourself in the business of my demesne."

Her shoulders stiffened at his order. "I cannot do that." She turned to face him. Standing toe to toe with him, she tipped her head back to hold his gaze. "This is my demesne and will remain so. Your rule is only temporary. Might does not make right, Norman." She put her arms akimbo and his mantle slid from her shoulders and hit the hard dirt floor, the knives sounding with a heavy thud.

With dread, she slid her gaze to his daggers lying in the dirt.

"What is this?" he asked, his eyes widening as he recognized his own weapons. Royce picked up the knives and held them before her. "Have you not learned yet that daggers and swords are not toys? Or do you require another lesson from me to curb your foolish penchant for carrying men's weapons?"

She did not answer him, but stood stock-still under his steely regard.

He moved the sharp edge of the knives closer until the light reflected off the blades in blinding flashes. "Did you plan to use these to regain your rule?"

"Nay, I do not have to kill you," she said while raising a hand to shield her eyes from the bright glare. "The people will follow my lead, not yours. Unlike you, I have their loyalty. You are the usurper here and, like any disaster, must be endured until the calamity has past."

"Annie, you are wrong," he said as he slipped the daggers into his belt. "You only prolong your pain by believing in foolish dreams."

"They are my dreams, Norman, foolish or not."

He shook his head. "Have it your way, Annie. Thank God all Saxons are not as stubborn as you."

"Because I do not agree with you does not make me stubborn."

"*Non*, it simply makes you wrong."

He took hold of her arm and guided her out of the stable before she could form a reply.

Chapter Nine

The castle's warmth closed around her as they entered the great hall. The returning men sat at the trestle tables eating voraciously.

It was disheartening to realize that since the Normans' arrival the people were faring better. One look at their grateful faces banished the selfish thought. It should not matter who provided for the demesne; only the people's welfare was important.

"Bring a trencher of cheese and meat up to my room. See that a flagon of wine is also provided, one that does not hold vinegar," Royce said to Bethany with a lighthearted grin.

Bethany ignored the jest and went to fetch the food. The smiles of greeting from the Saxon soldiers tore at her heart. These men were happy and content. It was humbling to realize that a mere meal, something she took for granted, could elicit such joy.

She returned their smiles and lingered to say a few words to those who spoke to her.

A glance at the warlord found him deep in conversation with his brother. They huddled together in what seemed to her critical eye a conspiratorial pose. If he had wanted, he could have demanded a harsh recompense from these returning men. Instead, he had offered them an honorable truce, one that left them with their pride intact. She did not understand the Norman, nor did she want to, but she could not help admiring his skill with people. Enemy though he was, the fact remained he was a fair ruler and they were fortunate he was so made.

Suddenly, Bret yelped and ran across the floor toward her. Friar John tried to intercept him, but the little boy evaded the cleric's grasp.

Bethany could see the tracks of tears on his face and knelt to meet him. This was the last time she would comfort him, for tonight he would leave for Scotland. She hugged him to her breast and tried to still the misery that mushroomed from the coming separation.

"My arm," he wailed, showing her the bruised and slightly red skin.

"Oh, Bret, 'tis nothing." She tried to rise with him in her arms, but his weight threw her off balance and she would have stumbled if Royce had not steadied her.

"Warriors are very brave and do not cry when they are hurt," he said to Bret and nudged Bethany, prompting her to translate.

As though God had spoken, Bret sniffed back his tears. "I am a warrior and I do not cry," he said. When Bethany hesitated to speak his words to Royce, Bret grabbed her shoulder. "Tell him, lest he think I am a coward," he insisted.

She could not resist the imploring look in her brother's eyes and complied.

"Verily, Bret of North Umberland, you are indeed a warrior. I have need of such courage in my army."

As she relayed the Norman's message, a smile split Bret's face so that she could hardly believe this was the same tearful child who had flown into her arms for comfort.

"Now, I have a job for a strong soldier," Royce said, and Bethany repeated the French words into Saxon.

Bret puffed up his chest, trying to look more impressive. "What is it?"

"See my brother, Guy? He is in charge of the new recruits." Royce turned and winked at his brother. Guy's answering nod acknowledged the silent communication.

His hurt forgotten, Bret wiggled to be free of her arms and charged over to the big handsome Norman by the fire. A pain sliced through Bethany's heart at her brother's admiration for the Normans. Thank God Bret was going away to Scotland; he would not be raised among the enemy.

Still, she shook her head in wonder at the magic Royce had worked. Without thinking she said, "You have a way with children."

"Do I, now? And do I also have a way with maidens?"

Her face warmed, and she turned away rather than answer him.

She felt his breath on her neck, and her skin tingled.

"Make sure you do not forget the food," he whispered, then moved away.

She resisted the urge to rub her neck and soothe the goose bumps. The telling action would give him the satisfaction of knowing he had disturbed her.

"My lady, is there anything we can do?" one of the returning Saxon soldiers asked.

"Nay," she responded to the concerned faces that met her gaze. Before any more well-meaning inquiries could be made, she gathered Royce's food and headed for his room.

In the master chamber, she stared gloomily at the bath. Knowing the task had been left for her, she filled buckets to empty the tub. It was an arduous chore, but she did not want the Norman insisting on another bath, or worse, insisting on bathing her again. Her face flamed at the memory.

As she lifted two brimming buckets of water from the floor, her arms felt as though they were being pulled out of their sockets. "Lord, I never knew how hard the servants worked," she muttered to herself.

"Bethany?" a tentative voice asked as the tapestry in front of the window moved and her sister peeked out.

"What in St. Bede's name are you doing?" Bethany gasped, startled by the sudden appearance.

"I wanted to see you in private. I am to tell you that Maida will set the sleeping brew out at eventide. The potion will act as the food is digested. Bret and I will leave in four hours time," Mary said, taking a bucket and leading the way out of the room and down the stairs. When she reached the bottom step, Mary turned back to Bethany. "This will be the last chance I have to say goodbye. Oh, Bethany, I worry so about you!"

Royce's deep voice rang out from across the great room. "Your sister is not a servant here. Tell these men that they will not be treated like slaves just because they are Saxons—and why you are."

Bethany burned at his order. Taking the bucket from her sister's hand, she grumbled, "The lord and master refuses to allow you to do menial work." Then she turned and addressed her men. "My sister surrendered and is treated fairly. I did not and am treated thusly."

Mary's face drained of color at Royce's approach. Quickly, she said. "Be careful, sister. The warlord strikes terror into my heart."

"Do not worry. I will keep him busy so he does not suspect you are leaving." The thought of truly matching wits with Royce frightened her, but for her sister and brother she could do no less.

"I love you, Bethany." Mary was on the verge of tears.

"Do not give us away," Bethany warned, then turned and found the Saxon men studying them. She noticed the sorrow in their loyal gazes but refused to respond in kind. Thank God her parents were dead so they could not witness how low their daughter had fallen. She was, in truth, in jeopardy of slipping into Hades.

"What did you tell them?" Royce demanded.

"Just what you ordered. Verily, your nature is like the apostle Thomas, you doubt everything. Or is it that your conscience is blacker than pitch and you suspect everyone of being the same?" she taunted. When he refused to rise to the bait, she felt disappointed and added with a sullen tone, "If you wish to know every Saxon word spoken, I suggest you learn our language posthaste."

"Mayhap I will."

Under his scrutiny, Bethany felt a sudden chill.

"Bring the wine upstairs," he said with a slow grin that fit smoothly and naturally into place.

Royce's pleased expression, and she was coming to know them all, unnerved her.

"And, Annie, bring a good wine. I am sure this land can produce a fine vintage. Why not take pride in it?"

"I will see what the cellar has," she said through gritted teeth.

"Hold!" His command stopped her. "Vachel will escort you."

Bethany whirled around, reading the look in the warlord's deep, blue eyes. There was no mistake. Vachel was not a courtesy escort, but a guard. Clenching her fists and closing her eyes, she took a deep breath to bring her emotions under control.

"Come along, my faithful watchdog," she grumbled to Vachel in Saxon, knowing he could not understand her and needing to vent her ire.

Bethany found the best wine in the cellar and filled a wineskin. If Vachel were not her shadow, she would have sought Maida's sleeping draught and Royce would have ceased to be a worry tonight. If only he were a drinking man, perhaps he would spend the night with his wine instead of her. The thought intrigued her, but she had already noticed that he did not overindulge. It was a pity. Then she wondered if she could goad him into drinking more. It might have the desired effect, but 'twould be dangerous. Still, it was worth a try. After all, she had no plan for escape tonight and it was doubtful he would let her out of his sight. Assigning his man to escort her to the cellar had proved that much.

With wine in hand she ascended the stairs, trying to ignore the echo of the soldier's footsteps behind her. A guard! The very thought infuriated her. As if she would run away. She did not have that luxury. Too many people depended on her.

She marched determinedly through the great room without as much as a look in anyone's direction. Her head held high and her eyes focused on the stairs, she moved through the busy hall of curious eyes.

At the chamber door, Vachel stopped her and knocked. "My lord, she is here with the wine," he announced, no doubt to discharge his duties and make sure that if the woman were lost again it would not be considered his fault.

"Enter."

At Royce's command, Vachel opened the door and stood back, motioning for her to precede him in.

"Come over here, Vachel, and tell me what you think of this," Royce said, motioning for his soldier to come and view something on the bed.

Curious, Bethany followed in the soldier's wake.

Royce pointed to the rumpled linen. Bethany stood on tiptoes trying to see over Vachel's shoulder. The breath caught in her throat as she viewed the deadly snake cut in half.

"It would seem some Saxon coward thinks to do away with his overlord. There can be no mistake. This viper was taken from its winter sleep and placed here to do the knave's evil deed."

Bethany's stomach churned with fright. Mary had been here and in danger! God's blessing that she had not been bitten. But if the warlord ever learned of her visit, with his suspicious nature, he would blame the innocent girl.

"I will take care of it, my lord." Vachel said as he folded the linen sheet and carried the dead serpent to the door.

"Thank you, Vachel," Royce said. "If you would be so good as to guard my door tonight."

Bethany stiffened. She had not expected that order.

His soldier nodded, then shut the door behind him.

"To insure, my dove, that you do not slip past me again," Royce said. " 'Tis a disquieting habit you have."

Bethany turned around, unable to face him. Even if she managed to get him drunk, she would still be trapped with him all night. Even if he were well into his cups, to spend a night with Royce was unthinkable. Her mind rushed on frantically to figure out a way she could leave the room.

"Why do I have the feeling you are contemplating another escape?"

Her face flamed and she quickly poured the wine. "A refreshment, my lord?" she asked, hoping to take his mind off such matters.

"I never drink alone." He held his goblet, waiting for her to fill hers.

"Very well." She poured a tiny amount in the very bottom of the cup. "To your . . ." She raised her goblet in a familiar toast and then realized she could not in all good conscience offer that sentiment.

He laughed at her predicament. "To my what?"

"Health," she ground out, knowing that this drinking contest would be harder than she imagined if she could not even offer an honest toast.

"To my health," he said, then touched her goblet. He drank his wine, and when she lowered her cup, he refilled her goblet to the rim. "To your good health, slave."

She could not refuse to drink that toast, but the wine would surely have tasted better without the word *slave*. When she took a sip, he did the same. Good Lord, she could never hope to match him toast for toast.

Distract and disarm your opponent. Her father's words came to mind. She looked up and stared into eyes the color of ocean waves at night. Midnight blue, she thought, described the unusual shade exactly, and they contained just as much depth and mystery as the sea. These eyes could look into your soul and, for a frightening minute, she thought they had. Being this close to the man and not the soldier, she realized she could never act coy with him. That would not be dangerous—it would be suicidal.

"Where is your home?"

"In Normandy," he said, his knuckles brushing her temple with a light touch that sent a shock through her system.

"I know that, but where?" she asked, ready to scream at his clipped replies and trying subtly to move out of his reach.

"In a small town by the sea." His fingers traced the line of her jaw, then stopped to linger on the pulse beating in her neck.

"You do not wish to talk about it," she said as perspiration dotted her forehead. She felt scorched by his touch.

"Non. This is my home now. I would rather talk of the present and future than dwell on the past." He moved closer.

Why did this warrior refuse to relive his past? A man always drank more when reminiscing!

"Do you find it hard to adjust to England's weather and ways?" she asked inanely.

"Non. The weather I can do nothing about, and the customs I can change."

She racked her brain for topics in which to engage him, but nothing inspiring came to mind. As she sipped her wine, the room began to feel extraordinarily warm. She fanned herself and noticed the smile her action brought to the Norman.

"What amuses you?"

"If I told you, I am sure you would not find it as amusing as I do." His smile broadened. Whatever struck his fancy truly tickled him.

"Aye, I would say we are unalike in many ways."

He reached over and withdrew her wine goblet. "I think you have had enough of this very excellent wine. You would not wish to lose your wits when dealing with me, would you?"

"It is not my wits that are in danger. Still, I agree. When one faces an adversary, it is best to remain clearheaded." Her words seemed heavy and her thoughts muddled, as though cobwebs hung in the way of reason.

"Too true." He reached out and smoothed the hair away from her cheek.

She tried to brush his hand away, but he stroked her skin in a soft caress. "You worry overmuch, Annie. If you'd let yourself relax, things would take care of themselves."

"If I relaxed my vigil, you would have my demesne completely taken."

"Little Saxon, already I have full control. 'Tis a losing battle you wage."

"If you were me, would you surrender?"

"*Non,* I would not." He smiled, obviously conceding the point. "Still, 'tis not the same for us. I am a warrior; you are but a woman."

" 'Tis of no importance. You would out of honor and responsibility protect your people. I can do no less."

"Very well, Annie. But a good soldier knows when to accept defeat."

"I never said I was a good soldier."

With that, Royce's hand slipped to her neck and softly massaged the tense muscles. Even though she wanted to push his hand away, his touch worked magic on her stiff and sore neck.

"Have you always worried about everything?" he asked, continuing to stroke her tender flesh.

"Why is it that a man may express concern for his duty, but when I exhibit the same emotion it is silly fretting?"

"Truce," he said. "I am not used to any woman caring about others outside her family. It is a new experience for me."

Bethany shook her head sadly to convey her opinion of the women he had known. "It may amaze you, but women have just as many virtues as men."

"And just as many vices," he added.

"True," she conceded slowly, edging away from him.

"Forsooth, then we have much in common. Can we not put aside our differences?"

"It is easy for the victor to say that. I would wager the words would stick in your throat if you were the vanquished."

"Verily, Annie, you are a woman of intelligence and logic. We must work together for the sake of your people." His hands started massaging her back, working their way down her spine.

"How?" she asked, suddenly intrigued.

Royce merely smiled, his expression too pleased and knowing for her liking. "Peace. Would not you agree 'tis needed in this land?"

"Aye, sorely."

"Good," he murmured, then pulled her into his arms before she could offer a protest.

The moment his lips touched hers, a current ran through her. They were warm and smooth, and as the kiss became a sensuous union of taste and texture, a strange sensation tingled over her nerves, evoking a shiver that was both colder than a winter's night and hotter than a summer's day. Why had she ever tried to match wits with him?

"Please," she managed to whisper between ragged breaths. "This has nothing to do with peace."

"Oh, Annie, this has everything to do with it."

"You were talking about my people, not us."

"Peace includes everyone, or it fails. Will you surrender to it?"

"Nay."

"Then I must see this through." His lips once again covered hers, and this time resistance became even harder than before. His mouth moved over hers, demanding a response she fought not to give.

She almost sighed in relief when his mouth stilled and she could gather her turbulent thoughts. But suddenly his tongue touched her lips and slipped into her mouth, and she was lost. His erotic exploration dazed and excited her; and though she wanted to slow everything down, she also inexplicably wanted to speed them up.

It was uncanny, but he seemed to know her thoughts. "Trust me," he said, "and all your fears will be put to rest, all your questions answered." Then his lips returned to tantalize her.

How did he know? Her thoughts whirled about with frightening speed. Yet through the confusion, one tenet remained constant: She wanted this man. It was simple and direct—and purely forbidden. Of all the men in Christendom, she must not choose her enemy.

He would not force her. She had to be strong. But strength had nothing to do with the power and magic of his heady kiss. Surely if the man's sorcery could be harnessed, there would be no need for conquest.

She did not resist when his hands slipped like a tight-fitting garment over her hips and waist, clinging softly, but momentarily, then trailing up with exquisite feather-like strokes to the soft under-curve of her breasts. His touch sent ripples of delicious pleasure racing through her. If she thought she had been warm before now, she felt on fire.

His lips travelled from her mouth to her throat. The warmth of his touch combined with the heat within her to ignite her senses. Consumed by the flames of her passion, she submitted when his hands slipped beneath her tunic and gently slid the material from her body. His fingers caressed her breasts, gently massaging the peaks until she felt a red-hot wave surge through her. A soft moan escaped her and his lips devoured the sound as he continued to stroke and caress her.

The sensations overwhelmed her. She tried to hold onto her will, but her traitorous body surrendered to the pleasure offered and slowly responded. Her kiss, though shy at first, soon matched his ardor as desire coiled within her. Instinctively, she molded her curves to him, touching, stroking, and caressing every inch of his superb body, bespeaking her need for him in a sensual language that was far more eloquent than words. Long and languidly, she kissed him, her tongue stroking his lips and making gentle forays past his teeth to caress the warm recesses of his mouth.

She felt bereft when he pulled away, but then his lips travelled lower, his teeth taking little nips from her shoulder and grazing across her breast. A shiver of pure delight shot through her. His hands slipped further down her body. Slowly he peeled her tights off and they joined the pile of clothes pooled at her feet.

"Touch me, Annie," he whispered.

She reached out and met the stiff material of his tunic. With slow, tentative movements, her palms slipped beneath it. Lord, but his body held a fascination as her fingers traced every rib, every rippling muscle on his chest.

He swore softly under his breath and helped her remove his tunic and tights.

Whispered words of endearment floated to her ears as he picked her up in his arms and carried her to the bed.

Tentatively she touched his skin again. The warmth beneath her fingertips did not surprise her. His skin was bronzed by the sun, and the hard firm strength of his muscles was a temptation she could not resist.

Like developing a taste for an exotic wine, her exposure to the beauty and sheer size of the Norman had stimulated an appreciation for his magnificent body; in truth, she seemed addicted to touching him.

He shuddered as her fingers stroked low on his chest, and his powerful reaction excited her. The building pressure within her peaked with each sound and shiver he made.

"Annie."

He reached for her, his gaze scorching. His hands and mouth covered every inch of her. There was a breathless moment when his head was between her legs that she tried to stop him, but resistance died as an incredible warmth poured through her. Her gasp clearly inflamed him. He moved to cover her. Lowering his lips to hers, he whispered, "I will take you to heaven, Annie."

Then he moved closer, his kiss not merely exciting but commanding and forceful. The tender lover was gone, and in his place was a man who needed and demanded more of her. She felt the sudden urge that was driving him on, but she did not know how to meet it.

"Annie, wrap your legs around me." His voice was husky and a bit sharp.

Without thought or resistance, she complied.

His hands softly caressed the line of her chin, then cradled her face. "I wish there were a way to do this so there would be no pain. It will last only a moment, Annie, then it will be replaced by pleasure. Trust me."

Like dim sounds in a deep fog, his words confused her. Pain from him? It did not seem possible. He had given her so much pleasure.

Then he thrust into her and she felt ripped asunder. His mouth swallowed her painful cry. When he was imbedded, he stilled. Softly, he kissed her cheeks and the tears that had fallen. "I am sorry, Annie. There was no way to avoid it."

Bethany did not answer him. In her pain, all she wanted was for him to get away from her and even tried to push him off, but he remained.

"Shh, little Saxon, it will be better from here on."

His kisses and soft caresses helped to ease her mind. The fire he had started began to build again. The tender kisses grew more urgent and consuming. And for some unknown reason, she responded to that urgency, instinctively knowing that what she craved was there, just beyond her reach.

When he moved again, her soreness had passed. She tried to match his rhythm, but he abruptly stilled her hips. "Too fast, Annie. You are driving me mad."

What on earth did he think he was doing to her?

Once kindled, the flame of her passion did not simmer but burned out of control. Engulfed by a fever that was fueled by need, she pushed his hands away and frantically met each thrust. Harder, faster, she hastened the pace, racing for release.

Then she stilled as though her whole body had gasped.

As if overtaken by a sudden storm, she was showered with turbulent emotions. She could not understand it, but held on to him as he cried her name into the air, then shuddered and collapsed on her.

As she floated downward, she sighed, utterly content. So this was lovemaking. Now, all of the stories she had overheard in the kitchen made sense. No wonder people did it often and with such fervor.

"Annie." He caressed the side of her cheek. She moved as close as the embrace would allow, curving to his hand and relishing the feel of his touch.

As though he could not bear to be parted from her, he rolled to his side, gently taking her with him.

His smooth, light finger-strokes slid over her shoulders and back, feeling as delicious and delicate as fine silk over her naked skin. Little circles drawn up and down her spine grew larger each pass until his hands no longer massaged but fully embraced her in a passionate caress. Whispered kisses that began feather-light became long, slow, and deep. She returned his ardor with a passionate response that drove him wild.

They made love again, this time with an exquisite tenderness and exploration that left her breathless. When Royce cried out in fulfillment, her voice joined his.

Exhausted, Bethany fell asleep in his arms. For the first time in a long time, her dreams were peaceful. At daybreak, his gentle kiss awoke her. Lingering in a sleepy haze, she basked in the glow of his lovemaking; then, slowly, reality intruded and the memory of the trouble and problems that beset her before retiring last eventide returned.

She was about to push out of his embrace when a hard pounding on the door startled her. He pulled away slightly, but kept her within the circle of his arms.

"Who dares disturb me?" Royce bellowed.

"Brother, I must see you, 'Tis important," sounded Guy's urgent reply from the other side of the door.

"It had better be or, so help me, I will see you staked out and spitted."

Guy opened the door and smiled at the sight of them in bed. "Your pardon, brother, but we have a visitor."

Bethany's heart skipped a beat. She was reminded of their last visitor.

"Who is it, Guy?" Royce asked, his weariness and frustration unmistakable.

"Your betrothed has arrived."

"Damiana?" Royce asked, instantly alert.

"*Oui*, and she wishes to see you posthaste. Should I send her up to your bed chamber?"

"*Merde,*" he answered, clearly annoyed by his brother's jest.

Bethany raised her face from the covers. Burning with humiliation and mortification, she turned to Guy. "Aye, send his fiancee up. 'Twould be interesting to see how much she desires him," she said, throwing Royce's words back in his face.

Guy smiled, but Royce did not. "Hold your tongue, woman," Royce ordered. "Remember you are a slave and do not give orders. I will go downstairs." He leapt from the bed and dressed quickly.

After he tied his fastenings, he turned to his brother. "Stay with Annie. Make sure she does not cause trouble."

Chapter Ten

"Are you going to cower beneath those covers all day? Or are you going to get dressed and satisfy your curiosity about Royce's betrothed?"

From Guy's tone, it was apparent that he did not like this Damiana and that he was not afraid of his brother's ire. Of course, he would not suffer for it the way she would.

Bethany did not answer, but shooed him away with a wave of her hand, trying to gain some privacy to dress. She was not about to leave the bed with the Norman soldier watching her. But reminding her very much of his stubborn brother, Guy just stood there and shook his head.

"Please," she said, "I cannot dress with you standing guard."

"I promise not to peek," he said with mock solemnness. At her glare, his handsome smile surfaced, exposing briefly the charming devil that lived beneath the tough exterior. "I would not believe me, either. But I cannot leave you alone. Go behind the screen to seek your privacy."

Bethany wrapped the covers tightly about her and rose from the bed, then gathered the discarded clothes to take behind the tapestry.

"Hold." Guy took the clothes from her hand. "You will need finer raiment than these to meet the impeccable Damiana. Would you not face the flawless fiancee on equal ground?"

"I have other clothes." She pointed to the chest, then went on, reluctantly, "but your brother only gave permission to wear my normal dress."

"I will take responsibility." Guy moved to the chest and pulled out gown after gown of her everyday wear until he reached the bottom of the chest where her finer, more costly gowns were stored. He dropped one after another to the floor until he found a style that finally satisfied him.

He held up a dark-green overdress with a pale, spring-green undershift, one of Bethany's favorites. Then with a frown he fingered the frayed hem.

"You do not concern yourself with clothes as other women do," he said, handing her the woolen dress. She could see by his features that he found even this garment sorely lacking.

" 'Tis the best I have," she said defensively. "All the finery in the world would not change who I am."

"*Non.* You would still be the Saxon woman who dared champion a Norman warlord so her people could escape. I shall never forget the sight. You were barely able to hold that sword aloft."

" 'Tis unkind of you to remind me."

"There was nothing in your actions to regret," he said with a sincerity that surprised Bethany. "I admire your courage and honor."

She accepted the dress and went to change behind the tapestry. She did not understand Normans. Sometimes they actually seemed compassionate, like Saxons. Still, she was sure Guy had his own reasons for being charitable. Though he could be quite chivalrous, it was only when it suited him. Her dress on, she came around the tapestry looking for her comb, but Guy stopped her from grooming her hair.

"You look like you just rose from a lover's bed. I would have Damiana see you thusly."

Her face warmed at the reminder that she had indeed just risen from a lover's embrace. But her brother and sister were now in Scotland and the sacrifice was worth it.

Godalmighty, she was a hypocrite. The truth stood far harder to face. 'Twas no sacrifice at all to lie with the Norman. But she would never, never let that arrogant devil or his brother know it.

"Do not distress yourself, my lady," Guy said as he arranged her long hair to fall down one shoulder and spill across her arm. "There, you look beautiful."

Bethany tossed her hair back over her shoulder where it belonged. "What game do you play, Norman? Why are you putting yourself to such lengths to see this done?"

"Because, bold Saxon, I do not like Damiana." He held out his hand to her. "But come and make your own judgment about the lovely spider."

"Why should I care?"

"If for no other reason than the welfare of your people. Lady Damiana can be cruel."

He hit a nerve. Thank God he had not mentioned jealousy. She certainly did not care whom Royce married. Still, the pain of betrayal ate at her. She had been no more than the spoils of war, and her pride burned.

Bethany said nothing as they left the room and walked down the stone stairway. She did not relish meeting the woman and could only imagine Royce's anger over her rebellion and what he would term her disobedience in leaving his chamber. But she felt bold with her sister and brother safely away.

The great hall was filled with Royce's men. As they parted for Guy, Bethany had her first glimpse of the lovely Damiana. Sultry dark eyes and shiny black hair made her white skin stand out with striking clarity. She stood a full head above Bethany, with far more generous curves. Dressed in fine white linen with gold embroidery outlining the hem, she was the image of an aristocrat.

"Who is this?" she asked imperiously, glancing at Bethany.

Royce slowly pivoted and faced Bethany and Guy. His stern features gave nothing away as he turned back to his betrothed. "Merely the former lady of this demesne—and now my slave."

"Mon dieu, but she is not much more than flesh and bone." Damiana strolled around Bethany, taking her measure with a seemingly critical eye. "Are all the Saxons so poorly formed?"

Bethany bit back a retort as she met Damiana's malicious glare. Guy was right. It was clear this woman would be her enemy.

With a look of pity, Damiana lifted Bethany's arm. "Her arm is so thin it could not heft a dust linen."

Guy chuckled as Bethany pulled her arm free of the Norman lady's grip. "Verily," he said with laughter in his voice, "nor even a sword."

Royce smiled at his brother's private jest, but his silence made it clear the joke would not be shared with Damiana.

"Secrets," she said, raising an eyebrow. "I see." Damiana turned back to Bethany. "Courtliness and gallantry often are casualties of war. Without the influence of fair maidens, men fall into boorish ways." Damiana tapped Bethany on the arm. "Now that a lady is present, that will change."

She glided passed Bethany and stood in the center of the room. Running her finger over the top of a table still laden with the morning repast, she raised her hand and stared disdainfully at the results. " 'Tis bad enough the place is little more than a hovel, but I will not tolerate a slovenly home."

Bethany gasped at the insult. Renwyg might not be a Norman castle, but it was her home and had always been scoured and cleaned with scrupulous care.

Damiana shook her head sadly. "Thank God, my parents do not arrive for weeks. I thought to come ahead to oversee the preparations for our wedding, but now I fear that time will be needed to make this place fit for habitation." She pointed to each lovely tapestry. "An abomination to the senses, they will have to go," she said scathingly, then turned beseechingly toward Royce. "Did I leave my beloved Normandy to bear the rigors of this uncivilized island, Royce?" The arrogance in her voice permeated the air like a damp, chilling mist, leaving those it touched uneasy and uncomfortable.

Bethany was shocked that Royce would allow anyone to address him with such insolence in front of his men. But if he were content to remain silent, Bethany was not about to stand still while her land and people were insulted by this condescending sow.

"Nay, Lady Damiana," Bethany said, her tone unmistakably dry. "I heard you left Normandy to marry your beloved." Bethany extended her hand toward Royce. "However, if you find the hardships here outweigh your desire, then it would be prudent of you to return home."

The woman's face mirrored her disbelief at the rebuke. Guy appeared pleased while Royce remained impassive, yet a hint of humor sparkled in his midnight eyes.

Damiana's rage flickered across her countenance, but she maintained a tone of bored disinterest as she turned to Royce.

"I am very disappointed, *cheri,* that you allow your slave to be so disrespectful." She then glared at Guy. "I am not surprised *you* are pleased by this peasant's behavior. Crudity is something that I would expect you to enjoy."

"My lady, you are mistaken. It is not I but Royce who is pleased by Bethany." Guy raised Bethany's hand and placed a chaste kiss on her palm.

By the quick tightening of her expression, Bethany could see that Damiana grasped Guy's meaning.

"It would seem that this isle holds more for the men than I had thought." She stared at Bethany with a pitying look that said far more than words.

With a long-suffering sigh, she turned to Royce. "I had not realized that the campaign was so long. Now that I am here, things will be different."

Though he remained silent, Royce raised an eyebrow at the last remark.

"Are you giving Royce orders?" Guy asked.

Damiana shot Guy a sharp glance but turned a contrite face to Royce. *"Mais oui.* I am sorry, *cheri.* I am truly not myself from this dreadful travelling. Please forgive my incautious tongue."

"Damiana, do not worry yourself. I will have a room prepared for you." He turned to Bethany. "Tell Maida to see to our guests' needs."

"Tell her yourself." A smile of pure satisfaction curved Bethany's lips. When Royce did not react to her defiance, she tried to goad his temper further. "I no longer will act as your interpreter," she said with a great deal of delight. Her family was safe; he no longer had leverage over her.

"Are you daring to challenge me?" Royce asked quietly while every Norman looked on in shock.

"Aye. There is nothing you can do to force me to your will."

"The insolent wretch," snapped Lady Damiana, and the deep-throated voices of his soldiers grumbled in agreement.

"Vachel," Royce bellowed.

At the summons, the soldier appeared. *"Oui,* my lord. What say you?"

Staring stonily at Bethany, Royce spoke to his man. "Bring your charges here."

"As you wish."

A moment later, Bethany looked up to see Vachel escorting her brother and her sister back into the hall. Her breath caught in her throat as she blinked to make sure she had seen right. Dear St. Bede, her eyes had not played her false. With a sinking feeling in her stomach, she knew she had failed—again.

Royce looked at Bethany pointedly. With an angry oath, she spun about and ordered Maida to see to the Norman lady's needs. Ignoring Damiana's gloating expression, Bethany held her head up, refusing to act humbled or defeated. When Damiana had departed, Bethany tried to move away, but Royce clasped her arm and restrained her. "We will discuss your rebellion in a minute." With a slight incline of his head, Royce signaled Vachel.

The soldier immediately escorted her sister and brother toward them. Bret ran with the free abandon of a youngster unaware of the intrigues around him. Mary followed cautiously, as though dreading the moment she would face her sister.

"What happened?" Bethany asked as her brother ran around her and Royce.

"We were followed," Mary stated simply.

"How could you be? No one knew of your departure."

Bret pushed his way between Royce and Bethany and pulled on her gown for attention.

"It was the warlord," Bret said. "He knew."

"What are you talking about, Bret? He could not have known."

"He told me that as the man of the household I had to take care of my sisters. He said that running away solved nothing."

It *sounded* like Royce, but how could he speak to her brother? He did not understand their language. Suddenly, an ugly thought occurred to her.

"Bret, when did he talk to you?"

"Ever since he first came. 'Twas a secret. We played a jest on everyone."

"Impossible," Bethany muttered, trying to still the fear that this was not a game. "Little boys who make up stories often find themselves going without dinner," she warned.

"Little girls who call the lord and master a *dim-witted lout* often find themselves in a more precarious position than going without dinner."

She heard Royce's voice—clear, crisp, and concise as he uttered each word in Saxon. Not only did he speak her language, but he did so flawlessly. God's teeth! What a fool she had been. Humiliation burned deep within her, her pride ground beneath a Norman boot. Slowly, she tried to pry Royce's fingers loose from her wrist, but to no avail.

Mary picked up Bret and held him to her breast. "What will he do to us, Bethany?"

There were times when she wanted to box Mary's ears. *Ask*

the warlord yourself. He understands our language! Bethany
wanted to scream, but instead held her tongue. If Mary were
to challenge the warlord, he might take his anger out on her.

Swallowing her pride, and giving Mary a reassuring look,
Bethany took a deep breath. "I am responsible for their actions
and will bear the punishment."

Royce ignored her and spoke to Mary. "You will retire to
your rooms."

The frightened, pleading look Mary sent Bethany wrenched
at her heart.

"What do you plan to do?" Bethany demanded of Royce,
unable to keep the touch of panic from her voice.

"Whatever I decide, the boy will not suffer. I hold him
innocent—unlike those who unwisely controlled his actions."

"And my sister?"

"Mary is not bold or smart enough to execute the escape.
Still, I cannot let her actions go unpunished."

"You could show mercy."

"I will think on the matter," Royce replied.

Bethany felt her stomach roil with fear and resentment. Her
sister's fate stood undecided.

He turned to Mary. "You will await my decision in your
room."

Mary nodded, then scurried out of the hall with Bret in her
arms.

Bethany tried to follow, but Royce's tight grip on her arm
held her back.

"I want you where I can keep an eye on you. You will
accompany me all day and await my pleasure," he said. He
pulled her through the great hall and passed the milling crowd
to the lesser hall, where he took his seat behind a small table
for the grievance proceedings.

A chair was not provided for her, and it became clear that
she would stand throughout. When Guy entered with a long
list of cases waiting to receive judgment, Royce sent her for
wine and cheese. She returned before the hallmote began, and

Royce kept her at his side for the rest of the day. Bethany had presided over these functions many times and she resented another settling her people's disputes. But though she was loath to admit it, she learned a great deal about the man as he dealt with the problems placed before him.

After the military infractions had been dispensed with, the civil disruptions were brought before Royce. Vachel announced the first transgression. "Thievery," he bellowed.

A young boy of seven summers stood before Royce. The terror in his eyes shone like the stark whiteness of a full moon on a clear night.

"This Saxon whelp is accused of stealing food, my lord," Vachel said.

"Why did you steal the food, boy?" Royce asked.

Though he was afraid, the boy managed to stand tall. "I was hungry."

The voice was small and the answer so simple, Bethany felt her chest constrict. Not caring if she interrupted the manorial court or showed disrespect, she turned to Royce. "Ram is a good child. You must not punish him."

Royce ignored her and motioned for Guy. With their dark manes bowed together, they conferred in soft whispers that did not carry to Bethany. Resentment filled her that it took two strong warriors to condemn a child. She seethed with ire at Royce and in that moment knew she would never forgive him.

Guy left and Royce, either unaware of her anger or uninterested, turned his attention back to the child. "Tell me, boy, have you been hungry before?"

"Aye, my lord."

"Have you stolen food before?"

"Nay, it was wrong."

"Then why now?"

"There was nothing for my mama and sister. With my father gone, I am the man now."

Royce leaned back in his chair and studied the boy.

"Why is there no food?"

The color drained from the boy's face and his gaze travelled to Bethany. The beseeching look tore at her heart as he silently pleaded for her intervention.

Royce's grip warned her to remain silent.

"Why is there no food, boy?" Royce repeated his question, leaning slightly forward in his chair.

Under the weight of Royce's authority, the boy crumbled. Huge tears slid down his cheeks as he knuckled them away. "The soldier sells it," he spat, half in fear, half in belligerence.

Guy entered with a soldier at his side. They walked through the lesser hall, their footsteps echoing in the sudden silence. As he stood before his commander, the young soldier glared threateningly at Ram and only when the boy seemed properly cowed turned his attention to Royce.

"You wished to see me, my lord?"

"This boy says you starve them," Royce said. "Is that true?"

"*Non,* my lord. You have ordered all soldiers who live with the villagers to provide for them."

"Then you swear you have done so."

"I vow it on all the holy saints," the soldier said sincerely, then held out his hand to indicate the child. "This boy is a Saxon. Would you take his word over mine?"

Bethany closed her eyes and begged God to strike the Norman dead for his blasphemy.

Vachel approached Royce and leaned forward to whisper something. Bethany could not hear this conversation, either. Curse Vachel for his covert ways.

"Since you have sworn before me that you provided for the Saxon family and the boy has denied it, we will go to your lodging and see how the hut fares."

The soldier looked around the room as if seeking help from the other Normans gathered in the hall. When no one came forward on his behalf, he spread his arms wide and took a hesitant step forward. "*Non,* my lord. That is not necessary."

"I insist on seeing your abode," Royce ordered. "That way

the question of lies will be put to rest and these people will see Norman justice firsthand."

"Pray forgive me, my lord. But 'twould serve no purpose." The soldier looked uncomfortable, and Bethany noticed a sheen of perspiration on his forehead.

"Is there a reason why you do not want us to see where you live?"

"I yield, my lord. The boy spoke the truth."

"Then, this is my decree. You will vacate the abode to an honorable soldier. Then you will repay this family. Every night you cheated them will cost you. They were forced to open their home and you took the very food out of their mouths to support your gambling habit. Do not looked so surprised. I am aware of your vice. Henceforth, no soldier will be allowed to gamble with you."

The soldier's face turned beet red and his hands clenched into tight fists held rigidly at his sides. "My lord, this is not fair."

"Then find yourself another army. Mine does not tolerate your kind of behavior."

Bethany was shocked that Royce had ruled in favor of a Saxon against his man. It showed a side of him she did not want to see. Royce was an honorable man.

As quickly as the kind thoughts entered her mind, she rejected them. Royce was her enemy. She would not be fooled by one gesture. Did he, with Norman arrogance, think Saxons were so shallow-witted that they would believe his ploy to win their loyalty?

When the last case had been settled, Bethany felt the weight of their coming meeting. She stood as much on trial as those who had laid their problems before the lord for justice. But justice for her would not be forthcoming.

As if reading her thoughts, Royce turned to her. "Would you like to state your case here before everyone or privately in our chamber?"

"Here," she said, refusing his kindness.

He merely inclined his head, acknowledging her wishes. "Now, what did you hope to gain? If your sister and brother escaped, you would still be a slave."

Bethany refused to answer him.

"Ah. You would have your family and fortune safe from my greedy hands. And with that burden removed, you could openly defy me."

At his perception, Bethany met his harsh glare. "Aye."

"I know, Bethany." He reached out and clasped her arm.

She tried to pry his fingers loose. "I have duties to attend to," she said with unconcealed irritation in her voice.

"No escape is possible, my little Saxon. You have much to answer for and the time of reckoning has come."

Standing, Royce headed toward the stairs, pulling her behind him as if she were no more than a pet being made to heel.

Thinking he entertained amorous thoughts, Bethany began to resist with all her might. She did not want to go to their chamber to settle this matter. "Nay, 'tis not fitting, 'tis daylight!"

He chuckled. "Lovemaking is the last thing on my mind. You deserve not a reward, but a punishment."

The arrogant beast thought his lovemaking a reward. Before she could say anything, Lady Damiana's voice rang out from the balcony above them.

"Royce, can you not see that the child is afraid of you? Leave be and find some more mature sport."

She started down the stairs with a sultry walk that would fairly singe a saint. Lord, had the woman no shame? Any minute Bethany expected to see the wide, swaying, motion of her hips hit full momentum, bouncing from wall to rail with her exaggerated stride.

"Let the little slave go and seek your pleasure with a woman who has been alone for far too long."

A smile spread over Royce's lips, but did not reach his eyes. "Alone, Damiana?"

"*Oui*, alone. Who has been telling falsehoods? Guy?" she snapped.

"Damiana, you take the bait so well, I cannot help but tease," Royce quipped.

Bethany looked from one to the other. Lady Damiana wore a satisfied expression, while Royce's was, as always, unreadable. No one knew his thoughts. But it was plain to Bethany that the woman's reaction to Royce's teasing came from guilt, not coyness. Clever and cunning, this woman would bear watching.

In Saxon, Royce ordered Bethany to see to her chores and make sure she awaited him tonight when he would mete out her just deserts. Then, with a sweet smile, he gallantly offered his arm to Damiana. "Let me take you on a tour. After all, this is your new home."

As Damiana brushed passed, Bethany felt a nasty sting. The prettily dressed lady with the honey voice had pinched Bethany on the arm.

Bethany rubbed her arm and resisted the urge to stick out her tongue at Damiana's back. She turned around and found Guy smiling at her.

"Let me escort you, Lady Bethany." He offered his arm as if he believed her a true woman of station.

She studied his face. The mockery she expected to see was surprisingly absent. He offered her a courtesy and meant it.

"As if you have seen, and felt—" He lifted her arm to examine the red Mark. "—Damiana is a true bitch. Royce is blind to it."

"Why are you telling me?" Bethany stared at him, trying to discern his motives.

"It seems strange to enlist the help of a woman—and a Saxon at that . . ." When she started to protest, he held up his hand. "I think you will see the prudence of it . . . if for no other reason then the welfare of your people."

"Your brother is a man full grown. I think he can take care of himself without your help."

"And your sister is a woman full grown. Yet you rescue her continually. Where is the difference?"

Bethany conceded the point with a slight nod. "I will not help the enemy."

"Think of it as helping your people."

Bethany thought about it. "I cannot promise to help you. What do you wish?"

"I want you to make my brother fall head over heels in love with you."

"Are you mad?" She pushed away from him.

"Think of it, Bethany—Royce so smitten with you that when you reject his love, you destroy him. Does that not sound to your liking? He has taken everything away from you. All you need do is seduce him."

"Forsooth! And what am I to gain, besides revenge?"

A soft chuckle escaped his lips. His dark, blue eyes sparkled as though he held the secrets of the world and they amused him. "Your kingdom. Your freedom and that of your people. A man who loves would deliver the world to his beloved's feet."

It sounded wonderful, but she knew her limitations and found herself wholly inadequate for the task. Woefully, she looked at Guy.

"I have never tried to—attract a man. I would not know how to go about it."

"Leave everything to me," Guy said with an air of assurance that was truly annoying.

"Why should I trust you?"

"Because, my dear, I can help. You will not find a better teacher in all of Christendom."

At the sly smile and the pleased look about him, Bethany could not stop from speaking her thoughts. "What manner of man were you before you became a soldier?"

His face actually turned red. " 'Tis of no consequence."

At his evasion, she pushed on. "What were you, Guy? A courtier?"

"*Non.* I entered the seminary to study for a life within the church."

"A priest?" she gasped. She shook her head in despair. "I am truly doomed if my teacher of vice is a near-friar."

"Worry not, my dear. Who else to teach you about sin but a man who failed to be a saint? My spirit was willing but my flesh was, oh, so weak."

Chapter Eleven

"This ring is the answer to their prayers," Bram muttered to himself. Bethany was a smart one, thank God. He held the ring up to the light. " 'Tis no mistaking the emblem. 'Twas William's ring."

Obviously, Bethany had heard the story. The lass knew William remained their last hope. Though a Scotsman dinna like to admit to defeat, Bram would have to depend on the Norman King to honor the debt he owed to his late brother, Gowain. He had little choice but to leave for London, England.

By this time next month he would, God willing, right the injustice done to his relatives. He looked around his empty room and recalled a time when Bethany's mother had lain in his arms after a passionate night of lovemaking. He had failed her once; he would not fail her children. He owed it to his brother to protect Mary and Bret, and he owed it to Hayley to protect Bethany.

He closed his fingers tightly around the ring and made a silent vow. He had failed his lover in her time of need. He would not do the same to their daughter.

* * *

The hours had dragged as Bethany waited for Royce to return and announce her punishment. Suddenly, she heard the unmistakable sound of crying outside her chamber. She pulled the wooden door open and found little Bret covering his cheek trying to stifle a sob. She knelt and hugged the child to her breast. "What is it, Bret?"

"That bad lady hit me."

The words chilled her. "Who?"

"The one who wears all the shiny stones."

Only one woman had jewels in Renwyg castle. A Norman woman. "Shh. It will be all right." She rocked her brother in her arms. When his sobs quieted, she whispered. "Why did she strike you? Were you bad?"

"Nay! I was bringing you this from the warlord. 'Tis your punishment." He held out his hand and she grasped the missive.

Bethany quickly scanned Royce's directive, written in Mary's distinctive script, her jaw tightening at the tone and list of instructions detailed as her chastisement for the escape plan. Her only consolation was that he held her accountable, and not Maida, for drugging the guard's wine. "God's teeth," she muttered, thinking that cleaning his armor and weapons, the very instruments of her vanquishment, was a task designed to remind her of her status. Seething, she refolded the note and placed it in her smock.

"What was Mary's punishment?" she asked.

"Mary must rise early to help Maida with the bread." Bret sniffled and, through his hiccups, he added, "When Damiana saw me, she said I must read her Royce's message. She hit me when I could not."

"Do not worry, Bret. I will deal with her." A red haze slipped over Bethany's vision as rage welled in her heart.

"I want her to go away," he wailed.

Bethany rose with her brother in her arms and went down the stairs. Long past midday, the night meal was being placed upon the table. Damiana sat between Guy and Royce. Bethany walked over to Mary and handed Bret to her, then turned and approached Damiana. When she glanced up, Bethany slapped her hard across the face. "If you ever touch my brother again, I will kill you. Remember my threat," she stated in a low, even tone that belied the turmoil roiling inside.

The noise in the room ceased. All Norman eyes turned toward her as two soldiers grabbed her arms. Held fast, she stood silent under their appraisal, not caring what would happened. "What Norman law allows a brute to abuse a child?" she addressed Royce.

He tried to answer, but she cut him off.

"Know you well, I will take care of my own."

Royce turned toward a gasping and sputtering Damiana. "Did you strike the child?"

"Oui. The whelp refused to do my bidding. But 'twas just a tap."

Royce turned to view the red mark that covered half of Bret's face. He held out his arms for the child, who flew off Mary's lap into Royce's waiting embrace.

"What happened, little soldier?"

"She," he pointed determinedly at Damiana, "hit me when I tried to deliver your missive to my sister." He turned tearful eyes to Royce. "She called me a lack-witted oaf when I could not read your message."

Royce turned to Damiana. "You dared to interfere with my business?"

"Cheri, you misunderstand. 'Twas not my intent to intrude on your domain. I assumed the letter had to do with the operation of this castle, the province of its mistress."

Royce turned to Bethany and she merely held his gaze. Seemingly satisfied by her placid regard, he turned back to Bret. "Did you say or do anything to the lady that was disrespectful?"

Wide-eyed, Bret shook his head from side to side. Royce touched his cheek gently. "You call this a tap, Damiana?"

She glanced at the child with a nonchalance that chilled Bethany to the bone.

"What care you for this Saxon whelp? Properly disciplined, he will be more careful in the future not to incur my wrath." She massaged her cheek. "I want that whore punished. How dare she strike and threaten the future mistress of this castle!"

Royce's tone was flinty as he replied, "I decide the punishment here. No one else has that authority, and my men will act only on my orders." He turned to the guards holding Bethany. "Release her."

Lady Damiana drew back in shock. "Royce, are you mad? This slave must be taught her place."

"If it comes to my attention that you have raised your hand against my people again, I would advise you to seek a convent to hide from my wrath," Royce said dispassionately.

All the color drained from Damiana's face. "You have been too long among these peasants."

She rose from her seat and started for the stairs.

"Do not think if you leave my table you will be allowed to eat in your room. I tolerate no disrespect."

With a coy, almost superior smile, Damiana turned back to face Royce. "If you wish to marry me, *cheri,* you had best not forget yourself. Remember how close my family is to the queen."

"Make no mistake, Damiana, what I want I will have, but not at the price of anyone's flesh. You *will* marry me because you have no choice. Your family is without coin and all you have is your name. I am not blinded by your beauty or your charm as I once was. Years ago I saw a lovely woman." He paused. His gaze travelled from the top of her head to the tip of her shoes, inspecting her as if she were a piece of merchandise. "Today I see a selfish one."

Damiana faced Royce with her nose high in the air. "If that is all, my lord, then I will retire for the night."

Royce merely inclined his head and, enraged by his lack of reaction, Damiana's lovely face contorted in frustration as she left the great hall.

"Thank God you came to your senses." Guy gave his brother a mock salute. "For a time I feared you were smitten with the vixen's charms."

"Guy, what I once saw in her I can no longer find. Time has changed us both."

"The passage of time has been a blessing. I believe you have changed and matured. The same cannot be said for Damiana."

"That may be, but my plans remain the same. I will still take her as wife."

"But why, brother? At court you will always be a bastard. Nothing you do will wash that clean," Guy said.

"I cannot leave that legacy for my sons."

"You are a stubborn man, brother. Better you should leave them a legacy of love and understanding. Teach them by the example of the man you have become. That should mean more to you than a title."

"Title is not what I seek. 'Tis acceptance. No man will look down his nose at my offspring. No child of my loins will ever be ashamed of his heritage. With Damiana's bloodline, my sons will never be treated with contempt."

"Then it is not for yourself that you do this?"

"Non. It never has been," Royce said, then shrugged his shoulders. "Long ago, I gave up caring what they thought of me."

"I think it still bothers you," Guy said.

"I have learned to live with it."

Bret started to fidget in Royce's lap.

"What is it?" Royce asked.

"Will she hurt me?"

"Non, mon petit, never again will you have to fear punishment unless you have done a wrong."

"I will be good." Meekly Bret raised his eyes to Royce,

hesitated, then blurted out, "You will not punish my sister, will you?"

"*Non.* She did but protect you," Royce said with a gentleness that was absent when he addressed others.

He looked at her, but Bethany did not acknowledge the reprieve. Let him be Solomon the Wise. It did not change the fact that if they were to know any peace and safety, they would have to escape the Norman's control. Their well-being rested on another's whim. She could not let her family live like that.

"From now on you will bring your grievances to me. Do you understand?"

Bethany raised her chin. "Has the master spoken?"

"*Oui,* he has. You would do well to remember it."

"Listen to me, Mary." As early-morning sunlight filled the room, Bethany stopped folding the clothes strewn on the bed and shifted to face her sister. "I know you do not like Lady Damiana." The name soured in her mouth, but she forced herself to continue. "She has no one to talk to and no one she considers an equal. I want you to befriend her. Since the Normans have been here, the language is coming back to you. I know you understand far more French than you let on. You must do this."

"She is horrid," Mary protested, her lovely mouth turning down with a pout.

"I know; but if she trusts you, we will have firsthand knowledge of what the Normans plan to do. I do not like asking this of you, but I must."

"Nay, you have all of our well-being at heart. I will do what you ask, but I think we would be better off planning our escape."

"We have tried that twice and failed. I have not given up, but I fear the only way out is if the warlord releases you when the wealth of the demesne is in his hands."

"Uncle Bram will never agree to that," Mary said.

"Perhaps someday he will, when all avenues are exhausted.

'Till then we must live by our wits. I, for one, do not want to be surprised by the Normans again."

A knock at the door interrupted Bethany's thoughts. "Enter," she called out, knowing it was not Royce. He would have barged in.

Guy opened the door and, upon seeing Mary, he paused. "Your pardon, ladies, but if I could have a word in private with you, Lady Bethany."

Mary rose and curtsied. "By your leave," she said to Guy, then turned, her face mirroring her curiosity as she took her sister's hands. "I will see you later," Mary said warily, before leaving the room.

"What is it Guy?" Bethany asked.

"Not here," he said, opening the door.

"Whatever is wrong?" she questioned, growing alarmed at his secretive manner.

"I will tell you when we are alone and safe from discovery. Trust me." Guy escorted Bethany from the master chamber toward the commander's room, a small circular chamber inside the left tower.

"Guy, 'tis late. I will be missed at break-the-fast," Bethany said, hearing the voices of the men gathering in the great hall.

"Do not worry. We have plenty of time before the morning meal is served. Royce will never know."

"What game are you up to, Guy?"

His soft chuckle echoed in the narrow stairway. "The oldest one in the world, my lady. It started with an apple."

"An apple?" she questioned as they passed the tower guard.

"*Oui.* But unlike you, Eve had no competition for Adam."

"I will not participate in a contest for your brother's affection."

"Oh, pretty Saxon, you are already a player and need to prepare. 'Tis a match you must win or yesterday's incident will become commonplace."

Silence met his statement as she remembered Damiana's cruel treatment of Bret.

He opened a door and extended his hand for her to precede him. "We will have a lesson today, my lady," he said, closing the door and securing the wooden bar in place.

"A lesson?" she asked as he approached.

"*Oui*, an exercise in portraying the perfect image of nobility which Royce thinks is necessary. Damiana is a master at exuding superiority—and sensuality." He walked around her, looking at her attire as he stroked his chin, "You are sorely at a disadvantage. Your tunic is cut so loose that it hangs like a sack."

Her face burned at the insult, and she glared at him. She was not ashamed of her garb. "I will not change my manner of dress."

"Royce is accustomed to the finery ladies at court wear. Attired in this shapeless apparel—" He lifted a loose draped fold of her tunic with distaste. "—you look as alluring as a poor peasant covered in rags."

"I am Saxon, and I will dress as a Saxon," she said, pulling her tunic free of his grasp.

"I am asking you to compromise and wear a flattering garment."

"Nay, I am not ashamed of my clothes."

Guy shook his head. " 'Tis too bad Royce allowed you to wear your own gowns. Your charms were enticing displayed in the squire's tights and short tunic! They certainly left little to the imagination." He chuckled.

Her face burned as she recalled the male costume and the embarrassing looks it had elicited. Tears actually gathered in her eyes at the memory of her disgrace and humiliation.

"God's teeth, Bethany, 'twas not meant as a insult, but a compliment," he said, handing her a cloth to wipe her tears. He sighed. "You are a stubborn mademoiselle. Very well, if you refuse to dress up the package, we will concentrate on presentation. You must change your manner when he is about."

"How?" she sniffled.

"Dry your eyes and give me a smile, and I will instruct you

in the fine art of dallying. Once learned, my lady, the amorous skills will win you the admiration of any man."

When she brushed the moisture away and looked at him, he lifted her hand and led her to a small writing table.

"Have a seat and listen, my lady. This is how you entice a man."

"Entice a man?" she queried.

"*Mais oui.* Have you forgotten, my lady? I said I would teach you the finer points of seducing a man. Paramount is capturing his eye and keeping his attention."

Wary of Guy, she leaned back. "Seducing?"

"My lady," he said, chuckling. "I am not going to participate in this exercise unless you wish me to. Your honor is safe."

She sighed. "Very well, show me how to interest a man."

"First," he said, "you must walk differently."

"Differently?"

"*Oui.* When you march through the castle, you defy Royce as though you, and not he, were in authority. You have to adopt a gentle swing to your gait."

"A swing?" she asked suspiciously, hoping he would not suggest Damiana's scandalous walk.

"*Oui,* a swing. Bethany, you must walk as though you wished to draw a man's gaze, not stroll through the castle unaware of him."

"How?" she insisted.

He ran a hand through his hair. "I suppose I must show you," he said in exasperation. Then he placed one hand on his hip and the other he extended forward, holding it up preposterously high in the air. "Like this." He moved across the floor, swinging his hips in an exaggerated wiggle as his hand swayed in a counterpoint.

She could not help but giggle. He looked ridiculous.

"You dare laugh when I am endeavoring to enlighten you as to how some of my countrywomen, one you have met, act before chivalrous men?" The mock admonishment was given with devilment shining in his eyes and a teasing smile that she hoped bespoke his jesting.

"Verily, I am truly sorry. Please continue."

He grabbed a mantle from the table and draped it around his waist to hang like a woman's tunic. "Every now and again, show a little ankle," he instructed as he walked across the floor.

Ankle, indeed. She smothered another giggle as he strolled in a circle, flipping the mantle up here and there.

The Normans had strange ideas. "Is this truly what interests a man?"

A broad smile creased his face as he walked back and placed his hands down on the table. With his palms resting at either side of her hips, he leaned forward, forcing her back. *"Non,* Bethany, 'tis only some womanly wiles that I have shown you to acquire a man's notice, but keeping a man from becoming bored is another matter." His face sobered. "A man chooses a woman who completes his needs. Royce's mate would have to offer—" He paused, looking straight into her eyes. "— unconditional love, and loyalty."

On a swiftly indrawn breath, she gasped, "He is my enemy." She lowered her eyes and whispered, "I could never give him my heart."

"Very well, if you cannot give my brother love, than give him what Damiana offers . . . an enticing woman who moves her body sensuously, leaving a man in little doubt that she craves his touch."

"Sensuously?" she squeaked.

"Oui." He chuckled. "When Damiana walks or talks, there is always seduction present. She wears her clothes tighter than fashion dictates, revealing every curve of her generous body. If you cannot love my brother, then you must compete with Damiana on her own ground." His gaze traveled to her breast and, with a mock leer, he suggested again, "You must wear your tunic a little snugger across your top."

Her face burned with embarrassment. "Guy, cease," she said, pushing him away.

" 'Tis true, Bethany. If you are to vie for and win Royce's favor against Damiana, you must find and flaunt your sensuality."

Why had she asked? "I understand. Are we done?"

"For now. You will try these suggestions out on Royce?" he asked.

Ha! Never would she behave in so ridiculous a manner. She would be scandalized.

"Bret told me you would be at the stable." Friar John furtively scanned the area before leaning close to Bethany. "Here," he said, handing her a sealed missive. "From your Uncle Bram."

Excitement bubbled within her as she opened the letter; and after she had read the contents, a smile slipped into place.

"I think God is answering our entreaties. Uncle Bram has gone to London to seek help," she said, slipping the secret communication into her kirtle.

"I will keep your uncle in my prayers." The friar squeezed her shoulder and left.

She strolled from the stable and stopped at the open corral.

The spirited, midnight-black destrier circled the closed pen. Eyes flashing with a wild sheen and nostrils flared, the animal galloped around the other horses, hemming them in better than the fence.

Bethany missed riding her favorite mount. "Come here, Morlock, and let me see your ugly face." Obediently, the horse trotted over. "You are my little love. If only I could take you out. A vigorous exercise would rid your restlessness as well as my anger. How we used to fly over the fields when trouble chased our heels! Now there is no escape from the problems at hand."

"Would you like to take your horse out?"

Bethany jumped at the sudden intrusion of Royce's voice. Her shock was quickly replaced by wariness, and she turned to face him. "I would, indeed."

"Then I shall take you myself." His self-satisfied expression boded ill for Bethany.

"Nay. 'Tis not necessar—"

He held up his hand, silencing her. "I wish to speak privately with you."

Although still wary, Bethany felt anything would be acceptable for a chance to ride her horse.

"Verily, I shall be spoiled by all the partiality you show me."

"Do not let it go to your head, Annie. You are still a slave."

"I shall not be in peril of forgetting it with you around to remind me."

"Morlock is a strange name for a horse. What manner of temperament inspired such a name?" he asked, ignoring her barb.

"My first choice was Warlock, but Father did not like to tempt fate."

"Ah," **he** said with a soft chuckle. "He is a magnificent beast. Worthy of any name."

"Aye. I do love him." She rubbed the horse's side in a gentle caress. "Every day we would chase the wind and ride for hours. I miss that freedom. There is nothing like it."

"Most woman view riding as a necessary evil."

"Nay, not I. It is a pleasure beyond compare. Morlock is a beauty both in strength and stamina; and when you have that combination, you have a rare horse, indeed. But Morlock possesses one thing even rarer. He has heart. This horse will die before he gives up a race or delivers a mild ride."

Royce looked thoughtful. "You have much in common with your animal. Neither one of you knows defeat."

"We are Saxon."

"Verily, you are. The war is over, Bethany. When will you surrender? Your country and people are already conquered by Normandy."

"Surrender is for those without hope. I have never lost faith. I will give up when there is nothing left for me to do but lie down and die."

"I fear, my little Saxon, that the end is closer for you than you think."

"Do you think I will tremble and shake at your words?"

"Non. But for the sake of those who follow your lead, I am afraid you must compromise your principles."

"Do not lecture me on principles," she declared, knowing that attempting what he asked would be pure hell for her and carrying it out would be damnation itself.

"You are a leader and, like it or not, others follow your example. My men inform me that every time you are reprimanded there is civil unrest. I cannot afford to have that in my demesne," he said, motioning for the stable master to ready the horses. "If you cared for your people, you would surrender."

"You dare speak of caring? My life has been devoted to my people."

"Then this will not be that hard to endure," he said.

"I cannot."

"You will, or be responsible for the needless suffering of those who are loyal to you."

What he said tore at her sense of duty and honor. The legacy weighed heavily on her mind. She could not let her people suffer for her stubbornness.

"I will make you a bargain," he said, as if sensing her dilemma. "If you do not challenge me, I will send your sister and brother to Scotland. On that day, in accordance with our laws, you will swear your fealty to me."

His words stunned her. To have her family safe she could endure anything. "You swear it on everything you hold holy?"

"Oui I do."

"What assurance do I have that you will fulfill your promise?" Bethany persisted.

"You have my word, woman. That should be assurance enough!" he said angrily.

Strangely enough, his indignant manner convinced her more than his words. Only a man of honor would have been offended by her question. "Then I will not challenge you," she said, feeling a growing elation. "My sister and brother will leave tonight."

"Non. They will leave when I am convinced you mean to keep your vow."

"I have given my word, Norman. My honor is as important to me as yours is to you. I have never broken it."

"I will only know that in time."

"You will see that a Saxon takes his oath as seriously as a Norman."

"Then I have your solemn word of honor—Saxon honor, that you will not oppose me or offer resistance to what I impose for a period of one year?"

A year! The sound echoed in her mind. Twelve long months of bowing and scraping before this man without uttering one word in protest. 'Twould be a miracle. "Six months," she said, hoping to bargain down the time to a more realistic goal.

"Non. A full year is the term," he said, then his voice softened. "I have nothing to gain here, Annie. I am offering you an honorable solution."

Bethany hesitated a moment before nodding. "Know you well, Norman, I only do this to see my family safe."

"And after they are and a year has passed?" he asked.

"We did not bargain for beyond that time. To purchase my family's freedom to Scotland, I have given my word to render you your due only until then."

"Very well, I will accept that," he said. Apparently amused at her smile, he added, "Do not worry, little Saxon. I consider this a challenge and will find a way to make you toe the mark even after our bargain is fulfilled."

"You think it will be that easy?"

"Non, but I do not doubt myself or my capabilities."

"Nor do I doubt mine," she said, feeling euphoric and for the first time at ease.

He chuckled. "If the situation were reversed, you would act the same as I."

"Aye, I would. But it is not. I must do what is best for those I love."

"Would you give me your hand on this?"

Bethany extended her hand. She could not believe he would accept her word as if she were a man. That only heightened him in her estimation and she did not want to see him in a favorable light.

" 'Tis done," he said. "Now, to the matter of this morning. I will, this time, let the disrespect go. Since we have settled our differences, I suggest we have a truce for the rest of the day."

"Truce." She echoed his word as she considered it. "You mean, we will not talk about Normans or Saxons?"

"*Oui*, that is exactly what I mean."

She shook her head at the enormity of the request. Still, if they could ignore the world around them for a little while, it would be wonderful and so peaceful. " 'Tis a dream to be hoped for."

"All you have to do is agree."

"Aye. Why not?" she said, smiling in spite of herself as the stable master brought their horses.

He helped her up onto Morlock, then he mounted his white warhorse. "Follow me." He kicked his horse and took off at breakneck speed.

Bethany was not troubled; Morlock could easily catch him. She gave the horse a gentle nudge with her knees and he reacted instantly, racing over the fields in hot pursuit of the Norman.

But Royce's white stallion, a magnificent beast, kept the lead, proving her assumption wrong. She had to admire the Norman horse and its rider.

After a while, Royce pulled back on the reins of his spirited animal, allowing her to catch up so that they rode abreast.

"It is very different here from my home, but I find it remarkably beautiful."

She chanced a glimpse at Royce. He sounded like a visitor paying a compliment instead of the conquering lord of the manor. She looked around, trying to see her land through his eyes; but staring back at her stood the familiar scene of autumn fields, bare from harvesting, the black soil rich and moist, filling the air with earthy scents. Each crop plot of exposed earth fell away in the distance and slipped beneath the rolling hills covered in the light-brown grass of November.

The day was unseasonably warm, providing a very pleasant and comfortable ride. They rode over the empty fields and through the forest until they came to a small pond.

"How did you know it was here?" Bethany asked, wondering if the warlord had explored every inch of her land and knew all its secrets.

"Why, Annie, you have been leading the way since the race, not I."

She had, and the realization stunned her. This Norman—no, this man, she amended, keeping with the truce—constantly surprised her.

"I think this would be a good place for a rest," he said, looking around at the glen. "I wonder how many times you stole away to this private haven?" he asked. Dismounting, he helped her from Morlock.

"Many times," she said, a smile slipping easily into place at the pleasurable memories of her favorite spot.

He took in his surroundings with more interest. The dark pool was ringed by sparse trees which, in summer, would be full but now were bare and ready for winter's sleep. "It is so peaceful. Did coming here help?"

"Usually. Here, in this quiet sanctuary, I seemed to find the answers that at home evaded me." She lifted her arms up and turned full circle. "This is my own special place."

"And now you have no place to hide and nowhere to go," he said.

His uncanny insight touched a tender chord within her. Bethany looked at him, wondering if there were any secrets left in her soul.

"Why do you not simply accept your lot in life? You would have less misery."

"In case it has escaped you, I am not a horse and will never be broken."

"You have given me your word. Would you go back on it?"

"Nay," she said, shaking her head in denial. "But if there were another way, I would take it."

"Then, you see, there is little to be gained from fighting me," he said, taking hold of her hand.

"Nay," she responded, pulling free of his grip to face him. "For the moment there is more to be gained by not fighting you. There is a difference," she said with impertinence.

"*Oui,* you are right," he conceded, but this time he reached out and grasped her shoulders.

"What?" she taunted, looking pointedly at where his hands held her, then back to his face, "Will we now agree?"

"We have done so already," he said, sliding his hands up and down her arms in a gentle caress. "I believe the politicians call it peace—or, at least, the beginnings of a negotiation."

Unable to think with the delicious sensations he created, she blurted out, "I wish you would keep to your word. We were not to be Saxon and Norman today, but merely a man and a woman."

A smile that revealed too many of his perfect teeth warned her.

"Again, Annie, you are right," he said, his hands moving up from her arms to cradle her face.

"Royce," she cautioned, knowing that she could not resist his allure.

"I will never forget the differences between the sexes," he said, his voice slightly husky. "That is something we can both appreciate." His eyes reflected a hidden fire as his gaze met hers.

"How do you do it?"

"Do what?" he asked with an innocent expression that was both endearing and intriguing.

"Make me feel uncomfortable," she said, turning away from his midnight gaze.

"Annie, *ma cherie,* I only wish you to feel safe. Do you not feel desire when you are within my arms?" he asked. Taking her into his embrace, he slowly turned her back to face him. His hands moved up and down her back, gently massaging.

His earthy male scent aroused her senses, and passion ignited from even the slightest contact. She longed to be with this man and literally ached for him. But she could not, would not, admit it and tried to pull away.

"You agreed to the truce, Annie. I am merely proceeding with peace talks. One must make certain concessions when negotiating with the opposite side. I have agreed to let your sister and brother join your uncle in Scotland without payment for their release," he said.

"Aye, but—"

He pressed his finger to her lips. "What did you promise me in return for your family's freedom?"

Bethany hid her smile and replied, "Not to fight you."

"Then it is simple. Do not resist me."

His lips covered hers in a scorching kiss. She needed air and yet she could not pull away to draw a breath. Slowly, he traced a path from her mouth to her ear with soft, hot kisses that were butterfly light. "You want me," he whispered. "Why fight it, little Saxon?"

She would not give him the words he asked for. Even if it were true, she would not say it out loud. Instead, her lips sought his in utter surrender.

Slowly, with infinite care, he drew her tunic up, depositing kisses each inch of the way. Her skin tingled as he lowered her to the ground onto his open mantle. With deft movements, he slipped from his clothes and joined her on the soft robe.

A tingling went through her as he slid his hands lower on her body. Every inch of skin he touched flared to life, warming and awakening to his gentle administrations. Exhilaration washed over every nerve as a tidal wave of emotion flowed through her veins.

Heat surrounded and engulfed her as he moved lower, his lips trailing across her skin and lingering at her breast. When his teeth grazed her nipple, a shock streaked through her. His tongue circled the peak, drawing a moan of ecstasy from her throat. Clearly driven by her response, his mouth closed over her breast and he gently applied a tugging pressure that had her arching her back and reaching for him. Her nails raked his skin and she clasped his shoulders when he moved to her other breast.

She tried to pull him to her, but he held her down, his hands continuing to roam over her body with seductive caresses. His tongue lavished attention on her navel as his hand settled between her legs, not moving, just resting. The sensual pleasure intensified to a near-painful pitch.

"Royce, please," she begged, not knowing if she wanted him to hurry or slow down.

"What do you want, Annie?"

I want you to love me with your mind, heart, soul, and body, she replied silently. *Love,* the word echoed in her mind. Had it happened? Had she fallen in love with her enemy?

That was not the plan. He was to fall in love with her.

God's teeth. She had fallen into her own trap and was lost in his caress.

"Royce, do you care for me?" she asked with hope and fear, knowing that either way she had condemned herself to a purgatory worse than damnation.

Rising up, he gazed at her, his eyes dark and intense. "I shall care for you all the days of our lives. But will I choose you above others? *Non, cheri,* I cannot."

His lips touched hers and he whispered against her mouth, "I will stop if you want me to. Tell me what you want, Annie."

She closed her eyes and knew she was lost. A trade had been

bartered today and Bethany would never be the same for it. But pride and station mattered not. Royce had become the single-most important need she had.

Mayhap on the morrow she would feel differently, but she doubted it.

Two tears slipped down her cheeks. "God help me, I want you."

Her words released his control.

His callused hands scraped over her sensitive skin with a primitive urgency that made her shiver with anticipation. Lightning bolts of white-hot desire streaked through her with every stroke of his rough-textured caress.

Reacting to his passionate skill, she moved sensuously against him. Rubbing her thigh against his, then seductively trapping his leg between hers, she squeezed firmly and felt the agony of her own need. Frantically taking little nips at the corner of his mouth, she snuggled closer to him, molding her breasts against the abrasive hairs of his chest and sinuously sliding her curves to fit against his hard muscles. Not an inch of space remained between their bodies as she ran her hands over the bunched muscles of his shoulders, letting her nails rake the skin of his back and buttocks. She ached with a burning need and reached between them, guiding his manhood to her. Royce grabbed her hips and lunged forward, joining them with savage force. He kissed her with a ruthless need and she responded to his reckless demands. The ripples of desire quaked through her as he started to move within her. His rhythm was fast and hard and she matched his fury, meeting his every thrust with a desperation borne of her unbridled passion. Their frenzied lovemaking unleashed a startling climax that sent tremors of ecstasy through her. She clung to Royce, feeling wave after wave of pleasure wash over her. Seconds later, his muscles tensed beneath her grip as he found his release.

"Annie," he gasped as he collapsed. His breathing labored, he hugged her in a tight embrace that barely left room to breathe.

* * *

Bethany drew her smock over her head. Her efforts were hampered by a playful Royce who fought her attempts to dress. " 'Tis too nice a day to return to our duties," he said, nuzzling her neck with kisses as his fingers stroked long, full sweeps across her back.

"You should be ashamed. 'Tis midday," she said, then blushed and changed the subject. "You would lie about all day when there is work to be done?"

"Oui, with a winsome woman such as you by my side."

She shook her head, still stunned that they had made love in the full light of day.

As if he could read her thoughts, he smiled. " 'Tis a misconception I took delight in correcting."

"What a jest I must have been to you. An ignorant Saxon needing to be instructed by the wise Norman." Tears were actually welling in her eyes and she brushed them away. To play the fool for this man above all others was more than she could bear.

"Bethany, do not rob the joy from the day. I will admit that I found your inexperience refreshing." He raised her chin to meet his gaze. "There are those who would trade a fortune to lay claim to such innocence. It was nothing of which to be ashamed."

"My experience is."

Her statement seemed to take him by surprise.

"I cannot change what has happened. Nor do I think I would if I could. What other Norman when he laid eyes on you would not have taken what, by right, was his due?"

"Should I feel grateful that I have been so graced with your favor?"

"Do you mean to tell me you did not enjoy it?"

"I will not lie. But I do wish I did not feel this need when you are about. You are more pleasure, and pain, than I have ever known."

She pulled away and reached for her kirtle. Uncle Bram's letter dropped to the ground.

Royce picked it up.

"What does this say?"

"Can you not read our churlish language?" she asked, knowing Mary had written his instructions. "Forsooth, what a shame."

"I did not say that I could not read. I asked what it said. You will read it to me and remember I have your word, if that means anything, that you will obey me in all things."

She looked over the letter. It was entirely possible that he could read their language; then again, he could be ignorant of the letter's contents. If not for her word, she could tell him anything.

"My Uncle Bram is going to petition William the Conqueror for our release."

He stared at her for a moment as if she had taken leave of her wits and left all sane thoughts behind. Then he looked at the letter.

"It is too wild a story to conjure up. But I will have Guy look into it."

"You do not believe me?" she asked with hands on her hips. "I have given my word."

"And I will see if it can be trusted."

"You are indeed a man of mistrust."

"I will trust you, little Saxon, when you have earned my regard and not before. I can hardly credit your Scottish uncle travelling across England to ask a Norman king to grant freedom to a Saxon slave."

"Then you are not well versed in my family history, but you will be soon."

From his dark expression she could tell that he liked neither her tone nor her words. "What mean you?"

"Norman, hear me well: I am neither mighty nor powerful, but I will be free. I am a woman to be reckoned with, and even your king will acknowledge this."

"You have surely hit your head."

She ignored his sarcasm. "Nay, I *will* be free."

He held the note up. "You put false hopes in a kinsman who brought half a man to save you."

"You should not bray so loud, my lord. That catamite nearly defeated you."

Chapter Twelve

Hungry flames licked the walls and greedily devoured the dried straw and brittle reeds in the Saxon's thatched roof. In the black night, the crofter's cottage burned bright yellow, illuminating the surrounding area in a queer glow.

The Widow Chadwick stood with her child and stared in a bewildered daze as everything they owned was reduced to flames. With the help of Royce's men, the villagers worked to put out the fire, but the hut was a loss.

Bethany wiped her brow, leaving her sleeve soiled with soot and perspiration. With the cattle missing, there could be little doubt that the fire had not been an accident. "Why would someone do such a thing?" she asked, then shook her head in weary resignation. Desperate men without a country and king would steal to survive.

As the lean months stretched ahead, the attacks would only increase as wanderers headed north. The North Umberland land stretched across the top of a natural corridor to Scotland. What bitter irony! Their Norman enemies were now their only protection against their own displaced Saxon army.

Royce shook his head in obvious disgust at the lost home,

then turned and mounted his horse. At his signal, an attachment of men fell in behind him and Guy. He guided his horse over to Bethany. "See that you offer comfort to my serfs."

Bethany bristled at the command and crossed her arms over her chest. Did he think she would not take care of those in need?

He chuckled. "Have you forgotten your vow in only a month?"

"Nay, my lord."

"Annie," Royce said in earnest, "it may take weeks to catch the outlaws. In my absence, Vachel will be in charge. If my luck turns bad and fate lays me low, I have left orders concerning your family."

The thought of his peril snapped her head up. She did not want to think he would not return, but an inner voice warned her of the possibility. Had her father not marched out confidently, only to be defeated? His position and status had not saved him. War knew no titles, taking men indiscriminately and leaving their loved ones to mourn their loss and survive alone. Bethany had learned that bitter lesson.

"Cherie," he whispered, using the endearing term that once had irritated her. "Would you not send me off with more than an angry glare?"

Unable and unwilling to deny his request, Bethany looked away to hide her weakness.

He leaned down from his horse and swept her off her feet. With care, he pulled her onto his lap. Before she could react, she felt his lips on hers and could not resist responding. His kiss was warm and wonderful, making the coming separation all the more heartbreaking.

"The best decision I ever made was to extract your vow not to fight me." Royce said, his forehead touching hers. Then with evident regret, he pulled away and gently placed her on the ground. "Remember, you are my slave and, as such, you owe your allegiance to me." He chuckled and easily evaded her slap. "Remember," he repeated.

His eyes darkened into a serious expression, his gaze holding hers until he seemed satisfied that his meaning had been understood. With an authoritative command, the warlord wheeled his horse around and rode out after the uprooted Saxons who had resorted to thievery to survive.

Bethany watched until he was out of sight, then helped the tired family gather what they could and led the way to the castle. She would find a spot for them.

With Royce's departure, Bethany felt empty and hollow inside. She offered a silent prayer for his success and safe return—whether he was Saxon or Norman did not matter; he needed divine help. After all, it would be a long winter if this raiding did not stop.

Inside the castle, the warmth roared from the hearth, a welcome respite after the biting cold.

Norman soldiers staggered in and warmed themselves with a cup of ale while they sat by the fire. Yawning, Damiana was making her way down the steps, apparently having just awakened.

"What is all the excitement?" she asked from mid-stairway. "Has someone of importance come to visit?"

"*Non*, my lady, 'twas only a fire," a soldier responded.

"Oh, such distress this inconvenience has caused me," Damiana whined as she straightened the folds of her dark-blue overtunic. "I had no one here to wait on me."

Bethany shook her head at Damiana's self-absorption. Without a thought for those who had fought the fire or those who suffered from the loss, the Norman woman stood on the stairway overlooking the hall, primping and preening as though she were the queen making an entrance.

Maida entered the great hall carrying two trenchers of meat. When she handed the food to the widow and her son, Bethany touched the cook's arm. "Take them to the armory and see if a place can be found."

"Hold! How dare you bring that filthy baggage in here?" Damiana pointed to the widow and her son. "On whose authority do you presume to act?" she demanded with a thin-lipped sneer as she descended the long stairway to the great room.

"On Royce's," Bethany responded.

"I do not believe you. There is barely enough food in the larder to see the soldiers through the winter. Throw that scum out. I will not see good food wasted on the likes of them." Damiana paced the great room while she surveyed the trestle tables and the wares upon them as if she owned every grain and seed.

When no soldier moved to do her bidding, Damiana's face turned bright red. She pointed to the biggest Norman at the table. "You. Did you not hear me? I said, *Throw that scum out.*"

"My lady, 'tis not my wish to disobey you. But I heard my lord command his slave to oversee the welfare of this family. My loyalty is to my soverign lord."

Relieved that Royce's soldiers only took orders from him, Bethany turned her attention to Damiana. "Through these good people's efforts, the fruit of the field has been brought forth. You have no right to begrudge them the bounty of their labor."

Damiana's face, usually so smooth, contained pinched lines as her gaze bore into Bethany. "When I am mistress of this castle, I shall see you whipped for your insolence."

Though it was no idle threat, Bethany refused to show her fear. There would be a time when Damiana held power over her, but that did not bear thinking about. "If and when you are mistress here, you still will not be given free reign."

"Do you think your charms are such that they bend Royce to your will? He will grow tired of you," Damiana said.

The barb found its mark, but none knew it as Bethany raised her gaze and met Damiana's contempt with dignity. "Whether or not Royce grows tired of me, one thing is certain: *Your* place will be as it is now," Bethany said, letting her disdain sound in her voice.

"How dare you?" Damiana snatched up a brass candle-holder from a table and heaved it at Bethany.

Bethany easily sidestepped the poor throw. " 'Tis a pity your aim is not as sharp as your tongue. Then perhaps you would be feared—for you are not respected."

Entering the hall, Vachel chuckled at the scene. "Ladies," he intoned dryly, "this is not behavior I, or anyone, would expect from the gentler sex."

"Shut up, you lackey! I do not answer to underlings," Damiana screeched. Her hate-filled gaze aimed at Vachel like an almost tangible weapon.

Bethany waved her hand as if she were shooing away a fly. "Be gone, Damiana, unless you wish to actually work and help us settle this family in."

"By His wounds!" Damiana's strong curse drew every gaze. "You will rue the day you challenged me." In the sudden silence, she flounced to the stairs and, in a dramatic state of indignation, ascended the steps.

With her departure, the mood did not linger, but cleared, like a dark storm that had blown over. Bethany turned to Sumar Chadwick and her son. "Do not worry. You are welcome in Renwyg Castle," she said—and noticed that Vachel seemed to be taking an uncommon interest in the young widow. The seasoned soldier, sprouting silver in his dark mane and beard, was no callow youth to have his head turned by a pretty face barely half his age. Yet so enraptured was he that Bethany surmised it would take a fire-breathing dragon to gain Vachel's attention.

"Let me see what can be done, Lady Bethany," Vachel said suddenly, surprising her with the respectful title of address. He held out his hand for Sumar to precede him. It was obvious he would deal with this matter personally.

Sumar hesitated, her anxious gaze darting from the Norman soldier to Bethany. "Is it all right, my lady?

Bethany knew the weight of her word. She noticed the anticipation in Vachel's eyes. "Aye. Vachel is a good man."

Relief spread across Sumar's face and Vachel smiled.

Once alone, Bethany wondered how much longer it would

be before Royce took his betrothed's behavior in hand. Bethany had given her word not to defy Royce and she would die before she broke it.

But Damiana was not part of the bargain.

William studied the ring. "How did you come by this?" he asked.

"My brother received it in payment for helping a young lad when he needed assistance. Had my brother not drawn his sword, Normandy would be without a duke," Bram stated, neither afraid nor intimidated by the man before him.

"*Oui*, Gowain Mactavish did me and my followers a service that day and I do not dispute that my life is owed to this man."

"Then repay your debt. His family is in need of your help. Do not turn your back on them." When William nodded his head, the Scotsman relayed the plight of his kin.

William shook his head sadly. "A slave, you say?"

"Aye, a brave and bonnie lass she be to meet your man on the field of honor."

"Then you would have me rescue Gowain's children?"

"Aye, you owe their father that much."

"The debt is to the father, not his children." William said as he paced the floor. "I will think on the matter. Return home, Bram Mactavish; and when I decide what is owed this family, a messenger will be forthcoming."

When the Scotsman had left the room, William motioned for his trusted advisor. "Ancil, send a man to North Umberland. I will have the truth of this matter before I make a decision."

Ancil bowed his head. "I would trust the job to Verdon, but Royce knows him."

" 'Twill make no difference if they are acquainted. You would be hard-pressed to find someone Royce does not know. Send Verdon; he is the best man for the job. If the truth supports this Scotsman's story, I fear Royce will never forgive me for what I must do."

* * *

The hoary breath of winter swirled around Renwyg Castle, turning the warmest room into a chilly den. In the week since the fire, the weather had worsened.

In the great room, servants prepared for the midday meal. By the huge fireplace with its full log blazing, Lady Mary sat with her Bible and sewing while Lady Damiana sipped the last drop from a chalice of warmed wine. Finally, after seven cups, a warm glow had begun to dull her senses. The empty container dropped from her hand and rolled across the table, then over the edge.

A loud clatter sounded when the metal chalice hit the stone floor. Then it noisily swayed back and forth in a small arc without anyone rescuing the fallen cup. Damiana knew the servants despised her. Bethany, that slut, had turned the serfs against her ever since that incident with the widow. Damiana's hatred grew as she thought of the thousand-and-one humiliations she had suffered. She ticked them off mentally: her tea being served lukewarm, her fire never blazing hot enough to last the night, her . . . Surely there were more, but when nothing else came to mind, she ground her teeth. Oh! the inconveniences were too numerous to name anyway. It was intolerable.

Suddenly, Sumar Chadwick came into view. The little vixen had the audacity to pick up the fallen wine cup, flaunting the fact that no one else would. The Saxon peasant dared to smile, but she did not fool Damiana with her happy appearance. The filthy slut blinded Royce's man with her duplicity, but Damiana knew a fake when she saw one.

She picked up a red woolen mantle and wrapped it around her shoulders as she walked around the widow. "See you that my room is well heated or, by heaven, you will wish you had never inhabited this miserable isle."

Sumar bowed low and had turned to leave the great room when Damiana grabbed her hair and yanked it with a vicious pull. "Remember who is the mistress of this castle," she said, venting her frustration on the servant.

Tears appeared in Sumar's eyes as she stared beseechingly at Mary, but Mary remained seated.

When no help was forthcoming, Sumar took a deep breath. "Aye, I know my mistress, the one who has my loyalty. Her name is Bethany of North Umberland," she exclaimed with pride.

At such outright insolence, Damiana shrieked, "Saxon slut, you need a lesson in manners." She had lifted her hand to strike when Bethany entered the great room followed by Bret and Vachel.

"Hold, Damiana," Bethany commanded.

A nasty smile curled the Norman lady's mouth. "I am in charge here."

Vachel's voice rang out in anger, *"Non,* I am in charge with the lord away. Enough, Lady Damiana. Cease, I say."

But Damiana ignored his command and drew her hand back to deliver a blow.

Bethany leapt across the space and shoved Damiana hard, freeing the frightened servant.

Released, Sumar fled to Vachel's side.

Enraged that a slave would dare interfere, Damiana delivered the blow meant for the servant to Bethany. 'Twas not a slap but a vicious gouging, with fingers curled so her nails raked deep into Bethany's flesh.

When Bethany staggered back, Damiana lunged for her with a cry of triumph. Catching Bethany off balance, Damiana wrestled her opponent across the floor in a fierce struggle.

The sound of scuffling and high-pitched screams drew a crowd of eager onlookers. Soldiers and serfs stood side by side with anticipation in their eyes and cheers on their lips for their favorite. The two women, locked together in anger, fell to the floor, brawling and fighting like men as Royce entered the hall.

He and Guy gaped at the spectacle.

"Five gold coins on Bethany," Guy said, clearly delighted by the bout.

Royce shook his head at his brother's jest. "I thought the Holy Mother Church considered gaming a sin."

"You know well I am no longer in training for sainthood."

"You will have to find your pleasure somewhere else, brother. This fight must end before one of them is injured. Lend a hand, Guy."

"Royce, just a minute. Let the women have at it," Guy cajoled as he stared mesmerized at the two combatants, watching the hair-pulling and the clothes-tugging. Suddenly, the sound of rending cloth filled the air and Guy pointed at the tantalizing glimpse of Bethany's breast showing through her ripped tunic. "This, dear brother, is not only entertaining, but educational," Guy said with a devilish grin.

Before Royce could move, a hand was lightly laid on his arm in a gesture of caution. "My lord," Vachel said. "A lesson is sorely needed here. Lady Bethany could teach it far better than you or I."

Royce looked sharply at his man, surprised by his defense of Bethany against a Norman mistress.

"You would also like to wager five gold coins on the Saxon maid?" Royce asked, tongue in cheek.

"*Non,* my lord," Vachel replied as expected, then looked his leader in the eyes. "I wish to wager *ten* gold coins."

The amount was no small bet for a man-at-arms.

"You two are witless dolts," Royce said in mock disgust and turned to Bret. "Come, young soldier, let us break up this unseemly display."

Royce stepped forward and Guy followed, placing little Bret behind him and out of danger.

To much shouting, Royce grabbed Damiana and wrestled her free of Bethany. Denied her prey, Damiana howled like a wounded animal in Royce's arms, then bit his hand.

Guy held Bethany easily in his massive arms, but she twisted and struggled to his obvious delight. He turned to his brother.

"What say you, Royce? Would you sell me this slave? I have heard of the pleasure of your baths and wish such ease for myself."

Damiana shrieked. "I forbid her to bathe you. Do you hear me, Royce? I forbid it!"

Royce smelled the wine on her breath. No wonder she was overwrought, but he could not in good conscience allow the future mistress of the castle to further humiliate herself. "Damiana, control yourself," he said, trying to calm her down.

"You do me dishonor," she said, her expression raw and ugly. "Sell this witch. This Saxon she-cat has bedeviled you."

Royce paused at her wine-soaked words. It was true. He cared uncommonly for the wench, but he was not bedeviled, nor would he be goaded into giving her up. "Annie will attend my bath as long as I wish. These are not matters that concern the lady of this house."

"Make peace with your betrothed Royce," Guy taunted, his eyes twinkling with amusement. "Sell Bethany to me."

"You forget yourself, brother. I will share many things with my kin, but not my slave. Annie is mine and mine alone. Do you understand me?"

"Verily, I do," Guy said with a smug smile of satisfaction curving his lips, clearly pleased by Royce's response.

Royce released Damiana, and she fairly spit her words at him. "Though I must suffer your weight in bed after we are wed, I will not welcome it. I care not how many mistresses you have as long as you do not flaunt them before me."

Royce remained unmoved by her tirade, and she ran from the room, leaving a relieved ensemble behind.

Much to Royce's irritation, Guy still held onto Bethany. "The danger has past. Let the slave go."

"Must I?"

At Royce's warning look, Guy released Bethany.

Vachel stepped forward and offered Bethany a linen cloth. "Your face, my lady. That cat has clawed you."

Royce spun her around and, gently pushing her hair back, examined the cuts.

"I am sorry, Annie."

"Do not apologize. I am but a slave and must be at the mercy of my betters," she said, clearly satisfied by the anger it produced in Royce.

She tried to pull free, but he held her tight. "What happened here?"

When she remained silent, Vachel spoke. "My Lady Bethany defended the young Widow, Chadwick from the cruel hand of Lady Damiana."

"Is that true?" Royce asked.

"What does it matter to you?" she asked, a line creasing her brow as she met his gaze.

"Maida," Royce bellowed.

When the cook scurried out of the kitchen, Royce pointed to Bethany's face. "See you to this wound," Royce commanded as he ushered Bethany toward the servant. "Make sure Annie listens to your advice."

Maida's eyes rounded in surprise. "Aye, my lord. I will see to the lady." With an arm clasped firmly around Bethany's middle, the cook dragged her complaining mistress away.

In the silence, a wood chair scrapped the floor and Mary rose from her seat to leave the great hall.

"Hold, Lady Mary. how could you sit by and let your sister be abused?" Royce asked harshly, stopping her retreat.

Mary's face paled. "My lord, I could do nothing."

"My sister is making the adjustment you wanted me to." Bethany's voice rang out from the far end of the hall. "You have no right to judge her."

Though he glowered at Bethany's back, Royce dismissed Mary with a wave of his hand. When the women were out of hearing, he turned to Guy. " 'Tis strange for Annie's flesh and blood to behave in that manner. If ill-will existed between them, then I could understand it, but they are, for all to see, two loving sisters."

194   *Marian Edwards*

"If you acted that way, I would disown you," Guy said.

"I would expect you to," Royce said, stroking his chin in quiet contemplation. "I wonder . . ." Royce mused, then seeing his brother's curiosity explained. "It is possible Bethany's fine hand has created this ruse."

"Bethany?" Guy questioned doubtfully.

"I think every intrigue, whether minor or major, that occurs in this demesne has Bethany's approval."

A soldier entered the hall, his heavy footsteps echoing in the great room as he approached. "My lord, there is a Saxon soldier at the gate. He wishes an audience," the gatekeeper's underguard said.

"Send him in," Royce said, exchanging a meaningful glance with his brother. This land would never bore him.

A tall, gray-haired solider marched in. His manner did not indicate subservience in any way. Holding his head erect and shoulders straight, he approached the lord of the manor as an equal.

"My lord, my name is Cedric. I have come home to the land of my birth. I will vow allegiance to you if it will not interfere with my prior oath."

"What, pray tell, is that?" Royce asked, hiding his curiosity behind a bland expression. A Saxon to put conditions on his vow of loyalty!

"Not to Harold," Cedric answered, clearly guessing the lord's puzzlement. "I have sworn to protect the woman of North Umberland. I owe Lady Bethany my life and have returned to offer my service to her and you—if a conflict does not exist."

"I do not think one vow will interfere with the other. Your mistress is in no danger. But Bethany of North Umberland lives as a slave under my protection and I will brook no interference with her status. Do you understand?"

"Aye, my lord. 'Tis good to be home and fulfill my oath."

"Then kneel, Cedric, and swear your fealty to William and his men."

With some difficulty, the older man bent one knee, then

bowed his head. His voice was strong and clear as he spoke the words sealing his allegiance to the Normans.

"What position did you hold in this castle?" Royce asked as Cedric raised his head.

"Captain of the castle guard and, before that, armory," Cedric said with pride.

The Saxon soldier was long past his prime, but Royce did not have the heart to turn him away—besides he could prove invaluable. Cedric probably knew every glen and dale in the area.

"Rise and take your place among my men."

A flash of surprise glimmered in Cedric's eyes, and a watery sheen of gratitude followed as he quickly paid homage to the new lord then went to a side table. The Normans made room for him. Though Saxon, Cedric was a soldier, and there existed a deep camaraderie among men who had made their livelihood protecting others.

"A slave with a protector? 'Tis a first," Guy said.

"Verily," Royce said speculatively, almost as if he spoke to himself. "Methinks there is nothing common about my little Saxon slave."

"*Oui,* she is different. Even her coloring is uncommonly strange," Guy said.

Royce raised an eyebrow at his brother's observation. " 'Tis odd that you notice so much about my slave."

Guy smirked and raised his chalice in a toast. "I am not blind. Bethany of North Umberland is a beautiful woman in a queer sort of way. Her looks seem to grow on you," He said, then took a slow sip of his ale, clearly mulling over his words.

"I think you need to find yourself a woman posthaste." Though a jest, Royce's earnest tone made the statement a warning.

"Would it bother you, brother, if I had an interest in the Saxon maiden?"

"Not at all, *brother,* for your interest would remain only that. I will not tolerate *anyone* taking what is mine."

Chapter Thirteen

"Lady Bethany. If you would be so kind," Vachel said, holding his hand out for her to follow him.

"What is it, Vachel?" she inquired, walking before the Norman soldier. The solemn and steady man had won her affection for being so helpful and kind to Sumar Chadwick.

"I wouldst see you prepared when you have to fend off that cow." He looked at her cheek, and she knew the marks were unsightly.

"I can take care of myself," she said defensively, unwilling to admit that Damiana had indeed bested her.

"Verily, I never doubted that, but I would feel better and am so ordered to see that you can do so in the Norman fashion."

"Royce wants me to know combat?" she asked, stunned that the warlord would issue such a command.

"*Non,* it is Guy. Begging your pardon, my lady. He said that he could win many a voucher if you only had a good left hook."

Bethany chuckled, that sounded exactly like Guy. "Now I must know the manly arts?"

"*Oui,* mademoiselle. I am afraid so."

"Before the Normans came to my land, a lady never needed

to know such barbaric things! Saxon men displayed gallantry and chivalry. All a lady ever required for safety was a protector."

"You may find, my lady, that it is better to know how to protect yourself than to rely on others."

She mulled his words over. He made a good argument. Knowledge of this type would allow her more freedom.

"Very well, Vachel. Shall we make Guy a lot of coin? I intend to be your best student."

"Verily, my lady. If not my best, you surely are my prettiest."

She smiled at Vachel. When she'd first met him, she had thought him the fiercest old man in all of Christendom. Now he seemed infinitely less terrifying.

"Now, my lady, this will be very hard. I have never instructed a female soldier, and never one so puny."

Bethany's head snapped up. She knew she lacked the beauty her sister held, but puny? 'Twas a bitter blow.

Reading her shock, Vachel shifted from foot to foot. "Sorry, my lady, but you are little more than a mite."

Vachel's apology took the sting out of his words, and Bethany smiled as she said, "I am petite. Remember that word, 'tis one of yours and much more flattering."

Vachel chuckled. "Whether 'tis petite or puny, you are still the same size—too damn small to do any damage."

She looked down at her toes and slowly back up. He was right—she was too small. "I suppose it is useless."

Clearly moved by her dejected voice, Vachel spoke quickly, rushing to make amends. "It is not for want of effort and determination, for I have seen you fight. You do not give up. But your size will act against you every time. You need something to give you an advantage."

"Perhaps a weapon?" she asked eagerly. "A sword or dagger would lend strength."

Vachel roared with laughter at her suggestion. *"Non,* putting a sword in your hands would be courting disaster." Then his features sobered. "You have neither the muscle nor the strength to swing the blade. Do you not remember how you felt when you so rashly challenged our overlord?"

"I had no choice, Vachel. My people's welfare was at stake."

"I know, Lady Bethany, but 'twas a foolhardy action," he said, his voice softening with his sincerity. " 'Tis lucky the lord discovered the deceit before he decided to end the fight."

She shuddered, remembering how powerfully Royce had swung his sword and knew 'twould have been her last breath had he not discovered her masquerade.

"What say you, Vachel? What could I use as an advantage?"

Vachel rubbed his face and walked around her, studying her as carefully as a monk studied an ancient scroll. " 'Twill have to be your size. 'Tis a disadvantage if you are in close quarters, but it can also be a boon if you use your speed and agility. Pay attention and I will demonstrate. I do not tolerate lazy daydreamers in my ranks."

He talked to her as if training a raw recruit, moving close to her and quickly withdrawing. "Now, come at me and see if you can land a blow," he ordered.

When she charged him, he neatly sidestepped her.

"Lady Bethany, you must watch me for a sign. I will drop a shoulder or shift my weight before I move."

"This is hard, Vachel."

"Oui, but if you are to do it right, you must practice. Now, we will repeat this exercise until you can anticipate my move."

By the end of the day, she understood why Vachel held every man's respect. "Until I am satisfied, we will meet four times a week." Vachel handed her a linen cloth to wipe her damp face as Guy entered the training room. Upon seeing Royce's brother, Vachel winked at Bethany. "When next you have an altercation, Lady Bethany, I will wager you will come away without a scratch."

Guy chuckled as he approached. "With Vachel as your instructor, I am assured of making a great fortune." He lifted her hand and deposited a light kiss on her fingers, then led her to a small table. "Sit and rest, my lady, while I learn of your progress."

While Vachel explained her prowess to Guy, she let her thoughts wander and smothered a yawn. Overtired and drained from the exertion, she let their voices recede from her awareness.

"Are you ready, my lady?" Guy asked.

She opened her eyes to find that Vachel had left while she had dozed. She did not respond, but jumped down from the table. Suddenly, a wave of dizziness assailed her and she would have fallen if Guy had not steadied her."

"Are you all right?"

" 'Twas only the excitement today. The shakiness is over," she said.

At his look of doubt, she linked her arm through his and flashed him a bright smile "I am fine." But even though she reassured Guy, a niggling of doubt remained, which she quickly pushed to the recesses of her mind. There was no reason for anyone to know that this spell had not been her first.

As Guy walked Bethany back to the chamber she shared with Royce, she had difficulty keeping up with his pace. She hurt in places she had not known existed until today.

"I vow tonight you will need the healing benefits of a bath more than Royce," he said, then—clearly taking pity on her tired expression—added. "The soreness you feel will lessen in time."

" 'Tis little comfort to me now."

"*Oui,* the pain diminishes the merit, but 'twill serve you well someday."

They ascended the staircase and with every step Bethany was winded. But her silence was not due to fatigue but Guy's reminder of the baths. Until this moment, she had been able to put Damiana's nasty tirade from her mind. Never could she admit how much it had bothered her.

Royce opened the door and threw a sharp look at his brother and slave. "What is amiss?"

Bethany held her breath.

"Rest your sword, brother—nothing that needs your attention. I was merely seeing this lovely lady to her door."

" 'Tis good she arrived, my patience is at an end," Royce said.

Guy raised an eyebrow as Royce rubbed a hand along the muscles of his neck. "What has put you in a foul humor, brother?"

"My bath is long overdue."

Bethany closed her eyes at the thought of carrying all the buckets up the stairs. Even worse than the labor was the knowledge that she would not be allowed to bathe after her chore was completed. She buried the thought deep within her mind and concentrated on the problem at hand.

Disheartened, she opened her eyes and encountered Guy's understanding gaze. Abruptly, she turned to begin the task. She dared not beg Royce's pardon. He would never understand what she was doing tonight, nor would he approve. Royce would look poorly on Vachel and Guy for teaching her how to defend herself.

"Where were you, Annie?"

" 'Twere only the duties of the day that delayed me. I will have your bath ready soon," she replied.

She tried hard not to give a hint of her languor, but she failed.

"You do not look well. What ails you?"

"Nothing, my lord, 'tis only fatigue."

He held her arm when she would leave. "Then, rest tonight." Royce turned to his brother. "See to it that water is brought to my chamber for a bath."

Bethany's mouth fairly dropped open in surprise.

"Do not act as if it is impossible for me to do a kindness," Royce grumbled.

Guy burst out in laughter. "Verily, brother, she is no more stunned than I."

"Did it ever occur to either of you that though Annie is too exhausted to bathe me, the reverse is not true?"

Guy smiled broadly. "I do not suppose you would let Bethany attend *my* bath?"

"Non, but if you wish, I will send Damiana."

"Heaven forbid. I wish to enjoy my bath, not hate it."

Royce did not rise to the bait. "See to the bath." When Guy left them, Royce escorted Bethany inside the room and closed the door.

"Now, you will tell me what my brother was about."

When she remained quiet, he said. "No one will suffer for your honesty. I give you my word on it."

At her continued silence, he sighed, "Very well, but you know I will find out eventually. Why not save yourself, and Guy, the trouble, and just tell me."

" 'Tis not trouble, and I have kept my bargain," she said.

"Verily, you have, and with remarkable restraint. I am both surprised and impressed."

She looked at him, unable to decide if he jested or were serious. With Royce, it was very hard to tell the difference.

The sun was high in the sky and the midday light poured into Lady Damiana's bedchamber as she took an aperitif from her private stock brought from France. "Mary, this is brandy. I will not drink that filthy swill the Saxons serve," Damiana said.

Mary flinched at the disparaging reference to her people but, said mildly, "Do you think it prudent to drink before riding?"

"Mary, dear, I know you think this is the devil's own brew, but civilized people indulge in libation. I could ride in any state. I am an excellent horsewoman. You will understand that your betters are bred for this." Damiana took another hearty swallow of the brandy and made an elegant sweep of her hand, spilling several drops of the dark liquid on her lovely cream-colored gown. "If only I could return to my home. Traveling with me in France, you would see the difference at court and how ladies are treated. I could, with my connections, make a good match for you ... one that would be a far sight better than you could ever receive here."

"My lady, I do not seek a reward from you. The Almighty will see that my needs are fulfilled."

Damiana rolled her eyes. "God save me from the righteous. Here, fill this again," she ordered as she handed her chalice to Mary. "If you will not join me in a toast, at least let me drink in peace."

Mary accepted the cup and poured the liquor to the brim, then with a demure smile handed the drink back to the Norman lady.

Damiana raised her brandy to her lips and studied Mary over the rim. Overly devout people made her uncomfortable. She had allowed the Saxon maiden to spend time with her only because it served her purpose.

"Do you ride, Mary?"

"Nay. My sister loves riding, but I am not so inclined."

Though it was as she expected from this timid mouse, Damiana said "forsooth" with feigned surprise, then inquired with false brightness, "Did your sister have a favorite mount?"

"Aye, she was partial to a high-spirited horse she raised from a colt. Morlock."

The woman's French grated on Damiana's ear. Stupid Saxon, the name *Morlock* did not even exist. "Well, if it has the temperament of its master, it would not suit me."

Mary look relieved. "A lady needs a gentle horse."

"*Oui*, I am a lady," Damiana said with sugary sweetness, feeling the effect of the spirits. She tipped the chalice up and swallowed the last golden drops. "What other pursuits did your sister and you have before the Normans conquered this pathetic land?"

Mary wrung her hands together. "I was in the convent learning the ways of the church for eight years. My sister learned how to rule and govern this land."

"I am not surprised," Damiana said as she handed the brandy to Mary. "Put this away from prying and pilfering eyes. It is my own piece of Normandy."

Mary rose and placed the brandy in its hiding place behind the tapestry. In the stone wall was a depression that acted as a shelf. Unless someone knew the bottle was there, they would not discover it. Mary dropped the tapestry in place and turned around.

"It is away, my lady."

"Then lend a hand so I may stand. I will ride now."

"Lady Damiana, I do not think you should after imbibing so heavily," Mary said as she offered her hand for assistance.

Once on her feet, Damiana slapped Mary's hand away. "Run and tell your sister that I will ride her favorite mount as soon as I can change and arrange an escort."

Mary's face drained of all color, and Damiana thought it did her justice. Since she acted like a holy saint, she should appear as one—ghostly and pale. As Mary ran from the room, Damiana laughed and tried to unlace her tunic. She would have her revenge on that damn Saxon slut, Bethany. The very thought drove her onward as she ripped her ties, then stripped her clothes from her body.

Wobbling with numb limbs, she managed to dress herself in a tunic designed for riding. Nothing seemed to fit right, and she staggered to the polished metal to check her appearance. Her image wavered in the reflecting surface with dizzying speed. When she finally caught a fair glimpse of herself, she thought the mirror must be vastly distorted to reveal her clothes draping in such uneven folds with tabs and ties misaligned. The Saxon quality was inferior to Norman.

The comforting effects of the brandy lasted long after the time required to redo her hair. Standing straight, Damiana managed to walk the distance to the door without incident. She would have to remember her brandy was superior and, therefore, more potent than these damn Saxon wines.

The courtyard teemed with villagers and soldiers. Saxon and

Norman melded together into a crowd that struck a harmonious chord. As Damiana made her way to the stable, the crowd parted. A sure sign of quality, she thought.

When the stable master had Bethany's stallion saddled, he said, "My lady, this horse is a mite spirited. 'Twill do well to see that you use a firm hand on him, but nay the whip."

"Do not presume to instruct me, oaf. Breeding and quality will always tell. Now see to your duties."

The stable master smiled and slapped the horse's flank when Damiana's seat hit the saddle. She struggled with the horse, unable to maintain control, then she raised her whip and brought it down viciously across the horse's backside. Morlock reared, then bolted from the stable.

The stable master chuckled as he watched the thoroughly inadequate rider. "Ah yes, my lady. Quality and breeding are very telling traits indeed."

Just then Bethany arrived, breathless, accompanied by Vachel. "You must stop her," she said, looking after Damiana. "Morlock's temperament will not tolerate a whip."

" 'Twill do her good, my lady, to see that she cannot beat the spirit from the horse." The stable master dusted his hands on a clean rag. "A lesson to be applied to all else."

Though Vachel smiled at the stable master's words, the Norman soldier motioned for a contingent of men to give chase to the runaway rider.

"Sometimes a lesson is learned only when it is felt. Mayhap the spirited mount will teach the lady a whip is not for Saxon flesh," the stable master continued, placing a piece of hay in his mouth and chewing thoughtfully.

Bethany touched the stableman's arm. "I fear that lady knows only severity. My worry is not for her, but my horse."

Vachel shook his head. "Do not fear, my lady. Norman soldiers will not allow her to abuse a good piece of horseflesh. Animals are too important."

"Unlike Saxons, who can be beaten?"

"I did not mean that, my lady! Do not judge us by that one's behavior. We are as different in temperament and philosophy as you and your sister."

"Aye, you are. But I fear many Saxons will have to bear the heel of Normans who feel the same as Damiana."

"Fortunately, my lady, Royce de Bellemare is a fair and just man."

"As I am sure the lady knows, Vachel," the warlord said.

Startled by the sound of Royce's voice, Bethany turned around. "If it were your horse, you would not be so cavalier."

Royce's features tightened at her words. "Do not chastise me, my lady. I will deal with those who abuse *my* possessions."

Morlock is mine, Bethany wanted to scream, but instead she lowered her head and gritted her teeth. She had promised not to contest him in front of others.

Keeping her own counsel was brutally hard, and she kept her eyes focused on the ground. Rebellion surfaced in her like a piece of wood tossed into a stream, but she tamped it down. Her brother and sister's freedom depended on her submission.

"As you wish, my lord. I will trust in your judgment." The words choked her, but she spit them out.

She heard the stable master's gasp of surprise, and his reaction tore at her heart. Did her people think she was deserting them?

Chapter Fourteen

Detached from the broken horse-saddle, two leather strips stained with horse-sweat and age hung in Royce's hand. A line of concentration marred his brow as he examined the snapped rawhide in the dim yellow light of the sputtering candle. His finger ran across each end. Both edges were smooth and straight, not jagged. His fist tightened around the evidence. Morlock's saddle cinch had been cut.

"Royce, do you need my help?" Guy hailed as he approached the stable.

"Is Damiana all right?" Royce asked in reply, relieved he could take Guy into his confidence.

"*Oui*, Royce. 'Twas not a serious fall, but your dear betrothed is carrying on and complaining as though she suffered the pains of death." Guy shook his head, clearly disgusted. "More is the pity the accident did not end her miserable life."

Royce slowly handed his brother the leather cinch of Morlock's saddle. " 'Twas no accident," Royce said.

The shock on Guy's face sobered his handsome features. Apparently, enough of his religious training remained to make his brother ashamed of his remarks.

Royce snatched the evidence from his brother's hand and flung it across the stable. "I will not be robbed of all I have worked for. If Damiana dies, so, too, does the opportunity to link our name to her noble line."

Guy nodded. "Even though I cannot abide the woman, this cannot go unpunished."

" 'Tis good you see the heart of the matter," Royce said, reassured by his brother's support. "I want Damiana guarded both day and night when she leaves the castle."

"Though the men will grumble over the duty, I will assign my most trusted soldiers. 'Twill be as you wish, Royce."

"Then you will delve into this matter. I need to know who is behind these *accidents.*"

"Accidents?" Guy questioned. "You mean there have been more than one?"

"Oui." Royce felt the stab of his brother's censuring stare and reluctantly relayed the incident of the poisonous snake left in his bed. " 'Tis time to find the traitor in our midst, for he grows bolder with each attempt."

The disgust on Guy's face was well deserved. It had been foolish to keep the first attempt a secret.

"I am sorry, Guy. At the time, I thought it was unimportant."

"Stubbornness has always been your failing," Guy said, his gaze intent and features solemn. "Is there someone you suspect?"

"Oui, I have someone in mind, but I would wait upon your findings. Then, if we are in agreement, there can be no doubt. I need proof." Seeing the confused look on his brother's face, Royce added, "Without evidence, the accusation would seem ludicrous and open a hornet's nest."

"Then you shall have your proof," Guy said.

Royce rubbed his temples, trying to ease the ache within and soothe the weariness. "Who is with Damiana?"

"Mary and two serving girls. Damiana would not let Bethany attend her."

"Damnation." Royce's vehemence surprised his brother.

With a deep sigh, Royce raked his fingers through his heavy hair. "Damiana is crippled by her prejudice," he said with disgust. "Bethany's skill would ease her misery."

"Nothing will ease that woman's misery. She revels in it."

Royce shrugged his shoulders. "As long as she speaks her wedding vows, she can be the worst shrew alive."

Guy shook his head in commiseration. "Brother, you have chosen a strange fate, a marital life that rivals your martial career. Both offer hardship fraught with battles. In other words, a Hades of your own making."

Royce ignored his brother's barb. "Next month, when Damiana's family arrives, the marriage will take place. Keep her alive until then, brother."

"Verily, Damiana's safety interests me little. I must confess that given the opportunity, I might even side with her enemies." A serious expression stole over Guy as he extended his hand and grasped Royce's forearm. "However, with your life in the balance, I swear I will find the coward who would harm a woman."

For a brief moment they stood and gazed at each other. In that silent communication, Royce felt the power of his brother's conviction and loyalty. Then, Guy walked off, his steps hard and fast.

Royce shook his head at his brother's determination. Even as children, Guy's passionate tenacity to an endeavor, to the exclusion of all else, was his only fault—one which worried Royce. He thanked God that Guy was his brother and, luckily, his friend. Royce would not want to find himself with such an opponent. Many underestimated the former seminary student. Royce knew better.

He walked through the stable to Morlock's empty stall, where he had thrown the cut straps, and retrieved them. Hoping his suspicion was wrong, he tucked the evidence into his tunic and marched off to his room to write a detailed report to William.

The months had been profitable, but William was not short-sighted. The king's concern involved more than coin. A strong monarchy could not tolerate insurrection and intrigue, no matter how small the incident, if it were to survive. Royce admired his liege, both as a man and a king, not only for William's accomplishments, but for thumbing his nose at the world and attaining the highest office in the land . . . a bastard's revenge, legitimized by success and power that none could dispute. Thanks to William's example, Royce planned to place his name where it would be respected. He needed Damiana for that end. Up until now, he had acquired everything on his own, but he was not fool enough to think he could cross certain thresholds without the right social ties.

Royce had just finished a detailed account when he heard the hesitant sound of someone's throat-clearing.

"My lord?" The stable master stood in the doorway to Royce's chamber with his hat in his hand. "Your men have returned with the runaway steed. What do ye want me to do with the injured horse?"

Irritated by the interruption, Royce affixed his name to the missive then put down his quill. "Morlock?" he questioned.

"Aye, my lord. 'Tis the law that the mistress of the . . . begging your pardon, my lord, the master decides the fate of injured animals," he said, twisting his hat into a tight wad.

"See to the wounds and treat the horse till he recovers," Royce ordered.

At Royce's command, the stable master's face beamed. The strangled hat was untwisted and placed upon his bare pate. " 'Tis glad I am not to put down Lady Bethany's favorite mount. For sure no stomach would feel full from an animal taken before its time."

" 'Tis a fine-spirited beast." Royce smiled wryly. "Unfortunately, like its mistress, I fear Morlock is too stubborn and temperamental to be tasty fare for any man's appetite."

The stable master chuckled at the jest.

Surprised and pleased that they could share humor at the expense of a Saxon, Royce returned the laughter.

"Aye, Lady Bethany is a stubborn lass. But there is naught

other who would be so true. Morlock is the finest horse in the stable, and Lady Bethany is the finest woman in the land. Take care, my lord, that she does not roast you alive for letting her love get hurt today."

Royce considered the old Saxon's reply and his jovial mood died. For an instant, he entertained the thought of sparing her the painful news. As quickly as the idea appeared, he dismissed it. Grasping hold of the wind would be easier than silencing the gossip in this shire. Bethany would have to be told.

"My lord, will ye be needing anything else?"

Jarred from his reverie, Royce met the man's speculative gaze. "*Oui*, I would see the animal," he said, deciding it would be best if he inspected the injuries before telling Bethany.

Though the stable master bowed his head, his puzzled look did not go unnoticed.

" 'Tis not that I doubt your skill," Royce said, slapping the man on the back. "Merely my need to satisfy my curiosity."

The stable master's relief spread across his wizened face, showing a toothless grin and sparkling eyes. " 'Tis well known I am good with animals, but 'twould be best if Lady Bethany treated her stallion."

The Saxon had a very good point. Though difficult, treating her horse's injuries would keep her busy. Since Damiana had refused Bethany's care, Morlock would benefit from her talents as healer.

She would prefer treating her horse over Damiana and would be much gentler to her beast than to his betrothed. The irony did not escape him, and a lopsided grin formed on his lips.

The stable master led the way to Morlock's stall, where he soothed the stallion with soft words and a firm, even stroke on the horse's uninjured back. Impressed by the stable master's gentle skill, Royce entered the stall and examined the horse. For the most part, Morlock's injuries were minor. Only one caused concern, a deep gash on his back leg.

" 'Twill need to be bound tight." Royce looked up and caught a glimmer of respect in the experienced horseman's eyes.

"Aye, I will fetch the wrappings," the stable master said with eager agreement.

Royce ran his hands over the animal, searching for further injuries. The scored marks damp with blood on the horse's flanks disturbed him more than the minor cuts. The signature of the whip was unmistakable, and Royce knew Bethany would never forgive this wanton cruelty. Nor would he.

He turned to call after the stable master to bring the ointment on his return, but the words died in his throat when he saw Bethany standing in the opening of the stall, her eyes round and moist with tears.

"How could she?" she whispered, her sight fixed on the heavy weals on Morlock's flank.

"Annie," he implored, trying to gain her attention so he could explain, but she refused to meet his gaze.

"I swear on all I hold holy, I will make that woman suffer," she said in a low voice that he had to strain to hear.

Trembling slightly, Bethany stepped into the narrow stall to examine her horse. Royce obligingly moved out of her way. At once, her hands moved with loving care over the animal while tears slipped over her lashes and ran unchecked down her cheeks. Softly, sweetly, she crooned the same words the stable master had earlier, and Morlock responded to her voice with soft neighs.

After she had examined Morlock from head to tail, she glanced up and gave Royce a look that chilled his blood. As long as he lived, he would never forget that expression—rage, naked and raw with pain. He blamed himself for the horse's senseless injuries. Though he could not have known about the cut strap, he should have anticipated Damiana's abusive treatment. Strange he should feel more compassion for Bethany's horse than for his betrothed.

"My lord, I think Morlock will also need ointment," the stable master suggested as he approached with the leg wrappings. Upon seeing his mistress, he bowed and handed over the supplies before leaving.

Without a word, Bethany accepted them.

"Here, let me," Royce insisted, grabbing hold of the medicine.

Shaking her head, she pulled free. "Morlock is my horse."

Royce sighed. "Let me assist you, Annie."

She looked up, revealing shimmering eyes that held his gaze. "I would like that."

As she bent to treat the injured leg, Royce knelt down and handed her the wrappings one by one. He anticipated her needs so perfectly that she never once had to ask for anything. When she ran her finger along the heavy weals, Royce had the ointment waiting. With a tenderness that touched his heart, she nibbled her bottom lip as she gently applied the salve to the open wounds. When the last mark was treated, Royce handed her a rag, and while she wiped her hands clean, he put the supplies away.

Returning, Royce watched her as she crooned another tune to the huge beast. Ever so gently, she rubbed the horse's nose and offered him an apple.

And like any male, Morlock ate out of her hand. The analogy hit a tender nerve. He would have to be very careful around this mademoiselle. She had a way with men. Hell, she had a way with everyone. The trouble was, he enjoyed her ways and did not mind the effect she had on him.

Bethany tried to smother a yawn and failed. Her shoulders, normally held so straight and proper, were now rounded forward in fatigue.

" 'Tis late." He slung his arm over her shoulder and turned her in the direction of the keep, but instead of leaning against him, she dragged her feet in resistance.

"Royce, I would like to sleep out here tonight."

The way she looked at him tore at his heart. Her beseeching gaze spoke more eloquently than words. Obviously, she expected a denial of her request. He wanted her in bed next to him, but he understood precisely how she felt.

He smiled down at her. "Very well. We will sleep under the stars tonight, Annie."

A gasp slipped past her lips. "You would stay out here with me?"

"*Oui,* I would. Your place is beside me. Since I choose to sleep here, you will not deny me," he said with mock authority.

"Royce de Bellemare, I could come to love you, if I let myself." She stretched up on tiptoes and brushed his lips with hers. It was not the most passionate of kisses he had known, yet it touched his very soul. For the first time, Bethany had bestowed a kiss for the sheer joy of it.

He stared into her lovely brown eyes, surprised by her honest admission and regretful that he could not return her words of love.

"What shall I do with you, Annie?"

" 'Tis a problem." She sighed. "Perhaps in the next country William invades there will be a procedure for taking away maidens' hearts along with their lands." She looked away, clearly unable to hold his gaze with the unsettling truth of her words.

He brushed his fingers gently across her cheek, trailing down the line of her jaw to stop beneath her chin. He lifted her face to his. "Do not torture yourself, or me. All we have is what we take from life." His lips caressed hers, softly, sweetly. "If it were another time, another place, we could suit. You are the essence of all I hold dear in a woman. But 'tis our lot to meet now."

"If you could, would you change what has happened?" she asked, gazing up at him as though her life depended on his answer. She wound her hands around his back and tantalized the muscles of his shoulders with soft smooth strokes that sent chills of desire through him.

"What do you mean?" he asked hoarsely, trying but failing to bring his desire under control.

"If it were in your power to go back in time and change the

way and circumstances we met, would you?" she asked as her hands slipped beneath his tunic.

"You talk in riddles," he said, unable to concentrate because her fingers played a sensuous dance over his skin. "History cannot be changed."

"I know that, Royce. I am only dreaming of what might have been. 'Tis a secret pastime of mine."

He cradled her face in his hands and gazed into the loveliest eyes he had ever beheld—so true and trusting, a man could lose his soul. The words formed in his mind, but he could never say them. *If I could change the laws of nature and alter time, then yes, Bethany, I would choose you over all the women I have met and all those yet to come. If God could make a miracle, then both of us would be high-born Normans and free to marry. He could surely grant us a small time and place in which to live and love only each other.*

Aloud, he said, "My destiny is cast for the good of my offspring. I will marry a Norman lady. That cannot be changed."

Her hands slid down his chest, slipping from under his tunic to drop to her side. "You have stated it often enough. I know it well." She paused and drew a deep breath. "I do not ask to be chosen over your glorious plans. I only meant, do you wish otherwise? A lady can have her dreams, or would you deny me those, too?"

The pain in her eyes wounded him deeply. "Keep your dreams, Bethany. But know they are only dreams. I do not want you hurt believing in that which can never be."

"Norman, do you see a woman or a child before you?" she asked, but did not allow him to answer. "I know the difference between dreams and cold reality. I have been raised to be practical. I cannot betray my people, nor would I ever beg a man to marry me."

He could not ignore the glistening in her eyes, but he had to admire the way her chin rose and her gaze never wavered from his. Humor, he decided, would lighten the mood. "What woman would not wish to marry me? I am an excellent prospect."

Bethany chuckled. "What a spoiled child you must have been."

He was glad his ploy had succeeded. "Actually, I was a serious little boy. Do not look so surprised," he said with an air of feigned indignation. "I was not always the jovial fellow you see before you."

"Oh, were you more somber than now? I do find that hard to believe. Was it not you who locked me in the tower, threatening dire consequences?"

He smiled at her stern account. "I am a warrior, *cherie*, but you also know there is another side of me. You are one of the few who has seen it."

"I know, Royce," she conceded, then looked at him with a seriousness that touched his soul. "Were you unhappy in your childhood?"

"I knew what destiny awaited me. I accepted it."

She waved her hand in dismissal. "I know that, but what were you like?"

As he gazed into her eyes, his fingers massaged seductive little circles on her temples. "I was lonely."

The compassion that welled in her eyes was unexpected. He quickly released her and changed the subject. "And you? I would think as the privileged daughter of North Umberland that you laughed and played all day with your friends. Am I right?" he questioned as his hands slipped to her shoulders.

She laughed. "This will surprise you. I was very serious."

"Non, I expected as much. You seem to think you must shoulder all the burdens of this borough."

"I must. 'Tis my responsibility."

"Then it is good I came to this part of England. Now you are relieved of the burden."

"Only a Norman would think with such arrogant logic!" She looked at him askance, and he knew he had travelled on dangerous ground.

"It is truth, *cherie,* you could not have protected the castle from the marauding bands."

"Are you telling me I should be glad I am a slave?"

"If there ever existed a woman who could twist words!"

"You do not like what is said for it has the ring of truth you wish to silence."

"Perhaps." He conceded the point. "Still, it does not change our destinies."

"Royce, destiny is changed with every breath. I do not believe our lives are mapped out by some greater design. Do I think you control our destiny? Never."

"Annie, as far as you are concerned, I am your destiny. You would do well to accept the present and let the future take care of itself."

"I have always believed in lending a helping hand where needed. My destiny is not written by God, or you."

He put his hand out and held her arm when she would have turned from his embrace. "My sweet, stubborn Saxon, I vow if you were docile you would not be half so interesting," he said, drawing her close and whispering. "Every hour spent with you is magical—fresh and new."

The look in her amber-flecked brown eyes said more than words could; and coward that he was, he refused say what was in his heart.

"Just take the day as it comes, Bethany. No one knows the future," he murmured and lowered his lips to hers.

The touch, feel, and taste of her sent hot currents of passion through his body. She was more potent than any wine he had tasted and far more satisfying. He could not get enough of this woman and, by her eager response, he realized the same held true for her.

Tonight their joining was different. He sensed it, and knew why. He loved this woman, wanted her by his side as his wife. But he kept the knowledge deep in his heart where he could guard it. Or hide from it.

Chapter Fifteen

Verdon, the king's emissary, arrived at Renwyg Castle in the wee hours of the morning. After he had satisfied the gatekeeper of his identity, he was admitted into the courtyard.

Frost tinged the air and his breath appeared as a white cloud surrounded by the darkness. Verdon huddled into his mantle as he led his horse to the stable. Chilled to the bone, he shook his head in consternation as he spied two people sleeping in the hay.

Though Verdon created only a slight noise in the still barn, the male figure came awake, lifted his head, and stared directly at the intruder. Once satisfied that there was no danger, the awakened soldier resumed his comfortable position, but not before drawing his companion close in a tender embrace.

Repeatedly, Verdon's gaze travelled to the figures curled up together as he unsaddled his horse. As the moonlight filtered through the clouds, he picked out the features of the lord of the manor. He could not place the woman, although he knew it was not Lady Damiana. Obviously, de Bellemare's taste in women had improved. The red hair and pale skin fairly glowed in the obscure light, giving the woman an ethereal, almost angelic quality. The loving couple lay partially under a fur robe, the lord's arms and leg sheltering the woman, who snuggled deep within the folds of the covers.

She sighed and turned in her sleep, curling into the warlord. In response, Royce tightened his arms around her, hugging her closer. It was obvious that this woman meant a great deal to the warlord and that the reverse also held true.

Verdon smiled. William would find this an interesting development.

Yawning, Bethany knuckled the sleep from her eyes. Her stomach roiled at the sudden movement and she knew the nauseous feeling would pass if she remained still. The tensions of late were having a strange effect on her. If these symptoms did not disappear, she would be forced to ask Maida for a potion.

Beneath her cheek, she felt the steady rhythm of Royce's heart. His presence comforted her. He had chosen to be with her in a cold stable instead of inside the warm castle with Damiana.

Though the weather was overcast and the smell of rain hung in the air, she thought it a magnificent day. The queasiness in her stomach subsided and she drew in a deep breath. A warm glow engulfed her as she recalled their lovemaking. Last night had been special. The hope she nurtured in her breast had grown last eventide when he had chosen a slave over his betrothed. She had won a small battle in the war that raged within him. For the first time in months, her heart felt unfettered and free. If it would not have wakened Royce, she would have sung a morning tune, instead, she hugged the happiness to herself.

Royce's arms came around her and held her tightly. "Good morning, Annie."

The name that had once annoyed her now filled her with joy, for his husky voice softened when he said it. She stretched and smiled. "Good morning, Royce."

"I have decided that it is time to send your brother and sister to Scotland. On the day of their departure, you must swear fealty to me. You have kept your word. I know you will honor the full agreement."

A constricting band tightened around Bethany's chest, and a huge lump formed in her throat. She was unable to stem the riotous emotions that welled up inside her; her eyes stung, and his image blurred.

"Here, stop that. I thought the news would gladden you," he said, trying to wipe the tears away. He rubbed her cheeks as fast as the tears appeared.

Laughing and crying at the same time, she took a deep breath and explained. "I have not held hope that you would keep your word. I wanted to believe you would play true; but, deep down, I did not know," she said.

"Annie, you wound me. I gave my word."

"Aye, but a promise from a Norman meant nothing to me."

"Then, like the apostle Thomas, you doubted me," he said, giving her a quick kiss to soften the words. "You will have your proof. By mid-morning, they will be on their way to Scotland."

Bethany wrapped her arms around him and snuggled deep into the welcoming heat of his body. The cold air swirled around them, but she felt nothing but the warmth of happiness.

In her private chamber with Mary and Bret, Bethany savored the image of her family. This memory would have to sustain her for the years to come. "Here, Mary, you must take the girdle," she said as she handed the gold-embroidered belt to her sister. "The legacy must be passed on."

Mary pulled her hand away, cradling it against her chest as if the very cloth were a snake that would bite her. "Nay, sister, it is yours until your death." Mary dabbed a linen cloth to the corner of her eyes. "I do not understand why you are sending us away."

"Mary, how can you be so naive," Bethany said, retying the girdle around her own hips and giving the knot an extra tug. "It is not safe for you and Bret here."

"That is not so. The warlord fairly dotes on Bret, while Damiana, though not devout, is very kind to me. Did you know she has friends who have met the Pope? Bret and I shall miss them dearly."

The loss of Mary's loyalty hurt Bethany to the bone. "When Damiana becomes mistress of this castle, your place will not be secure."

"Oh, sister, I will pray for you. Envy is an ugly sin."

Exasperated, Bethany grabbed her sister by the shoulders and shook her. "Mary, you have never been able to see the bad side of anyone; but I tell you true, your newfound friend is cruel. Trust me in this. I am your flesh and blood and would not lie to you."

"You are hurting me." Mary cried out at the rough treatment. "You are the one who bid me act friendly toward Damiana," she accused, huge tears hovering in her eyes.

"I am sorry, Mary, you are right," Bethany replied, instantly contrite for her uncharitable thoughts, yet frustrated that her sister could be so muddle-witted.

"I wish you would not have asked this of me. Our people do not like it."

"They know it was my plan. Believe me, sister, they hold you innocent," Bethany said, giving Mary's arm a comforting squeeze.

"I wish they felt as kindly towards you. Bethany, our subjects think you betray them. They believe it is because you have found pleasure in the master's bed."

Bethany quickly covered Bret's ears. "Mary, how can you say such a thing?"

"Because it is true," Mary said quietly, then lowered her eyes and whispered, "They say you enjoy fornicating."

Glaring at Mary, Bethany slipped her hand to Bret's shoulder.

"Bret, will you check and see if your favorite cookies are ready? If they are, you have my permission to have two."

Bret smiled wide. "I will bring you back one," he said, then scampered out of the room.

The moment Bret disappeared behind the door, Mary, wearing a childish pout, turned back to her sister. "I only repeated what everyone else is gossiping about. Is it the truth?" Mary asked with an edge to her voice.

When Bethany did not respond, Mary shook her head sadly. "Not once in the last month have you challenged the warlord. Did you think no one would notice?"

Bethany felt her throat constrict. She took a deep breath to relieve the pressure. "I cannot help what people think. I am doing what is best for all."

"I do not understand you, sister. Once I thought your people were all that mattered to you. I think Mother and Father would be ashamed of their daughter."

Bethany swallowed the lump in her throat. That her own sister would think she was a traitor tore at her, but Bethany had given her word to Royce not to mention their bargain and she would not break her promise. "Mary, if you ever rule a kingdom, you will find there are sacrifices that must be made. Do not question me on this again."

Mary touched her arm. "Do you speak of martyrdom? Bethany, confide in me, please. I promise, I will understand and forgive you."

Bethany shook her head in denial. "Do not badger me, Mary. Though I wish to tell you, I cannot."

"Very well, if you will not share your burden with me, I shall pray for guidance," Mary said, humbly. Her eyelids slipped down and her hands clasped in prayer. Suddenly, a frown marred her brow and her eyes opened. "Bethany, have you done something you are ashamed of?"

Bethany remained silent.

"You have!" Mary said, misconstruing her sister's secret. "I can tell by your face, it is so. Oh, sister, what did you do?"

"Mary," Bethany said forcefully to stem her sister's rising agitation, "I have done nothing I am ashamed of and need not the office of a confessor. Please, just trust me."

Maida suddenly burst into the chamber with her usual bustle and energy, wearing a smile as bright and warm as a summer's day. "I have been trying to open yon door for several minutes," she said, jostling the laden trays on top of her arms for emphasis. "But with my hands full, I found the door latch hard to grasp."

Bethany rushed to relieve the cook of her burden. "Maida, you should have called out for help," she said, thankful for the timely interruption.

"I tried, but you two were so involved in your conversation you did not hear me, although I could hear you both quite clearly."

"I am sorry, Maida. If I had known you were there, I would have helped you," Bethany replied, placing the tray of bread and cheese on the table.

"Aye, my Lady Bethany, you would have. 'Tis your nature."

Mary took a hunk of bread, then brushed by Maida. "I must spend time in the chapel before the journey. Prayer will offer solace and comfort," she said, then nodded to her sister. "Pray you seek Friar John's counsel. I will keep you in my prayers always. Do not worry, Bethany; God forgives even the most wretched sinners. See to your immortal soul." With a serious expression in her eyes, Mary held her sister's gaze for a moment and then, without another word of explanation, whirled about and marched out.

As the door closed behind Mary, Bethany wondered if her pious little sister should find another interest. Too much religion could surely be as dangerous as too little. Mayhap the pagan influence of Scotland would have a beneficial effect.

Bethany looked upon her bed at the heap of Bret's belongings which she had gathered and brought into her room to sort.

She turned to the cook. "Maida, I know you are busy, but do you think you could pack Bret's clothing? I wish to spend as much time with my brother as I can."

"Aye, my lady, I would be glad to." The cook's smile seemed full of meaning.

Bethany heard the sound of running footsteps outside her chamber, and a second later Bret burst through the door with a cookie in his hand. At the sight of Maida, he skidded to a halt. "I waited until they were cool. I did!"

Though Maida's eyes sparkled with amusement, she maintained a serious mein and nodded her approval.

Bethany led her brother over to the window. She accepted the cookie and broke it in half. Giving Bret a piece, she nibbled on hers, trying to find the words that would help ease not only his separation but hers. "Bret, if Father had lived, you would have been sent to foster at another castle in a few short years. Though it would have been hard on all of us, it would have been your duty."

She put her cookie down and knelt beside him. She could not imagine life without him in it. "As much as I would like to keep you here always, I cannot. And instead of leaving in two years, now you must leave sooner. You must journey to Scotland."

"Nay. I will not go," Bret stated. Slowly, his chin began to quiver and his brave front dissolved. With an anguished cry, he threw his cookie down and pummelled his little fist into her.

Her arms encircled her brother in a loving but firm embrace. "Hush, I have not bartered away my freedom so you could throw a tantrum," Bethany murmured, kissing the top of his downy head.

"What is this, Lady Bethany?" Maida asked, pausing in her task and looking up.

"Nothing, Maida," Bethany said as, tenderly, she soothed her little brother's fears.

"So that is why you have not challenged the lord. My ears did not deceive me."

Bethany could not deny it. Maida would see the lie.

"It does not matter." Bethany stroked Bret's fine hair off his forehead. "Bret and Mary will be safe."

"Aye, they will. But what of you, my lady?"

Bethany ignored the question. "Mary will need help packing," she said, not willing to debate another word with Maida when there was so little time left with her family. "Now that you have finished with his bag, would you direct a servant to assist my sister? I fear she will spend all the time allotted in the chapel."

Bethany picked up Bret, who had tears in his eyes. "I love you," she whispered, her heart aching from the separation to come.

His arms slipped around her neck and he hugged her in a tight embrace. "I want to stay with you."

"I know, but it is not possible." Bethany blinked to clear the tears forming. "You must stay with Mary. She will need you by her side."

"Mary prays all the time. She does not need me," he said with childish honesty. Then he looked at Bethany as if an idea had suddenly occurred to him. "Is it the warlord's fault?"

"Nay, 'tis important for you to go to Uncle Bram," she said, trying to keep the emotion out of her voice.

"Does he need my services?"

"Aye, he does," Bethany lied. "When you are old enough, you can come back for me."

"I will," he said in a voice that suddenly sounded adult.

Bethany hugged him once more, then took his hand and led him to the staircase. As they descended the steps, she noticed Bret's and Mary's bags by the door. Her gaze scanned the crowd in the great room, but Mary's face was not among them. When they stepped onto the main floor, Mary rushed into the room carrying her Bible.

"Is your family ready?" Royce asked as they approached him.

"Aye."

But Bret again balked at the news. Royce knelt down to him.

"Brave soldiers do not disobey commands. I am giving you a chance to prove how responsible and courageous you can be. Will you follow my orders on a hard and dangerous mission?"

Bret nodded his head in wide-eyed agreement.

Leaning forward, Royce whispered in the boy's ear.

Bethany did not like the secrecy, but knew it was better that Bret left willingly.

Mary stepped forward and, with tears in her eyes, hugged her sister. "Forgive me, sister. I have meditated and been shown the way. Take comfort, Bethany; God will right the wrongs done," she whispered in Bethany's ear, then added breathlessly, "I shall miss you."

"Take care of yourself and Bret," Bethany managed to choke out. Suddenly the sacrifice of not fighting with Royce seemed nothing at all.

Mary pulled out of the embrace and reached for Bret's hand, but he pulled free of her grasp.

"I am not a baby," he said and marched from the great room toward the courtyard.

Bethany smiled at her brother's courage. She did not want to credit Royce with the improvement, but she could not deny his influence had indeed helped Bret's temperament.

She followed her brother and sister out of the great room to find the courtyard lined with servants and the center occupied by the mounted escort.

"I have kept my word," Royce said. "Will you trust me now?"

"Aye, I will," Bethany whispered.

He smiled at her response, and they both turned and watched her brother and sister mount their horses. The crowd smiled in approval, and Bethany knew they admired Mary. How could they not? Only a saint commanded more respect. She wished her people felt as kindly toward her.

She waved farewell to her family, pain stinging her nose and throat. In all likelihood, she would never lay eyes on her beloved brother and sister again.

Royce handed her a small linen cloth and whispered close to her ear, "Are you ready?"

She refused the cloth, rejecting his kindness. She could not think of him in a warm way, knowing the gesture ahead would humble her.

Royce folded the linen cloth and slipped it into his tunic. Then he turned to Bethany and commanded her to kneel. The sadness reflected in his blue eyes was the only sign in his stern face that he regretted this necessity.

She knelt and touched her head to his hand. Though it choked the very pride from her lungs, she said the vow that bound her loyalty to this man.

Her voice echoed in the silent courtyard. She felt the quiet censure of every villager as she spoke her solemn oath to her enemy.

Bethany could not look any of them in the eye. The Lady of North Umberland, like her long dead ancestor, was a slave at the feet of the conqueror.

"Rise, Bethany of North Umberland. Know that as you do, you are my vassal and under my protection for life." Royce's voice rang out, cutting through the silence like a sword slashing through chain mail. Despite his confident tone, he felt strangely awkward, and he moved away and sought out the king's messenger. "What brings you to Castle Renwyg, Verdon?"

The man hesitated. "My lord, could we speak in private?"

"*Oui,*" Royce said, motioning for the man to follow him to his apartments.

Bethany turned and stared to the north. Mary and Bret would be with Uncle Bram by sunset. She smiled. Her family could grow and prosper without the fear of reprisals from the Norman invaders. Then she turned around and looked at all the people in the courtyard.

They watched her carefully as though they were considering a deep problem. Finally, the Widow Chadwick stepped forward. "My lady, we are beholden to you. Some of us are ashamed of our thoughts and actions this past month. Any one of us would have done whatever 'twas necessary to save our family."

At Bethany's look of surprise, Maida, joined the widow's side and said, "Though I overstepped my place and surely deserve punishment, I told them what I overheard. They had a right to know." Maida's demeanor, however, did not appear one bit repentant.

Feeling humbled by their support, Bethany scanned the crowd. The sea of familiar faces blurred, and she quickly wiped her eyes. "I should have done more for you. Now that my family is safe, I will work harder on your behalf."

"My lady, we should be begging your pardon for thinking you would abandon us to your own selfish desires," Sumar said. Then her gaze lowered and she sheepishly shuffled in place. "Not that you do not have a right to find a mate. But, my lady, we know that no man would ever take the place of your people."

"Nay, my people have my loyalty." Even as she said the words, she wondered if Royce truly had her heart. Would there come a time when she would have to choose between them? In truth, Royce was a good military ruler who had never misused his power. It was a shame they could not combine their individual strengths and rule together. What a force they could be.

But that was impossible.

Chapter Sixteen

In the Scottish stronghold, Mary paced back and forth before her Uncle Bram. Her shadow floated across the floor in the torch and firelight like a ghostly presence. "You must understand," Mary implored with her arms outstretched, "it would be for Bethany's good."

"Dinna think age has robbed my wits, lass. Coveting Bethany's wealth canna be in her best interest," Bram said acidly.

"I fear my sister is bedeviled," she said, her worry evident as her soft, modulated voice rose almost to a wail. "You do not understand, Uncle Bram. She has sold her soul to Lucifer."

"Bethany?" he scoffed, growing weary of Mary's self-righteousness.

"Aye, Uncle Bram," she said, emphasizing her words with a vigorous bob of her head. "You must contract a marriage between myself and a high chieftain. As my husband, he would be honor-bound to rescue my sister."

"Mary, lamb, do you kin? There is nay a chieftain who will have you without a dowry."

"That is why I am begging you to use the wealth from our demesne to procure a husband for me."

"Nay, 'twould be wrong," he said, waving his hand in the air as if to dismiss the idea. He walked over to the hearth and checked on young Bret. Curled up with a wolf skin, his nephew slept through the discussion.

" 'Tis the only way I can save my sister." Tears formed in her bright-blue eyes and shimmered like precious jewels. "By all that I hold holy, I fear for her immortal soul." Mary's gaze darted to her brother, then back to her uncle. She took a hesitant step forward, holding her hands out half in prayer, half in pleading. " 'Tis our duty to save Bethany from falling into an ungodly state of sin at the merciless hands of that devil."

Tears had never moved Bram. "Lassie, I have been to William's court. We canna fight him. His army could crush Scotland if he had a mind to conquer us."

"Uncle Bram, Bethany willingly and unselfishly sacrificed herself for our sake. Please, I beg of you, arrange the match. Verily, a marriage can be made without involving your clan."

" 'Tis not the fight I mind," Bram said as he ran a hand through his hair, trying to find the right words for his Saxon niece. "A Scotsman is no a coward. 'Twould be foolhardy to attack William's forces. A good soldier does not take on a hopeless cause. 'Twould not be a battle, lass; 'twould be a slaughter, and all we would reap would be bloody fields."

"I am ashamed of you, Uncle Bram." Mary's head bowed in defeat and her shoulders slumped forward as she inhaled a deep sigh. "I will pray for your soul."

With restraint, Bram stayed his hand from delivering a well-deserved slap. So, little Mary was as spirited as her sister—though he much preferred Bethany's spunk to Mary's spit. "I will honor your request—with one provision," he said, holding up his hand at her excited expression. "I will arrange a marriage, but without the dowry. A northern chieftain might be willing to overlook the lack of dowry if there were the possibility of reward later." He paused and studied Mary, sizing her up. "However, know you well that a man from the high country might not fear William, but he will likely be harsh and unforgiving as a husband. Think you well on the matter."

"I will take the heathen for master whether he be cruel or kind. My sister's only hope is to be rescued."

The Scotsman in Bram winced at her coarse choice of words. Heathen, indeed.

As she stormed across the floor, Bram watched Mary's angry steps carry her dainty form from his great room. He tried to like Mary as much as Bethany, but of the two sisters there was little question who held his admiration. He hoped it was not because Mary was his brother's child and Bethany his; he did not think so. As a leader of men, he prided himself on being an impartial judge. There existed something about Mary that set his teeth to aching.

He would, however, arrange a match as his niece requested. Even if William freed Bethany before Mary's wedding, no harm would be done. Mary needed a husband. A little healthy male lust might dilute the self-righteous mein that Bram found so distasteful.

In any case, a plan acted upon made him feel less useless. He had not heard a word from the bastard-king. God willing, Bethany was keeping her mouth shut until rescue was possible. But the women of North Umberland were not known for their tact. He smiled as he picked up his nephew. Bethany would be just fine. In fact, it would not surprise him if she conquered the Norman warlord all on her own.

In Renwyg's spacious, great room, Bethany sat alone with Vachel. With the lateness of the morning hour, the castle occupants were about their business and the cavernous room seemed twice the size. The huge, darkened, oak-beamed ceiling and rough-hewn, gray-stone walls—like the roof of a cave—echoed the tiniest sound made.

To the right of Bethany's elbow lay her morning meal, cold and untouched as she sipped her hot cider. Her stomach was so upset this morning that she could not tolerate the thought of food, let alone its smell. She motioned to Sumar. "I am not hungry. Please, remove my trencher."

When the servant had cleared the table and left the room, Bethany offered Vachal a weak smile for the interruption of their game. The gray-haired soldier leaned forward over the trestle table and studied her last move. With a sad shake of his head, he captured her light-colored pebble and removed it from the game cloth.

With the patience she had come to associate with this bear of a man, he moved his piece, then looked at her. "Bethany, it takes time and concentration to master this."

Bless his heart, all morning he had tried to teach her Twelve Men Out. But the game, created to sharpen a soldier's strategic skills, evaded her. She smiled at him, grateful for his concern and time. Though Bethany tried, she really did, the game could not hold her interest. Her thoughts centered wholly on Royce.

With a renewed effort, she moved a light pebble and watched the play of the game. Her interest lasted only seconds before Royce's parting words echoed in her mind, *Mademoiselle, I wish you glad tidings today.* Was he mad? Misery filled her heart. Royce was spending the day with Damiana at his betrothed's insistence. No doubt the sudden interest in this game was Vachel's way of occupying her time. Vachel's sincere concern touched her. Even Guy had surprised her by suggesting and initiating several diversions. For their chivalrous efforts, they had both won a place in her heart. Though each man had done his best to get her mind off Royce, nothing had worked.

Like a self-imposed purgatory, visions of Damiana placing her palm upon Royce's hand haunted her. The thought that Damiana would spend time with him hurt, but the knowledge that Royce acceded to her wishes created more than pain. It devastated her.

In an effort to banish Royce from her thoughts, she redoubled her resolve. Though poor competition, she managed to finish one game with a reasonable showing.

Guy entered the hall and walked over to the table. With a good-natured smile and wink for Bethany, he turned his attention to the old soldier, saluting Vachel with a slap on the back. "You have spent enough time with this beautiful lady. I have come to rescue her from your boorish ways."

Accompanied by Vachel's feigned blustering, she accepted Guy's offer and, though it took a great deal of effort to put up a cheery front, she maintained a smile. With her hand in Guy's firm grasp, she walked with him to the stable.

Riding would be a good diversion. She loved it so—but not as much, a little voice whispered, as she loved Royce.

Tears welled up in her eyes and she took several deep breaths to stem their flow. Damn Royce de Bellemare and Lady Damiana. Ever since Mary's departure, Damiana had craved attention.

Bethany knew that the pain she felt must be borne in silence. Royce had never lied to her; she knew all-too-well that her status would never allow them to be together. At least, her mind comprehended this—her heart could not.

The ride took them over the same ground she had covered with Royce. "He *will* marry her." The words slipped passed her lips before she could stop them. Then she turned to face Guy and finished her thought. "Will you help me when he weds his betrothed? I must be away."

"I cannot help you escape. If it were in my power, Bethany, I would see you as his wife. But you and I know Royce will make up his own mind without counsel from anyone."

"I cannot stand to see him with her." All the anguish she felt was reflected in her tone.

"You would not do anything about it, would you?" Guy inquired, eyeing her cautiously.

"What mean you?" she asked, trying to understand the unexpected change in his manner. Suddenly, he was sounding more like the Norman soldier who had conquered her land than the genuine friend of late.

He shrugged his shoulders. "Only that some would take

matters into their own hands." His face remained expressionless as he waited for an answer.

"Nay, Guy," she answered, wary but determined to state the truth. "I may not like her. In fact, I despise her. But her fate rests with God, not me. When she meets her maker, he will hand out far more punishment than I could ever conceive."

Guy pulled up on his reins and brought his horse from a slow walk to a stop. When she followed his lead, he turned to her, and his gaze, devoid of its usual humor, pinned her with an intensity that brought an icy shiver to her spine.

"Some think you are behind the accident that befell the lady. It has been mentioned, more than once, that you are the one with the most to gain if Damiana were to die."

Bethany swallowed her fear. " 'Tis true, Guy." She paused to gather the right words. "But my character is set. As you should recall, I met your brother in yon field, not sheltered behind some tree with a bow and arrow."

"Verily," he said, a slow smile spreading across his handsome face. "You did, indeed, challenge him."

"Then you have your answer," she said, still indignant and trying not to let his boyish charm influence her.

His smile beamed bright and full now, relief shining through. "I never thought you were behind it, Bethany. But someone is, and the person must be stopped before he succeeds."

Bethany hung her head. "I could not tell you even if I knew his identity. I will not betray my people," she said, knowing her answer put a strain on their relationship.

Guy reached over and lifted her chin with his finger until her downcast eyes met his gaze. "It may not be one of your villagers."

"This is not London, Guy, but a small borough. An outsider would be noticed. What stranger do you see? Except for the one who arrived the other night and has a penchant for asking questions."

"*Non,* it is not he," Guy stated emphatically. With a sheepish

smile, he reluctantly explained, "Verdon is the king's man."
Guy took a deep breath. "Bethany, Royce is in danger."

"Royce?" she repeated, unable and unwilling to believe harm
could befall him.

"*Oui*. Remember the snake?"

She shook her head in denial. "Nay, Guy, the snake was a
mishap of nature. No Northumbrian would dare harm the warlord. Do you think Saxons are senseless?"

"Then you must help discover who is behind these attempts,"
Guy pleaded. "At least try to dissuade your people from any
foolish attempts. The consequences would be devastating."

Bethany shook her head. Guy had missed the point entirely.
"If my villagers were responsible, I would have knowledge of
it. Believe me, Guy, it is no one from this shire."

"For their sake, I pray you are right. However, my duty is
to find the culprit, and I shall. Justice will be served."

"What if the villain is a Norman?" She held up her hand to
forestall his objection. "I know it sounds farfetched, but it is
possible. How would your justice deal with one of your own?"

"The same, mayhap harsher. Traitors are never received
kindly."

"Of this I have firsthand knowledge."

"*Oui*, the bargain," he said.

"I knew it would not be easy, but my brother and sister are
safe."

"I wonder if they would have done the same for you."

"It matters not. I did not ask for a sacrifice from them, nor
did they ask one of me."

"They asked with every look and every deed," he said with
derision. "Your sister plays you like a well-worn mandolin."

"What mean you, Norman?"

"She knows your weakness and uses it. I suspect she is not
as helpless as she appears. Perhaps you have done her a service."

Bethany raised an eyebrow. "How is that?"

"Now, Mary will have to rely on her own wits. She does not

have her big sister there to rescue her every time life deals her a hardship."

"You do not understand her. Mary is sensitive," Bethany said, but could not entirely deny Guy's words. There had been times her sister had surprised even her.

"I think I understand her character well enough. But, as you say, she is your sister. Who else would know her better?"

Bethany found Guy's remarks strangely disturbing. He possessed a way of posing a question so that the answer haunted you.

Stranger still was his disregard for Mary's devout manner and sweet, even-tempered charms. Most people respected and admired her after only one meeting. Guy, obviously, did not.

Bethany had little time to ponder the conversation, for it was at that moment that Royce and Damiana decided to join them.

The sight of the approaching Norman warlord with his betrothed made Bethany's stomach turn. Every inch the fine aristocrats, they were clothed in splendid garments covered by thick fur mantles, their tunics woven of the richest fabrics and dyed the brightest hues. She lowered her gaze to her own raiments. Next to Damiana, Bethany looked like a milkmaid in her loose-flowing tunic adorned only by the elaborate embroidery that the Normans had not comprehended or mastered.

Guy's hand squeezed hers. "You need no jewels to shine, Lady Bethany," he said, as if guessing her thoughts. "You are truly beautiful."

She returned the comforting squeeze and let her hand rest in his. Taking a deep breath, she raised her chin to meet Royce and Damiana's arrival.

Determinedly, she settled her gaze not on their finery but on their faces and she noticed something interesting. Though it was of little compensation, she took some satisfaction in their strained expressions. They were miserable.

"What, pray tell, are you about, Guy?" Royce asked his brother as he reined his horse before them.

In contrast to Royce's displeasure, Damiana lost her sour expression and looked positively pleased.

"I desired a pleasant companion for the ride, Royce, nothing more," Guy said, his voice and manner remaining easy and relaxed.

Though he addressed his brother, Royce looked at Bethany. "I did not realize your day was so free from work that you could wile the time away with a beautiful woman. From now on, brother, I will have to find more duties for you to perform."

Bethany shivered from the cold look in Royce's eyes. His anger sliced through her as effectively and sharply as his sword had slit her clothing on their first meeting. Suddenly, she was aware of her hand in Guy's. She tried to pull free from his grasp, but he held on tighter.

Guy raised her hand to his lips and deposited a light kiss on her fingers, then released his hold and threw his brother an almost challenging look.

"I told you, Royce," Damiana purred in a voice that set Bethany's teeth on edge, "the little vixen is already feathering her nest for another."

Guy's deep laughter filled the air. "Would that were true, Damiana. I would gladly fly to this dove's nest. But she is ever faithful to my brother, much to my woe," he said. Then the laughter left his eyes. "And even if she were not, I would never trespass on my brother's domain. To suggest so insults not only the lady but also myself."

Damiana gasped. "How dare you, you—"

"Enough," Royce roared, cutting off Damiana's tirade. "I suggest we all enjoy what is left of the day."

Slowly, Damiana regained her composure. "Are you suggesting that we ride with them?" she asked, the distaste dripping from her every word.

"No, I am commanding it," Royce said, his voice now a full-blown bellow.

" 'Tis bad enough that I must endure the rigors of this uncivilized land, but to be subjected to this crude and vulgar association is really too much to ask of me. By your leave, my lord, I no longer find the company enjoyable," Damiana said imperiously.

Bethany could hardly believe the brazen insult. Her gaze traveled to Royce. Not a sign of what he thought or felt showed on his enigmatic features.

"My wit has lost its appeal, Damiana?" Royce asked with a raised eyebrow.

"I wish to return to the castle" was all she said. With a delicate sniff, Damiana raised her nose in the air.

Guy chuckled. "By all means, Lady Damiana, we shall try to survive without your charming company."

Royce noticed the satisfied look on his brother's face. "Guy, accompany Lady Damiana back to the castle."

"Royce, you cannot mean to send me back with your brother while you stay with this slut?"

Though the word, as always, succeeded in wounding Bethany to the very core, she refused to lower her head and give the bitch the satisfaction of knowing she had hurt her prey.

Guy snorted with disgust. "Follow me, woman, and mind you stay on your horse, for I will not stop if you should become unseated."

With that, he turned his horse and headed for the castle at a full gallop.

At that moment, Bethany loved Guy for the chivalry he had shown her.

"He is not doing you any favors," Royce said, following her gaze.

"You mean a slave should not grow used to such kindness?"

"When Damiana becomes mistress of the castle, your life will be very hard. It would do you well to make peace with her now."

Bethany could not believe her ears. She stared at Royce, wondering if he truly had lost what little wit God had seen fit to give him. "Aside from the fact that I am your mistress, do you really think your Norman wife and Saxon slave can have any relationship other than hate?"

Royce knew she was right, but being just and fair did not appeal to him in his present mood. He had to meld this land together and suppress any insurrection. To insure peace, he must guard against marauders and protect his borders. Now, as warlord and overseer, he had to deal with the king's embassy, who carried news of a prior claim to this land.

"Just get along with Damiana. Do not cause me grief in this matter. I have kept my word; keep yours."

"I have. My loyalty was bought and paid for. Perhaps you seek from Damiana what you have purchased from me. But then, I always thought a betrothed's loyalty was given freely."

The truth of her words angered him. When she turned her horse to ride away, he yelled, "Hold! I have not dismissed you."

She pulled back so hard on her reins, the horse reared, nearly unseating her. With cheeks flushed and red hair unbound and blowing in the wind, she turned to face him. "I am not at your beck and call, Norman, and never will be."

"Annie, you are exactly that," he retorted, watching the healthy red glow slip from her face. "By my will, what I wish becomes fact." Though he knew he played with fire, he could not stop himself from baiting her. "My lady, I will enjoy your charms when and wherever I so desire."

"Very well, warlord. Would you have me disrobe here in this field?" she challenged.

The thought was tempting, but he noticed the slight glimmer in her eyes and knew his crude, unchivalrous manner had caused her humiliation. Her chin wavered, but she kept it raised and held his gaze.

"*Non*, not here, there is too much chance of being interrupted."

The relief flowed across her features, softening the tense lines about her mouth and jaw while smoothing the frowning lines above her brow. Never had he wished to cause her embarrassment. He simply had so much on his mind, and the pulse at his temple was pounding.

"Forgive me, Annie," he said as he ran a hand through his hair. "I am taking my ill-humor out on you."

Bethany's mouth dropped open in surprise at receiving an apology.

"I am tired of bickering," he went on, thinking of Damiana's constant complaints.

Her hand strategically covered her lips, trying but failing to hide a grin. Clearly, she was pleased his day with his betrothed had been ruined.

He gave Bethany a sheepish smile. "Annie, if I promise to be on my best behavior, would you spend the afternoon with me? I value your company and need your counsel. Guy offers his opinion, but I would have yours."

Her features changed before his eyes. Her skin fairly glowed and the sparkle returned to her eyes. God, she was lovely. But her beauty was the last thing he needed to consider. His concentration belonged on the problems at hand, yet she captured his mind and heart like no one else.

"What is it, my lord?" she asked.

He almost blurted out the truth, then said instead, "The soldiers fleeing William are one of the problems, while storing enough food for the winter is another."

"You have men posted to intercept the raiding soldiers. What else can you do? As for the food, there is enough grain and vegetables stored. What is needed is meat."

How simple she made everything sound. He decided to ask her the one question that haunted him. He had worked too hard for his land to lose it; she above all others would understand his fears.

"William has sent a man to see about my claim to this land."

Her eyes widened momentarily. "Was not the land given you as reward for your efforts during the war?"

"*Oui.* But there is another to whom William owes a prior

claim." He took a deep breath. "Probably a high-born lord with powerful alliances who has distinguished himself."

"Is that why the stranger ask questions of everyone here?"

"Verdon will send a full report to William when the investigation is finished."

She turned away from Royce, but he claimed her attention, needing to see her reaction. There were tears in her eyes.

"You mean you could lose my land? My people would be thrown on the mercy of another master! What kind of king gives a reward, then meanly snatches it back?"

Her words pleased him. He knew they were from her heart because her people and her cause were included.

"William will be fair. He is a good ruler. In time, you will find this so."

"You defend a man who could strip you of everything you hold dear?"

"*Oui.* I would follow that man into hell itself. He has earned my loyalty."

"Royce, I will never understand Normans. If a Saxon king tried to take that which was mine I would fight him to the death."

"There can be only one leader if a land is to prosper. Only the people suffer when men fight over power. I am content. Greed is for those who are dissatisfied."

"You truly care about the people," she said, amazed, then paused as if to consider her revelation. "I hope the land falls to you."

Her words were said begrudgingly and, therefore, meant all the more. He smiled. "Better the devil you know than one you do not."

An almost melancholy look crossed her face. "Aye, that is true."

She looked so forlorn and vulnerable, a rare expression that he had never seen before, that Royce wanted to comfort her; then, as quickly as her deep look of sadness had appeared, it vanished.

Royce still had an overwhelming urge to hold her in his arms, but consoling thoughts had fled with her transformation from self-pity to self-possession. He wanted her, badly, but he owed her more respect than to take her in the field like a rutting animal. Still the memory of her charms played about his mind, teasing him with her sensual delights. The soothing comfort of her silken skin next to his and the sound of her voice whispering warm, loving words in his ear tantalized his senses. Later, he promised himself, when they could enjoy the privacy of their room without the possibility of interruption, he would take her.

"Come and ride with me," he said. "I have a hunger to view this land through your eyes."

A soft smile spread across her ripe lips and, though she was unaware of the picture she presented, it took all his willpower not to kiss her.

"You do not need my eyes to see the beauty here. It is either apparent or it is not." She pointed to the far-off horizon, the empty fields back-dropped by the dark forest. "Can you sense the miracle of the winter's sleep?"

"Miracle? What miracle?" Royce asked, suddenly very curious about her thoughts.

A little shyly, she faced him. "Winter holds magic and wonder. The long cold months bring the promise of rebirth. Faith and hope are borne on winter's breath," she said as they rode slowly over the sloping hills and viewed the barren landscape.

"You really love this season," Royce said in awe.

"Aye. 'Tis a special time of rest for the body, spirit, and mind. It makes me long to curl up in a fur robe before a warm hearth on a snow-covered morning or cold, frosty evening and do nothing." She laughed self-consciously, clearly embarrassed by speaking such whimsical thoughts. Then she turned to face him. "North Umberland, my lord, is much colder than you are accustomed to."

"I can think of ways to keep warm," he said, noticing the bright color climbing her cheeks. Still, she amazed him. He would not have thought such romantic nonsense existed in such a practical mind. And yet, when she said it, it did not sound like nonsense, but poetry.

"My favorite season is summer," he said, sharing his thoughts. " 'Tis the only season a warrior does not have to guard against the elements." Looking over the landscape that had become rockier as they'd ridden west, he pointed ahead. "Did you come to the cliffs often?"

"Only in the summer, my lord. My family favored a sheltered cove to the north."

Though he had explored all of his demesne, this area he would know blindfolded. Breathing deeply, he tasted the tang in the air and knew the sea was close. It reminded him of home. What a strange and diverse land was this North Umberland. He wondered what the crop yield brought in and if the villagers that bordered the sea were adept fishermen. "If the crops fail, there is bounty from the sea."

"Aye, the people of North Umberland are blessed by a benevolent Lord."

" 'Tis a rare and wondrous land," he said, seeing all that she had envisioned and more.

"Aye, my lord. That is why its loss hurt so much."

He noted the sadness in her voice; and though he agreed wholeheartedly, he thought it prudent to divert her.

"We had best be away," he said, noticing that the shadows had lengthened and darkness would fall long before they retraced their way home. "The castle needs my presence."

She did not argue with him, and he was relieved. She seemed to sense his needs with uncanny perception.

Finally the torch-lit castle came into view. Every time he saw his home, he was filled with a sense of accomplishment and pleasure. That he could lose it all did not bear considering.

Strange that a man who had spent his life as a mercenary would think of Renwyg as home. He wanted to tell Bethany how he felt, but knew it would be salt for wounds that had not healed. Suddenly, he understood her. He would never accept another's claim to a place he loved. Though he would, if William asked, give up his ownership to North Umberland, his roots would never take hold again. No other plot on God's earth would ever bear the name home.

It disconcerted him to have so much in common with his slave. Given the rare opportunity to see the world from her view had crystallized many problems, while making others more difficult. He could not change her plight, yet he could understand it. This must be what his brother, Guy, talked about—compassion and judgment.

God's teeth, he was not born to be a savior! He was a soldier with a duty to perform.

He would marry Damiana and secure his children's future. Nothing and no one would ever change that. He had worked too hard and sacrificed too much to lose sight of his dream. Though noble blood from the best house in Normandy coursed through his veins, his father had publicly disavowed siring him and, forever after, the condemnation *bastard* had followed him and Guy. In one ugly moment of time, their world had turned upside down and they had gone from the privileged elite to little more than common serfs, forced to take their mother's name. Losing his home and his rank were blows that could be overcome, but his father's betrayal had left its mark. Never would the wound that had scarred him ever touch his children.

As the gates opened, Bethany turned to him. "I am always filled with pride and thankfulness that Renwyg exists. Do well to pass it on to one who cares."

Her words said what he had tried not to. Damn if he did not feel a lump in his throat. The land, the people, meant far more than they should have. He belonged here. When had it happened?

She had not asked for her freedom or worried if he would provide for her well-being or take her with him. He stared at Bethany and really saw her for the first time. Unselfish, loyal, kindhearted, and truly lovely. Aye, she was lovely, but her inner beauty shone like the sun. A man would be blessed to call this woman his own.

Her gaze held his, and he could not allow himself to be lost in the warm, brown mist. He could not, would not, fall under her spell. She was his slave, nothing more . . . no matter what the king had in mind for him. He had never considered dragging a woman on campaign. But that had been before Bethany. Suddenly, he could not think of a future without her in it.

That was a disturbing thought. He immediately looked away and urged his horse into the castle courtyard.

"Royce, if you have a minute," Guy called out as Royce dismounted.

"What is it, Guy?" Royce responded, irritated that he would not have a moment's peace.

"There is trouble."

Immediately, Guy had Royce's full attention. "Is it raiders?"

"*Non*, 'tis a private matter," Guy said, glancing beyond Royce to Bethany.

"Very well," Royce nodded, then turned to Bethany. "Await me in our apartments."

Bethany dismounted with the stable master's help and left the men alone.

When the horses had been led away, Guy looked around to make sure no one could overhear their conversation.

"You have found something out?"

"*Oui*, but you will not like it."

"What is it?"

"After I escorted Damiana to her room, I left to be about my duties. Just a few moments ago, Maida bid me to return to Damiana's chamber and I discovered an interesting piece of information."

"My lord," the stable master said, "will there be anything else?"

At the interruption, Guy's features formed an impatient mask.

"*Non*. Seek thy rest." Royce turned back to his brother and leaned closer.

"As I was saying, Royce—"

"My lord." Vachel approached. " 'Tis well you are back. There is a matter that cannot wait."

"Not now, Vachel." Guy pulled his brother from the stable and into the courtyard. He surveyed the area, his gaze travelling full circle to guarantee privacy.

Royce's impatience could not be contained. He slung his arm over his brother's shoulder and pulled him near. "Do you think you could manage to tell me in this century?" he whispered.

Guy gave his brother a long-suffering look. "From Damiana's room came the unmistakable sound of a tryst."

"What?"

"She was not alone. It would seem Damiana is enjoying her moments when you are not around."

"Who is the varlet who would dare usurp my place?"

Guy smiled. "The varlet is still with the vixen."

"Let us away. I wish to catch the man when he emerges from his rendezvous with Damiana."

Guy looked at him with a strange expression. "You do not seem upset."

"About her having a lover? I could not care less. But I will not be cuckolded."

"Has it occurred to you that you would feel differently if it were Bethany?"

"You think I value my Saxon slave above all others?" Royce asked, knowing even as he posed the question that the answer was something he could not explain.

"Normally, you are not so dim-witted," Guy said with a raised eyebrow.

Royce recognized the gesture. Guy always knew when he had his older brother. " 'Tis true I have formed a tenderness for the mademoiselle, but she will not stand between me and what I want."

"Royce, you cannot have them both."

Royce stopped and looked at his brother. "Why not?"

"Because, if it has not escaped your notice, the lady will leave before she subjects herself to such humiliation."

"Damiana will not leave," Royce stated emphatically.

"I was not talking about Damiana," Guy replied with a knowing smile.

"Bethany has no place to go and no one to take her in."

" 'Tis not so. She has kinsmen. Bethany stays because of her people. The moment Damiana has dominion over them and her cause is lost, she will leave."

Royce could not deny the truth. "Come, we will see to one lady, then I will attend the other. You need not concern yourself about Bethany again."

Though he told his brother to forget about the Saxon maiden, it would be difficult to do the same. But he would not allow her that much power over his thoughts and his life and vowed to place her in the back of his mind. Never again would he waste another moment dwelling on the delightful pleasures of her lovely face and delicate body. There, he was through with thoughts of her. *Liar,* his mind screamed. He ached to be with her, to be in her. It was a foul mood that led him to Damiana's door.

A quiet stillness met them as Guy dismissed the guard he had left in attendance.

"Shall we?" Guy asked, bowing in mock deference for Royce to precede him.

Royce kicked the door open. Two people bolted up in bed at the resounding crash.

Royce's mouth thinned when he saw Philip Gaston, the man Damiana had chosen, the hearth fire and burning candles illuminating their nude bodies.

"Well, well, my secret is out," Damiana said with easy confidence, her relaxed air an insult in itself.

" 'Twas no secret, Damiana. Everyone in the castle knows that this room is not occupied by a lady but a whore," Royce said in disgust.

"I will make you a bargain, Royce," she said, halfheartedly

covering her breasts. "I will send Philip back to France if you will give up that slut."

"You are not in a position to make demands."

"Do not be so sure," she said, caressing the side of the man's face. "Philip brings news from Father that another has offered suit. You need my name, but you will never have it unless I have your vow that Bethany will be cast aside. I will not suffer humiliation in my own home."

She had bested him, and he hated her for it. He needed her name and would do anything for it. The thought of giving up Bethany tore at his insides, but it would be one way to be over the enchantress. He had vowed that no woman would mean that much to him. Now, he would put it to the test.

"Give the Saxon slave to Guy," Damiana said. "He seems to be enamored of her soiled charms."

Guy turned to his brother, awaiting the words. There was no derision in Guy's eyes. Thankfully, he understood this was not a jest.

But Royce could not give her to another, not even his brother. Though the practice was common, he would not sleep knowing she lay in another's bed. "I will send her to her sister's room."

"Non," Damiana shrieked. "A slave is not my equal to be given a honored room in the family quarters. Send her to the dungeon."

"Non! She is not a criminal," Royce declared. Then he took a deep breath and slowly released it. "I will send her to the tower."

"The tower sounds delightful," Damiana purred. "I do not care if you have your little affairs, Royce. But no one will usurp my position and power in this household."

"You have your bargain, my lady, but should you choose to betray me again 'twill be your very life that is forfeit. Remember that."

Never had he hated a woman so much.

Chapter Seventeen

"The tower?" Bethany asked, stunned. She looked from Royce to his brother, feeling as if her world had collapsed. "Why?" she questioned, wondering what sin she had committed to warrant such a harsh sentence from the warlord.

Royce stood solemn and uncommunicative, refusing to even meet her gaze. She noticed the tense lines fanning out from his eyes and the taut muscles about his mouth and jaw. His angry expression worried her.

She turned to Guy. "I do not understand."

"I will see you to your room." Guy stepped forward and gently took her arm.

"Wait," she said, pulling out of his hold. She walked over to Royce. "Is it something I have done?"

"*Non,*" he said, but refused to elaborate.

She caught a glimmer of guilt in his eyes and spoke her suspicions.

" 'Tis because of her, your betrothed. You have put me from your side at her request."

When he remained silent, she knew. A mixture of shame and

betrayal boiled up in her. Before she could stop herself, her hand swung and connected with his cheek.

He did not move, and her palm stung from the blow. But the pain helped ease her anger. "What now my lord? Am I to go to Guy—or someone else?"

"You dare ask?" Royce roared.

"I dare," she responded, unmoved by his wrath.

Royce reached out and clasped her shoulders. Closing the space between them, he leaned forward until his face met hers. "You will never belong to anyone but me."

"I am not yours, not after being put out like yesterday's meal."

"Take her," Royce rasped, shadows of regret darkening his eyes as he pushed her toward his brother.

Guy gently pulled her from the room.

As they moved up the stairs side by side, Guy's hand steadied her movements. "He had little choice, Bethany."

Bethany shook off his hand. "Everyone has a choice. He made his," she said, refusing his explanation as she did his help. "Am I to be held prisoner?" she asked.

"Non, just given your own room so Damiana can sleep easy."

"I see," Bethany said, her chest constricting as she thought of the new arrangement, Damiana in Royce's bed.

"Non, I think you do not. Royce is blind when it comes to his ambition. He may have discovered what a witch Damiana is, but he will still take her as wife. Understand, Bethany, as the eldest, his life differed greatly from mine. He has never forgiven those who treated him like dirt beneath their feet."

"Am I to pity him and pay for the cruelness of others?" she asked, then rushed on before Guy could reply. "Hardship does not seem to have affected you."

"Royce and I, like you and Mary, approach life in different ways. Unlike Royce, I do not care what others think. In truth, he is the better Christian."

"It is too bad that he cannot look at life the way you do."

Guy shrugged his shoulders. "He would be happier, but

Royce has always been the serious one. Mother thought she should have laughed more when she carried him."

The reference to their mother piqued her curiosity. "What does your mother think of his quest for acceptance?"

"Mother has a partiality when it comes to her sons. Royce has fallen from her favor only once, and by now I believe she has forgiven him for rescuing me from the seminary."

"It would seem that even the saints smile on your brother." Her hand slipped to her stomach, sheltering the life that grew there. Earlier that day, she had finally accepted that the symptoms of nausea and dizziness that plagued her of late could not be attributed to illness and she had planned to share the joyous discovery with Royce at a special time. A tightness gripped her throat, and she swallowed the lump that formed there. If he cared so little for her, he would not be concerned for their child. "I will never forgive him for this." The fine embroidered girdle beneath her fingertips spoke silently of the magnitude of her folly. She had not only betrayed herself with this man, she had forgotten her responsibility to her people.

"Bethany, Christians forgive their enemies."

She stared at him. "Aye, they do. But I fear you have me confused with my sister, Mary."

As he opened the door, the chill of the tower room encompassed her. She stepped into the dark room. A feeling of dampness, like an evil specter, permeated her clothes and passed over her skin. She started to shiver and hugged herself to stave off the goose bumps.

Guy followed her in. *Merde*, I will see about a fire."

Rubbing her hands up and down her arms to warm herself against the cold, stagnant air, she paced about the small room. Royce had banished her to this prison, as he had at their first meeting. She could have no illusions about her place in his life.

Guy's voice drifted to her ears, but she ignored him. Her whole world had shattered. Never would she be able to piece the shards together. Love was a lie. She had believed in one man, hoped that somehow they would be permitted to be together. And what was her reward for loving her enemy? To be locked away in a damp, dingy room—worse, she had made her own prison, more binding that these stone walls. She could escape a tower, but not the enslavement of her heart. How did one forget such a love? In time did the terrible ache disappear? Pain as blinding as the sun shot through Bethany, and she moaned with the realization. Royce did not love her. Probably never had. Oh God! What a fool she had been.

Suddenly she felt the warmth of strong arms enveloping her. Bursting into tears, she turned into Guy's solid chest and sobbed uncontrollably for her dream of the future, of lasting love—all of which were lost to her.

"There, there, Bethany, do not carry on so."

She heard Guy, but could not stop crying. She tried to pull away, but his arms tightened on her. "Shed your sorrow and be done with it."

"Guy, I . . ." She could not tell him. No matter how caring and kind he was, her pride would not allow her to share even the most ordinary pain, let alone this earth-shattering anguish.

She felt him pick her up, and she clung to him as he carried her to the pallet. A blanket of despair descended on her, smothering all concentration, as if her mind and heart would not allow thought to enter.

He held and rocked her for an endless time. She was aware of his closeness but drew neither solace, nor sanity, from it. The pain she felt did not stop. Her unborn child needed her to be strong, yet she had never known such heartache. Like an endless cycle, the memories washed over her, reminding her with excruciating clarity of what she could never have.

"I am worried about you, Bethany. Look at me."

She heard the words, but could not respond. Guy's voice seemed to come from a long distance away, then fade.

"Bethany, you must stop this now. Please, my lady, answer me."

Bethany's stomach roiled and churned with dangerous waves

of nausea. "Please, let go of me. I am going to be ..." She covered her mouth as Guy released her, and she dashed for the chamber pot.

"Maida!" Guy bellowed and continued to call the cook's name until a guard responded and sent for the woman.

When Maida entered the room a few minutes later, she gasped. "My lord, what have ye Normans done to my little love?"

"She has cried uncontrollably and now she retches as though she cannot stop. I fear for her."

"My lady, can you hear me?" Maida asked, walking to Bethany's side.

Bethany could not answer, for her heaving seemed to continue without end.

"My lady, Bethany." Maida knelt down and brushed the hair away from her mistress's face. "Let me help you."

Bethany's eyelids fluttered, then lifted to meet Maida's worried gaze. "Leave me be, Maida. I hurt." Bethany took deep breaths to stem the retching, but it started anew.

"Aye, my lady, you must calm yourself," Maida soothed, laying her hands on Bethany's shoulders and massaging with a light touch the tense and tired muscles. "My lady, your heart will mend. The Norman is nay worthy of your love."

"Maida, leave me be, I say." Bethany gasped for air. "I just want to die."

"Stop, my lady, 'twill do you and your baby harm to speak so," Maida said.

First surprised by Maida's astute perception, then panicked at the revelation of her secret, Bethany met Maida's concerned gaze.

"You must say nothing, Maida," she said urgently. Then, noticing Guy's shocked reaction, she reached for his hand.

"Promise on everything you hold dear that this will remain a secret."

"A pregnancy cannot be kept a secret," Guy scoffed. "Time will betray you, not I."

Bethany gripped his hand tighter, trying to convey the importance. "Guy, for the sake of the child who will call you uncle, please understand. I wish to tell Royce myself when the time is right."

"Uncle," Guy echoed in awe.

He squeezed her hand in reassurance, then turned to Maida. "Stay with her," he said thoughtfully as he left the room.

"What do you mean, Guy? Is she ill or no?"

"She has made herself sick. Maida is with her, but I fear you must come," Guy said as he led the way.

Royce dreaded seeing her as he climbed the stairway to the tower. Each step brought him closer to a meeting he wished to avoid. He realized, to his shame, that he would rather face a horde of seasoned warriors than one Saxon lady.

Guy's words echoed in his mind, but he could not match them with the mademoiselle he had known. The moment he entered the room he understood. She had given up. He could not believe this of the woman he knew.

"A martyr? Bethany, I would not have thought it of you."

Her head raised at his voice, and tears glistened in wet paths down her lovely, pale face.

"Poor little *mademoiselle*, are we to feel sorry for you? Do you send my brother to fetch a strong shoulder to cry on?"

"Royce, you go too far," Guy warned.

"I know what is needed here," Royce snapped at Guy. As a commander in more campaigns than he wished to remember, he recognized what had happened. He had seen soldiers with this malady. Though his tactic would seem cruel, it was the only way. She could not be allowed to wallow in her own pity.

"Bethany must be cared for, Maida. See to it that she is treated like the invalid she is," Royce mocked.

"How dare you come in here and speak like this to me?" Bethany replied defiantly, though her voice was weak and her eyes red-rimmed.

Maida angrily jumped to her feet and, with her hands on her hips, spun to face Royce. "You son of Satan. Have you not done enough to harm this poor innocent? Leave be or, by all I hold dear in this world, I will take you to task."

Royce was stunned by the servant's vehement defense. "Bethany, your people do you proud service, but I think you should remind Maida who is in charge."

"Maida, thank you," Bethany said. She tried to stand but began to sway.

Royce leaped forward and caught her as she fainted.

"Dear God, what is wrong with her?" He laid her on the pallet and pushed her soft red hair off her forehead. Had he made a mistake? Was she truly ill?

"Annie," he whispered.

When she remained unresponsive, he turned to Maida. "Tend your mistress."

The servant snorted at the unnecessary command and pushed him aside. "Be gone and let me be about my business."

Royce raised an eyebrow at the disrespectful servant, but said nothing. He would deal with her later. Right now, he needed her services. He stepped back from the bed and paced the room, waiting for Bethany to wake. Never had he felt so useless. The feeling was disquieting. "By His wounds, what illness has she contracted?" he bellowed, but no one answered his command.

Guy glanced from Bethany to Royce. "You can do nothing here. Let Maida treat yon lady."

"*Non*, I will stay until I am assured she is better."

"I will need my tray," Maida said.

Guy left to do Maida's bidding.

Time seemed to stop. Not until her eyelashes fluttered did the normal tempo return, and seconds once again passed as she opened her eyes.

"Annie, what ails you?" Royce asked.

She looked at him as though he were a stranger, then turned away.

"She will recover, my lord," Maida offered.

Royce knew Bethany would not answer him and she was too sick to force the issue. Stubborn woman. Quickly, he turned away from Bethany and bumped into Guy returning with the medicine. Without saying a word to his brother, he left the room. The hardest thing he had ever done was to walk out and leave her without comfort or solace.

The hallway echoed his footsteps as he charged down the stairway without a destination in mind. He needed to collect his thoughts. For that he required solitude and room to pace.

To protect his family, he needed a Norman woman of noble birth. Bethany could not and would not understand that. Yet, she would do anything for her people. Strange, she could not see they were just alike. Both had bartered away a piece of their soul for another's benefit.

Bethany could hate him, but it would change nothing. His plans were in motion, and he would let nothing go awry. If he could put up with that shrew Damiana to gain his children's future, then, by God, Bethany would have to be content with her bargain.

It was a world of trade-offs—you gave up something to gain something. Of all people, did not Bethany understand that?

"Royce, wait," Guy hailed as he stormed across the great room to catch up to his brother.

At the summons, Royce came to a halt and slowly turned around.

"What is it?" he asked, wishing, not for the first time, he could dismiss his brother as easily as he could any soldier in his service.

Guy folded his arms in front of his chest.

Royce recognized the gesture from childhood. His brother had taken a stand and would not budge.

"I respect you in all things, Royce, and because I do, I will say this whether you take offense or no. You are wrong about Bethany—terribly wrong. If you cannot see the injustice of the situation, then I beg you, release her into my care."

"Into *your* care?" Royce asked sharply.

"*Oui.*"

Royce studied his younger brother. Guy's good looks and easy manner with the ladies had never been in doubt. Half of Normandy had gone into mourning when he entered the Church, the rest had breathed a sigh of relief. But he had not thought his brother had formed a serious tie to the Saxon woman.

"I have already told you that you are not to desire her."

"I care for her, but not as you think."

"I do not understand you, Guy."

Guy rubbed a hand across his face, took a deep breath, then met Royce's glare.

"If I thought she would consider me as a lover, I would defy you. I admire her. I simply wish to protect her."

"Mayhap I will send her to Scotland," Royce said, walking away from his brother.

"Do it! Send her away . . . if you think you can bear to part with her," Guy replied.

Stopping in his tracks, Royce turned around slowly, surprised by his brother's tack. "If you think I cannot, you are mistaken."

"Then prove it. Banish her today," Guy challenged with a self-satisfied smile.

"I need not prove anything to you or anyone else," Royce stated in a quiet commanding voice, the voice of battlefield orders and life-or-death decisions.

"You are a master at avoiding a trap, brother. Do you think I do not know the love that exists between you two?"

"You are a fool. Love can have no place in my life."

"There is a fool in the room, brother, but it is not I. If there is no place for love in your life, only hatred and despair will grow and prosper in your heart."

"Save your sermon for the gentle Saxons who fill the chapel, not me. I am a soldier. Men of war have no time for softness."

"Royce, men of war need softness and warmth more than others," Guy argued. "Their minds and bodies have experienced horror and need the tenderness to heal."

"I need no one," Royce growled, and walked away.

"Then it is good you have Damiana," Guy shouted at his back. "She will not waste one moment soothing your brow or helping you forget the past."

The king's advisor, Verdon, peeked around the high-backed chair when the brothers stormed from the room.

The de Bellemares were quite entertaining. Guy especially interested him. He must remind the king that Guy was once in training for the cleric's life. He would be perfect for a certain delicate task, and land and a title should overcome whatever moral objections he might have to kidnapping a nun from a convent. After he settled this business of Royce de Bellemare, Verdon would bring up the younger brother's usefulness.

As a diplomatic emissary, he had learned what he needed to, and far more than he wanted to know. Listening at doors had revealed a great deal, and the rest of his information had been supplied by the helpful cook, Maida. Now, *there* was a woman to set a man's heart afire.

Though he had acquired sufficient intelligence for the king's dossiers, he decided there was no rush in getting back. He wished some time to explore the lovely Maida's charms. The king would not begrudge him the dalliance, and the information could wait a week or two.

Mary could not wait for her uncle. Bram Mactavish believed William of Normandy would act on their behalf, but she would not leave their fate to speculation and the good intentions of others. Though she had begged her uncle to arrange a marriage for her, he had dragged his feet.

Now she wrote a letter to Hugh Sinclair, a laird of the north country, whom her uncle had proclaimed the fiercest chieftain in all the land. Pretending to be her uncle, Mary finished drafting her proposed betrothal to his clan, then affixed her uncle's seal with his ring. He had left it in plain sight. She should lecture him about such carelessness.

God would surely forgive her, for she was acting in the best interest of those involved. Did not the Bible say, God helps those who help themselves? As she folded the letter, she promised to do penance for her deceit. The chapel would be her home until she had atoned for her sins.

Dear Lord, I pray this will solve the problem and put aright what has gone awry.

With her petition winging its way to heaven, she gave the messenger the letter and one gold coin to insure his service. "Remember this must be placed in Laird Sinclair's hand and his reply brought back to receive the other gold coin."

It was all Bethany could do not to lose her midday meal. Watching Damiana prance and preen in the great hall before the eventide meal made her grit her teeth. The Norman lady had been drinking wine for the better part of an hour. Her eyes were glazed; her steps, awkward and exaggerated.

"Come here, slave," Damiana commanded, as to a hunting dog. Heads turned at the summons.

Bethany obeyed, cautioning herself not to lose her temper. A scene would only please Damiana.

"You see who is mistress here. When I marry, your room will move from the tower to the dungeon." She took a sip of wine, then let out a vicious laugh. "Whore, in my room behind a wall covering is a cask," she said, shoving an empty flagon into Bethany's hands. "Fetch my brandy, and be quick about it, or I will have your flesh stripped."

Bethany did not say a word as she turned and saw Royce and Guy standing in the doorway of the great hall. The warlord's arrival would signal the start of the meal.

"Damiana, you make yourself the fool. With power there is responsibility," Guy said.

Damiana made a little-girl pout. "Guy, do not lecture me on

how to treat the servants. Tonight, I plan to celebrate and I will not allow you to spoil my good mood."

Guy shook his head in disgust. Bethany's gaze sought out Royce. The lines around his mouth were pronounced and, for one heart-stopping moment, she thought he might say something, but he did not. She passed him without a word.

When she returned to the great hall with Damiana's brandy, dinner had begun. She tried not to notice the seating arrangement which placed the Norman lady at Royce's side in a position of honor.

When Bethany approached the main table, Damiana ripped the brandy from her grip and poured a liberal amount into her chalice.

"By my decree, you will wait upon my table. And mind, Saxon, if you are clumsy or lazy, you will be taken to task for it," Damiana snapped.

As dinner progressed, not a platter of meat or a bowl of vegetables, that Bethany placed upon the table met with Damiana's approval. She criticized the service and the preparation while never touching the food, preferring to gain sustenance through the fermented grape and grain of the field. The ordeal was a trial, but Bethany would not say a word. The experience was meant to humiliate and humble her. Damiana would not be pleased that it did neither.

Royce said nothing about the treatment or the change in their relationship. His silence hurt Bethany more than any of Damiana's vicious words.

After the meal had been consumed, Verdon was in exceptionally high spirits as he raised his glass high for a toast. "To the Norman Empire."

"Hear, hear," the Norman soldiers responded.

Bethany ground her teeth at the merriment.

"What is wrong, Bethany? Do you not share our happiness?" Damiana asked.

"Nay, I do not," Bethany said politely.

" 'Tis treason! Royce, what is the penalty for treason?"

Royce glanced up from his trencher; his eyes blazed dark blue. "Damiana, you have overindulged. I suggest you keep your own counsel."

"Ah! So you will do nothing against a traitor if she be a beautiful whore. William should hear of this, Verdon."

Verdon looked at the lady with disbelief. "What would you have me tell the king?"

"Tell him that Royce and his band harbor traitors in their midst."

At the outrageous charge, loyal Norman soldiers looked at the lady with open disgust and anger in their gaze.

"Enough," Royce bellowed. "You will leave my table."

"How dare you? I will leave when I am ready."

Royce slammed his palms down hard on the table and stood up, his anger making him seem even taller. "You are ready now."

Damiana tried to stand, but could not gain her feet. Her angry expression dissolved into a frightened mask. "Royce, something is amiss. Terribly amiss."

"You have had too much to drink," Royce said, unmoved by her changed manner.

"*Non,* 'tis not that. Something else is amiss." Damiana ran the back of her hand across her forehead. "I do not feel well. I feel . . . Good God, I think I have been poisoned!"

Royce shook his head at Damiana's weak attempt for attention. "Go to your room, Damiana."

"I tell you, I have been poisoned!" she exclaimed with a great deal of force for one who was dying. Damiana looked up and down the table, a red stain of fury climbing up her cheeks when no one believed her. She pointed at Bethany. "She did it. She is responsible. Verdon, promise me, if I do not wake, you will arrest and try Bethany for murder."

Verdon looked at her with pity in his eyes. "I think you should rest now, Lady Damiana."

She swayed back and forth, making several failed attempts

to reach her private flagon. "Bring my brandy. I cannot possibly rest without it," she snapped.

Bethany shook her head at the woman who could not make the stairway without grabbing onto every handhold and soldier in the room.

"Mind you do not spill any," Damiana ordered.

For a moment Damiana's drunken weaving and wobbling ascent of the stairs held Bethany's attention, then pointedly her gaze travelled back to Royce. She smiled and raised the flagon high in salute, silently congratulating him on his choice of ladies. She knew by the way he stiffened that he understood her gesture of contempt.

After Damiana had taken to her bed with the brandy clutched in her hands, Bethany stepped outside of the room and closed the door. Guy was coming up the stairs, his face drawn and his serious expression so different from his usual affable smile.

"Damiana could be dangerous to your health. The charge of treason is nothing to jest about," Guy said.

"No one will take her seriously. Seasoned warriors I have seen well into their cups, but Damiana puts them to shame." Bethany shook her head at the total disgrace Lady Damiana had made of herself.

"*Oui,* that may be true, but if the lady should suffer an untimely demise, you would be suspect."

"She is not ill!"

"Verily. I know that well enough. But Damiana is contrary enough to die and leave you to answer for the death," Guy said, chuckling softly.

"Guy, you jest. No one would go to such lengths for spite."

"*Non,* no one in their right mind. But methinks Damiana is unbalanced."

"If you are looking for an argument, you will not find one from me. What on earth does Royce see in the woman?"

"If you had a bloodline as long as hers, my dear, Royce would already have claimed you as his wife."

Bethany's laugh was bitter. "My line is known far and wide

in England. I enjoy the highest rank and respect among my people. Strange that I am not worthy of such a lofty position as wife to a conqueror—a man who has no claim to anything other than his brute strength."

"The world is not a fair place, Bethany."

"Aye. I know that well. If it were, Royce would recognize the regal standing of my house."

"Come, my lady. I will see you to your room."

Bethany pulled back. "Why?"

Guy hedged, " 'Twould not be amiss, a man seeing a maid to her quarters."

"Am I to be held prisoner there?"

"Not exactly."

"Guy, what exactly are you trying so hard to avoid saying?"

"Royce has ordered, for your own safety, that you be shown to the tower room and a guard posted so there can be no question of your loyalty."

"Who will be the guard?"

"Myself, Vachel, or Royce."

"He once asked me to trust him. I gave him that trust unconditionally. Now he treats me like the traitor he wishes to prove I am not." Bethany drew a deep breath to get her turbulent emotions under control. "He does not trust me, Guy, and nothing he can say changes that. I am the dreaded Saxon and must, therefore, be suspect."

Her head hung downcast like a hapless pennant without a breeze. "Pray forgive me, master jailer, but I must first retrieve the empty brandy container before I am jailed. Damiana would be in an awful fit come morning if the evidence of her overindulgence is left for all to see."

"Bethany," Guy said in a warning tone, clearly feeling the thrust of her sarcasm.

"Aye?," she responded with innocent demeanor.

Guy shrugged his shoulders and shook his head as if he had lost the argument. "Never mind, my lady. I will fetch the brandy container. 'Twould be best if you stayed out of Damiana's sight.

As vicious as her tongue is, she would slice your hide for the sheer pleasure."

"As you wish, my lord."

Guy placed his hand on Damiana's door, then turned back to Bethany. "My lady, do I have your word you will not escape, while I perform this service for you?" he asked puckishly.

"How could I ever hope to evade the whole Norman army?" Bethany replied, feeling an answering smile slip past her control.

"How could you, indeed?" Guy mocked.

"You have my word. I will not this night escape."

"Very well," he said reluctantly. Opening the door, he peeked inside. "Thank God, she is sound asleep. This may come as a surprise, but I did not relish facing her waspish tongue," he admitted as he entered.

After several minutes, Bethany began to wonder what was keeping Guy. She was about to open the door and investigate when he came out, his face white and his expression dazed.

"Well?" she asked.

"Damiana is dead."

Chapter Eighteen

"Dead?" she repeated, feeling the blood drain from her face and rush into a roiling pool in her stomach. If Guy thought this was a jest, his humor was poor. She ran past him into the room, praying to find Damiana passed out in a drunken stupor. But her form was too still; all movement was absent from her chest. Nay, she was dead.

Guy ushered the profoundly shocked Bethany out of the room. A woman in her prime had died, nay not died, been murdered. The loss of life, even Damiana's, shook Bethany to her very core. Her stomach felt queasy, and she feared she would disgrace herself.

"What now, Guy?" she managed to gasp.

"My lady, if I were you, I would say every prayer I knew. And when I ran out, I would make them up."

Suddenly, her legs buckled under her weight. "But I am innocent."

His arm encircled her waist and he held her close, taking her weight with ease. "I know you are, but . . ."

He did not have to finish his sentence. She pulled away from his steadying embrace. "Whose mercy should I pray for? God's or Royce's?" Bethany asked, wanting it out in the open.

Guy drew a deep breath. "Whose do you think is the most powerful?" Then he ran his hands through his hair and looked at Bethany. "To be on the safe side, I would pray to God to intercede and protect you from Royce. I think you will have more luck gaining a miracle than Royce's forgiveness."

Bethany did not reply as he led her down the halls, their steps in cadence sounding a strange melody on the stone stairs. She knew the destination. The tower. At least it was not the dungeon. As she stepped inside the bleak room, Guy looked at her, then gave a sigh. "I am sorry, Bethany."

After Guy had locked the door and posted a guard, Bethany sat down on her pallet, unable to believe what had happened.

A numbing chill overcame her. If just one person believed Damiana's silly rantings, it would mean her life. Earlier this evening, the ravings of a drunk had seemed pathetic and sad. Not so now. Fate had played a dreadful trick. Deathbed confessions were considered gospel. Damiana's accusation, no matter how false, would carry weight.

Surely Royce would never believe it.

But Royce wanted only one thing out of life, acceptance at court. Without hesitation he had set her aside in order to attain his goal. Oh, yes! Royce would believe it. She began to rock back and forth. Royce would believe Damiana's last words.

If he believed her guilty, he did not know her. Her hand rested on her stomach. Her child, what of her child? She would have to protect the baby. *Oh, little one, you have chosen a poor parent, indeed. This world will not be an easy place for you.* Tears filled her eyes as she thought of the stigma that would follow the child of an accused murderess. *I swear to you, my little love, that no matter what fate awaits me, I will provide a better life for you.* Her uncle would take the bairn and, if not, perhaps Royce would feel duty-bound to raise the child.

She drew a deep breath. A bastard raise a bastard? Nay! He

could not accept his own birth, let alone acknowledge the same of his own seed.

Bethany curled up on the pallet and drew the fur robe over her. Rest, she told herself firmly. She had the child to worry about now. The fleeting memory of her parents slipped past her thoughts. How they would have doted on their grandchild! That was gone ... buried with the invasion and the Norman conquest. A whole way of life had vanished. Tears slipped past her eyelids. Without a mother, would her child ever know his history?

"Gaston wants blood," Guy said. "He has gone to the king to petition for Bethany's death."

Royce rubbed his eyes. He did not want to deal with this mess. "Verdon, what say you on the matter?"

"Given Damiana's status, William will have to act as judge and decide. In any case, you will have a revolt on your hands if Lady Bethany is found guilty."

Royce laughed outright at the pronouncement. " 'Tis only Saxon women left in the shire and a few returning soldiers."

"*Oui*, but they are fiercely loyal to their mistress and I am told she has ties with Scotland. In fact, this land, long fought over by both countries, has enjoyed peace because of her blood tries with a certain Scottish laird," Verdon stated.

"*Oui*, I believe he would retaliate," Royce replied, remembering his last meeting with Bram Mactavish.

Verdon held his gaze. "Then, for the time being, do nothing that threatens the lady's well-being. You can leave her in the tower until William has made a decision. But to satisfy Damiana's family, I believe Lady Bethany must stand trial."

Royce poured several goblets of wine and handed them out. "Will you journey to London to seek counsel with William?"

"I will leave tonight." He raised the goblet to his lips and drew a long drink. "I would know where you stand on this, de Bellemare?"

Royce picked up his wine and sipped it slowly. "I do not in my heart believe the Saxon maid did the deed." Royce rubbed his chin. "None-the-less, a murderer is loose among us and we must catch the killer."

"I am aware that every Saxon in this demesne hated Damiana, but, unfortunately, Bethany of North Umberland had the most to gain by her demise," Verdon interjected.

"She is no murderer, Verdon, even if she can drive a man to drink."

Verdon smiled. "As what woman cannot?" He took a large sip of his wine. "Do you think Bethany knew of the murder attempt?" he asked as he wiped his lips with the back of his sleeve.

"Non, 'tis not her way. If she confronted an enemy, it would be face to face."

"You cannot ignore such a possibility," Verdon insisted. "Her people still look up to her. Though innocent of the murder, she may be guilty of giving her consent."

"I disagree, Verdon," Guy said. "Bethany faced Royce out in the open. A woman who would stand up for her people does not sneak around in the dark, giving orders to pour poison in a drink. She is no coward."

"Non, the woman does not have a cowardly bone in her body, if the stories I have heard are true. But have you forgotten about the wine?" Verdon asked as he leaned forward, his gaze locked with Guy's. "The vinegar?"

Guy's features sharpened at the reminder. "That was but a prank. This is out-and-out murder. I do not believe Bethany would commit such an offense against God and her conscience."

"Guy," Verdon said patiently, "in the right circumstance, anyone can justify murder. As soldiers, we do. She is as capable of rationalizing another's death as we. You let her beauty blind you."

"I think it is you who are blind," Royce said vehemently. "Of all the Saxons I have met, this woman has honor."

There was a speculative expression on Verdon's face as he

placed his empty chalice on the table. "I will let William know of your belief in her innocence. It will not surprise him that the de Bellemare brothers, so close in battle, are united in their defense of this woman."

"Have you finished your report?" Royce asked, wanting to change the subject.

"*Oui.* I believe William will gift the land to its rightful owner."

Though disappointed over the noncommittal answer, Royce would never show it. "Damiana's parents should be arriving soon," he said grimly.

"You do not need more trouble here. I will see to it that they are intercepted and detained at court. Not even La Marche would be so foolish as to decline an invitation to join the royal entourage."

A knock at the door interrupted their meeting.

Guy opened it to find Cedric standing in the doorway, his face drawn and eyes cloudy. The old Saxon entered the room and knelt before Royce.

"My lord, when I swore my fealty to you, it was with the understanding that it would not interfere with my previous oath to Lady Bethany. Is there now a conflict between my vows?"

Clearly interested in the strange behavior of Royce's serf, Verdon poured himself another goblet of wine from the flagon.

Royce gazed at Cedric, wondering which of them was the bigger fool. "There is. I would release you from your vow to me, but to do so would make you an outlaw. You can not hold allegiance to a Saxon in a land ruled by Normans."

"Then I must be an outlaw. My duty to my mistress is clear. I will not desert her."

The words pricked Royce's conscience. He did not need to be reminded that the woman was alone and defenseless.

"Very well, Cedric, you are released. Go now. Do not remain in North Umberland. If you choose to help your mistress, I will be forced to deal with you."

"I understand, my lord. But a man without honor has nothing."

The old Saxon bowed once and turned, marching out of the room with the same dignity with which he had entered. Royce could not help but admire his loyalty. Bethany had earned the love of her people. Suddenly, Royce understood what resistance he might be facing by placing Bethany's life in peril.

"I fear we will weather a storm of outrage at her incarceration. We need not concern ourselves about outright rebellion in the village. 'Tis the outlying areas, where there are still men to put up resistance, that worry me."

"What if her uncle takes a hand in this?" Verdon asked. "Will William need to send reinforcements?"

"If the Scotsman marches, we will have a bloodletting on our hands." Royce turned the full weight of his gaze on Verdon. *"Oui,* William will need to fortify our position."

"Royce, I think you should reconsider keeping Bethany in the tower," Guy said, a warning note in his tone.

"Non!" Verdon interrupted. "No one outside this room except for William can know that you believe her innocent. After Damiana's accusation, everyone, including Bethany herself, must believe the suspect is in custody."

"Why?" Royce bellowed, knowing such a deception would not sit easily on his shoulders.

Verdon paced the room as he spoke. "Because if she does not believe the trial is in earnest and King William holds dominion over her very future, then no one else will be convinced either. It is for this very reason I am ordering you—in King William's name—to act as though you believe Bethany guilty of this crime. Bethany is a Saxon accused of murdering a Norman lady; this case has political ramifications. If, as I suspect, you and Guy are right about Bethany's innocence, then the killer is very clever to have poisoned Damiana and let the suspicion fall on Bethany."

"What in God's name are you talking about?"

"If Bethany is found innocent, it must not be because she

was your mistress. La Marche must be satisfied that his daughter's death is being handled fairly by King William. The Saxons will learn that the law is impartial, that Normans and Saxons will be judged equally."

Royce conceded the point, but the look on his face spoke volumes. "No one, including Bethany, will know that I think her innocent."

Guy shook his head, "Someday, Royce, you will rue this decision of yours."

"I have been willing to accept the consequences of all my decisions since I was old enough to be in charge of men's lives," Royce said, knowing his brother was right. He rose to escort Verdon to the door.

"I will proceed with haste," Verdon said and held out his hand in friendship. "There is still the matter of this demesne."

As Royce gripped Verdon's hand, he could not stop himself from asking the question that had haunted him since the emissary's arrival. "Who is the man who has laid claim to this land?"

A sadness entered Verdon's eyes. "I cannot say. That pleasure belongs to King William." Verdon started to leave but stopped and turned back. "Royce, I am confident in the king's judgment. He will make the wise choice."

In the back hallway, Maida met with several other servants. "Tell everyone the meeting is tonight after the main meal."

The servants whispered among themselves. The rumors were running rampant. There was not a woman in the village who did not know the Lady Bethany was imprisoned in the tower.

"Any more news, Maida?" the milkmaid inquired, wringing her strong hands together.

"Cedric has just left for Scotland," Maida said, raising her hands in a sign for the other women to lower their voices. The whispered talk died out as one voice rang out.

" 'Tis worried I am that we will be in a war," a wine steward said, voicing the concerns of many.

"Nay, Lady Bethany has assured me, the Scotsman will not involve his clan."

"What is the plan, Maida?" Sumar Chadwick asked.

"Tonight, we will consider how best to show the Normans our power," Maida said with a dramatic sweep of her hands.

"Are you mad?" the serving woman asked. "We women are going to show our power?"

"In a manner of speaking, aye," Maida countered.

The servants muttered their confusion. Though what she said seemed impossible, Maida held the highest rank among them and was greatly respected.

With her finger poised in the air, pointing in the direction of the village, Madia ordered. "Pass the word throughout the village. Everyone must attend the meeting.."

"Why?" a serving maid asked.

"If we make a stand, it will have to be united to succeed," Maida answered in a confident tone that never wavered or hesitated.

After the small crowd dispersed, the Widow Chadwick approached the cook. "Mistress, what are you planning?"

For a moment Maida debated the merit of disclosing her plans ahead of time. If people were given time to deliberate, they might resist. But she trusted this woman. "I have decided to make things uncomfortable for the Normans. Very uncomfortable."

"You do not mean to injure any of them?" The widow looked stricken. It was well known that Vachel had established residency in her home and bed; many soldiers had found companionship with Saxon women.

"No more comfort to the enemy until our lady is released. Do you understand?" Maida looked closely at the young woman.

The widow's eyes opened round and large. "You mean no more sharing our beds? The Normans will never stand for it."

"They have no choice. We are in this matter as strong as the most powerful army. Women possess a weapon that is more devastating than the best-outfitted forces. We can bring the Normans to their knees."

"I think you have the right of it. But who is to suffer for this? Not just the Normans, but everyone involved."

"Aye," Maida said with a sigh. "It will not be pleasant for any of us."

"Vachel will be most distressed," Sumar said reflectively.

"Mayhap it will make him more aware of how important you are to him."

Sumar looked up at the cook. "Vachel is very kind and most considerate. In many ways he is more of a husband and father than was my Nyle."

"Do not worry. This will be resolved quickly." Maida patted the young widow's arm. "I do not think there are many men who will relish the thought of spending a cold winter alone. They will know how to convince the master to resolve this matter— more than we ever could."

Sumar nodded in agreement, then left with hurried steps, and Maida turned and went in search of her rolling pin. She was going to make her mistress her favorite dessert tonight. And although she was preparing a feast for Bethany, the Normans would have the worst fare imaginable.

It was going to be a fine day, she thought as she smelled the acrid odor of food sticking to pots and meat scorching. *Ah, the scent of victory!* Maida chuckled, and hummed a Saxon tune that had a bawdy lyric.

Bethany smiled at Maida when she entered with the tray. The aromas would bring a grown man to his knees. And though she had no appetite, she knew her strength was necessary for the health of her unborn child. "You have outdone yourself, Maida."

Bethany watched the cook set the tray on the cot and seat herself at Bethany's feet.

" 'Tis the only way we can talk. Eat, my lady."

Bethany wished Maida had not remained. Though she planned to eat, her appetite could not do justice to the delicious-smelling trencher. A poor showing would do insult to the servant after the trouble she had gone to.

With resignation, Bethany picked up the bread and tore a piece off. "What is it, Maida? Have you news?"

"My Lady Bethany, I wish to tell you of our plan."

"Plan? What plan?" Bethany asked warily, knowing Maida's penchant for trouble. "You must not place yourself in danger."

"You did not put yourself in peril when you faced the warlord on the field of honor?" Maida asked, a raised brow arched over her questioning gaze.

"That is different. 'Tis my responsibility to see to your safety."

"My lady, whether you say yea or nay, the plan is in motion." Maida crossed her arms beneath her ample bosom. "Now, do you want to hear the whole of it?"

Bethany pushed the food around and sighed. "Go ahead."

"We, all of the women, that is, have decided to thwart the Normans in every manner conceivable. First, their comforts are to be ignored. The cooking will be burnt or underfired and the laundry washed in vinegar and dried herbs that will produce an uncomfortable rash. But the main strategy," she said, sounding like a military advisor, "is to deny the men any intimate rights."

"Intimate rights?" Bethany questioned, afraid she understood but wanting Maida to explain.

"Aye, until you are free, no bedroom pleasures. 'Twill be hard on all of us. But, my lady, 'tis a sacrifice we are willing to make for you."

Bethany's mouth dropped open. She could not believe her ears. She had worried that they intended to take up weapons and place their lives in danger, but this!

"'Twas my idea, my lady. What say you?"

"I am not surprised to hear this came from your imagination.

Though your intentions are good, I am afraid 'twill serve nothing."

"Oh, it will work. When you draw your first breath of freedom, you can thank me while you eat your words. For now, though, just eat your dinner."

The king made preparations to depart. Damiana's parents were a considerable thorn in his side, insisting that Bethany of North Umberland must stand trial—under his court and no other. In addition, there was the unfinished matter of Bethany's father and the debt to be repaid. William would see that justice was served and, at the same time, oblige his own ends.

He studied the ring again. Only two names were engraved in it. Strange that Bethany was not listed with Mary and Bret. One would almost believe Gowain had not sired her. He threw the ring up and caught it in his hand. No matter, the laird had claimed the child as his, and William would treat the girl as such. The king knew only too well a bastard's plight.

A knock on the door interrupted his thoughts. "Enter," he commanded.

Verdon opened the door and closed it softly behind him. "You have some questions about the report, sire?"

"Is Bethany of North Umberland a bastard?"

"That is what I believe. Her father is, from the hints left in my ear, Bram Mactavish."

"Thank you, Verdon. I appreciate your diligent work. I have also noted Guy de Bellemare's background, and I agree with your recommendation. We will set the rescue in motion after North Umberland is secure."

"As you wish, sire. Is there any other part of the report you wish clarified?"

William took a sip of his wine and mulled over his concerns. "What, in your opinion, is the greatest threat?"

"My liege, the Scots are the ones to fear."

"I know, but I doubt they will interfere with my men. I have met with her uncle, Bram Mactavish, and he understands my power. The Scotsman is first and foremost a soldier, not a fool."

Verdon rubbed a hand over his face. "The lady in question commands the strongest loyalty. She has many supporters. I would counsel you that her popularity is great and reaches very far."

"Thank you, Verdon. I will take that under advisement."

Verdon bowed and withdrew from the king's chamber.

Royce had more in common with the little Saxon than with Damiana. Royce and Bethany were the kind of rulers this country needed. Farsighted and just, they would build a future, while Damiana had only been interested in the present and her own selfish pursuits.

But Royce had never come to terms with his birth. In all things but this, William trusted de Bellemare's judgment. Royce lacked tolerance and breadth of vision when it came to matters of station. Bethany of North Umberland's status would be greatly diminished if the warlord ever learned of her illegitimacy. It would prejudice him toward her. The king shook his head. He would have to sit in judgment for Royce when such matters came before the warlord.

The king was well aware of the La Marches' influence and the outcry they would raise over their daughter's death. He had to satisfy everyone involved. It would not be easy to work out a solution, but he was confident he had an alternative that all would embrace. At least almost all. Royce would find the solution not to his liking. But de Bellemare would serve his king; and although he would not like the command, he would follow it.

Taking a deep, long, swallow of wine, the king considered his decision again. *Oui,* it was his only choice, no matter who was upset by it. A king had to rule for his subjects. This was the only way to maintain peace and avoid a war.

As an afterthought, he made a note to take Ancil and Oriel La Marche with him. He did not want them in North Umberland, but they would not be satisfied until they saw justice performed.

Philip Gaston could remain by their side. William did not like that one. A soldier who admitted cuckolding the man he laid charges against was not trustworthy. To think of the viper turned William's stomach.

Yet he was bound and determined to end this situation with all the players involved. He had even sent a communique to the Scotsman, Mactavish, to meet him at Castle Renwyg.

In two days' time, William would decide the fate of Royce and Bethany. They would not be grateful, but it would be over.

North Umberland had to be secured, and—by heaven—it would be.

When he left Renwyg Castle, it would be a house united. For now, and for all the future generations that would serve the crown.

In the Scottish stronghold of Bram Mactavish, during the darkest pitch of night, Mary met with her intended, Laird Sinclair. He was a brute of a man, but his size would only aid her cause *and* he had an army at his disposal.

"Do ye promise before God and this company all you say is true?" Hugh Sinclair asked with a voice that nearly shook the rafters.

Mary swallowed the knot in her throat and tried not to appear frightened. The course of action she had chosen was dangerous.

"Aye. Everything I have told you is the gospel truth. Will you help me?"

The northern laird circled her, making his inspection of her clear. A hot blush burned her cheeks, but she refused to look down at her feet as though she had been cowed. Instead, she faced forward and tried to ignore the humiliating regard.

"I will meet with my clan. If they are in agreement, we will have a match. But I warn you, lass, if you have lied about any of this, your life will pay for the deceit."

Mary nodded her head, unable to speak. Her uncle stood beside her, equally silent.

After Sinclair left, her uncle turned to her. "Mary, lamb, da ya ken what you have done?"

Mary looked her uncle in the eye. "Aye, I have set in motion the means to free my sister."

"Nay, lass. You are committed. If his clan agrees, the betrothal is as good and binding as a marriage contract; but when he finds out you have lied, you will feel his wrath."

"Perhaps he will die in battle with the Normans. I am willing to take the chance."

"Ye are a brave lassie. I would not have credited you with such resolve. What is it that you are really after?"

"What I have been after all my life—justice," she said with such conviction and vehemence that she stunned her uncle. With a tiny smile of satisfaction, she turned on her heel and left.

Chapter Nineteen

Bethany walked back and forth across the length of her prison. She had never considered herself weak, yet after several days of spending hour after hour wondering about her fate, she had little doubt that she was, indeed, a coward. If Royce meant to punish her, aye, steal her life from her, then—by God—why did he not do it and have done? This waiting was punishment in the extreme.

The tower room, though plain and drab, had become her entertainment. Not a crack in the walls had gone unexamined. She had only herself as company; and as pleasant as she had once thought she was, it was a revelation to find out how many irritating traits she possessed. *If only* and *what if* travelled through her mind a hundred times. But no matter how many times she pondered the past, she could not see how she could have avoided this fate. Maybe Royce was right; maybe the course of their lives had been decreed before they were born and nothing they did could change things.

His betrayal was painfully sobering. Her lover and friend was now her judge and jury. God forgive her, she had, for a short time, allowed one man and his love to overshadow her duty. That foolish oversight would cost her dearly. But the thought of forfeiting her life did not frighten her as much as the loss of Royce's love. What a fool she was. To mourn a man's love over her life. She truly must be touched.

A key turned in the lock with rusty clarity, and she jumped up from her cot.

A stranger stood in the doorway next to Royce. His clothes were costly and his carriage regal. In a heartbeat, Bethany was certain she knew his identity: William the Conqueror. He moved into the room with quiet control.

"Bethany of North Umberland, I have a few matters to discuss with you." The king's voice, though soft, held authority.

Bethany raised her chin. "What makes you think I will converse with you, Norman?"

"If you value your life, you will."

She nodded her head. Her rebelliousness quickly died under his cold assessment. She noticed Royce neither spoke nor offered support. Her fears were confirmed. She would face her fate alone.

"You had everything to gain with the Lady Damiana out of the way."

"I do not dispute that. But as much as I despised the woman, I did not kill her."

At her declaration of innocence, Royce turned away and she whirled on him. "Think what you will, warlord, but I do not fight my battles by deceit."

The king moved between the two. "What say you, Royce? Is she guilty of the crime?"

Bethany held her breath.

"Whether she is innocent or guilty, my liege, is not my place to judge but yours," Royce responded dispassionately, neither looking at her nor the king.

She felt crushed beneath the weight of his betrayal. With every heartbeat, her pain increased. Royce despised her so much that he could not even look at her. He walked across the cell and clasped his hands behind his back.

"We need solid evidence. Did anyone see her do it?" King William asked Royce.

"Non," Royce replied from the corner of the room. Without turning around, he added. "And if they did, none would testify against her."

"You must sweeten the pot. Offer coin for the information. Plenty will be forthcoming then."

Bethany shuddered. Poor peasants offered coin to give testimony? She would be condemned to die. One could not expect those who had lost so much to turn down a windfall.

"What troubles you, mademoiselle?" the king asked, guessing her emotions correctly.

"You would buy testimony of war-starved widows? Why not offer me the money to confess? 'Twould save time and effort. My family's needs are as great as any, especially since the mighty Normans have come to our shores."

At her insolence the king peered down at her with an icy stare. "Your tongue is sharp. 'Twould do you well to curb it."

"Verily, what more can you do to me? My life is already lost," she returned, not one bit intimidated, her hands resting on her hips. "If I behaved myself, what could you possibly offer me? A gentle death? One that is more humane than the Normans are used to meting out?"

"No, my dear, I could offer you life," he returned, the barest sign of amusement about his lips and eyes. " 'Tis a vast difference. To face death is one thing; but to face life—now, there is another proposition entirely."

"Why would you even think to offer a Saxon life, when every true Norman knows the only good Saxon is a dead one?"

"God's teeth, enough," Royce commanded her as he walked back, then turned to the king. "You see, my liege, this is her true nature. She is not a biddable slave."

"I have always admired those who do not cower before me. You of all people should know I value a courageous soldier above all else." The king turned toward Bethany. "Whatever my reasons for offering you your life, Saxon, I think it would be in your best interest to humor me."

Bethany could not dispute it. She sensed he was growing weary of her wit. She nodded.

"Wise choice, my dear. I knew behind that mulish facade was an intelligent mind."

She looked at him with open skepticism.

"If I judge you innocent before an assembly of Saxons and Normans, there will be a small favor in return."

"A small favor?"

"*Oui.*" The king smiled, but the expression did not reach his eyes. "*Mademoiselle,* nothing in life is without a price."

Bethany swallowed as the hair rose on the back of her neck. "I am aware of that. Only I cannot imagine what you would ask of me." All she knew was that whatever the man wanted would cost her, and cost her dearly.

"You already have guessed who I am. I knew that the moment I stepped into the room. So, if you think about what I am proposing, it should become quite clear why I would save you."

"You have nothing to gain by my life," Bethany said to the king, then pointed to Royce. "Thanks to yon warlord, I no longer have land or title."

"I have heard that you have ties to Scotland," King William said smoothly, almost blandly, but he held her gaze in a stare that conveyed far more interest than his voice had.

"Aye," she admitted with reservation. "That is right."

"Then I have much to gain if you live to keep the peace. I would not be here, Lady Bethany, if it were not to my advantage."

"What do you wish in exchange for my life?" Perspiration broke out on Bethany's brow and, though she longed to wipe her forehead, she refrained, not wanting to call attention to her fear.

"Of your own free will, you must agree to do a service for me. No one must know of our arrangement."

Oh, Lord! Another secret bargain. Were the Normans all

fanatics about silent oaths? She remembered only too well the last one and what it had cost her in pride and pain.

"You would have your life and your freedom," the king went on, "but more importantly, your land and rule over your people."

Bethany's mouth dropped open.

"What mean you, my liege?" Royce barked, startling her so that she jumped back.

Eyes on Bethany, William held up his hand to silence Royce. "What say you, *mademoiselle?*"

"I say, my liege," she replied, the form of address a subtle acknowledgment of her acquiescence, "I would be happy to serve you. What, sire, do you wish of me in return?"

"You must wed Royce de Bellemare."

"Never!" Royce yelled, the anger in his voice striking like a loud clap of thunder that reverberated off the stone walls and floor, then receded to a hushed silence.

Bethany met his hostile gaze and inwardly cringed from the wrath shinning in his storm-darkened blue eyes. His disappointment she would have expected, but not this loathing and contempt. Under his piercing glare, she lowered her gaze. Her stomach churned as she nodded her head in acceptance.

Royce turned to the king. "I will not marry the woman."

"If you do not obey me, Royce, you will lose everything you have worked for."

"If I marry this low-born Saxon peasant, I will lose it anyway," Royce replied.

"The choice is yours," King William said quietly.

"I am of nobler birth than *you,*" Bethany said hotly.

Royce rounded on her. Under his stern visage, her bravado deserted her. He towered over her and she was reminded of their fight, when he had stood over her ready to draw her life's blood.

"You would make me the laughingstock of Normandy? A slave joined to a bastard! What place would my children ever have in society? I will see that every hour you spend as my wife will be a study in pain."

Bethany did not answer him. She could not. Her chin quivered so badly that she bit down on her lip to still the trembling. His words and his expression had robbed the voice from her throat. He meant every word he said; and for the first time in his presence, she tasted the rising panic of true fear.

Bethany looked at the short, white over-tunic and rich, blue under-tunic and shook her head in wonder. The lush feel of the material slipped through her fingers like the down of a newborn chick. Even she, the lady of the manor, had never touched such a smooth fabric.

She felt a touch scandalous in the Norman costume. The Normans liked their clothes snug; their tunics revealed rather than concealed the curves and shapes beneath. 'Twas not the only difference she noted. Saxon gowns were simple in design, embellished only with the fine embroidery of one's hand. Looking at the Norman ensemble, she saw no comparison. The stylish white-and-blue tunic, blue embroidered girdle, lavishly appointed, white fur mantle, and sapphire broach were the height of luxury and elegance.

All the finery had been a gift from William's wife. It was clear the queen took an interest in her husband's affairs, and William not only allowed it but approved. Without a polished metal in which to view her image, Bethany turned back and forth, looking over her shoulder to get a glimpse of the long under-tunic. The outfit clung to her as closely as a damp linen sheet. But an independent streak made her place the embroidered girdle back in the pouch in favor of her own. She would not desert her heritage.

The finery had been a godsend, for every Saxon and Norman that could squeeze into the crowded great room—known during the trial as the hallmote—stood witness to the event. Gowned regally in the queen's gift, she knew that neither her people nor Royce's could find her lacking, and this knowledge added the confidence she so sorely lacked.

The trial itself was a cleverly engineered mockery of justice. Though Royce and Bethany were aware that William had made his decision before the verdict was read, no one else would have guessed. William went through the motions better than she had expected. All the witnesses were brought forward and gave testimony.

With the skill of a grand strategist, William arranged that every witness who testified on her behalf had something against Damiana. Bethany's heart nearly stopped when her old nanny was called. Poor old Tayte had not been right in the mind since the invasion. She did not realize that by voicing her deep hatred for the Normans, she could, in essence, place herself under suspicion. William, however, was not interested in finding the culprit. He merely wanted to introduce others who had as much motive as Bethany to see the lovely Damiana dead.

Bethany literally drew a breath of relief when the last Saxon testified. By giving testimony in a Norman trial, her loyal servants courted reprisal. She did not want to see her people in danger.

Then the Normans gave witness before the king. Bethany was shocked at how many soldiers hated the Lady Damiana. Apparently the deceased's cruelty had also extended to Normans beneath her station. Warrior after warrior repeated the same damning story, blackening Damiana's memory. Philip Gaston took the stand, and Bethany swallowed the huge lump lodged in her throat. Under William's questions, Philip admitted his liaison with Damiana, her penchant for brandy, and even her mean-spirited side. Though he did not paint a flattering picture, he was merciless in his venom, trying to convince the king of Bethany's hand in the terrible crime.

Finally, Royce was called to speak before the king. Bethany watched his hard, unemotional features as he recounted the cold facts about his dead betrothed—and shuddered. Marriage to this man would mean losing one's heart and soul, for it was obvious he had none. Under pressure from the king, Royce admitted that many had a reason to murder Damiana, but it was clear from his testimony that he suspected Bethany.

Royce's distrust wounded her, but she could never show how his betrayal hurt.

Maida wrung her hands throughout the day and Bethany wished she could ease her loyal friend's fear. But everyone in the hall had to believe that the trial was real. It would be disastrous if Ancil and Oriel La Marche learned of the sham. William would have no choice but to sacrifice her. Though they were shy in the pockets, Damiana's parents held considerable influence with the nobles of the court.

Politics, Bethany knew, played a greater role in this court than truth. That justice would be served by an innocent verdict mattered naught next to appeasing a powerful family. William would never jeopardize a kingdom for a peasant.

Not for the first time, Bethany wondered why William took such an interest in her plight. She did not believe for one minute that he wanted to unite the war-torn area. If that were true, her sister could serve the same purpose while avoiding a possible conflict with Damiana's family. She thought of her uncle. Had he persuaded the king of his debt to Bethany's father? Dare she hope that motivated him? 'Twas possible, but somehow the idea of the king repaying a boon over twenty years old seemed as magical and wishful as any fairy tale, indeed more fanciful than fact. Nay, 'twas more to it; she was sure of it.

Hour after hour, the king, acting as judge and jury, listened to testimony. Throughout, Royce remained stoic, his features solemn and stern. She had never seen him this unfeeling and uncaring. Not ever. She thought a statue would exude more warmth than her betrothed.

At the end of the two-day trial, King William announced his decision.

"Not guilty."

Upon hearing the verdict, relief soared through Bethany's veins and her legs nearly buckled. Though William had promised her freedom, she had not known if he would keep his word.

"What?" Philip's face contorted with rage as he stood and faced the king. "How can you find this peasant innocent?"

The king crossed his arms against his chest and raised one brow. "Do you question my decision?"

"Non, sire." Nevertheless, it was clear Philip was not happy about William's verdict.

Bethany turned to Royce, who stood stone-faced across the great room, leaning one shoulder against the fireplace. His very stance distanced him from her. He would not look at her. Despondently, her gaze fell on the one friendly face that returned her smile. Guy.

Vachel joined her side and gave her arm a gentle squeeze in congratulations. Then he led her toward the king.

"Bethany of North Umberland, you are cleared of all charges and need not fear the court or Norman law," William said.

What was the protocol? she wondered. Did one bow or curtsy when being exonerated of murder? She nodded.

With a slight tilt of his regal head, the king acknowledged her gesture, then raised his hands and addressed the assembly. "Let all here gathered know the rule of law prevails. Today's hallmote has rendered a verdict of *not guilty.* This judgment is as final as a fallen soldier laid to rest. Henceforth, when you will recall and recount this trial, it will be as the memory of a slain hero who, in death, is not remembered for his sins but for his honor. Lady Bethany is innocent, and her good reputation is restored. Let no man question it.

"So, too, as a nation we must bury our differences and march forth together if we are ever to attain our destiny. Only if Saxons and Normans learn to live together in peace will the wounds of this country heal. It is, therefore, my wish . . ." He paused, holding the crowd spellbound as he glanced at each face before continuing. "It is, therefore, my *command* to see this Saxon house of noble birth and de Bellemare's line joined," he said as his fixed look focused on her. "Are you so disposed?"

Ancil and Oriel La Marche gasped and jumped to their feet.

The king merely lifted his gaze and stared at the couple until he had their attention and silence. When they bowed their heads and returned to their seats, King William looked back to Bethany. "Well, *mademoiselle?*"

She stole a hasty glance at Royce and wished she had not. His expression, as threatening as a storm-darkened sky, struck terror in her heart. Quickly, she swallowed her fear. "Aye, sire. I will wed Royce de Bellemare."

Barely a glimmer of a smile showed on William's regal face, but she caught the sign of approval before he turned to Royce.

"And you, de Bellemare? Will you have the lady?"

"I already have." Royce's insolence and sarcasm rang out in the hall. Philip chuckled at the lewd remark.

"You shame yourself with your lack of grace," the king said, his gaze passing over the crowd until Philip's laughter died under the sharp disapproval.

"I thought you were interested in the truth," Royce said, undisturbed by the king's censure.

Tilting his head slightly, the king said wryly "Very well, Royce de Bellemare. Will you take Bethany of North Umberland for your wife?"

"*Oui*, sire. I will obey your command."

Deep down, where she kept her secret dreams, his dutiful answer robbed her of any joy.

"Then it is done. I would have the cleric brought to me on the morrow. The ceremony will take place before the eventide meal."

Bethany dared not look at Royce again. A death sentence would have been easier to endure. Ironically, in sparing her life, King William had condemned her to a lifetime of punishment.

Uncle Bram attended the wedding in full Scottish dress. The Normans stared, but the laird seemed unaware or unconcerned over the furor his kilt caused. Mary had wed Hugh Sinclair and appeared content on her husband's arm. Bret, as always, was exuberant and happy. Cedric, her loyal captain of the guard, returned from his exile to attend.

Bethany looked around her and knew that she had not made a mistake. Family meant everything. She turned to take in Royce's hard, handsome features. Would he ever understand?

Her betrothed stood with Friar John before the fireplace at the end of the great hall. The flames outlined his features, adding a glow to his silhouette, but it was hard to ignore the color he had chosen for his vows—from his tunic to his boots, he was dressed all in black. Yet, though he acted like a devil sometimes, he had never looked like one. Now, he was the very picture of a dark saint. Bethany's knees wobbled as she took a deep breath.

Normans and Saxons lined the hall and stairways. She did not care to lose face in the eyes of those who watched her. She tried to gather her courage and appear unconcerned. But the way Royce watched her approach unnerved her. He had not stopped staring at her from the moment she'd entered the hall, studying her as if she were a leper who dared trespass on his domain.

Bethany endured his contemptuous regard, too proud to allow the pain to show. Courage came from the familiar, and she chanced a look down at her mother's gown. It was a loose-flowing, light-green tunic over an under-smock of white, and along the hem and cuffs her mother had embroidered a row of spring flowers. The season in which her mother had wed represented a time of rebirth. It was, no doubt, prophetic that she was to be married in the dead of winter. But winter was her favorite season, a time of hope, she reminded herself.

Following Northumbrian tradition, she wore her girdle and dagger. With her long red hair unbound and held back by a rope of delicate pearls, she faced Royce proudly. He said nothing. She was not surprised. A man who wore black to his own wedding did not expect to enjoy the ceremony, or the marriage.

She knelt before Friar John. The sweet prayers he said

bespeaking the solemn, holy state of matrimony touched her very soul. But her heart was heavy. Royce did not want her.

Friar John's face was gentle and kind, as if he understood her fear. "Bethany, do you enter into this marriage of your own free will, without any coercion?"

Here was her chance for freedom! But she could not take it. She had given her word.

Still, for the briefest of moments the thought tantalized her. What would it be like to be free? To live only for herself, without the weight of responsibility? Her gaze flickered to Royce's face. At that moment she knew. God help her, she still loved him. She looked at Friar John. "I do."

"Royce de Bellemare, do you enter into this marriage of your own free will, without coercion?"

"I do," he said through clenched teeth.

"What God hath joined together, let no man put asunder. I now sayeth you are man and wife."

With Friar John's words, it was time to turn to her husband for the kiss of peace. Bethany took a deep breath and raised her face to accept the symbolic kiss.

But Royce only stared down at her. A slap would have been kinder. Tears stung her eyes as she turned away, humiliated before her people and her God.

Guy grabbed her by the shoulders and whirled her to face him, his eyes filled with compassion and understanding.

"I am not as shy as my brother," he said to the assembly, then gallantly lowered his face to hers. As he kissed her cheek he whispered, "Would you let that pigheaded lout best you? Do not give him the satisfaction."

When Guy released her, Vachel took his place. Glaring past her at Royce, the old soldier showed his displeasure, then his gaze softened and returned to her. "Courage, my lady," he added as he, too, kissed her cheek.

Then, Cedric stepped forward and bent his wizened cheek to hers. "My lady, your mother would have been proud."

Tears blurred the old soldier's image, but she heard him step away and another take his place. She tried to brush her eyes, but a hand intercepted her wrist. "Let me, Bethany," her uncle said, and gently wiped the tears from her eyes. "Lass, there hasna been a more bonnie bride than your mother, until now."

Uncle Bram's eyes were suspiciously shiny as he grasped her shoulders with his large hands. " 'Tis a wonder that lout of a husband had the good fortune to be gifted with such a precious woman. Hear me well, lassie. I am prouder of you than any man has a right to be. Ye have done the clan Mactavish proud." He leaned forward and gently kissed first one cheek, then the other.

At his touching words, Bethany swallowed back fresh tears. She had never known her uncle to be so sentimental.

When he moved away, she was surprised to see a long line waiting to congratulate her—Saxons, of course, but also Royce's loyal soldiers. Bethany accepted their well wishes with humble gratitude. At the end of the line, King William stepped in.

"May I also offer my congratulations?" Then the King of England also bent to kiss her cheek.

Bethany thought the kiss was offered to rebuke her husband, but the king surprised her by whispering, "I remember your father and consider the debt paid in full. Do not make me regret it." Over her head he placed a gold necklace from which her father's ring dangled.

Tears again blurred her vision as Royce took one step forward and joined her side. She had not expected the support of the Normans or their liege lord. Suddenly, Royce's arm captured her shoulders and he spun her around in front of the full assembly. There, in the middle of the great hall, he kissed her hard on the lips, not with tenderness or passion but with punishing force. The crowd cheered, but the voices sounded like a distant din to her. When she was, at last, released, she trembled at the look on Royce's face. Could it be that he truly hated her?

"Now, every man here knows you are my property," he

gritted. He was about to say more, but the crowd swept them away on a tide of well-wishing, singing, and dancing.

The Normans and the Saxons acted as one. The jovial merry-making and rejoicing had but a single sound—happiness. Glad tidings abounded and, for once, the separate loyalties did not impede the good feeling. 'Twas a miracle, but the castle was united. Their marriage had solved at least one problem.

She watched the Norman soldiers take turns slapping their warlord on the back. "Glad we are, my lord, that you have taken a bride." Royce's only acknowledgment was a nod as he raised his goblet.

Bethany knew Maida would consider her plan a success, and if the men's reaction were anything to go by, perhaps it was.

All too soon, the women whisked her away from the celebration to ready her for the wedding night. 'Twas a foolish custom, for she was not a maiden. But she said nothing. The women, it seemed, were as happy as the men that the sleeping arrangements would be back to normal.

In the master chamber, the ladies attended her bath and brushed her freshly washed and scented hair until it shone, then left her upon the master's bed, gowned in a sheer smock.

She shut her eyes and waited sadly. He would never forgive her, never. Marriage to a Saxon slave instead of a Norman lady had destroyed his grand dreams. How would the years pass with such bitterness between them? They would slowly grow miserably old and, leaving their loveless union like the unharvested fields, dried up and shriveled.

The noise in the hall warned of the approaching men. Bethany quaked, and her face turned bright red. She prayed the men would not remain until the marriage was consummated. Her gaze shifted to her lap; the ivory smock she wore was scandalously sheer.

The door burst open, and the laughing crowd entered with Royce held high upon their shoulders.

She ventured a glance at her husband, but the look on his face was so unpleasant that she quickly turned away.

His men deposited Royce on the bed and, after several ribald jests and lewd looks directed at her, they left.

Bethany waited for him to speak, but he said nothing. When she could stand it no longer and raised her head, she came face to face with Royce's gaze. She swallowed the lump in her throat, for he was staring at her as if he would strangle her.

"Royce, what is amiss?"

"My lady, did you think it appropriate that the men see you attired thus?" He pointed to her thin wedding smock.

She blushed to her toes. "I thought to shield myself from their eyes would have been an insult to you."

"Insult be damned. Now, my brother, Vachel, Cedric, and dear old Uncle Bram know exactly what you look like."

A flicker of hope burned within her heart as she looked at her husband. Never before had she seen this thunderous expression on his face, and she had weathered many storms. Though his features were drawn and taut, anger alone did not appear to be the cause.

"Royce, are you jealous?" she asked, elated by her suspicion.

"*Non,* I am but embarrassed to be saddled with an immodest wife."

"I see," she said, suspecting he lied. Though he acted indifferent to her, he was not. There was only one way to breach the defenses he hid behind. Taking a deep breath, she turned toward him, deliberately shifting the loose-fitting material so that the opening of the smock slipped down over her shoulder.

"Annie," Royce said, visibly swallowing as though his tunic were too tight around his neck, "Never let another man see you thusly."

His eyes, smoldering with inner heat, never left her as she provocatively shifted again, baring more to his eager gaze.

"I had not planned to let any man into the bedroom but you," she said, realizing that his emotional barriers were crumbling like the walls of Jericho from the blast of Joshua's trumpet. She wiggled, slipping the smock further down her arm, and watched his nostrils flare at the tantalizing sight of her bared breast. Though he willed it otherwise, his reaction proved he could not remain impervious to her charms. He wanted her.

"That, wife, is how it should be."

"Have you forgiven me, then?" she whispered as her hand slipped behind his neck and gently massaged the tense muscles there.

"Never," he half growled, half groaned as his lips descended on hers.

Chapter Twenty

Royce took her in his arms with such force that, for a moment, she actually feared him. When she trembled, he smiled. "Are you frightened, Annie?"

All the moisture in her mouth dried up and she could not have responded if she'd wanted to. Nor would she have given him the satisfaction of knowing what he did to her.

She shook her head nay, then, with all the bravado she could muster, looked straight into his gaze.

He laughed. "You think I cannot feel your fear? Though you try to hide it, I see it in your eyes. Oh, I will give you credit: you can bluff your way out of more trouble than anyone I know. But, my dear, I am onto your game. You wanted a powerful husband. A man who would give you all that you had lost."

That he could think her so cold and calculating! She pushed against his chest and wedged enough space to gain her freedom. Quickly, she flipped over in bed, presenting her back to him.

"Now, Lady Bethany, you have what you fought and schemed for," he said, drawing little circles on her shoulder with the feather-like touch of his finger. "Poor Damiana. At least she was honest about her intentions. You are now my wife, and I want to see a little appreciation."

"What?" Whirling back around to face him, she was stunned by the look on his face. The gleam in his eye left little doubt of his intentions or his interest. He looked every inch the warlord and every inch the conquering male.

"Don't be so coy. You have chased and caught me, mayhap even murdered for the right to bed me legally. Now that you have won your prize, is the passion you displayed gone?"

"You are despicable," Bethany gasped, unable to believe his baiting and unsure how much was in jest and how much in earnest. "You believe I killed Damiana!"

"No," he said softly, ignoring her surprise. "Did it ever occur to you that I had to behave so during the trial because of Damiana's charge?"

Relief soared through her, but it was short-lived.

"I have paid highly for the honor, or dishonor, of your hand. And you, my dear, must pay your portion."

"You mean, I must satisfy your lust."

"You are not as witless as one first thinks."

"Have you forgotten that you hate me? Aye, 'tis true, I can see it in your eyes."

"Then it is your job to make me forget what a cunning little schemer you are—at least, while we are in this room."

"You act as if all I have to do is bed you and all is right between us," she scoffed, feeling pain slice through her heart.

"It is a start," he said as his lips grazed the sensitive skin of her neck, sending ripples of warmth through her.

"You cannot be serious," Bethany said, jumping out of bed to put some much-needed space between them. She did not mind playing the vixen, but never would she accept treatment as a whore.

"I am, Annie. And I am also very impatient." He looked at her with such fervor that she literally shivered. His gaze slowly swept her from head to toe, igniting a flame of longing deep within her soul.

"Stop it, Royce," she demanded with false courage, power-less to deny her own passion and hoping to gain time to abate his ire.

He rose from the bed and stood before her with his arms folded across his chest.

"Annie, your husband is waiting," he said in a voice of liquid velvet.

"Then, you will wait all night." But deep inside, she knew the battle was lost. She ached for him.

"*Non*, I will not," he said with a wicked chuckle that mocked her.

"Royce," she said, backing away from him despite the pull of his sensual charisma. "We need to bury the animosity between us before—"

"Do we?" He stalked her, pinning her body up against the wall; then, he lowered his lips to hers. "Why?"

"Because we are husband and wife now. We must work together."

"I am more than willing to . . ." His lips touched hers.

His kiss held none of the anger she had tasted after their wedding, and she felt herself responding as she had so many times before. He deepened the kiss, slanting his mouth over hers and gathering her in his embrace. A swelling wave of sensation broke over her, and she fought to keep her reason. "Please," she breathed.

"Annie, the time for talking is over," he whispered, his lips covering hers again. Then, he swung her up in his arms.

As he carried her to his bed, Bethany could feel every corded muscle in his chest. The hard strength bespoke security. The musk she smelled had the scent of lust. And the taste of his kiss, passion.

The sensation of floating ended when she felt the fur cover beneath her. Climbing up onto the bed, Royce leaned over her. His gaze, followed closely by the gentle caress of his hand, slowly travelled up the length of her, stopping to inspect her hips and breasts with an intensity that seared her. Desire, hungry and hot, glowed in his feverish eyes as they met hers. When she moistened her lips, a smile spread across his.

He cradled her face in his rough callused hands, his thumbs gently tracing the line of her jaw. "My beautiful little Saxon. Though lovely, you are a willful little witch who meddles in my life, questions my decisions and shamelessly offers her opinions whether I ask for them or not. You are the worst possible match, and you have ruined my plans, taken away my sons' future; but God help me, I still desire you more than any other woman I have known."

His lips descended on hers, the scorching kiss taking the bite out of his reluctant admission. A secret joy bloomed within her as she realized Royce did not fight her, but himself. His mind might reject her, but his body did not. With languid ease, his tongue sensuously stroked her lips, sliding back and forth, his warm touch and sweet breath creating a delicious sensation that made her quiver. The very air she drew carried his taste and touch. As the tip of his tongue grazed past her teeth to caress the moist warm interior of her mouth, she moaned, feeling a million tiny waves of desire flow through her.

Royce's essence filled her, and her senses responded as she imitated his movements. Their tongues danced and mated in a ritual of lust and desire, of love and passion. Suddenly, Royce's kiss changed from long and drugging to sweet and savage. A sizzling excitement streaked through her, leaving her nerves raw and exposed, their perception heightened to every sensation.

His lips moved from hers and nibbled a path down her neck to her collarbone. A shiver of pure pleasure flowed through her as she caressed his neck and ran her fingers through his thick, ebony mane. He slipped her curls aside, removing her smock, and his mouth travelled to the valley between her breasts. Suddenly, his teeth gazed the tender skin of her breast, from the base to the crest. When the rough texture of his tongue circled and then stroked the delicate tip, jolt after jolt of pleasure shot through her.

"Royce," she half whispered, half cried.

"Do you want me?" he asked, his lips and tongue returning to caress her breast.

She tried to speak, but the words caught in her throat as he drew the peak of her breast between his teeth, sucking softly until she nearly fainted with pleasure.

"Do you, Annie?"

Her fingers curled and grasped his hair as she arched her back. His lips rained gentle kisses on her flesh, his mouth moving languidly from one breast to the other as a shiver travelled through her. He could drive her insane with the sweep of his tongue or the caress of his lips. Indeed, he seemed intent on doing just that.

His lips returned to hers in a kiss that made her perspire from the heat.

"Tell me, Annie," he whispered against her mouth.

Tell you what? she thought. Then, suddenly, she knew. Like her, he needed to hear the comforting words of love. Strange, to think Royce experienced doubt. With half-parted lips, she grazed his cheek and made a path to his ear, her breath raising goose bumps on his skin. "Norman, you may be the worst possible choice for a husband, but I would not have another."

Whether it was the sound of her voice or the reassurance of her words, Royce's manner changed. The gentleness disappeared, replaced by raw hunger and need. She revelled in the way his hands moved over her, urgent and possessive. The excitement that surged through her caused an answering response to his cadence and tempo. When his fingers dipped low to the crease between her legs, wave after wave of intense desire surged within her. The slow, teasing strokes of his hand quickened until the physical need had her thrashing about. As she moaned her pleasure, he slipped a finger deep inside her, nearly driving her over the edge. He stoked the heat that blazed within, needing release, needing fulfillment, needing him. Suddenly he withdrew.

Unable to bear the separation, Bethany reached for him as she crooned his name.

In his haste, Royce half-ripped the clothes from his body and returned to her embrace. In the firelight, his eyes shone like rare sapphires. He kissed her, entering her with as much need as she.

In a rhythm as old as time, they danced to a sensual tune, clinging to one another physically, but—more importantly— with bonds of love and hope. If those tender emotions existed, surely trust and tolerance would follow.

Whether he sensed the difference or not, Bethany did. She hoped that the regrets Royce harbored in his heart would lessen. For herself, there could be no regrets.

Suddenly, all thought fled her mind as she experienced an exquisite release filled with a rush of color and sound. In the throes of her own climax, she heard Royce's muffled roar, his husky voice rumbling through her like a strong wave crashing against the shore. Bethany hugged her husband to her, slowly drifting back on a cloud as light and wonderful as any she had seen in the sky.

In his arms, she reached heaven. Bethany did not look to any other salvation.

Awareness intruded on her dream-filled mind, and Bethany stirred slowly. By the amount of light in the room, she judged it was late in the morning. She reached over for Royce, but his place was empty and cold. He must have risen early as was his custom. Remembrance of the passion shared in his embrace stole through her, and she hugged the knowledge to herself.

Maida entered the room without a warning or a knock. "Ye are awake. The master said to leave you sleep. He seemed to feel you would need your rest," she finished, chuckling at her jest.

Bethany felt a blush steal up her cheeks.

"What are ye so pleased about, my lady?" Maida asked as she prepared the morning bath.

"Maida, I cannot believe how happy I am. This marriage is a godsend for our people."

"The Saxons will benefit from this match, to be sure. But what of you, my lady? Is it a trial for you to bed the enormous beast?"

Bethany gasped in feigned outrage, then broke down into a fit of delighted laughter. "You know me too well. Aye, I am happy. Happier than I have a right to be."

Maida turned away, wiping quickly at her cheeks. "Hush now, my lady. Let me help you with your bath. The midday meal will be on the table soon."

Bethany threw her arms around Maida. "No tears today, Maida. 'Tis too joyous an occasion."

But Maida met her mistress's gaze, her wise, old eyes brimming with moisture. "You have a right to be this happy, and more. No one in this demesne deserves better." Breaking free of Bethany's embrace, Maida began to pour fragrant herbs and spices into the bathwater. "Hurry up, my lady. Ye be mistress of this castle as ye should be; but, even so, ye do not want to keep your lord waiting."

Once again Bethany donned the queen's gift, the beautiful Norman tunic. Attired in the rich fabric, her hair combed and held securely in the snood, Bethany could not believe how different the dress made her feel. She looked every inch the lady of Renwyg Castle, the dignified wife of the austere Norman warlord, Royce de Bellemare, and she was filled with a new confidence born of the station. She only wished the ribbing due a new bride were behind her. Royce would beam from ear to ear and she was glad of that, but the teasing embarrassed her. She offered a prayer to St. Bede for courage and patience.

Descending the staircase, she heard Philip's nasty voice and stopped to listen. "Damiana would be happy for she has had the final revenge. No offspring of a bastard and a slave will ever be welcomed at court."

The man's harsh words sliced through her as the noise of a scuffle sounded from below. Several blows were dealt out before the fight ended. Quietly moving halfway down the stairs, she peeked through the stone opening to view the great room.

Royce stood over Philip, clenching and unclenching his fists. Testing his jaw, Philip glared up at Royce with a look meant to lay him low.

King William approached and said to the soldier lying in the rushes, "How dare you? Need I remind you that your sovereign lord is also a bastard?"

"Your forgiveness, my lord," Philip said petulantly.

The king scowled. "You will leave here immediately. Accompany Ancil and Oriel La Marche now."

When Philip scrambled to his feet, Bethany stole back up the stairs. She did not want to enter the great room on the heels of this disturbance, but her delay could only be temporary. Taking several deep breaths, she reached the top of the stairs and came face to face with Maida. The cook's look of dismay indicated she had overheard the trouble downstairs.

"My lady, 'twill be all right."

"Nay, Maida, it will never be made right." Bethany sighed, her lips trembling. Philip's hateful words were true, and the bitterness they resurrected would linger long after his departure. "I need a moment," Bethany said, offering Maida a weak smile. "Would you fetch me a cup of water?"

"Aye, my lady."

When Maida left, Bethany stood alone, her heart aching with the acceptance of the truth. Royce would never truly forgive her. He might love her, but love was not what he sought. Their marriage had destroyed his lifelong dreams.

Maida returned and, nodding her thanks, Bethany took a grateful sip of water. But the cool liquid did not wash away the bitterness. She swallowed the taste of defeat, resolving to make the best of their marriage. She had little choice. She loved him more than her life.

The head table held her husband, his brother, the king, his emissary, and Vachel.

"My lord." Bethany curtsied low before the king.

"Lady Bethany, 'tis happy I am to see you could join us," William said with a broad smile that gave no indication of the unfortunate incident.

She took her place between the king and her husband. Royce barely acknowledged her, a telltale sign that Philip's words had struck home. Though his retreat from warmth to indifference broke her heart, she could not show she was aware of the reason. So, assuming an uncaring air and smiling as though her world were naught but happiness, she turned to face her husband. "Royce, I overslept. You should have awakened me."

"'Twas not necessary," he answered curtly.

"My lady Bethany." The king claimed her attention. "Would you do this sovereign a favor? My little wife will join me in a week's time. Could you possibly be prevailed upon to entertain her?"

"Aye, my lord," she said, shocked that she would meet the queen.

"Good, Matilda travels overmuch. I fear she is often worn out."

"'Twill be no trouble, my liege. Long has this hall been known for its hospitality."

Without glancing in her direction, Royce stood and spoke to the king. "My liege, we must be about our business if you want to be done in a fortnight."

The king smiled at Bethany and gave her hand a comforting squeeze, then he rose to join Royce. As Bethany watched them go, she marveled at how attuned King William was to those around him.

Every soldier, save one, followed their liege from the room. No sooner had Royce shut the main doors than Guy pulled out the chair beside her and sat down. "My lady, you missed the excitement."

"I did not miss it," she replied with quiet dignity.

"Have patience, Bethany. 'Tis not everyday that Royce discovers he is in love."

"Love!" Bethany scoffed. "He does not know the meaning of the word."

"Oh, he knows the meaning now. Before meeting you, he never had occasion to."

Bethany shook her head in denial. She wanted desperately to believe Guy. Her heart, her very soul needed to believe, but fear of betrayal and rejection kept her from it.

"He will change his mind about your lineage. Give him time, Bethany. It takes awhile to get over such a disappointment."

"Does it? I seem to remember a Norman lord taking my home and my demesne and expecting me to accept my lot."

"Then have pity on your husband. To my knowledge, he has never been in love before. The shock might kill him."

Chapter Twenty-one

Guy shook his head at his brother's surly behavior as they walked the battlements together. Like a dog unable to scratch an itch, Royce's bark nipped all. "Brother, the men will revolt if you do not get your temper under control."

"Mind your own counsel, Guy," Royce warned.

Royce had been in a foul mood since Philip's departure a week ago. "If your Saxon wife displeases you so much that your waking hours are robbed of joy, then give her over to the convent."

"Guy, leave be; I warn you."

Guy did not acknowledge the request. But when Royce started down the stairs leading to the courtyard, Guy merely fell into step behind his brother.

"On further thought, Bethany's charms would be wasted in a convent." In the dim circular stairway, Guy's voice echoed off the walls.

"Guy," Royce gritted as he walked through the doorway into the weak light of the winter's day.

"Apply for a dispensation to dissolve the marriage, then you can charitably dispose of the girl. Gift her to one of your men, preferably someone who will appreciate her."

A fist crashed into Guy's mouth. "Enough! Do not dare to lecture me about my wife."

Lying on his backside, Guy rubbed his jaw to ease the pain radiating from the powerful blow. Thank God Royce had not thrown his fist in earnest or his jaw would not be throbbing but broken. "Royce, if you have a problem in the bedroom, solve it there. Not here, before the men and me."

"If you wish to remain in one piece, you will keep your mouth closed," Royce snarled.

Guy rose, brushing off the dirt and twigs from his clothing. "Are you not content to make the lady's life miserable? Is it now necessary for everyone who crosses your path to suffer your wrath?"

"I said, *enough!*"

"I will say one more thing, then gladly take my leave of you. Do you plan to treat your child with such cruelty?"

Royce rounded on him with such force that Guy literally jumped back.

"What child?" Royce hissed, his eyes narrowed suspiciously.

"The child your wife carries."

"What do you know of this?"

Guy fingered his tender jaw, hesitating while considering the wisdom of broaching the subject, then shrugged. "When you locked Bethany in the tower, she became sick. Maida guessed her condition, but Bethany made us promise that we would not tell you."

"And you felt honor-bound to her, not me? You would be wise to reconsider your loyalty," Royce fumed.

"I kept my word," Guy snapped. "She wanted to break the news to you when the time was right. I assume you have given her no opportunity to share such happiness."

"You do not know what you are speaking of."

"Are you still punishing her?" Guy asked with uncanny insight.

Royce cleared his throat and pointed to the practice field. "Look you to where your talents are needed. The raw recruits remind me of you when, years ago, you chose soldiering over salvation. Perhaps you can make them see the light. I have other duties I must attend."

Guy's gaze was long and measured. Whenever Royce had a problem, he covered it with arrogant bravado and confident bluster until he found the solution. Satisfied by the telling reaction, Guy nodded his head in acknowledgment and turned to do his brother's bidding.

Royce found Bethany hunched over the chamber pot, retching into the container.

"Lord but this is draining the life from me," she whispered. Leaning back, she tried to straighten but could not manage it in her weakened state.

Without a sound, he walked over to her and lifted her delicate body into his arms. Ignoring her startled protests and squeals of resistance, he carried her to the bed.

"What is it, Annie?"

She looked at him, misery and anxiety clearly exposed in her eyes. "Royce, why have you returned so soon?"

"I forgot my gloves," he said, the lie coming easily to his lips. "Now, tell me, why are you sick?"

" 'Tis nothing. I do not feel well."

"I can see that, but what ails you?"

"Royce, please. The reason will not bring you pleasure, and I am too weak to fight with you."

Her statement sent a stab of guilt through him. "Could it be you carry my child?"

She stared at him, clearly wondering if he knew or had only just guessed.

"I know you hate me, Royce. I would not want our child to feel the same wrath."

"I would not hate a child," he said, taking her hand in his.

Tears slipped down her cheeks. "The secret will be out in time. Aye, I am in the family way. If you wish to deny the child, that is your choice. Surely all your Norman friends will understand your reluctance to claim a baby of mine."

Royce scowled. "Stop it, Annie."

"Stop telling the truth?" she asked, pulling her hands free of his grasp. "You did not wish to wed me. Everyone knows that you do not wish a child of our union. You can say the child was conceived before we wed, which is true."

"Annie, I swear, you would try the patience of Job."

"If Job were here, I am sure he would be easier to live with than you."

With a sigh, Royce leaned over and gently kissed her lips. "I am sure he would be, too, but I am afraid it is your lot to be married to me."

She took a deep breath, then suddenly reached for his hand and placed it over her stomach.

In wonder he felt the baby's movements beneath his palm. "My child!" he said in awe. The moment the words left his mouth, he envisioned his future as a father. With a frown, he prayed he could spare his son the pain he had known. Bethany looked at him warily.

"Verily, you do not want our child?" she demanded, her hurt, angry gaze burning into his.

" 'Tis not that. No matter if I claim our son or not, he will never know acceptance at court."

Her expression dissolved from hurt into lines of hopelessness. "Will we always have this between us, Royce? Will it forever be there for our children to witness?"

"I do not know." He looked away and stared at the wall, the pain of childhood returning. "I have lived with the misery all my life."

She pulled out of his embrace and scrambled off the bed. "Because your sire abandoned you, bitterness clouds your reason. If that is your wont, then do not bother to claim the child. Bastards make out very well in this world."

Royce's anger exploded. "You go too far, wife," he snarled and followed her.

She whirled around to face him. "Do I?"

"*Oui*, you do," he said, stopping just inches away.

As in their first encounter, they faced each other as combatants. "Annie, you will learn that I do not give ground."

"I have already learned that by the boot-marks on my back," she returned.

"Enough," he bellowed. "I have told you I will give you and the child protection." Suddenly, he was thrown back into the past and heard his father uttering the same words to his mother. He was reminded of the bitter fights between his parents before his father left. Angry and frustrated, he ran a hand through his hair. He did not want to repeat his sire's mistake, but could think of nothing that would change things.

"I do not believe you, Royce. You want neither me nor my child." Bethany looked at him with tears clouding her eyes. "There was a time when I thought you were the fairest man who walked this earth. How disappointing to find you are not."

Bethany's words stayed with him long after he had left her side. He had once been everything to her, but had now fallen so low that in her eyes he was less than a knave. Conversely, her worth had risen in his estimation. Her people loved her; his own men adored her. There were none who met her who did not come away thinking she was a precious jewel. Saxon heritage could not dim her brightness or tarnish her luster. She was a rare and beautiful woman, and he had callously thrown her regard for him away.

He walked the battlements wondering what he could do to win her affection back.

"Did you put your foot into it again?" Guy asked from behind.

Irritated, Royce whirled around at the interruption. "Someone should tie a bell around you."

Guy chuckled. "You were so deep in thought you would not have heard it."

"Perhaps you are right."

"Bethany?" he guessed.

Royce nodded. "I do not know what to do about her. I swear a band of savage Celts would be easier to face than her wrath."

"Did you tell her Philip's words meant nothing to you?" Guy asked.

"Are you lack-witted along with ill-humored?"

"Then you have a dilemma. You want the pleasure of marriage without the payment."

"What payment?" Royce asked, impatiently.

Guy smiled. "The currency of love is trust and respect." He slapped Royce on the back in fellowship. "You are unwilling to part with those for fear they will not be returned."

"You talk in riddles."

"Do I?" Guy held Royce's gaze.

"Non, you speak the truth. But 'twill be hard to change after all these years. You might find this hard to believe, Guy, but I do not like change."

"Verily?" Guy put his hand to his forehead as if the news shocked him. "You, who are so open to new ideas and tolerant of those who do not measure up to the mark? Why, I find that hard to believe."

Royce chuckled, enjoying his brother's sarcastic wit. "Only you would dare bait me."

" 'Tis necessary. You take yourself too seriously. 'Tis simple," Guy said as he threw his arm around Royce's shoulders. "Decide and be done. Or the Saxon maid might tire of waiting for you."

"I doubt that," Royce said, walking toward the turret.

"Would you like to risk it?" Guy inquired.

"Non," Royce said with a finality that surprised even him. Suddenly he knew the truth. He would surely die if Bethany were not in his life. The depth of his feelings for this woman shook his very being. Yet, how to come to terms with her

heritage? Perhaps as the weeks and months passed, so, too, would the fresh hurt of his broken dream fade into a dull pain. He looked up at his brother. "When the day dawns that this marriage is more a blessing than a curse, I will proclaim my love to Annie. But baring my soul to a woman, let alone a wife, is unknown to me."

"I know. But you must speak the truth to keep Bethany and attain that which you search for."

"How do you know what it is that I desire?" Royce questioned, raising a skeptical eyebrow.

"All your life you have wanted respect and acceptance. I tell you true, if you cannot find it with Bethany, you will never find it at court."

Bethany checked her tunic and under-tunic. Her mother's finest white and violet gowns were her most prized possessions and worn only on special occasions. Though she preferred the Saxon style of clothing, in a show of courtesy to her new queen, Bethany ignored her own girdle and attached the jewel-encrusted one the Norman sovereign had sent as a gift.

Bethany hoped Royce would notice her concession along with the endless hours of preparation she had expended on the night's festivities. She took a deep breath. If tonight proved a success, Royce's fears might be put to rest.

William's queen, Matilda, had arrived with a small entourage. Though it had been a daunting task, Bethany had supervised, planned, and helped to prepare a fine feast for all the Normans in attendance tonight.

She would *not* be found lacking. Not because of Royce; Saxons had their fair share of pride. With her chin raised and shoulders squared, Bethany smiled. Tonight's dinner would be the best ever presented in North Umberland. Although Renwyg Castle lacked the luxury of Normandy, it was far from a heathen hovel. Besides, Bethany never intended to match the Normans' sophistication. Experience had long ago taught her to do what she did well rather than imitate others. Bethany had never been a follower; she knew only how to lead. After tonight, the Normans would remember her hospitality.

Finally, all was in readiness. Night had fallen and every candle and torch burned, lighting Renwyg Castle with a soft warm glow.

Poised at the top of the balcony, Bethany looked down and saw Royce standing like a statue at the bottom of the stairs. Though a tiny part of her screamed to flee from this night, it could not be put off or avoided. Royce waited.

Her husband's stoic front made it evident he thought he would be martyred today, pitied for making such a poor match. The thought nearly made her laugh. A Norman bastard marries the eldest daughter of the highest family in all of England, and he thinks she is below his station. Ha! The extent of his snobbery was ludicrous.

Tonight she would show her condescending husband, and the pleasure of proving him wrong would warm her pride for months. Aye, even a lifetime to come.

When Bethany descended the last step, Royce offered his arm to her. She could not discern from his enigmatic expression if he were pleased with her efforts or not. The warrior's mein was in place.

Across the room against the far wall, four tables held the bounty from the fertile fields. Early that morning, Royce had sent his men hunting; and thanks to the Normans' skill with the bow, there was game and fowl aplenty while, under Maida's experienced eye and more-than-capable hands, servants had roasted the venison to succulent perfection, prepared the aromatic spiced vegetables, baked the dozens of platters heaped with hot breads, and decorated all the trays with sweet pastries.

A hush fell over the crowded great room when Royce gravely entered with his wife. The curious Norman visitors looked with open interest while those of better breeding did not. Royce presented her to the King and Queen of England.

William and Matilda made a striking couple. Though William

and Royce shared the same stature, Bethany, who was accustomed to being one of the smallest in a crowd of women, could see clear over Matilda's head. But the queen's petite size did not diminish her radiant power and energy.

"I am honored to be welcomed into your lovely home, Lady Bethany."

Bethany curtsied, thrilled beyond words by the woman's praise and acceptance.

"Thank you, your highness."

The king stepped forward. "Lady Bethany, would you do me the kindness of sitting to my left?"

"Aye, my liege, the pleasure would be mine." Not only had the queen honored her, but so had the king! Royce must, indeed, be one of the king's favorites to warrant such partiality, Bethany thought, for she was not fool enough to believe that the compliment was to her. She stole a glance at her husband to see if he realized the great tribute paid him. His face remained expressionless. If Royce were aware of the King's fondness, it did not show. In truth, his silence near stretched her patience to an end. She longed to give him a swift kick in the backside, but the status of their guests made that out of the question.

Dinner began without mishap, but Royce scrutinized every dish presented as though he expected a catastrophe to occur at any minute. His watchful eye made the servants wary but, thankfully, not clumsy.

When the minstrels Bethany had engaged for the evening began to play during dinner, Royce nearly choked on his food. Bethany pounded on his back and glanced quickly at their guests. The visitors were surprised but delighted. The soft music of the mandolin and harp filled the room, making conversation possible, yet providing a comfortable and relaxing ambience. Bethany was not afraid to be innovative, and the effort won praise among all.

Under the gentle spell of the music and soft candle glow, Renwyg Hall took on an ethereal quality. This was the scene she had imagined, where everything was perfect and everyone happy under her rule. Her eyes met her husband's, and Bethany was touched by the admiration that shone in his gaze. He raised his wine in salute to her, then sniffed the goblet suspiciously.

She chuckled at the reminder of her prank, enjoying not only the memory but his good cheer. Her smile widened and heart fluttered as he took a sip, then offered her a drink from his cup.

The festivities Bethany had planned did not disappoint. Normans wore approving smiles, while pride and dignity shone on the faces of the Saxons who served, and those who shared, the bounty of this night. A lump filled her throat at the sight of her people's joy and the justification of her risky choice to present Saxon entertainment rather than French. The music, plays, and stories handed down for generations captivated the Norman audience, who listened with rapt attention.

First a bard recited Bethany's favorite poem, "Beowulf." The epic, with its themes of love of battle, loyalty to one's lord, and the implacability of fate, found a familiar chord among the Normans.

After dinner an historical play was performed. The players, all wearing full battle dress, lamented the loss of their home and hearth while fighting the dreaded northmen. The pain and savagery of war touched every soldier in the room, whether Norman or Saxon. The beginning and middle of the play dealt with the effects of war on men; the end concentrated on those left behind. As one of the women wailed over the loss of her husband, the queen wiped her eyes and leaned toward Bethany.

"Home," Matilda whispered in Bethany's ear, "is where William lies his head. I cannot bear to be separated from him."

Bethany smiled and looked at the king. A leader of men, 'twould never be doubted, but a loving partner? It was hard to imagine. Yet, that these two loved each other was plain.

She then glanced to her husband and was surprised to see a smile on his handsome face. Could it be that he was truly enjoying himself?

Thunderous applause ensued at the play's end, and people

crowded in to congratulate her. Bethany could barely catch her breath for all the unfamiliar faces that sought her attention and conversation. After more names and faces then she cared to remember had passed by, Guy pulled her aside.

"See that man talking to Royce? He is one who sought to prevent my brother's acceptance at court. Perhaps time has mellowed the old reprobate or perhaps he is enamored by this country. But whatever the reason, your party has impressed everyone. Thanks to you, dear sister-in-law, my brother may get his wish after all."

Bethany turned to Guy, voicing a question that had long plagued her. "Guy, if the king himself is a bastard, why does Royce so fear judgment?"

"Even though the king is followed because he is a great leader, there are those who speak spiteful words because of his birth."

Bethany sensed he held something back. "There is more than just that, is there not?"

A sheepish smile slipped over his lips. "*Oui,* 'tis not just his place at court that burdens Royce. Royce was much older than I when our father abandoned us. He harbors deep scars from the betrayal. Not only did he loose his status, but his security."

Thoughtfully, Bethany turned to watch her husband as he moved among his contemporaries. If she had known that a successful banquet would be so pleasing to him, she would have arranged one long ago and invited every royal subject who laid claim to a title. Though one night could not cure what ailed Royce, it went a long way to ease his pain.

After that, she relaxed and enjoyed the evening and readily leaned against her husband's chest when he slipped his arms around her. It truly took so little to make him happy and she'd found that when he was happy, she was overjoyed.

"Thank you," he murmured in her ear.

"For what?" she questioned. Even though she knew the answer, she wanted to hear him say it.

"For the one thing I wanted all my life," he said huskily, "a place to belong. I may never be welcome at court, but you have accepted me."

Even though the party was a success, he still believed he would be an outcast at court. In time, she prayed, it would not matter.

Royce looked at her so intensely that she could not hold his gaze. Something had changed between them. All of a sudden, she felt unsure and afraid to put a name to the reason why.

The dancing and merrymaking continued and, for the first time since the invasion, she felt at ease. Perhaps, she had found her destiny. Lord, she hoped so. Matilda had said it herself: Home was where her husband laid his head.

North Umberland belonged to Royce; and whether she willed it or nay, she loved him. Was it not fortunate that the king had seen fit to make them man and wife? If only Royce would come to terms with his devils.

The royal couple approached them, and the king slapped Royce on the back. "I knew this match would benefit both of us."

Matilda smiled with benign patience at her husband. "I am sure your words are a great comfort to the bride, husband." She reprimanded William in such a sweet voice that it had no sting. Then she turned to Bethany. "I have learned much from you."

"From me?" Bethany squeaked.

"*Oui,* my dear. A wise person never stops learning. You have shown me much about graciousness and hospitality. I thank you."

Bethany felt truly humbled. Norman society was the most sophisticated on earth. "Thank you, my lady. I shall never forget your kindness or your wisdom."

Bethany knew she would always harbor a warm place in her heart for this night. She tucked the memories safely away where they could not be forgotten or robbed of their importance.

As the festivities died down, Cedric appeared at the door, his expression anxious as he scanned the gathering.

Sensing something amiss, she walked swiftly to his side. "Cedric?"

"My lady," he said, breathing a sigh of relief. Then he leaned forward and whispered in her ear. "'Tis Mary. She is poorly disposed and asks your protection from her husband." Bethany felt the blood drain from her face. Suddenly, the joy of the present was replaced with the worry and fear of her earlier days. Her hands began to shake, and a cold clammy feeling stole over her.

Biting her lip, she turned to Royce, who had followed in her wake. "Warlord, my sister is at the gate asking asylum."

"What?"

"Gentle Mary is at the gate. She has left her brutish husband and asks, nay begs, asylum. Will you grant it?"

Royce took a deep breath and caught the king's attention. This was a volatile diplomatic matter.

The king gave an almost imperceptible nod. Royce repeated the gesture to Cedric, and Bethany gave a deep sigh of relief.

She reached out to her husband and gave his hand a squeeze. "Thank you," she whispered.

When Cedric left the room, Bethany was right behind him. "Did Mary say what happened?"

"Nay, my lady, but it is apparent a beating took place."

Bethany nearly choked when the gate opened and, by the light of the gatekeeper's torch, she viewed her sister's lovely face. "Good God!" she whispered. So distorted and misshapen were Mary's features, Bethany barely recognized her own flesh and blood.

"Sister," Mary whispered.

"Shh," Bethany soothed, her heart breaking. "Cedric, take her to the tower," she ordered. It was the only empty room, and fortunately it was far removed from the main rooms and prying eyes.

Bethany followed behind as he carried her half-conscious sister to the tower room.

Though heads turned as they passed the great room, only

Royce joined her on the steps. "What happened?" he asked, escorting her up the stairs.

With tears blurring her vision, she could not see Royce's features or gauge his reaction to her sister's plight. " 'Twas a mean-spirited man who did this."

"That may well be. But what happened to provoke this beating?" Royce asked, his words measured.

"Royce, I do not know." Bethany snapped loudly in her frustration. Ashamed at her outburst, she took a deep breath to calm her racing pulse and continued. "I will find out when Mary is stronger. But nothing she did could merit this kind of savagery. Nothing!" she said as she entered the tower room and knelt by the straw pallet.

Her sister moaned. "Oh, Mary, do not worry," Bethany soothed. "You are safe with us. Royce will never allow anyone to hurt you again."

Then she turned back to Royce. "Will you, husband?"

"I may not hold with beating a woman, but the law is explicit. I must know Mary's offense."

"Husband, what could ever justify this?"

"Before I make a decision that places this demesne in danger, I must know the whole truth. Is it worth imperiling every man, woman, and child for the beating your sister took?"

He was right. But Mary needed her.

Mary's strained voice croaked, "We are together now. That is all that matters. Bless you, sister."

Leaning over, Bethany kissed her sister's badly bruised brow. As she closed her eyes, tears of anguish trailed down her cheeks. "I will protect you, Mary," she vowed. Dear Lord, what had she allowed to happen to her family?

Chapter Twenty-two

Mary's black eye and swollen face bespoke a brutal assault. While waiting for Maida to bring the sleeping potion, Bethany wiped the blood away from her sister's cheek. When Mary flinched from the gentle touch, Bethany's stomach turned and she feared she would be unable to tend her sister. All the while, Royce hovered in the background, waiting for an explanation.

Mary's whimpers continued, and every sound drove a sword into Bethany's heart. What manner of man could abuse someone so sweet? The monster need only raise his voice to make Mary cower.

Anger, red-hot and burning, flowed through Bethany's veins. She could gladly kill Mary's husband. "Let him pick on me next time." She spoke her thoughts aloud, too enraged to care how they sounded.

Mary cringed and wept softly.

Royce snorted. "He would snap you in two. Or had not you noticed that Mary and you share the same size?"

"Aye, but not the same temperament."

"True. You would have provoked this man long ago." Royce spat out his reply.

"What will you do?" Bethany asked, needing to know if her husband would defend her family honor.

Before Royce could answer, the door opened and the queen entered. "Royce, lower your voice or the whole castle shall be privy to your conversation." Then, Matilda turned to Bethany with a gracious smile. "I have learned, my dear, you cannot outshout a husband, because his voice is too deep."

Bethany felt her cheeks grow warm from the queen's chastisement. "After my sister's injuries are attended, she will be able to give a full accounting," she said in a softer tone. "Royce will have his answers. When he does, I expect him to attack Laird Sinclair, ensuring he never harms Mary again."

"Think, Bethany," Matilda cautioned. "Royce is responsible for all your people, not just Mary. Though I sympathize with your sister's plight, her husband is within his rights to discipline her."

"He is not a man if he has to use such force to discipline," Bethany argued, tears clouding her vision.

"I agree," Matilda conceded with diplomatic skill. "But that does not justify sending an already war-weary people into another conflict to seek revenge. We are talking about invading Scotland, are we not?"

Bethany took a deep breath. Though she saw the wisdom of Queen Matilda's words, she still wanted to strangle Mary's husband with her own hands.

A quick rap sounded on the door, and the king entered looking for his wife. At the sight of both her guests of honor crowding into the tower room, Bethany wondered when the entire court would arrive to join them.

"There you are, my dear. Are you ready to retire?"

In answer to William's questioning look, Matilda continued, "I think you will find this young lady's story of interest."

The king nodded his head and waited along with everyone else for Mary's explanation.

"He struck me again and again." Her swollen face emitted

tears. "My crime," she said, looking up at her sister, "was trying to save you."

"Save?" Bethany asked in confusion, wondering what danger existed that Mary feared.

"Aye," Mary said. "How could I believe that you wished to marry this devil? A Norman, let alone a bastard? Nay, 'twas not possible." Mary paused to take a deep breath. "I was aware of the bargain you entered into to gain our freedom and could only assume you did so again for another concession."

"Mary, is that why you married?" Bethany asked, her insides twisting at the irony of it all.

"Aye. 'Twas to save you. My betrothed promised he would take up your cause, but after the wedding he changed his mind. If I even brought up your name, he considered it a reprimand and would beat me. Not even Bret's name could be mentioned. It was as if my family ceased to exist else they would remind him of his broken vow."

"Mary, 'twill be best to put all this ugliness to rest. You are home now." Bethany looked at Royce as she spoke to Mary. "And home you will stay."

"I have failed you, sister," Mary sobbed. "I am so ashamed."

"There was no need to sacrifice yourself," Bethany said, tasting the bitterness of the waste. "I am quite content."

"Truly, he does not abuse you?"

"Nay," Bethany said, gazing over her sister's head to see a fleeting glimpse of regret in Royce's gaze. A wry smile formed on her lips as her husband's mask of indifference quickly fell into place. "Royce would never wound me with his fist when his tongue is so elegant."

"What do you mean?" Mary asked, claiming Bethany's attention.

"Never mind, 'tis a joke between my husband and me." Bethany patted her sister's hand. "You must try to rest now."

When Maida arrived with the drugged wine, Bethany went to listen to her husband and the king, but when she approached, both men stopped talking.

Presently, the queen joined her. "Your sister is sound asleep. I suggest we take this discussion downstairs."

"What discussion? You see, my lady, when I am around, my husband is afflicted by a strange disease of silence."

The queen chuckled. *"Naturellement!* He does not want you to overhear his plans, for either your tiny brain will not comprehend his strategy or else you will see the flaw in it." She turned to Royce. "Which is it, my lord?"

The king chuckled as they walked out of the room. "I have learned, Royce, that it is less taxing to keep my wife informed than to hide things from her. The first is often a sharing of good ideas, and the latter expends more energy than it is worth."

Royce did not looked convinced. "Our quarters would serve better than the common room." Royce opened the door, and they entered the warm, cheery room.

"What do you plan to do?" Bethany demanded as they walked inside, unable to hold her curiosity another minute.

"I will do nothing. If Mary's husband has the brass to come for her, then we will decide what course of action to take. She is not a blood relative, and I am not honor-bound to seek him out."

"Well, I am!" Bethany cried. "That should be enough. He has dishonored this house and, by so doing, dishonored you."

"Non. 'Tis not the way of it."

"I vow, husband, you are as stubborn as you are handsome," she snapped as she paced the floor.

"Royce may be stubborn, I will not argue the point. But, handsome, Lady Bethany? That is stretching it a bit, do you not concede?" the king asked.

The queen hid her smile behind her hand, but her choking mirth could not be silenced. Royce joined the queen in laughter, but his was full-blown. "Handsome? Why, thank you, wife. I do agree."

Bethany's cheeks burned with embarrassment. She could not believe her inner thoughts had slipped from her lips. But to have Royce tease her in front of the king and queen was more than she could bear. In that moment, she could have cheerfully pushed him over a cliff without a shred of remorse.

Matilda diplomatically laid her hand on Royce's arm, bridging the awkward moment. "Never mind, it is settled. If this brute of a man shows his ugly face in North Umberland, I am sure you will handle him with Norman justice." Then, with a smile, she turned to Bethany. "That will satisfy you, my dear, will it not?"

"Aye." Bethany said, regaining her composure. "But I wish I could mete out justice. Saxon justice."

The king placed his arm around Bethany's shoulders. "Royce will take care of it, though he is stubborn and handsome." The laughter that followed proved her remark would be a source of amusement for some time to come.

"I will leave a complement of men," the king said, cutting off further comment with a raised hand. "Royce, I would see this territory defended."

Royce acquiesced by a nod of his head. "Guy will attend the quartering."

"Ah, Guy," the king said, stroking his chin as though an idea had suddenly struck him. "I have been hearing interesting tales of your brother. I have a boon to ask of him when he is free of his obligation here in North Umberland."

"Guy would serve you with honor and courage," Royce said neutrally, but the questioning tilt to his head showed his curiosity.

"The mission he would undertake is particularly suited to his talent. In all of England, I could not find another with such excellent credentials," the king elaborated. It was clear that would be the only information forthcoming.

Royce smiled at the explanation that explained nothing. William the Conqueror, renowned as a great soldier, also exhibited the skills of a master diplomat.

The king took his lady's hand. "It is late."

Matilda looked back over her shoulder. "Do not worry about

your sister, Bethany. Leave her safety to Royce. He is nothing if not a great warrior."

As the royal couple left the room, Bethany turned to her husband.

"What?" she asked, noticing the devilish grin on his face and bright twinkle in his clear, blue eyes.

He slipped his arms around her and pulled her into his embrace. "Do you think I am a great warrior?"

She smothered a soft giggle. "Aye, warlord, I never doubted it." She leaned into his chest and looked up at his face.

A huge grin spread across his lips. "And my little wife thinks I am handsome."

Bethany slapped his arm playfully and walked out of his embrace. "You are so swollen-headed, I should never have said that."

"I am glad you did. But did you mean it?" he asked with a suddenly serious expression, the easy humor gone from his manner.

"Aye, I did. I wish I did not feel this way about you, but I cannot help it. You are beautiful."

He actually blushed.

"Women are beautiful, not men," he said gruffly. Then his features softened and he cradled her face in his hands. "And none of the ladies of the land are as lovely as you, Annie," he whispered.

Embarrassed, Bethany turned away. "You do not have to pay me compliments just because I have so honored you."

"Surely you are aware of your beauty?"

She shrugged her shoulder. "My sister has the beauty in the family," she said. Her thoughts sobering, she had to swallow the lump that had formed in her throat. "At least she did before that man beat her."

His arms enveloped her once again, this time offering her comfort in a gentle cocoon of understanding as he pulled her close until her back reclined against his chest. His chin rested on her head as he hugged her in the safe shelter of his arms.

"Mary will fare well. Her face will heal, and her husband will not be allowed to disfigure her again. This I promise you."

"Would you ever strike a woman in such a fashion?" she asked, leaning back and looking up at his face.

"You want to know if I would strike you?" His finger trailed her cheek as he held her gaze.

"Nay. I know you would never harm me. I would know if you have ever felt that kind of rage."

"*Non.* But I am curious. How do you know I would not strike you? Lord knows, you could drive a saint to violence."

She let the comment pass, though she thought it singularly ungentlemanly of him.

"Royce, you have a good heart. I have seen it with my people, and I have seen it with my family; but most of all I have witnessed it between us," she said, then turned to whisper, "You are a good man."

" 'Tis truly a day of revelation! I have learned that you find me handsome but stubborn, a brave warrior, and a good man. I think, Annie, I will never understand you."

Lost in the wonder of Royce's surprise and open honesty, she took a moment, a very telling moment, to respond.

"Is it necessary that you do?"

"It is!"

Bethany chuckled, "I wish you luck, then."

" 'Tis not luck but skill that is needed. I have a lifetime at my disposal."

"It will take you that long."

Royce picked her up in his arms. "Then I shall get started right now. 'Tis a strange contradiction, Annie, but 'twould seem the more I discover about you, the more I realize how little I know. Now, all I want is the soft woman who makes me believe there is a heaven on earth. Take me there, Annie."

She wrapped her arms around his neck, knowing that when they were making love, what was Norman and Saxon lay stripped away, exposing only a man and a woman. " 'Twill be no trouble at all, my lord. After all, I do find you the handsomest man I have ever beheld." She meant to laugh but could not, for it was true. Her heart beat faster when she looked into his eyes. Lord, but she had trouble breathing when he was around. "I will take you with me to paradise, and I hope you find the journey as pleasurable as I do."

She stretched against him, sensuously moving her body to fit his. Closing the whisper of space between their lips, she tantalized his with a feather-like touching and tasting, teasing but never fulfilling, until at last she kissed him fully and soundly.

A growl deep within his chest voiced his hunger, and she was filled with a delicious sense of excitement and power.

Again she leaned forward and joined her lips to his. This time, the kiss started slow and sultry, growing until neither one could draw a breath. When she leaned back in his arms and met his gaze, a burning desire glowed deep within his eyes.

He carried her over to their bed. With one knee on the pallet, he leaned forward and placed her gently on the fur robes. Slowly, he unlaced her tunic, his fingers trailing across her skin followed by his soft kisses.

Her breath became uneven as every garment was sensually stroked from her body by soft brushes of his palms or sweet languid sweeps of his lips.

Heart pounding, she reached for him, slipping her fingers beneath his tunic. Her hands explored his body thoroughly while removing his clothes, and she heard his moan before his lips descended on hers.

His kisses were hot and hurried with a hunger that had to be met, and she felt the same need as desire built within her to a fevered pitch. Her nails raked his bare flesh as his hands caressed her with a sensuality that near drove her mad.

"Do you love me?" she whispered, needing to hear his avowal of love.

"I need you, Annie," he growled as he entered her.

Those were not the words she longed to hear. Still, it was all he could give and she would accept what he offered freely.

"I need you, too," she whispered as she met and matched

his rhythm. Her climax occurred at the same time Royce met his peak. At least physically they were in perfect harmony.

After a week, Mary's injuries had healed, but she was not yet on her feet.

"Come with us tomorrow," Bethany implored her sister, who reclined comfortably in bed.

"Nay, sister, I do not feel strong enough to ride the country-side. You and the queen will not enjoy your outing if you have to wait for someone who cannot keep up," Mary said, picking up her embroidery.

"Very well, we will tell you about it," the queen remarked with less compassion.

"As you wish, your majesty," Mary replied.

"Please reconsider, Mary. Though your sewing is lovely," Bethany said, looking at her handiwork, "truly the best in the shire, you need the fresh air."

"Do not plead with her," the queen admonished Bethany in a soft voice. "It is obvious your sister enjoys praying and stitching more than riding."

"Aye, I will spend my time thanking God for all his blessings. Do not give me a thought, sister." Mary bowed her head.

"Enjoy your day tomorrow, Lady Mary," the queen said drily. Then, with a smile on her face, she pulled Bethany away from her sister's side. "I will see you when we break the fast. Sleep well, Lady Bethany."

The queen opened the door to leave and, almost as an after-thought, turned around to face the room. "Good night, Lady Mary."

Bethany looked back at her sister. Why must she act the martyr? When she was stronger, Bethany would bring up the subject. She did not like to see her sister behave so.

"The queen does not like me," Mary blurted.

"Rest, dear," Bethany said, refusing to deny the truth. "I will see you after the ride tomorrow."

Bethany went to her room, wondering if Royce would be there. The king had kept Royce engaged and from her side. Since Matilda's arrival, they had spent only two nights together. The others she had been long asleep when he finally came to bed. She opened the door to her chamber and was disappointed to find it empty. She changed into her nightclothes, then, on a whim, stripped the clothing from her body. Perhaps, if her husband found her waiting for him in all her naked glory, he might not come to bed so late. Draping herself over the fur robe atop the bed, she threw her hair back over her shoulder and, half-reclining, leaned into her arm and thrust her breasts forward.

She looked down. Perhaps this was a trifle too brazen. After all, she did not want to appear anxious. She drew a long strand of hair over her shoulder and laid it down her front. The red hair draped over one breast and pooled in a soft stream at her waist, the end trailing down between her legs. Now let him neglect me, she thought smugly.

She was beginning to hate his dedication to duty, but she had seen that there was a way to broach his iron determination and was not above using her wiles to have her husband's attention and lovemaking.

The fire burned low and the hour was late when she smothered a yawn. The room was decidedly cool, but she did not want to stoke up the fire. When Royce retired, he would be forced to cuddle to stave off the chill. Telling herself he would be along soon, she closed her eyes to rest, stubbornly lying atop the covers in the cold, lonely bed. Royce had important business with his liege and there was nothing she could do about it. But she missed him so.

The morning found her still alone. She lifted the fur robe and wondered how she had come to be covered. She remembered drifting off to sleep waiting for her husband, seductively clothed in nothing but a welcoming smile.

A warm feeling encompassed her. Royce had covered her.

The morning meal found only the queen and Bethany surrounded by the Norman soldiers assigned to guard her majesty. Royce and the king, along with a complement of men, had left early to survey the region.

After their repast, Vachel and Guy ordered their horses brought to them. Standing with Matilda on the stoop to the courtyard, Bethany drew a deep breath of the clear, crisp air. Though the morning was cold, the sun broke through the dingy tufts of clouds, making it a lovely day for a ride.

At the stable master's approach, they descended the stone steps to the courtyard.

"Oh, what a beauty your horse is," the queen said, admiring the stallion's color and breed.

"Do you like Morlock?" Bethany inquired, pride filling her at the queen's praise.

"Oui, very much." The queen stroked Morlock's nose and patted his neck. "I would love to ride such a fine beast."

Bethany felt the guilty weight of obligation and good manners. "Are you an experienced rider?" she asked, hoping the opposite would prove true. She could not help but remember the last time a Norman lady had ridden her fine steed.

The queen laughed. *"Oui,* I have ridden with William, so I have to be."

"Then with my blessings you may ride Morlock, but use a firm, not forceful hand," Bethany warned. "Damiana did not heed my advice."

"Do not fear, my dear. I do not use a whip. If you like, you may inspect my own horse to see the truth of my words."

As Bethany walked around Matilda's mount, she wondered if that were a rebuke for the fading weals on Morlock's flanks or if the queen had heard of Damiana's meanness. Bethany rather guessed it was the latter. This monarch had her finger on the pulse of the country. No doubt the king's man had not only detailed a report about North Umberland, but also about its people.

" 'Tis a well-cared-for animal, your majesty." Bethany patted the sleek ebony steed on the neck, impressed with the horse's lines and carriage.

"Then if Nightwind meets with your approval, I would be pleased if you rode him."

"I would be honored to be so favored. Thank you."

Queen Matilda chuckled softly. "Fairness, Lady Bethany, is not reserved to Saxons." The queen mounted Morlock. "May you always feel that my judgments are just."

Bethany smiled at the subtle reminder that a new monarch and regime had been instituted.

"Aye, my lady. I hope your wisdom will last as long as your rule," Bethany said as diplomatically as she could, considering she was the vanquished.

The queen inclined her head in appreciation for Bethany's response. "Let us be away, Lady Bethany."

The minute Bethany mounted, the horse suddenly reared and bolted from the yard. The guards and the queen gave pursuit, but Nightwind's speed and Bethany's slightness kept her far out of their reach.

She simply could not bring Nightwind under control, and the huge black beast galloped over the fields, seemingly hell-bent on destruction. She pulled on the reins with all her force, but the animal did not respond to her commands. She soon realized how fruitless her efforts were. The only thing she could do was use all her considerable skill to stay seated in the saddle until Nightwind ran himself into exhaustion.

Although she was sure the guards would not be able to catch Nightwind, more riders suddenly appeared, approaching from the opposite direction. From high on the hill they galloped down the ridge to intercept the wild beast.

Bethany barely dared a glimpse at her rescuers before Nightwind bucked and shied. "Please help me, husband," she whispered to herself.

Suddenly, as if sensing the other horse and rider, her mount reared and pawed the air. Bethany could not maintain her tight grip on the reins. "Royce!" she screamed as Nightwind threw her from his back.

Royce thought his heart would stop as he watched his dainty wife being violently thrown from the horse. Unable to reach her in time, he heard her cry out his name as she fell to the ground.

Leaping from his horse before it had even stopped, Royce ran to her, his heart pounding with fear. "Annie, Annie, answer me!"

As William slid from his mount, he directed a soldier from his guard to catch the runaway horse, then joined Royce's side. "How does she fare?"

"I do not know," Royce snapped as the soldiers crowded around the injured woman.

She lay on the grass, still and silent. He quickly checked for any breaks in her bones and found none, then gently lifted her in his arms as the other riders from the castle arrived.

Through the growing throng, the king's soldier led Nightwind back, then handed the reins to William.

" 'Tis most strange, Nightwind is not given to wildness," the king said.

Royce heard nothing. He carefully mounted his horse with Bethany and cradled her in his arms. Good Lord, what had happened? This made no sense. Bethany was an expert rider.

The royal entourage—along with the warlord's private guard—rode ahead, but Royce held his horse to a gentle walk. He feared any more injury to Bethany and would not let his thoughts wander to the health of his unborn child. Panic visited the battle-hardened soldier for the first time.

On their arrival at the castle, Royce refused all help and dismounted with his wife. "I will take her to our chamber," he announced to the milling crowd of concerned Saxons. "Maida," he bellowed on his way through the great room.

Wringing her hands in her apron, the cook escorted them up the stairs as the queen followed.

Carefully laying Bethany atop the covers, Royce tenderly brushed the hair from her brow, willing her to be well.

"Move aside, Royce; we will do what must be done for her," the queen said.

Reluctantly, Royce shifted out of the way to let the women tend his wife. He caught Maida's attention. "What of the child?"

"'Twill be known in time, my lord. If your seed is planted well, then the fall will not have disturbed it. If not, we will have a sign by morning."

Bethany moaned and Royce's gaze slanted to his wife. "And my wife?"

Maida's face showed her apprehension. "A fall can injure some and not others. We will know when she awakens from this deep sleep."

Something in the cook's manner made Royce voice the question he did not want to. "Do you fear she will not awaken?"

"I am only a healer, my lord. Her fate is not mine to decide."

After a quick knock on the door, Guy entered and pulled his brother aside. "We must talk. Come with me."

"I will not leave my wife," Royce said tersely.

As Guy ran a hand through his hair, his gaze travelled from Royce to the bed. "You are needed," he implored, and caught the monarch's eye.

The queen left Bethany's bedside and joined the brothers.

"Royce," Matilda said with gentle authority, "you can do nothing for her now. Go with your brother; and when there is news, we will bring it."

Royce nodded his head, suddenly feeling helpless and intrusive. "You will send word the moment Bethany's condition changes . . ."

"You have my promise."

Guy held the door open, and together they marched down the stairs. In the great room, William held a tankard of ale and sat at the main table.

When Guy and Royce approached, the king poured two more tankards. "Did you tell him?"

"Non, sire." Guy turned to his brother. "His majesty found this sewn into the blanket beneath Nightwind's saddle." He handed Royce a cushion that at first appearance seemed to be a light pillow of fabric.

No sooner had the innocent-looking sack dropped into Royce's palm then a look of surprise crossed his face and he flung it to the floor.

Guy carefully picked it up between two fingers as the queen joined them.

"Maida is tending the Lady Bethany. She has not lost the child yet," the queen said to Royce, then turned her attention to Guy. "What is that?"

" 'Tis filled with sharp pins. This is what caused your gentle mount to react so violently."

"Good Lord!" The queen glanced toward the master bedchamber. "Then by changing mounts with me, Lady Bethany saved my life. I doubt I could have handled Nightwind's wild run as well as she."

"Lady Bethany's bravery has been tested more than once," the king agreed. "With this incident, no one can doubt her innocence in Damiana's murder."

Saying nothing, Royce accepted the pin cushion as the king put his arm around Matilda.

"We are indebted to Bethany." William's sharp scrutiny held his warlord's gaze. "Royce, make sure you guard her well."

"How?" Guy exclaimed. "The coward strikes without warning."

"Then I would tell her husband not to leave her alone for a minute," Matilda remarked drily.

When the king and queen took their leave, Royce turned to Guy. "Is it not strange that with Mary's return unfortunate accidents have started again?"

"Mary was not here when Damiana drank the poisoned brandy," Guy answered and took a deep drink of his brew.

"True," Royce said slowly, "but perhaps the brandy held the poison before Mary's departure."

Lowering his tankard, Guy stared at Royce, then he nodded his head thoughtfully.

"See to it, Guy. Assign someone to watch her," Royce said. He slammed his tankard on the table and marched to the stairs.

At the threshold of his room, Royce took a deep breath, then opened the door and looked at his wife, lying quietly asleep. She seemed so helpless. It occurred to him that she had never known the safety of a protector. She had always watched over and cared for her family and her people. She had no one, save him.

With a nod of his head, he dismissed Maida and sat by Bethany's bed.

His gaze lingered on her soft features and smooth skin. Though she was far from angelic, he had never before known a woman this close to perfection. Unbidden, the picture came to him of the way he had found her the other night, sprawled out above the covers, naked as the day she'd entered this world. There was a memory that would never fade with time. He would never be able to see her in bed and not picture her thusly. Desire filled him, and he chastised himself for having such thoughts while his wife lay helpless and unaware.

Suddenly Bethany began to stir, and he moved closer to the bed.

As she moaned, he hovered over her, gently brushing aside the light hairs that clung to her brow. "Annie," he whispered.

Her lashes fluttered, then her eyes opened and a smile spread across her lips. Love and tenderness shone in her eyes as she gazed at Royce. Then her expression clouded and she lifted her head to sit up, her hands flipping back the covers and protectively covering her stomach. "My baby?" she sobbed, looking at Royce with fear and apprehension.

"Hush, wife. Our child still rests snugly," he soothed.

Tears seeped out of the corner of her eyes. "Thank God," she whispered.

"You want our baby?" he asked, unable or unwilling to believe the depth of her commitment.

A bittersweet expression veiled her joy. "More than anything in this world. I will have someone to love and be loved by."

The truth of her words disturbed his conscience. She gave her love unconditionally. "Lie back and rest," he said more gruffly than he intended, and the earlier image of a seductress vanished with the reality of his injured wife.

"Royce, hold my hand." She extended her fingers to him.

He cradled her hand in his. "Rest, Annie. I will not leave until you fall sleep."

She smiled. "Husband, I know you have other matters that are more important than I. Your kindness is appreciated."

God, her response humbled him. She was grateful for what other wives would expect as their right. He treated her without the respect due a warlord's wife, and yet, he seemed powerless to change his behavior.

He sat by her bed and held her hand. How readily her fingers curled about his. She was a trusting and loving woman. If only he could accept her Saxon heritage, the barrier between them would be removed.

"Royce, you are so good to me," she whispered as she slipped off to sleep.

His heart responded, *you, my love, are more than I deserve.* But he whispered, "And you, my Annie, are bad for me."

Two days later, bright and early, huddled in a soft mantle of rich fur, Bethany stood on the stone steps overlooking the courtyard. With Royce beside her, a bevy of servants crowding in behind her, and Norman soldiers assembling in the yard and gateway, all of Castle Renwyg turned out in honor of the departing King William and Queen Matilda.

The gray, swirling clouds overhead, along with the cold-blowing wind, carried the biting promise of snow through the courtyard. At her shiver, Royce hugged her close to his side and she nestled into the crook of his arm, glad for the warmth and consideration. Bethany would miss the royal couple, especially the queen, a woman of rare humor and wit and such unexpected kindness that Bethany's eyes filled with tears at the farewell. At times her emotional state seemed uncontrollable, and she prayed that as her months with child progressed, this penchant for tears would diminish. 'Twas truly undignified.

Without comment, Royce slipped her a small linen cloth and she gratefully wiped her eyes. She wondered if anything missed his attention, then took a deep breath to gain control as the queen approached.

Matilda pressed her gold broach into Bethany's hand. "It matches your girdle so well. Please accept it from a grateful houseguest."

"Please, my lady, you do me dishonor. A reward for good manners is unnecessary." Bethany tried to return the gift.

"William." The queen beckoned her husband to her side. "Truly, I am vexed. Our host will not accept a token of our gratitude."

Bethany was dumbfounded that the queen would persist.

"My liege," Bethany said. "I mean no disrespect. Please understand that it is bad form for a Saxon to accept such an expensive gift."

"Are you not Norman by marriage?" the queen asked sweetly.

Bethany could not have been more thunderstruck. The woman had tricked her in a most becoming way.

"Aye, my lady. I am. And I shall graciously accept the gift in the spirit it was given."

The queen chuckled. "You are learning, my dear. After your child is delivered, you must come to London and join us at court. I truly did enjoy our stay." Then Matilda leaned forward in a loving gesture and hugged Bethany. "Have patience with your husband," she whispered. "He is stubborn, but I have found that the most loving and caring men are those of strong conviction. He will love with more passion than others, and the energy he expends in his causes is the same he will devote to you. Keep your sense of humor, my dear; it will see you through far more than this."

When the queen pulled free of the embrace, Royce and the king looked at her questioningly. " 'Twas motherly advice," she quipped in answer to their unvoiced question. But only Bethany saw the monarch wink before she turned to leave.

Bethany smiled at the way the king helped his wife mount her horse. They were an inspiring picture of wedded bliss. She wished Royce would understand that differences could exist between loving partners. But then, according to Matilda, William did not always understand his wife. A smile spread across her face as Royce hugged her to his side.

"I am glad they visited."

"Why?" Royce asked, his eyebrow lifting slightly as if her response were suspect.

"Because I did not know such cultured and refined Normans existed. If I had not made their acquaintance, I would have thought all Normans behaved as badly as you and your brother."

Royce threw back his head and roared with laughter, causing the soldiers in the courtyard to turn and stare. Clearly not many were used to seeing the warlord in a happy mood.

Guy joined their side. "I do not know what you said to my surly brother, but I beg of you, do it once a day so the rest of us can stand to be around him."

"Guy, you would recant your plea if you knew what aspersions were cast against us."

"Royce, please." Bethany placed her hand on Royce's arm and looked up at him, begging him not to repeat her private remark.

He stared at her so long that she thought perhaps he had forgotten what had been said. "Very well, wife. But if you wish to curry my favor, a kiss would not be amiss."

Standing up on tiptoes, she kissed his cheek. "When have I not been a model wife? I have sought your favors every night, in case you have not noticed," she whispered, reminding him of the late nights he had spent in the king's service.

"I noticed," he muttered.

He sounded so frustrated and disgruntled, Bethany's spirits lifted immediately.

Chapter Twenty-three

"Rest, Bethany. I shall return with something to help you sleep," Mary said as she gathered her sewing.

Tearlach, the big Norman soldier whom Guy had assigned to guard Mary, stood staunchly by the door. His size and determined silence made the sentry's presence rather conspicuous. Mary leaned close to Bethany and whispered, "He even follows me to chapel, but never prays."

Bethany chuckled as Mary left her bedside and walked to the door, where she was joined by her shadow, Tearlach. Poised and confident, her sister paused in the doorway. "Mother would have been very proud that you upheld the legacy and protected our people. You are the daughter she wanted," Mary said, then turned and left. Tearlach, trailing in her wake, bowed in deference to Bethany, then softly closed the door.

Radiant was the only word that described her sister of late. 'Twas not her beauty that accounted for the glow, for the evidence of her brutal assault remained, though the unsightly purple bruises had faded to yellow. Nay, the joy came from within. Mary's state of mind improved with each passing day, and Bethany thanked God her sister had suffered no lasting effects from her short-lived marriage. No doubt, being surrounded by her family helped Mary. Bret's visit could not have been more timely. They were all together, drawing and giving each other the love necessary for happiness and good health.

A month had slipped by since Mary's return, with no sign of her brutish overlord and husband. Royce believed the bad weather had delayed him, but Bethany hoped Laird Sinclair would simply put Mary from his mind. The thought did not comfort, for it reminded Bethany of her own uncertain future. Royce was not like Sinclair; but a woman, any woman, could find herself on the doorstep if her husband's affections changed.

She sighed. Perhaps it was the coming birth that made her so contemplative. Like a mother bird building a nest, Bethany had to feel that a safe haven awaited her baby. Her hand moved over her stomach as she felt a small flutter, and she wondered at the tiny being forming within her. 'Twas indeed life, a miracle that was no longer a mystery to her. She hugged the inner knowledge and pleasure to herself. She now knew what her mother and grandmother and all the North Umberland women had known. This was a link stronger and far more binding than the legacy . . . the greatest force in the world passed down through the ages until, suddenly, she was a part of the cycle of life. Humbled by God's grand design and thankful for His gift, she brushed at the tears that misted her eyes.

A sudden disturbance in the hallway caught Bethany's attention. "Nay, Bret, Bethany must rest. She is terribly ill with the child she carries. You may see her tomorrow." Bethany heard her sister's voice and wanted to intervene, but was too tired. Mary should not blame Bethany's illness on the unborn baby. Later, when she had a chance, she would correct the misunderstanding. Bret should not fear or resent this child.

Bethany sighed and turned in bed, trying to get the sleep she needed. Of late she seemed to drop off in mid-sentence. 'Twas normal for a woman in her early months, she was told. Still, this fatigue wore on her nerves. She was not used to inactivity.

The door opened quietly, and Bret peeked in. "Bethany?"

She heard the apprehension in his timid voice.

"Come in, Bret." She held her arms out wide and Bret raced over to the bed and hugged her.

"Are you truly sick?" he asked as a worried look crossed his features.

"Just a little tired," Bethany said to soothe his fears. "Sometimes, to have a miracle, one must rest." She smiled. "I am so happy. Soon I will have a baby for us. And you will be an uncle."

His face beamed. "Truly? I will be an uncle?"

"Verily," she affirmed.

"Wait until I tell everyone. Does Royce know?"

Bethany hid her smile. "Aye, he does."

At that news Bret's expression fell, but soon his eyes brightened. "Can I tell Uncle Bram?"

"Aye."

With his status and self-importance intact, Bret crawled up to the bed and snuggled close to Bethany. "Can I stay with you? Mary is so mean."

After overhearing Mary's reprimand, Bethany was not surprised by the remark. "She is just concerned for me, Bret."

"Nay, lately she is so bossy and mean. I hate her."

"Bret, you cannot mean it."

Bret's chin jutted out stubbornly, and he glared at his sister.

Bethany recognized that mutinous look. Today, she did not feel like challenging it. "Mary loves you," she said. "And I think it would hurt her very much to know you did not love her in return."

Bret squirmed uncomfortably and finally looked at Bethany. "I love her," he said reluctantly, then added, "But, I do not like her."

Bethany shook her head at his willful ways. She thought Uncle Bram and Royce would be better suited to deal with this side of his nature. In any case, she had missed her brother. "Very well, Bret, you can stay with me for a little while."

A smile split his face. "I want to tell you all about Uncle Bram's castle."

As Bethany listened to his eager chatter, a warm feeling encompassed her. Soon, she would have her own child—though Bret had been her responsibility for so long, he seemed like her firstborn.

He yawned, and Bethany smothered her own reaction. "Did you not sleep well last night?"

"Uncle Royce took me with him on his rounds."

Uncle Royce, she thought. Funny that Bret had always accepted the Norman. From the first, he had seen the goodness and kindness in Royce. What an irony that truth was revealed through the eyes of a child. "Do you like your uncle Royce?"

"Aye. But not as much as you like him."

Ah, if only her husband could see that, but he was so blind. If not blind, then dim-sighted, she amended. Royce found change hard. But she could see the cracks in his armor. He was bending. God grant her the patience to wait until his last piece of protection fell away.

Bret returned to the subject of his trip and his wonder at the Scottish customs. Time flew by, and suddenly they heard the sound of approaching footsteps.

" 'Tis Mary!" Bret wailed, crestfallen.

Bethany did not like the dread she saw in Bret's eyes. She would settle this matter.

Her brother dove under the covers and lay close to her side.

Wearing a lovely smile, Mary entered Bethany's room carrying a tray. "I have brought you a warm drink of milk. 'Twill help you rest. I know you have had several restless nights."

As Mary closed the door, Bethany noticed the guard's absence. "Where is Tearlach?"

"I pleaded with him for a moment's privacy with my sister. Bless him, he agreed there would be no danger in here and allowed us this time."

Her sister was very beautiful and could charm the birds from the trees, but Bethany did not think Royce or Guy would be so pleased with their soldier's attitude. "Mary, it is his duty to guard you."

"I know. But I have not been alone with you since your accident." Mary placed the tray down and offered her sister the drink.

Bethany accepted the chalice and held it to her lips.

"Drink," Mary encouraged as she tipped the bottom of the goblet up.

The milk was sweet—too sweet. Bethany felt her stomach roil at the richness. "Mary, 'twill choke me," Bethany said, lowering the goblet. At her sister's downcast features she added, "I will drink it, but slowly. 'Twas very nice of you to prepare this toddy."

"I will wait until you finish it, then return the goblet to the kitchen."

"Nay. 'Twill not be necessary. But stay and keep me company. We have so much to talk about. You have never told me of your time in Scotland," Bethany said, easing into the conversation in order to broach the subject of Bret.

Mary turned away. "My marriage is not what I had planned. When I was young, I had such glorious dreams. But in maturity we often find, to our regret, that our childhood wishes never come true."

As Mary began to pace, Bethany quickly poured most of the sweetened milk into a covered bowl near her bed. She did not want to hurt her sister, but she would never be able to finish this drink.

"Everyone in the castle, Saxon and Norman, is excited about their mistress being with child," Mary said abruptly.

"Thank you," Bethany murmured with a yawn, wondering why she could not seem to think clearly.

"I cannot believe my sister is about to be a mother. I am so surprised. You hated that Norman."

"Aye, I did. But I think love and hate are very close indeed."

"As always, sister, you are right," Mary said with a trace of amusement in her voice. Then she glanced at her. "How do you feel?"

Bethany felt extremely light-headed, but she did not want to alarm Mary. "I am well." There was something she needed to discuss with her sister, but at the moment it escaped her.

"Have you finished your drink?"

"Aye," Bethany lied. She felt so dizzy. Glancing up, Bethany thought Mary looked terribly strange. Bethany must truly be ill, if gentle, angelic Mary looked evil.

"Father's ring? Do you have it?" Mary asked.

Struggling for understanding, Bethany lifted the gold necklace free from around her neck.

Mary snatched it away and quickly placed it around her neck, fingering it as if it were a precious jewel. When she looked back, her eyes had a vacant, glazed look.

"Now, I can tell you something I discovered many years ago, when I was forced to go to the convent." Mary turned back to the side of the bed and removed the goblet from Bethany's boneless grip. She smiled. "Very good. You finished every drop."

Bethany felt as though her limbs were weighted, then suddenly remembered Bret cowering by her side. She tried to open her mouth to speak, but Mary spoke first.

"You are not my sister."

"What?" Bethany managed.

Mary slapped Bethany hard across the face. "I said, you are not my sister, but my half-sister. Pay attention!"

The sound of the blow was loud, but Bethany's cheek was numb and she hardly felt the pain. The jolt momentarily helped clear her senses, however, allowing the realization of what was happening to filter through the cobwebs forming in her mind.

"You are my half-sister," Mary screamed again. "Mother was fornicating with Uncle Bram. Father married her to give you a name."

Her sister's words, muffled and slurred, seemed to float to her as though in a far-off dream. "What say you?" Good Lord, what was wrong with Mary? Bethany tried to call for aid, but could not find her voice. Suddenly, it dawned on her that it was she, not Mary, who had taken ill.

"You are a bastard, Bethany. I am the rightful heir to the legacy."

Fear rose in her throat, and her terror increased as Bethany realized not only her hearing, but now her sight, was affected by the malady. Mary's face swam before Bethany's eyes, her lovely features distorted into ugly bitter lines.

"Mary, help me," she gasped.

"I am here. I will not leave you until you slip into a deep slumber and have no way of warning the others of my plan."

Beneath the covers, Bethany felt Bret's arms hug her waist. She placed her arms over his, instinctively protecting him. "Plan?" she whispered, only half understanding her sister's disjointed conversation, but dreading a full explanation.

"I am going to attack this castle with my husband's army. I will rule through him, and everything I want I will have. Never will I be cheated again."

A tortured scream of betrayal silently sounded from Bethany's soul. "Mary, please," she implored, but her sister's features dissolved into a swirling black pool and she knew as she drifted off into darkness that Mary was the murderer Royce sought.

Mary smiled with satisfaction. Bethany would not last the night with so much poison in her system. She looked at her helpless sister, and not an ounce of pity stirred in her heart.

The goblet would be washed and placed back where it belonged. She would go to the chapel, say her prayers, then meet her husband, who was waiting for her signal to attack.

"Bethany, you were a fool," Mary said. "Sacrificing for others when all you really had to do was ask God what he wished of you. He answers you. The Almighty talks to me all the time. But then again, dear sister, you have to be truly worthy."

*   *   *

Royce and Guy looked over the field at the invading army. "Who is it?" Royce asked

Cedric joined them, scratching his head. "If I know my clan colors, that would be Hugh Sinclair."

"Mary's husband?" Guy questioned.

"Aye," Cedric confirmed, his tone laced with concern.

Royce turned to Guy. "Fetch Lady Mary. She will be with her sister," he said, wondering how to avoid a bloody battle.

When Guy had left, Royce concentrated his energy on the advancing horde, which was setting up camp some three hundred yards away. He had not expected their arrival until spring. A winter attack only proved how determined they were.

"Vachel, see that the walls are defended with extra men. Send the women in for boiling oil and water. Any ideas, Cedric?" "Aye, my lord, several. If you will come with me, I will show you how the old lord protected this demesne."

Royce walked beside the old soldier, marveling at the man's energy and agility.

"My Lord, we have not one, but two secret passages. There did not exist the need to impart this information before. But now that we are under attack, my first loyalty is to Lady Bethany."

Royce looked at the old Saxon soldier, momentarily stunned by the news. But as he thought it over, he smiled. In Cedric's place, Royce would have done exactly the same.

Cedric chuckled. "Once your men found one tunnel, they never looked for another. But it exists. Come, I will show you."

Royce was truly impressed. "You will stand by my side," Royce said, giving the soldier a high honor indeed. A minute later, Guy approached, his face ashen.

"Have you found Lady Mary?" Royce inquired.

"*Non,* not yet. She was not with her sister."

"And?" Royce prompted, wondering why his brother bothered to report unimportant details.

"Brother, I have something to discuss in private."

Royce looked at Cedric, who had proved his loyalty, and was angered that Guy would imply otherwise. "Guy, in case you have not noticed, we are under attack. I have no time for private conversations."

Guy took a deep breath. "Bethany is unconscious. Bret says Mary poisoned her."

"What?" Royce gasped in disbelief. A drumbeat reverberated in his ears, its rhythm growing louder with each breath, and he distantly wondered if it were his heart pounding out the cadence of his pain.

"*Oui*, poisoned. I found her in your chamber and could not wake her. Bret knelt by her bed weeping uncontrollably. Through fits of tears he managed to babble, ''twas Mary who harmed her.' But Royce, the boy is overwrought. I do not know if he even knows the truth."

"Who is with her now?"

"Maida. She said if she knew what poison was used she could possibly find an antidote."

"Then find the bloody poison!"

"Royce, how can I find the poison when I cannot find Lady Mary?"

Royce shoved by him.

"She cannot escape with the guard I assigned her. Royce, we might be wrong. How could Lady Mary poison her sister under the watchful eyes of our man?"

"We have a traitor in our midst and we both know it. If not Mary, then who? I would bet my last coin on her. Find her and we will have our answer."

"My lord," said Cedric, "if the traitor is Saxon, she will know about both tunnels. Her avenue of escape will be the undiscovered passage."

"See to it," Royce ordered Cedric, then turned to his brother. "I will be with Bethany. Do not fail me!"

Nodding, Guy rushed away.

* * *

In the dim light of the chapel, Mary bent her head in prayer as Guy stealthily made his way up the aisle. He had not heard Latin since his days in the seminary, but as he listened, his features hardened. Far from the standard prayers, these were pleas to God, not to spare her sister or save the people from attack, but to deliver divine retribution on the illegitimate whore and make her supporters suffer.

Guy was stunned. Royce had been right. Mary was responsible for everything—the accidents, even Damiana's murder. He felt sick.

Carefully, he approached her pew. "Lady Mary," he said, then glanced at the kneeling Norman guard.

"Tearlach, what is wrong?"

His forehead resting on his folded hands, Tearlach did not respond. Guy gestured to Lady Mary to step out of the pew and move aside, allowing him to slide into the bench and bend over the soldier. Frustrated, Guy pulled the man's shoulder back and Tearlach fell over, a dagger imbedded deep in his chest. Too late, Guy turned around just as a hard object smashed into his temple.

Mary watched the fool collapse. "They really are stupid, are they not, Lord?" A wild laugh echoed in the small chapel as Mary replaced the broken wooden plank that Friar John had never found time to fix.

She walked slowly down the aisle and, at the end, turned back and genuflected. "Do not worry, Lord. I shall be careful," she whispered." Then she stood and left without a backward glance at her victims.

Moaning, Guy came slowly awake. His hand rose to his aching head and fell away covered with fresh blood. Staggering out of the chapel, he called for help.

Vachel ran to his side and assisted him into the castle great room. Sumar Chadwick tried to place a wet cloth on his injury, but he pushed it away.

"Search Lady Mary's apartments," he ordered.

When the young woman stared at him as though he had lost his mind, he grabbed her by the shoulders. "Just do as I say. Lady Mary has poisoned her sister and we must discover what was used."

Stunned, the maid stepped out of Guy's hold. "I will have a girl check the kitchen and send other servants to search the castle. But, my lord, she could have hidden the poison anywhere."

"We must find it!"

"Leave it to me, my lord; I will not let my lady down. If the poison is still here, I will locate it."

When the maid left to carry out the command, Vachel turned to Guy.

"It is hard to divide loyalties, my lord. But Sumar is devoted to Lady Bethany."

Guy was well aware of that. But then, every Saxon in this shire was devoted to Lady Bethany.

"Vachel, Mary must not escape. Take a detail and find her," Guy ordered.

"*Oui*, I will see to it personally."

Wiping the blood from his brow, Guy left to check on the sentries. He would leave nothing to chance. Apparently, Mary was responsible for a lot more than Damiana's murder. With the arrival of her husband's army, she obviously planned to overthrow the Normans.

He shook his head. Everyone but Royce had been taken in by her saintly pose. He himself had wondered about her, but could think of no motive to make Mary behave in such an unconscionable way. Now he knew what drove her: hate and envy.

Vachel met him on the walkway. "Lady Mary escaped. I found Cedric in the secret passage. He has been stabbed."

Sick at heart, Guy went to Bethany's room in search of his

brother. Opening the door, he gasped. Royce, who seldom asked God for anything, was kneeling on the floor next to Bret.

He could not remember a single occasion that had warranted Royce's prayer. His gaze travelled to Bethany. She was the true essence of his brother's soul. If Royce lost her, he would die.

Bethany lay on the bed without movement, the rise and fall of her chest minimal. Royce stared helplessly at her. She looked like a maiden at peace—her skin smooth and free from lines of tension and worry, her expression relaxed, almost angelic. Like a woman bewitched, she awaited rescue from a sorcerer's curse.

He rejected the thought of her leaving this world. The idea of life without her was too hard to bear.

He did not have to be told her fate. When the healer, Maida, had tears in her eyes, there was little else to be said. He thought of the times he had been harsh with his sweet, stubborn Annie. She had not deserved his wrath. But she had weathered it well, unlike those who cowered in fear of him.

Rising from his knees, he sat on the bed, wondering what she had ever done to incur such hatred. As he picked up her hand and gently massaged the soft skin, Royce vowed that he would find and bring Mary to justice. He saw Bret out of the corner of his eye, huge tears sliding down the small boy's cheeks. Royce reached out and picked him up.

"Help Bethany," Bret implored, clearly frightened.

Help Bethany. Two simple words, but an impossible request. Royce raised his eyes heavenward, asking Bethany's God for mercy.

Then he looked back to the boy. "I cannot, Bret. Your sister needs a miracle. That is God's province, not mine."

"I do not want her to be sick."

The boy began to cry in earnest, and Royce hugged the little frame to him, trying to absorb the pain and anguish into his own.

Guy approached them and knelt by the bed. Bending his head, he said a prayer. Then he asked, "What do you wish of me, brother?"

"There is nothing but what you have already done. Prayer is all we are left with. Where is Mary?" Royce asked in French, rubbing his hand over Bret's hair.

Guy responded in kind, "She has escaped."

"And the poison? Has it been found?" Royce inquired.

"*Non*. But your suspicion was right. Mary is the assassin. I overheard her prayers. They were more homage to Satan than Christ."

"Do you not think I am aware of that?" Royce responded bitterly.

In a brotherly show of comfort, Guy rested his hand briefly on Royce's shoulder, then left the room.

Royce knelt back by the bed and Bret followed his lead. The warlord picked up Bethany's hand and tenderly placed a kiss in her palm as one tear fell down his cheek to her fingers. He drew a ragged breath as he carried her hand to his chest, holding it reverently over his heart. "I never told you that I loved you. But not until this moment did I realize what the words meant. Strange that I could feel so strongly. I shall never look on a day without wondering what you would have thought about it. You cannot imagine the lives you have touched." He thought of her people, her brother, her uncle, his men, his brother, and—lastly—himself. She had changed them all. There was not an eye that would remain dry when she left.

No, he would not think in these terms. Death came on the battlefield often enough—it could not creep up on his love. Damn! She lay here dying, and he was powerless. He had devoted himself to regaining all that had been ruthlessly stripped away by his father's defection—name, respect, power, and wealth—for himself and his heirs. But suddenly, like a bolt of lightning streaking across the sky, the truth was illuminated and he realized what would make his life complete.

Bethany! He needed her. Bethany's love and understanding created a world he longed to live in and share.

"Bethany, how can you leave me? You know I need you here to counsel me." He smiled at that. She always had something to say about how he ruled her people. For they were her people, her demesne. He had conquered the land, but she had conquered his heart.

He touched his head to hers. "God," he whispered, "do not take her from me. Whatever I have done, this punishment is too much. Take me if you must, but spare my love. She is all that is right and good with the world. She is needed here. There are soldiers aplenty. But a woman such as Bethany, who serves you by serving her people, would be sorely missed."

Bethany moaned, and he brushed the hair from her forehead. "How can I help you? How can I take away the pain?" He took a deep breath, then threw his head back and looked heavenward. "God," he cried. "Take me, not Bethany!"

His echo hung in the room, and Bret slipped his hand into Royce's. "She will wake if you keep yelling."

Royce smiled sadly, his tears blurring the boy's image. "*Non,* she is still asleep."

"Let her rest. Bethany is so tired," Bret said.

"*Oui,* she has earned her rest." The tears he felt choked him. She had, indeed, earned her rest. Their child nestled in her womb would also sleep. Both of his loves would pass from this earth without knowing how much he cared. He bent forward and whispered in her ear. "Bethany, I love you with my whole being. You and our child are the greatest gifts from God. If you get well, I will grant you whatever your heart desires. Anything within my power will be yours for the asking, even your freedom." His lips touched her cheek, then he rested his head on her pillow. God, how he needed her.

Memories slipped into his mind. If he received another chance, if God would grant him that miracle, he swore by his very soul that he would not make the same mistake twice. Even as he made the vow, he knew it was wishful thinking. God did not give you another chance to right the wrongs in your life. If you made a mistake, you lived with it. This error would cost him his very soul. Wiping the tears from his eyes, he lifted his head. He could not stop looking at her perfect face.

Someone's hand rested on his shoulder, and he glanced up to see Vachel.

"My lord, we—I mean, all your troops are praying for her recovery."

Royce nodded his head. That his men would offer prayers for his wife touched him deeply. Now, when the Normans were so close to battle and his valiant men might lose their own lives, they took time to think of his Annie. He was a man who had been blessed and had not recognized it until too late. Taking a deep breath, he rose from the bedside. Others depended on him. He could not let them down.

He brushed her cheek with the edge of his fingers, then lifted Bret into his arms. "You will lead the vigil until I return. I need a soldier I can trust with this duty."

The little boy nodded solemnly, for they both knew when Royce returned it could be too late.

Mary entered her husband's tent, and her lip curled with distaste as his leman scrambled off the pallet and scurried to gather her clothes. Mary glared at her angrily until the wench left the tent. Then she turned to her husband, who wore a satisfied smile, not one bit upset that his wife had discovered him and his mistress together.

"They will be easy to defeat," Mary advised, her tone as cold as a winter's night. She unrolled a document. "Listed here are the number of men and horses in the castle. I have marked the main defenses and the two passages. However, the tunnels will be useless now." She smiled and handed him the papers. "The only one with courage and honor is dead. I have eliminated our only obstacle."

"It amazes me, wife, that you can so easily kill your own

flesh and blood," he said, placing the report down and pouring a cup of ale.

Mary's back stiffened at the reprimand. "'Twas necessary. God instructed that the sinner be smote."

The big burly Scot advanced on his wife while draining his brew. "Did He now?"

"Aye, 'twas my duty."

"Did you not love your sister?"

"Aye, though she did not deserve it. Bethany stole what was rightfully mine. God made me see the light."

A wicked look crossed Hugh's homely features as he stood before her. Then, suddenly, he flung his cup across the tent. "We are ready to attack tomorrow. Have you prayed for our success?"

"Aye, I have. You will carry the day, and we will rule henceforth."

"Nay *I* will rule!"

Mary backed away, apprehension coiling in the pit of her stomach. "*We* will rule."

"Nay, wife." He raised his hand. "You have a lesson to learn."

She raised her arms to fend off his attack, but his blow sent her flying to the ground. Hugh continued to strike and kick her as Mary rolled into a ball, trying to protect her head. Though she had stoically accepted his earlier beating, knowing it was necessary to convince Bethany of her sincerity, this one was far more brutal.

When he was finished, he picked her up and threw her on the bed. Mary screamed, unable to believe what her husband intended. He had assured her he only wanted the land and the demesne, not her.

"Now that you have done as I wished, there is no reason not to enjoy your charms." He ripped the clothes from her body. She fought him, frantically but every small resistance earned her another blow. Her head fairly reeled from the force of the man's fist as he mounted her.

Pain, sharp and hard, pierced her body when he impaled her.

Sickened, she tried to push him away, but he would not be budged. When he finished, he grunted and rolled off her. So enraged was Mary to be used in this manner, she lifted her hand to strike. She never landed a blow. Her husband struck her so hard that her neck snapped.

Mary's last thought was a reprimand to God for deserting her.

Royce walked the battlements. Far below, he could see the enemy in the field. At first light they would attack. He had checked on his troops, on all fortifications, but while he planned strategies, Bethany's image would interrupt his thoughts. Her every smile, every sweet laugh, taunted him while he worked to secure her land.

Painful though it was, he pushed himself. Her image did not fade, but remained with him throughout the night. He realized that whatever happened, she would be with him always. Bethany was a part of him, belonging in his heart and soul.

Spirits could comfort or torment; she would do both. When he was alone, he closed his eyes and let the sorrow have full reign.

Guy found him in a corner of the battlements with tears seeping from behind closed lids.

His pride would once have been in the dust to be discovered like this. Strangely it did not seem so important now. Still, he took a deep breath and swiped the tears from his face, then met his brother's gaze.

"What is it, Guy?"

"Royce, I would rather cut off my arm than bring you the news."

The blood froze in Royce's veins and he felt a band constrict his chest. "She is dead." he declared flatly.

"Non," Guy said quickly.

Relief flooded Royce. "What then?"

" 'Tis the poison. We cannot find it." Guy sighed heavily. "I am so sorry, Royce."

"How does she fare?" Royce asked, holding his breath.

"The same. Her fate rests with the Almighty."

Royce nodded then looked away, deeply burying the pain he felt. Several minutes passed before he spoke. "At first light we will see our land under attack. I am glad you are here by my side."

"I will stand with you," Guy affirmed.

"Pray the castle is held, not for us, but for my wife. I owe her that much."

"Then you admit you love the Saxon?" Guy asked.

"Oui, but it is too late. I never told her," Royce said brokenly.

"You will."

Royce took a deep breath. "I do not believe God gives you a second chance. I had all I could ever want, and I did not recognize it. I have thrown away a valuable gift."

"God does not punish, Royce; that is left for man. God is merciful and understanding. Pray to Him. Ask for your gift back."

"I have, Guy. With all my heart, I prayed. I received no answer. Not that I expected one. The Almighty and your brother are not on intimate terms."

"Sinners usually have His ear."

"Do they? I am afraid my voice went unheard." Royce smiled sadly. "I never needed God before, and now I am sure He feels the same about me." He wheeled around and marched out of the hall, shedding his reflective mood as he donned his mantle of responsibility. "Come. We have a challenge to meet."

Chapter Twenty-four

"Thank God we have a fortified position to defend. I would not be eager to fight these men hand to hand on an open battlefield," Guy said to Cedric as he watched the vast number of celtic warriors from atop the battlements. 'Twas not cowardice, merely an accurate assessment of the enemy's ability. "They are out-positioned, but they simply do not give up." Wave after wave of fur-covered warriors attacked the walls as they had all day.

"They are from the north with the savage blood of the Vikings coursing though their veins," Cedric said with respect. When he turned to face Guy, the Saxon's features were drawn and gray. Though stabbed by Mary last night, the old soldier stood his guard. "They are merciless," Cedric warned.

Guy understood. Half of Normandy could trace their descent from Viking raids. No mercy would be given. Only a victory could be entertained. Guy scanned the enemy's position, dimming in the falling light of dusk. Thank God. Night would give a respite from the enemy's fury. "If not for the stone walls, we would find ourselves at a disadvantage." He looked up and saw Vachel approaching with haste.

"Royce has summoned you to the great room," Vachel said in a voice underlined by weariness, his face stained with sweat and dirt.

While they hurried to the great room, Guy wondered what his brother planned. As hopeless as their positions had been and as desperate as their chances seemed, Royce had never failed to come up with a brilliant strategy. Now would not be the time to ruin that particular record.

As they entered the room, solemn-faced Norman commanders looked their way. The deep lines that etched their foreheads and sullen gazes filled with trepidation bespoke their silent fear. Though doubt and apprehension tinged the air, Guy heard Royce's forthright voice ring out with authority as he spoke to a messenger.

"I want a double watch posted tonight. We cannot afford to let down our guard. This enemy would jump at any mistake."

"Oui, that they would," Guy added, recalling the crazed horde of half-naked warriors screaming bloodcurdling oaths as they charged the castle.

Royce nodded as Guy and the commanders joined him at the table. A roughly drawn map of the castle's fortifications and terrain lay on the surface. "Deploy your men here, here, and here," Royce said to his guard leader, Ferragus, pointing to an area that showed the castle defenses. "I will lead an outside attachment through the secret passage and out-flank them." His hand moved to cover the fields and hills to the left of the castle.

" 'Twould be suicide to meet them on their own ground," Guy insisted, and others mumbled their agreement. "Besides, Sinclair will know of the tunnels and be waiting."

"Au contraire. The plan will work if we have the element of surprise on our side. An armed guard of horsemen led by Vachel will charge out the front gate, drawing the enemy away from the castle. They will not engage the enemy but lead them in a circle back to my waiting troops and defeat. Caught between the castle and my ambush, the enemy will be crushed."

" 'Tis brilliant, but dangerous," Guy said, stating the obvious with a worried frown.

"Do you have another idea?" Royce asked, pushing the map toward his brother.

Silence reigned as the brothers looked at each other.

Finally, Guy shook his head in defeat. *"Non,* but I would go with you." He did not want his brother to fight alone.

"Non. You will stay and protect those within. Cedric will assist you. I will take only a small complement of men, the king's regiment."

Several of the men expressed reservations. Royce, a true commander, listened to each soldier's comments. He defended his strategy, then outlined the importance of each individual assignment and emphasized the key position his men would hold. When all were satisfied, he dismissed his men. Every soldier but Guy filed out of the great room.

"Royce, you do not expect to come back," Guy said, speaking his thoughts aloud. Unlike the others, he understood the plan too well.

Royce shook his head. *"Non,* I expect to win. The complement I take is the king's own guard. They are well-trained, seasoned warriors."

And strangers, Guy thought. Royce did not wish to watch his friends die alongside him.

"I would be happier if you sent another in your place," Guy said, gauging Royce's reaction.

Royce's features tightened slightly. "That is not possible. It is my duty."

Guy had his answer and knew it was useless to argue. Royce would follow his own dictates. A tightness constricted Guy's chest, and he reached out and grasped his brother's arm. "God-speed, brother. I will defend your land and your home with my life."

"I know you will. If we are victorious, I will return at eventide and we will toast our success." Royce pulled his brother into his clasp.

In the middle of the great room, the two soldiers stood alone. In that rare moment of privacy, knowing that this could be the last time they saw each other, they clung together for but a heartbeat. Then they parted, and Royce de Bellemare marched off without looking back.

The proposed attack would take place at midday. Every man and woman prepared for the onslaught. It was a tense night as Normans and Saxons spent their last hours together, afraid to speak of the possibilities of the future. Many of the men and women living together were hurriedly wed. The looming battle created a time of accounting, and every inhabitant undertook a self-examination.

Royce found no peace in the long night. He spent most of it in the bedroom with his wife. He stared so long at her that he thought he saw her move; but when he blinked, she remained in the same position. He regretted so many things. If God would only grant him a few minutes to tell her what lay in his heart! But God, apparently, was not listening now any more than he had been yesterday.

Still Royce could not accept that he had lost her. Though he had chosen the most dangerous command, it was not, as Guy had mistakenly thought, because he wished for death. Hope burned deep within his chest. Bethany would live. They were meant to be together. He would win this battle and lay the victory at her feet. It was the least he could do for his love. The Northumbrian bride, as he recalled the legacy, would wed the strongest warrior to protect her land. And, by God, he would not fail her.

When the faint light of dawn streamed through the window, he knew it was time to leave his beloved. He leaned over her and pressed his lips to hers. "We will be together for eternity, for there is not another who could ever hold my heart," he whispered.

He rose and touched the soft skin on her cheek. "Annie, I love you. To you, I give my heart and soul. Keep them with you always."

He turned, ignoring the tears streaming down Maida's plump cheeks. He had work to do.

Maida touched his arm. "My lord, Godspeed."

He nodded, unwilling and unable to voice his thanks for this woman's respect.

"Take good care of my lady," he said gruffly in an attempt to cover his raw emotions.

Maida smiled, unashamed of her tears. "As long as I have breath, my lord."

Small skirmishes had been occurring on and off since dawn. Guy and Vachel apprised Royce of the situation.

"My lord," Vachel said, "see you keep that stubborn neck of yours safe."

"*Oui,* and the same to you," Royce said as Sumar ran up and threw her arms around Vachel.

"Come back to me, Vachel. I could not bear to lose another husband," she said.

Vachel led her away, and Royce felt a tinge of envy that he could not embrace his own Bethany and hear her wish for his safe return.

Guy handed Royce his weapons. "Need I remind you that I would not care to send our mother news of your death?"

"Do not worry, brother; I will return." Royce assured him. As he turned to leave, Friar John approached.

"My lord, one moment. By your leave, I would offer a prayer for you and your men that all will, with God's help, have a safe return."

Royce knew the prayer would aid his men both morally and spiritually. He was surprised, though, that a Saxon friar would offer such a wish for Normans. It was another sign of the Saxons' devotion to his wife—and, once wed to Bethany, to him. No forced allegiance could produce the loyalty that the Saxons now freely bestowed upon him and his men. "*Oui,*

Friar, we will humbly accept any prayer for our safe return," Royce said.

Friar John bowed his head, and those who were so inclined knelt before the cleric to receive his blessing.

"May these brave and valiant men, with God's grace and mercy, succeed in His name."

The soldiers blessed themselves and went their way. Royce rose, and Friar John stepped forward. "I have been in the chapel praying for Lady Bethany; now, I will go to her and not leave her side until you return."

"Friar, if it is God's will that I do not return, I wish to be buried on yon hill." Royce said, pointing to the spot where he had first confronted his wife.

The friar nodded, his eyes misting over.

"And if my wife—" Royce's voice broke. "—does not live, I wish us to lie side by side for all eternity. You will see to it?"

"Aye, my son, I will." Then Friar John gave Royce Bethany's girdle with the legacy embroidered on it. "She would want you to have it. Royce de Bellemare, you are, by my blessing, her husband and champion."

Royce took the girdle in his hand and examined the story as he had a hundred times before. Now he was being honored as the first conqueror had been. Swallowing the lump in his throat, he tied the belt around his waist and slipped her dagger into his boot, then left to join his men.

Loud war cries filled the air as the enemy charged the castle's edifice. As Royce led his men through the tunnel, the eerie sounds of battle echoed through the earthen walls like the wailings of ghostly warriors crying out in pain.

Royce made himself a promise as he heard the warning voice of death. If he lived the day, never again would he hold life so cheap. Every sunrise would be a reason to rejoice. As he stepped out into the sunshine, he knew nothing would ever be the same for him. For never would he know the kind of love he had found with Annie.

* * *

Bram Mactavish heard the unmistakable sound of battle long before he saw it. Carefully cresting a ridge, he looked down in shock. The last thing he had expected when he journeyed forth to retrieve his nephew was to find Renwyg Castle under siege.

He recognized the Sinclair colors, and his heart sank. By His wounds, were they mad? Family attacking family? What was he to do? The attacking tide of northern clansmen would soon sweep the Normans away if help were not forthcoming. Bram watched the battle. Memories long since dead rose in his mind, haunting him with the bittersweet message he had refused to hear years ago. Now, he could not deny the sound of his ghost. A soft, sweet voice whispering, *Save her. Save our daughter.* The plea tore at his heart. Aye, he heard his beloved as clearly as if she stood next to him. His own flesh and blood needed him. He called his men forth, and they rode toward the fighting. Bram threw back his head and hollered the ancient Mactavish war cry, which was picked up and repeated by his clansmen. The heat of battle ran through the old man's veins as he remembered a face he did not wish to see and a promise he had forsaken. He raised his sword like a man possessed and entered the fray.

Royce fought in the thick of battle. Though his plan had surprised the enemy, the initial advantage quickly waned under the sheer numbers of the Celtic warriors. He knew the fight went badly for his men, but every last one was as loyal and true as any leader had a right to expect. They might not carry the day, but they would take as many Scots with them as possible and hopefully save the castle in the process.

All of a sudden, Royce heard a bloodcurdling scream and looked up sharply. His blood froze. Behind them on the ridge stood another army of Scots! He had miscalculated, and his men would pay dearly for it. They were surrounded on all sides, committed to a hopeless battle.

Briefly allowing himself the luxury of thinking of his love, he wished again to have a second chance. Perhaps, he thought as he looked at the overwhelming odds against his force, God had given him one. At least in death they would never be parted. Then, there was no time to think as a warrior charged through the line, aiming his claymore at Royce's heart. Royce pivoted in the nick of time, pulling Bethany's dagger clear of his boot, and turned to drive the blade deep into the wild Scotsman. As he pulled the ancient blade free of the soldier, he knew his Annie was with him and would be always.

Even as he fought against overwhelming odds, Royce watched the Mactavish entering the campaign. "Damn him," Royce swore, vowing his sword would wear Bram Mactavish's blood for joining the enemy. Royce's forces would not stand a chance against the added numbers. He raised his sword and let out a Norman war cry. He would take that heathen with him to hell.

Bram slashed and hacked his way toward Royce. They met in the middle of the fray.

Bram blocked a blow from Royce's sword. "I have come to stand by you, Norman!"

Royce was shocked, but when a Sinclair slashed an arc toward him, Bram's sword blocked the blow, confirming his words with action.

They raised their swords and fought together, protecting each other's back. With Bram's men, the balance of power in the fight shifted and, though it still took the better part of the day, the Northern clansmen finally retreated in defeat.

'Twas a sight to be remembered. It was not unusual for Scotsmen to fight Scotsmen, but to do so in order to aid Normans surely was.

By nightfall, the clan Sinclair was on the run and the union of two great houses had been sealed.

"I will be thanking you to tell me what happened here today," Bram said as he wiped the sweat and dirt from his brow.

" 'Tis a long story and one you need listen to over ale," Royce said.

"Aye," Bram said, slapping Royce on the back. "There is hope for you yet, Norman." He turned his horse slowly around. "I will meet you at Renwyg after I have seen to my clansmen."

Royce did not relish telling Bram of Bethany's illness and Mary's betrayal. 'Twas ill-timing for the Scotsman to learn that one niece was probably fleeing her home while the other was fighting for her life.

Just then a soldier approached, "A word with you, my lord," he said.

Royce nodded and received a full report, along with several papers and Bethany's ring.

Night had fallen when the good tidings arrived from the field, and the moon would be high in the sky before the army finished driving the invaders from their demesne and returned with their wounded. Yet with the successful outcome, Guy could only hope his brother found cause to rejoice on his arrival as he left the castle guard to check on Bethany.

Uttering a prayer, he opened the master chamber door and was gripped by terror when he saw Maida's splotchy cheeks and red-rimmed eyes. "Madam, what has happened?" he asked, fearing the worst.

Crying loudly and wiping her eyes with her apron, Maida managed to point a shaky finger toward the bed. " 'Tis surely God's will," she choked.

His heart ached, knowing that he would have to enter and find his brother's dear wife dead. But when Guy looked, his mouth dropped open and he stared thunderstruck.

Bethany sat upright in bed with the sweetest smile on her lips. "Whatever is wrong with you, Guy? You look like you have seen a spirit."

Guy looked from Bethany to Maida, shaking his head. "It is not that I am sorry to see you recovered, dear little sister. It is just that I am at a loss as to how it was accomplished."

Bethany drew in a long, deep breath. "My sister gave me a warm drink. I could not stomach the brew; but rather than hurt her feelings, I poured most of it out when she was not looking. I did not know she had poisoned it."

Guy walked over to the bed and gripped her shaky hands with his. "So, you know it was Mary?"

"Aye, when the drug took effect, she told me everything. 'Tis still a shock, Guy." Bethany took another deep breath, clearly trying to stem her tears. "In my heart, I cannot understand her hate."

" 'Twas her twisted sense of morality," Maida piped up, apparently already informed of the story.

" 'Tis no matter now. You have recovered. Royce will be overjoyed."

A bittersweet expression crossed her face. "Will he? I am a bastard, Guy." Bethany turned away and stared at the wall. One lone tear travelled down her cheek before she brushed it away. "While I slept, I dreamt of Royce. His words were so loving, so beautiful." She shook her head. " 'Tis just the sickness."

"Non, it was not delirium, but my lovesick brother you heard. He cares for you, Bethany. Truly he does. More than I thought possible."

"Guy, you do not understand," she said. "If Royce holds any affection for me at all, it will disappear upon learning of my illegitimacy."

Guy heard the despair in her voice and decided it was time for another tack. Sitting on her bed, he took her hand in his. "Now, my dear, you did not listen to me about trapping a man, but will you take my advice about getting Royce to admit his love?"

Bethany smiled, but the expression did not reach her eyes. Exhaustion and fear clouded her gaze. "Guy, I do not think it would be right to trick Royce. He would never forgive being the butt of a jest."

"Bethany, he is capable of more than you think," Guy countered. "I believe it would be in your best interest, and his, to hear him say what is in his heart."

"What good would it do?" she asked, her gaze dropping to the covers.

"Bethany," he said, lifting her chin, "it will free him."

She paused for a moment, her gaze holding his. "All right," she finally agreed.

He heard the reservation in her voice and patted her hand. In truth, it was for Bethany's benefit, not Royce's, that he proposed the plan. His brother had already accepted the truth. It was Bethany who needed to dispel any lasting doubts about his love.

"Good. Now, we must not let him know you have recovered."

Bethany gasped as he rose from the bed and turned to Maida. "Does anyone else know of Lady Bethany's recovery?"

"Nay, my lord. With the battle raging, there was no time to tell anyone," Maida responded, a curious smile lighting her face.

When Guy saw the approval in the cook's eyes, he pulled her over to his side. "We will keep it our secret." He turned to Bethany. "When Royce comes in, he will still believe you are hovering close to death. Then, dear sister, you will hear his heart speaking."

Suddenly the door burst open and Bret rushed into the room.

"Bethany," he squealed in delight as Guy nearly collapsed from the scare.

Bret dashed around Guy and jumped onto Bethany's lap. "I love you," he said, his little arms wrapping around her neck.

"I love you, too," Bethany soothed, hugging him close.

"Bret, I swear you took ten years off my life," Guy admonished, resting his hand on his chest. Then he turned his attention to Bethany. "If it had been Royce, our plans would have been

for naught." Guy walked over to the bed and held out his arms
for Bret.

After giving Bethany another big kiss, the child leapt into
Guy's embrace. "Now, Bret, we must keep Bethany's recovery
a secret."

"Why?"

"Because, we are going to play a little jest on Royce, something like the one he played on your sister. Remember when
he did not want Bethany to know he spoke your language?"
he asked, waiting until Bret nodded before he continued. "Will
you help us?"

"Aye, 'twill be great fun."

"Forsooth, Bret, that is the spirit." He grinned, then lifted
Bret high in the air and swung him around in a circle. "I am
proud of you, little soldier."

Bret beamed.

Bethany shook her head. "Are you sure Royce will consider
this amusing, Guy?"

But Bret answered. "Aye, he will. He loves jests."

"Even if he does not, can you afford to waste this opportunity,
Bethany?" Guy inquired. "Not only will you even the score
between you two, more importantly, you will know once and
for all if he truly loves you."

Bram Mactavish passed through Renwyg's gates and entered
the castle courtyard with relish. He could not wait to see his
family. 'Twas a wonder that they managed without him. He
smiled. 'Twould be good to reunite his kith and kin. But what of
poor Mary? Strange that he should consider Royce de Bellemare
above treachery, yet know instinctively the Scotsman Sinclair
was guilty. Still, he had no doubt. Royce was not a man who
would double-cross. The Norman had stood his ground and
confronted him face to face. He was indeed a braw man, a
perfect example of the good and fine traits a Scotsman
respected.

Sinclair was another matter. He did not even feel Mary safe
when she wed. No, the varlet was the Northern Scot, he was
sure of it, but he would wait until he heard all the details.
Heaven help the man when the truth came to light.

When the men returned, the plaintive cry of women filled
the air; but the tears shed were of joy, not sorrow. Warm
embraces and long kisses attested to the grateful relief that so
many returned unharmed from the conflict.

As they dismounted, a Saxon soldier approached Royce de
Bellemare.

"My liege, the castle is secure," the man said, taking Royce's
reins. "The enemy are either destroyed or running back to their
moors."

Then, with the business out of the way, the man knelt before
his liege. "I am sorry, my lord, but there is no news from your
chamber."

"Thank you, Cedric," Royce said wearily as the soldier rose.

Bram stiffened at the Saxon's words, but not knowing the
meaning, he looked to Royce. 'Twas then that he noticed the
deep sorrow in the young man's eyes.

"Follow me," the warlord said in reluctant response. Royce
walked into the great room and pointed to a chair. " 'Tis a
heavy heart I bear, Mactavish. 'Twill be the same for you when
you hear the whole of it."

"Then I best have a dram of fortification," Bram replied,
though he wondered what on earth could be the matter. With
the enemy subdued and the castle secured, there was naught
that could be amiss. This Norman talked in riddles. He poured
himself a tankard of ale, then raised it in the air. "Go ahead, I
am ready for bad news."

" 'Tis of your family," Royce said, then poured himself a
healthy drink. " 'Tis no easy way to deliver this tiding."

"Speak the truth, though 'tis rarely easy to say or pleasant
to hear," Bram said as he took a healthy swig of his brew.

Royce ran a hand through his hair. "Mary was the one who
betrayed us. When my men overran Sinclair's camp, they found

her, along with a detailed report of the castle's defenses and this ring." He handed the ring with William's crest to Bram. As the old man examined it, Royce continued. "Mary is dead, but, that is not the worst of it."

"What could be worse than the lass's death?" Bram choked, shocked that sweet little Mary was gone. "Nay, lad," Bram shook his head as he held the ring in his clenched fist. "Mary would not betray her own!"

"Mary had you, along with everyone else, fooled, Mactavish. Clever and crafty, Mary spun a web of hate and retribution. She poisoned her own sister, then fled before we could find the name of the poison."

"Bethany!" Bram gasped, staggering to his feet as his ale spilled over the floor. "Why?"

"Because she was chosen for the legacy. Mary has envied her for years."

"My bairn is dying?" Bram groaned, struggling to accept the horrible truth.

"Your bairn?" Royce could not have been more surprised.

"Aye, she is my own fair child," Bram declared. It was a secret he had sheltered too long. He rubbed his hand over his face, feeling much older than his years. "Have we lost her yet?"

"I do not know, but you are welcome to join me. I go to her now."

As they started for the stairs, Bram took a deep breath and said, "I dinna claim Bethany. Do ye ken? I loved her mother beyond any love I have ever known. Yet, in my foolish youth, I threw that love away and never found it again. I was a young laird and wouldna give up my clan for her while she wouldna leave North Umberland for me. We both lost." Bram shook his head at the truth of the matter, showing his deep regret. "True love comes but once, my lad. I hope ye do not lose your fair bonny bride." Then he shoved the Norman forward to precede him up the stairs. "Dinna give up hope. Mayhap the lass has recovered."

Royce merely nodded his head and climbed the steps, feeling

like each one was his last. He could not believe how he feared reaching the top of the stairs and his chamber. Suddenly, a thought occurred to him. He wheeled around and faced Mactavish. "I will not dispute that Bethany is from your loins, Bram. But 'twould be a great kindness to my wife when she awakens if she never learned she is a bastard."

" 'Tis not my intent to hurt the lass," Bram said.

With a slight incline of his head, Royce continued up the stairs. What irony to find his bride was also a bastard. Strange, but the prized lineage did not matter now. He would have her for his own if she were the poorest peasant in all Christendom. All he wanted was Bethany for his wife. He reached his chamber and laid his head against the door, silently praying. "God, give her back to me and I promise I will never take her for granted again," he mouthed. "Grant me this one boon, and I will fulfill my vow."

He opened the door and saw Maida in the corner. The moment the servant noticed him, she jumped up and scooted by him as though she feared facing him.

Fearfully, he turned toward the bed, and his breath caught in his chest. She lay like an angel adorned in a white smock, a single white ribbon embroidered with her name holding the vivid tresses away from her face, allowing the bright hair to fan out across her pillow and flow softly over the pristine sheets. Gently, he reached for her hand.

Bram approached the bed as Guy and the friar moved forward.

"She has not succumbed to death yet, brother." In a show of support, Guy laid his hand on Royce's shoulder and squeezed it. "Mayhap you should make your peace."

"By your leave, Norman, I would say my avowal," Bram interrupted. "I have waited too long to tell Bethany what lies in my heart."

At Royce's nod, Bram continued. "Bethany, you are the picture of your mother, whom I loved with every ounce of my foolish heart. In my youth, I made a mistake, and I have paid for it every day of my life. You cannot die. Fight to live, lassie. Northumbrian brides are special." Leaning down, Bram gave her a light kiss on the forehead, then moved back to make way for Royce.

Royce thought he saw her eyelids flutter; but when he looked again, her eyes were as peacefully closed as a child's in sleep. Yet a tear slipped from beneath the lids and slid down her cheek. A ray of hope warmed his heart. Bethany had heard her father, he was sure of it.

"I have saved your land," Royce whispered as he grazed his lips against her cheek. "Your people will live in peace. If you but open your eyes and smile upon me, I would gift you your land and title and be content to be your slave for the rest of my life.

"Open your eyes, little wife. Do not leave me in this valley of loneliness." He noticed her eyelashes flickering again as he rested his face on her pillow. "If the sum total of our lives together is weighed in heaven, then we have been blessed beyond compare," he murmured, his chest constricting with pain. Suddenly out of the corner of his eye he saw her eyes flutter open and was about to yell for joy when he saw the signal pass between his brother and his wife—a wink and then a caution of the hand.

"Royce, tell her how much you love her so she can go to her rest in peace," Guy insisted.

So that was their game. Love her? God, he would die for her! So they had laid a trap for him. He did not mind being caught, but—by God—it would be on his terms.

"Love her?" he asked. "Guy, you know I never really cared for the Saxon wench. She was but a slave who happened to bring me pleasure in bed."

"What!" Bethany cried, bolting upright in bed.

"I said you brought me pleasure in bed," he chuckled, feeling the joy pour from his heart as he gazed at her with a silly grin.

She frowned. "Before that, Royce."

He pulled her into his arms and smiled. "I said I never loved you, but 'twas only a jest to make you sit up and kiss me. Quit your game, Annie. I should throttle both of you for this deception. You are lucky I am too thankful to do so."

" 'Twas not Bethany's fault, Royce," Guy interrupted. "The moment she recovered I talked her into this deceit so she could know how much you love her."

" 'Twas not Guy's fault," Bethany quickly defended. "I needed to know you loved me. To know that what I heard before was not a dream."

" 'Twas no dream, my love. Though I must admit it came as quite a surprise to me," Royce said. "I may have been the conqueror, but you, my little Saxon, won a victory of the heart. The moment I laid eyes on you, I was lost."

Sighing, Bethany placed her arms around his neck, knowing that the legacy had been fulfilled. "No, my love, 'twas a victory for us both," she said, then kissed him with all the love she had stored in her heart.

Epilogue

Bethany's recovery spread joy and merriment throughout the castle. Soldiers and milk maidens danced in the hallways. This good news following the defeat of the Celtic warriors was surely a sign that, at last, the hard times were over.

Throughout the land peace and prosperity heralded the union of the Saxon and the Norman. North Umberland's nine-hundred-year-old legacy of a foreign conqueror being tamed by a Saxon maid had been renewed. But the real celebration occurred six months later when the lady of the manor was delivered of twin sons!

" 'Tis happier I am than I have a right to be," Royce said, gazing down at his wife, who rested in bed, nestling a baby in each arm.

"Nay, my lord. God has blessed us all. He sent us a Norman conqueror—" She smiled. "—who at first was terrible and frightening, but whom I came to know as the sweetest of men."

He leaned over and brushed the delicate red hair from her brow before gently placing a soft kiss there. "Please, my love, with such a reputation, I will never be able to hold this land safe."

She raised her gaze and held his with an intense look that captured his heart. "My lord, you are the kindest and gentlest soul I have ever known. Should anyone think differently, I would be forced to take them to task."

He grinned. "And how, my lovely wife, would you propose to do that?"

"I would serve them wine and vinegar to temper their sour dispositions. 'Tis a remedy I found most helpful."

"How well I remember," he said, chuckling. It was then that he realized her strength of character and indomitable spirit equaled his own. He kissed her long and lovingly. "I have found my reward. I shall search no further."

She offered her lips to his again and extracted more than a gentle peck. "I hope so," she said breathlessly.

"I wish Guy were here to see his nephews," he said to distract his thoughts. God, how he wanted her! But 'twas unseemly—the woman had just borne him twins.

"Shall we name one son after him?" she asked.

"Heavens no! He already thinks himself important enough after being chosen to do the king's mission. Nay, we will name one son after your father and one son after your uncle."

"What of your father?"

The concern in her eyes touched him. *"Non!"* he said, then tempered his voice. "Annie, he abandoned us, depriving us of his name—and his love. I will never forgive him."

"If we are to have a future, then you must put the past to rest. Name one son after your sire and one son after mine. 'Twill end the bitterness in your heart."

His chest tightened. She understood his pain and offered a way to heal the wound of the past. " 'Twill be hard for me," he said, caressing first one baby then the other, "but I will begin. We will, indeed, name one boy Lance and the other Gowain."

She shook her head. "Nay, Royce. I said we would name them after our sires—Lance and Bram," she amended.

"You knew?" he asked in wonder.

"Aye."

"Very well. From this day forward, we will start anew and our twins shall be known as Bram and Lance."

Tenderly he lifted one sleepy form onto his lap and reached out to stroke his other son's tiny hand. "Unlike the childhood Guy and I knew, yours will be blessed with the love and security of both parents. I vow on my very life that you shall never feel unwanted. Never will my sons doubt their heritage," he pledged.

He touched Bethany's cheek. "I love you, my little Saxon, and bless the day I met you." He kissed her, letting his desire show. "As soon as you are up to it, we will get started on fulfilling the legacy. A daughter should keep her brothers on their toes."

Bethany snuggled into his embrace, returning his kiss with tears of contentment gathering in her eyes.

Dear Reader:

Every now and again a character comes along who needs his own story. That is how I felt about Guy de Bellemare. While I was telling Bethany and Royce's love story, Guy turned out to be so charming that I knew he would have to have his own book.

Here is an excerpt from *A Prayer and a Promise.* Guy and Gabby are unlikely candidates to fall in love—which is exactly why their romance had to be written.

Sincerely,
Marian Edwards

*   *   *

England 1067

"You want me to do what?" Guy de Bellemare leaped out of his chair, dumping the generously endowed serving maid onto the floor as he glared at the king.

Lying in a heap of half-unlaced tunic and smock, the maid shrieked indignant curses at Guy until William handed her a coin and shooed her away.

When the door had closed, the King turned toward the fire, his features sharp in the glow of firelight. "You heard me. I want you to pose as a priest to kidnap a nun from a convent."